I0819842

# Koasati Traditional Narratives

KOWASSÁ:TI INCOKFA:ŁIHILKÁ

Translated by Geoffrey D. Kimball

*With the assistance of*
Bel Abbey,
Martha John, and
Sam Thompson

Published by the University of Nebraska Press
Lincoln and London

In cooperation with the American Indian Studies Research Institute
Indiana University, Bloomington

Manufactured in the United States of America
♾

Library of Congress Cataloging-in-Publication Data
Kimball, Geoffrey D., 1954–
Koasati traditional narratives / translated by Geoffrey D. Kimball . . . [et al.].
p. cm. — (Studies in the anthropology of North American Indians)
Includes bibliographical references.
ISBN 978-0-8032-2729-3 (hardcover: alk. paper)
1. Koasati Indians—Folklore. 2. Tales—Southern States.
3. Koasati language—Texts. I. Title.
E99.K77K56 2010
398.0897'38—dc22
2009021115

# Contents

Part Two
Semihistorical Narratives

# Illustrations

*(following page xii)*

# The Narrators

Bel Abbey (1916–1991)
*Kawaknasí aykisá.*[1] Grandson of Jefferson Abbey; great-grandson of John Abbey

Martin Abbey (1896–1991)
*Fi:tó aykisá.* Son of Jefferson Abbey; grandson of John Abbey

Ellisor Battise (1881–1943)
*Hapí aykisá.* Married to paternal aunt of Ruth Poncho

Solomon Battise (1911–2003)
*Nokkó aykisá.* Son of Ellisor Battise; son-in-law of Martin Abbey

George Henry (1854–ca.1925)
*Nokkó aykisá.* Great-grandfather of Sam Thompson

Martha John (1908–1994)
*Kawaknasí aykisá.* First cousin of Bel Abbey

Ed John (1909–1986)
*Nitá aykisá.* Step brother/cousin of Martha John

Azilie Langley (1883–1975)
*Cahtá aykisá.* Sister-in-law of Jackson Langley

Bertney Langley (1951– )
*Kawaknasí aykisá.* Grandson of Jackson Langley by his third wife; nephew of Bel Abbey

Jackson Langley (1873–1941)
*Fi:tó aykisá.* Son of Selin Williams; brother-in-law of Sam Thompson's grandfather.

Asa Poncho (1900–1985)
*Kowí aykisá.* Grandson of John Abbey; nephew of Jefferson Abbey; father-in-law of Ruth Poncho

[1]*Aykisá* 'clan'.

Ruth Poncho (1923–1991)
*Fi:tó aykisá*. Sister-in-law of Bel Abbey; daughter-in-law of Asa Poncho

Sam Thompson (1927–1998)
*Nokkó aykisá*. Brother-in-law of Bel Abbey; great-grandson of George Henry

Selin Williams (1836–1917)
*Fi:tó aykisá*. Mother of Jackson Langley; sister-in-law of John Abbey

Myrna Wilson (1945– )
*Fi:tó aykisá*. Daughter of Bel Abbey; niece of Ruth Poncho

Bel Abbey. Photograph by Debi Bennett.

Martha John. Photograph courtesy of Iwana Bernard.

Sam Thompson. Courtesy of Mrs. Marjorie Battise.

Jackson Langley and Selin Williams. Photographs by John R. Swanton; Plate 27, *The Indians of the Southeastern United States.*

# Preface

This volume contains a collection of Koasati traditional narratives gathered between 1910 and 1992. The Koasati speak a language of the Muskogean family most closely related to Alabama and more distantly related to Mikasuki, Creek, Choctaw, and Chickasaw—all of which are still spoken. At the present time, the largest community of Koasati speakers is found in the forests to the north of Elton, Louisiana, where they homesteaded land in 1882. Over the previous two centuries they had wandered far from their aboriginal homeland, the upper Tennessee River valley. Despite the great shifts in material and social culture in the past centuries, the Koasati have preserved their native language and traditional oral literature. Social change is still going on, however, and although the Koasati language is still vital, persons who know traditional narratives are becoming fewer, and the repertoire of those who still know them has diminished.

This work owes a great debt to John R. Swanton, who, in the first decade of this century undertook fieldwork, both ethnographic and linguistic, among the Indian peoples who had once inhabited the Southeast. When he came to work among the Koasati in 1910, he not only recorded their tales in English, but also laboriously took them down in Koasati (Swanton 1910), even though he knew almost nothing of the language. Many times I have struggled with garblings and errors in Swanton's texts, wishing that he had been a better linguist, or at least had had a clearer penmanship. Nonetheless, without his work, this collection would have been a poorer one, not only for the tales themselves, but also because reading them aloud to people often would bring to mind other stories, some of which Swanton had never heard.

There is a debt owed as well, to the late Mary R. Haas, who very kindly gave me copies of the texts that she had gathered in her short period of fieldwork in Louisiana in 1939. She also offered great encouragement for the grammar and the dictionary of Koasati that have been published (Kimball 1991, 1994a) and for the putting together of this collection of narratives. Together, these three volumes represent the ideal that she laid before her students at the University of California at Berkeley, and I am glad that I was able to live up to her ideal and only regret that she did not live to see its completion.

I was encouraged to persevere in this work by Bel Abbey (1916–1991), one of the best modern-day storytellers among the Koasati. He was enchanted by the ancient tales preserved by Swanton and felt that if such stories were written in both Koasati and English, they would be accessible for his children and their descendants, even if the language itself should fail. In addition to relating his repertoire of traditional narratives, he encouraged his cousin Martha John and other relatives to do likewise. Perhaps even most remarkably, he attempted to pass on traditional narratives in the old way, by teaching them to his younger relatives—two of the stories in this collection were preserved in such a manner. Bel Abbey acted as a friend and as an advisor to me in the process of doing this work, and was actively engaged in it at the time of his sudden and untimely death. The work is now finished, and perhaps the spirit of Bel

Abbey will be satisfied when he watches his family reading these ancient tales.

This project was supported by a grant from the National Endowment for the Humanities (RL-21726-91) and by a grant from the Phillips Fund of the American Philosophical Society. In addition, a number of the narratives were recorded during the course of the Koasati Dictionary Project, which was funded by a grant from the National Science Foundation (BNS 8719269). In addition to Bel Abbey and Martha John, much-needed help was given by Sam Thompson, Bel Abbey's brother-in-law, during the period after Mr. Abbey's death. To all these people I give my heartfelt thanks.

There are also a number of people worthy of thanks during the long process (interrupted by Hurricane Katrina and long exile without text, tapes, or notes) of bringing this manuscript to publication. I would like to thank Raymond J. DeMallie of the American Indian Studies Research Institute, Indiana University, for his care and encouragement. In addition, I would like to thank Mrs. Cherry R. Hudson and Dr. Stephen L. Pearce of Byers Green, Co. Durham, England, for reading over the manuscript carefully and offering much-needed proofing and suggestions. I also appreciate the assistance provided by Mrs. Kathleen C. White of Newfield in Co. Durham.

## On the Translation

Although translation is commonly assumed to be a science, it is rather more of an art, and a treacherous art at that. A word may well have one meaning on its own, but quite a different one in combination with other words. And the perils are well known, as the Italian proverb *traduttore, traditore* 'the translator is a traitor', attests.

The ideal translator is one who knows the source language and the target language equally well, and is at home in both of them. However, for an American Indian language such as Koasati, such a translator does not exist. This is due to the way that Koasati and English are used among younger people—the ones who are most likely to have been educated in English. For those people, English is used with English-speaking people, and Koasati is used with Koasati-speaking people, and in their minds there is no interface between the two languages. They rarely, if ever, consider how to turn a Koasati phrase into English or vice versa. On the other hand, the generation of their parents had parents or other elderly relatives who were monolingual in Koasati (the last monolingual speaker died in 1995), and who required interpreters for even the most minor transactions with English-speakers. However, this generation of interpreters sometimes lacked the most basic education in English, and though they could translate general meaning, they could no more convey the art of Koasati speech than they could write an English sonnet.

Bel Abbey was of this generation of interpreters, and he keenly felt the lack of English education. Highly intelligent, thoughtful, and meditative, he was excellently educated in the traditional Koasati way, and the fact that his English was broken and labored bothered him. Up to the end of his life he was interested in learning the proper English way of expressing some idea, especially if it were an idea that he knew well in Koasati. He is the one who sat down with me when I was faced with a difficult passage, and who carefully and thoroughly worked through it with me until the correct English translation appeared.

And this is my responsibility—all the translations are my own. Some persons seem suspicious that the translation is done by one who is not a native speaker of the language, but a native speaker's translations lack far more than they contain, and their very nonstandard nature diminishes the interest of the English reader and puts the material at a distance. Swanton's (1929) published translations of the Koasati narratives he gathered in 1910 present a good exanple of this. On the whole, they are dull, flat, and lifeless, and give a very wrong impression of the people who told them. I have studied the Koasati language for over twenty years, and I am considered by native speakers to have a tolerable command of the language and a very good vocabulary. Thus, these translations are what I feel that the Koasati would say, were English their native language. I have tried not to intrude my personality or beliefs into the translations, but, as I have acted as a lens to focus the light of the one language into the other, the lens may have added some unwitting distortion. If so, the fault is my own, but I trust that it is not great enough to distract from the intrinsic interest of these narratives, nor from their usefulness for Koasati and non-Koasati alike.

In the chapter introductions and textual commentaries I have touched on many features of Koasati life as they were understood in aboriginal times. All of this now is a matter of fading memory, which is why it has been written down—to help the reader understand the social situation in which the characters of the narratives live, and the underlying knowledge of the original audience. It is not to be understood that any of this is now living tradition, since Koasati culture has changed drastically—socially, economically, and religiously—between the last quarter of the nineteenth century and the first quarter of the twenty-first century. This also is to serve as a warning to any non-Koasati person who thinks that he can take this book in hand, go to the community, and ask if this is so, or please explain that in more detail. If so, he will find a very cool reception at best, and an active hostility at worst. As Bel Abbey once explained, there is some knowledge that is always the exclusive property of the Indians, and they have the right to remember it, or to forget it, without consideration of the value that it may have for the outside world. I learned a few things rarely told to non-Koasati, and I trust that I have not revealed anything that I should not have. If I have done so, I beg their forgiveness, and I will trust that this work, the preservation of these ancient traditions, will serve as an excuse.

## Koasati Versification

All Koasati traditional narratives, and to a degree all Koasati narratives of whatever genre, are in verse. However, this verse is not in the tradition of European verse—that is, it is not created by the use of meter or rhyme. Rather, the verse form is basic to the language itself, to which the narrator applies her or his art to create effects that are perceived as verse to the Western ear. The Koasati language possesses a syntactic device called *anticipatory switch reference*, which involves a group of verbal suffixes whose purpose is to indicate to the listener that the verb that is about to follow has the same subject as, or a different subject than, the previous verb. Because of this device, Koasati sentences in narrative may be extraordinarily long, occasionally, an entire narrative may consist of but one sentence.

The basic unit of Koasati verse, so far as I now understand it, is the phrase. A phrase can consist of what can be translated as an English sentence, or it may consist of just one nominal element. A phrase, or verse, is defined by intonational, morphological, or semantic factors, or all three. The beginning of a phrase bears a slight rise in pitch, unconnected with the pitch accent of the particular word at the beginning of the phrase, and the end of a phrase bears a slight fall in pitch. The end of a phrase can be, but is not always, marked by an extended pause. Morphological markers of phrases are the switch-reference markers. The suffix *-n*, which indicates that the following verb has a different subject, almost always ends a phrase. The suffix *-k*, which indicates that the following verb has the same subject, more rarely indicates the end of a phrase, although it always does when it is affixed to a verb in the h-grade ablaut form. The nominal suffix *-o:t*, which creates lists of nouns, also ends a phrase (see Kimball 1991 for the grammar of these elements). The primary semantic criterion for the formation of a phrase is that quoted speech—or reported thought, which is structured like quoted speech—form separate phrases.

Despite the use of anticipatory switch reference, or perhaps because of it, there is a plethora of conjunctions in Koasati that relate phrases temporally, sequentially, causally, and so forth. A rather difficult feature of Koasati conjunctions for the English speaker is the fact that they are full phrases (they are essentially inflected impersonal verbs). This explains the fact that a conjunction almost always forms a single verse whenever it occurs in a narrative.

I have been aided in the study of Koasati verse by the work of Dell Hymes (1981 and personal communications) and Dennis Tedlock (1972). Hymes (p.c., 1992) has also suggested the division of Koasati narratives into scenes, a structural feature that has turned out to be highly significant. The matter of the layout of the texts has been treated more as a matter of convenience than of structure. My Koasati consultants all wanted to have Koasati and English text on the same page, and parallel as much as possible. Thus, the first verse (phrase) of a sentence is flush left, and each succeeding phrase is indented two spaces. Verse numbers are given only to help keep track of the placement of the English translation vis-à-vis the Koasati original and do not have any structural function. I trust that this format will be useful to the Koasati speaker and the English reader alike, but I have no illusions that it is the final word in regard to the structure of Koasati verse.

## Koasati Pronunciation

ʔ glottal stop, pronounced as a catch in the throat, as in the English interjection "uh-oh."

*a* a low central vowel, like the *a* in English father. Long *a* is written *a:* and pronounced like the *a* in English *heart*. Nasalized *a* is written *ą*, and is pronounced like *a*, with some of the breath of its production passing through the nose.

*b* a voiced, fortis, and unaspirated stop, pronounced like English *b*.

*c* a voiceless, fortis, and aspirated stop, phonetically [č], usually pronounced like English *ch.* By some people it is pronounced *ts* as in English *bats.*

*d* voiced, lenis, and unaspirated, found only in borrowings from English.

*e* a mid front vowel, pronounced like English *ey* in the interjection *hey.*

*f* a bilabial fricative [ɸ]. Koasati *f* is produced by friction between the narrowed lips, unlike English, in which *f* is produced by bringing the upper lip close to the lower teeth.

*g* voiced, lenis, and unaspirated, found only in borrowings from English.

*h* a velar fricative with a number of allophones. Word-initially and intervocalically, it is a voiceless aspirate, pronounced similarly to English *h*. Word-finally, *h* is a voiceless continuation of the preceding vowel. In consonant clusters, *h* frequently has a pharyngeal allophone [ɦ], which is produced by a tightening of the larynx during its production.

*i* a high front vowel, pronounced very much like the *i* in English *pin*. Long *i* is written *i:* and pronounced like the *i* in English *machine*. Nasalized *i* is written *į* and is pronounced like *i* with some of the breath of its production passing through the nose.

*j* voiced, lenis, and unaspirated, found only in borrowings from English.

*k* a voiceless, fortis, and aspirated stop, pronounced like English *k.*

*l* a lateral consonant pronounced like English *l.*

*ɬ* a lateral fricative [ɬ]. It does not occur in English or in any European language with the exception of Welsh. It is pronounced by placing the tongue in the position for *l* and allowing air to pass voicelessly and with friction around the sides of the tongue. Many Koasati-speaking people think that is the same as English *th*; however, this is due to the fact that, in their dialect of English, they replace *th* [θ] with [ɬ].

*m* a bilabial nasal pronounced like English *m.*

*n* a dental nasal pronounced like English *n.*

*o* a mid back vowel, pronounced very much like the *o* in English *coat*. Long *o* is written *o:* and pronounced like the *o* in English *know*. Nasalized *o* is written *ǫ* and is pronounced like *o* with some of the breath of its production passing through the nose.

*p* a voiceless, fortis, and aspirated stop, pronounced much like English *p.*

*r* a rare variant of *l* and *s* found in a few native words. In native words, it is a buzzing continuant [ɹ], much like Chinese *r*; in borrowings from English, it is pronounced like English *r*.

*s* a dental-palatal fricative with a number of allophones. It has the dental allophone [s], pronounced like English *s*, when it occurs as any member of a consonant cluster or initially in a word before *a*. It has the alveolar allophone [ṣ], a backed *s* not found in English, in word-final position and initially in a word before *i*. It has the palatal allophone [š], pronounced like English *sh*, intervocalically and initially before *o*.

*t* a voiceless, fortis, and aspirated stop, pronounced much like English *t*.

*u* a high back vowel, occurring only in a few interjections, pronounced like the *oo* in English *food*. Long *u* is written *u:*. This vowel does not occur nasalized.

*v* a voiced bilabial fricative [β]. Though borrowed from the English labiodental fricative, it is pronounced by placing the lips in position for making a Koasati *f* and voicing the breath as it is expelled.

*w* a bilabial glide, pronounced like English *w*.

*x* a velar fricative, it does not occur in English. It is found only in a few interjections and is pronounced like the *ch* in Scots English *loch* or in German *Bach*.

*y* a palatal glide, pronounced like English *y*.

: an orthographic symbol indicating that the preceding vowel is long.

:: an orthographic symbol indicating that the preceding vowel is double long.

˛ an orthographic symbol indicating that the vowel beneath which it is placed is nasalized.

´ an orthographic symbol indicating that the vowel over which it is placed is spoken with a high pitch.

` an orthographic symbol indicating that the vowel over which it is placed is spoken with a low pitch.

ˇ an orthographic symbol indicating that the vowel over which it is placed is spoken with a pitch that begins on a high level, rises and then falls to a lower pitch.

# Part One

# Mythological Narratives

# 1

# Rabbit Stories

Rabbit is the trickster-hero of Koasati literature, as he is in all of the literatures of the Indians of the Southeast. He is a self-centered, overweeningly proud troublemaker, always playing tricks, and acting against the common good. However, his character is so identified with traditional narrative, that all speakers call traditional narratives "Rabbit stories" (*cokfa:łihilká* < *cokfí* 'rabbit' + *a:łihilká* 'story').

Rabbit stories are extremely popular, and there is even an interjection, *hé cokfí* 'go on, Rabbit!' that is used by listeners when he has played a particularly good trick. It is interesting how an essentially antisocial character gained such popularity; it seems that Rabbit Stories serve as a sort of social safety valve, allowing the expression and tacit approval of various sorts of socially disapproved behavior, such as lies, trickery, and unconcern for others. By allowing these behaviors to be acted out in fantasy, it defuses them from being acted out in society. Furthermore, since most Rabbit stories end with Rabbit suffering some severe punishment as a result of his behavior, the listener can also enjoy the triumph of virtue over vice.

The actual character Rabbit varies, primarily according to the date that a tale was recorded. In the earliest recordings, it is clear that Rabbit is both human and animal, with the ability to change back and forth at will. This is illustrated most clearly in *Rabbit Steals Fire*. In the later tales, it is clear that he is no longer considered capable of shape-shifting, but is confined to his animal form, albeit with certain anthropomorphized characteristics.

Rabbit as a trickster can have anyone as a foil, although his primary bête noire is Great-One-Who-Eats-Human-Beings (*a:ti:pacobá*). In the company of Rabbit, Great-One-Who-Eats-Human-Beings is very different from the monster that is described in *The Obstacle Flight* in chapter 3. In that tale, he is a powerful and fearful man-eater, completely beyond the control of any human. When he appears in Rabbit stories, however, Great-One-Who-Eats-Human-Beings, while usually maintaining certain of his cannibalistic characteristics, as in *Rabbit Switches Dung with Great-One-Who-Eats-Human-Beings*, is big, slow, and painfully easy to deceive. In a few Rabbit stories, Great-One-Who-Eats-Human-Beings displays no cannibalistic characteristics at all. This seems to be the result of a tendency to bleach his character of its more horrific aspects, and the identification of Great-One-Who-Eats-Human-Beings as Elephant seems to have furthered this process.

Although Rabbit sometimes comes out on top—usually when he is paired with Great-One-Who-Eats-Human-Beings—more often than not he suffers some humiliation before the close of the narrative, whether it is as minor as getting beaten up by his wives in *Rabbit Steals*

*Fire*, or as major as getting eaten alive in *The Bungling Host*. This is due to his overweening pride or hubris (*ilakasamotilká*), and to the Koasati, pride was as great a sin as it was to the ancient Greeks. Just as hubris was punished by the gods in Greek drama, so Rabbit's *ilakasamotilká* is punished, not by any particular deity, but by the natural order of the world. However, Rabbit, like other trickster characters throughout North America, never learns from his mistakes, and is always ready to make some more.

## RABBIT STEALS FIRE

narrated by *Sacowáyhki*

This narrative was dictated to John R. Swanton in 1910. The Koasati language text was not published, but a translation based on its interlinear glosses was published by Swanton (1929:203–4).

*Sacowáyhki,* whose English name was Jackson Langley, was, with his mother Selin Williams Langley, the principal consultant for both John R. Swanton and Mary R. Haas. He was of good family; his mother's sister was married to the Koasati *mikkó,* John Abbey, and not long after Swanton worked with him, *Sacowayhki* himself became *mikkó* after the death of John Abbey. However, some time in the 1920s, he was replaced as *mikkó* by the son of John Abbey, *Sacikílli,* also known as Jefferson Abbey. The reasons for this are no longer clear; some say that it was the result of a failed attempt to go to Washington, D.C. to obtain help for the Indians. Others say it happened after the death of his wife *Sihó:ki* while giving birth to their eleventh child, when he became enamored of a young Tunica woman and left the community to pursue her. This relationship did not last, and *Sacowáyhki* returned home and contracted a normal levirate marriage with his late wife's sister's daughter (as his wife had no unmarried or widowed sisters). He remained in the community for the rest of his life, although the loss of the position of *mikkó* rankled until the end of his days.

This particular tale seems to have had a deep psychological resonance with *Sacowáyhki*, as it focuses on the hypersexuality of Rabbit. *Sacowáyhki* is remembered as having an extraordinarily high sex drive; in addition to his eleven children with his first wife, he had six with his third wife, the youngest being born when he was 72 years of age. The act of running off after the young Tunica woman, abandoning all his responsibilities, could be seen as Rabbit-like behavior. In any case, the sexual content of this tale is much more elaborate than in the recording of the tale as narrated by Bel Abbey. In 1936, *Sacowáyhki* gave Mary R. Haas a truncated version of this narrative, one that ruthlessly edited out every reference to sex. Because sexual matters are freely discussed only among Indians themselves, or in sexually segregated groups of non-Indians, *Sacowáyhki* felt free to include the sexual element only with an adult male non-Indian audience (Swanton), and produced an edited version for an adult female non-Indian audience (Haas).

## Scene 1: The World without Fire

Yá:li tikbák íksotoho:limpatš.
Mó:tohon,
okicobá tałón má:lon ná:hoto:š tikbák.

Máhmin,
yá:lik tikbą́ ohimbànnatik,
inká:hį bánkoto:š.

Má:min,
í:sato:š tikbá-íkson.

It is said that fire did not exist here.
Later,
[people found out that] fire existed
only on the other side of the ocean.
Right away,
the people here wanted fire from them,
but the others did not want to give
it to them.
Then,
they lived without fire.

## Scene 2: The Quest for Fire Is Proposed

Mó:tohon,
cokfík ónkak,
"Anók ómmi:k, tikbá astiwwalí:kalik"
ká:hato:š.
Má:mo:sin,
á:ti ocotaykihák hasaykáhcok
cokkó:tohok ónkak,
"Naksók tikbá ostí:lan
tayyihá caffá:kan
ínkala:š" káhhan.
Cokfí:kok ónkak,
"Mántik tayyihá caffá:ka:sip
stamalpísko:š," ká:hato:š.

Later on,
Rabbit spoke,
"As for me, I can run with those people's
fire," he said.
Thereupon,
a person whose daughters were many
spoke:
"To whomever goes and brings back fire
I shall give one of the women," he said.

Rabbit spoke:
"But just one of the women is not
enough for me," he said.

## Scene 3: The First Quester Fails

Má:min,
"Anók," ká:hatoho:limpats a:ti:pacobák.

"Sti:lalíhc," káhhan.
A:ti:kok ónkak,
"Mó:li:p, isnók áłłok ohwíhlit stí:l!"
káhhan.
A:ti:pacobá:kok tayyihá bànnak,

bikkón ałí:yatoho:limpatš.
Má:mik okicobá ohto:cofóttoho:limpatš.

O:nakáłto:š.

Then,
"I," said Great-One-Who-Eats-Human-
Beings, so it is reported.
"I can bring it," he said.
"The person spoke:
"Well, as for you, go off, go and look
for it and bring it!" he said.
Great-One-Who-Eats-Human-Beings
wanted women,
and he went first, so it is said.
And at that he went and dived into the
sea, so it is said.
He disappeared into the water.

Má:mik,
íklot nakáɬɬan.

Then,
he did not come back and was gone.

### Scene 4: Rabbit Is Sent on the Quest

Cokfí:kok ónkak,
"A:ti ná:sok ɬóykat íklot,"
ká:toho:limpatš.
"Aná:ɬok ómmo:š.
Łóykat í:lahalpí:sak," káhhan.
A:ti:kok mán mattóhnoto:š.
Má:min,
cokfí:kok ónkak,
"Mó:li:p, tikbá stí:lali:p,
tayyí imaníhtaha óhyan
apoɬó:kallaho:š," ká:toho:limpatš.

Rabbit spoke:
"No one has come back," he said,
so it is reported.
"I alone am the one.
I can come back," he said, so it is reported.
The person also sent for him.
Then,
Rabbit spoke:
"Well, if I bring fire,
I shall have sexual intercourse with all of
the young women individually," he said,
so it is reported.

Má:min,
á:tik ónkak,
"Mámmitikš!" kahhan.

Then,
the person spoke:
"Let it be so!" he said.

### Scene 5: Rabbit Crosses the Ocean and Steals Fire

Má:mo:sin,
cokfí:kok yawophilkón
aɬíytoho:limpatš.

Thereupon,
Rabbit went quickly, so it is said.

Aɬí:yak,
okifón ó:ɬat,
holikfá síhlit apíslok,
ittó tospón pa:cokkóhlok,
sto:waɬíytoho:limpatš.
Má:mik,
o:ɬopóttoho:limpatš.
A:yatoho:limpatš.
Mó:tohon,
tikbán a:timbànnan,
ohįhíkkon,
astimíhsok,
astiwwalí:katoho:limpatš.
Má:min,
hoɬóhtoho:limpatš.
Má:min,
stá:yat
óhya ittohayó swalí:kat,

He went off,
and arrived over there to the ocean;
he took off his shirt and threw it off,
and sitting on a rotting log,
it is said that he went off sailing.
Then,
he forded the ocean, so it is said.
He went about there, so it is said.
And later,
he wanted fire from people,
and they did not give it to him,
and taking it from them,
he ran with it from them, so it is said.
At that,
it is said that they chased after him.
Then,
he carried it;
through the whole forest he ran with it

stá:ya:sin,
okicobafón óhłok,
oshaccá:lik.

and he really carried it,
and, having arrived over at the ocean,
he went and stood with it.

**Scene 6: Rabbit Swims the Ocean with Fire**

Mó:tohon,
coyyí nihán isbakkí obá:li,
coyyí mashamóhlit anóhlok,
hacca:tohon,
á:tik łóhli:k ilá:ci:fó:kon,
sto:cofóttoho:limpatš.
Ilbí abón swáylit,
tikbá stó:wałí:yato:š.
Má:máhpok,
lóhkat anó:kak,
isbakkí obá:lin tikbá masbatáplit
hiłi:lí:cit sto:wałíytoho:limpatš.
Kámmit sto:wá:yat o:łopóttoho:limpatš.

Then afterwards,
pine resin on the back of his head,
having rubbed it full of pine,
he stood there,
and when the people who were chasing him arrived,
he dived into the water with the fire.
He held it up in his hand;
he went in the water with the fire.
Nevertheless,
when he became tired,
it is said that he struck the back of his head with the fire,
set it on fire, and went in the water with it.
In such a way, it is said, did he carry it in the water and go in the water with it.

**Scene 7: Rabbit Receives His Reward**

Má:mok,
á:tifa:kon stí:lato:š.
Máhmin,
tayyihá imaníhta ínkak ónkak,
"Hiná:p yók cintayyí mó:š,"
ká:toho:limpatš.
Má:mo:sin,
cokfí:kok ayókpat ayókpat
á:tatoho:limpatš.
Mó:tohok,
tamóhkan,
bálká:hi:fó:kon,
cokfík ónkak,
"Hotahón támmillaho:š anók,"
ká:toho:limpatš.

Then,
he brought it to that person.
Right then,
he gave him the young women and spoke:
"Now indeed these are your women,"
he said, so it is reported.
Thereupon,
Rabbit was in a state of extreme happiness.
And then afterwards,
night having fallen,
when they were about to lie down,
Rabbit spoke:
"In the middle is where I shall be lying!" he said.

| | |
|---|---|
| Má:min, | Then, |
| tayyihák ittimmánkak anóskok cokfí ohimpátlin, | the young women having finished speaking to one another, made the bed for Rabbit. |
| "Híc!" hoká:n, ballá:kato:š. | "Now!" they said, and he lay down. |

## Scene 8: Rabbit Receives His Comeuppance

| | |
|---|---|
| Ma:fó:kon, | When that had taken place, |
| tayyihák ittimmánkak, | the young women spoke to one another. |
| "Cokfík balláhkan, | "Rabbit having lain down, |
| inna:łí:kat afá:kat stistílkan, | we are to continue to laugh and to speak to him, |
| cokfík ayókpahalpí:sat tàmmi:fó:kon, | and when Rabbit is lying down and sufficiently happy, |
| shompá:nit ittįhalátkok | we are to play with him, |
| ittaskáhhílkok, | and grab him together, and go out |
| acón stonłá, | and arriving outside, |
| holikfá įsíhhílok, | we shall strip off his shirt, |
| łómmit apí:hílá:š," | beat him, and dispose of him," |
| hoká:toho:limpatš. | they said, so it is reported. |
| Mó:tohok, | Then afterwards, |
| bálka:fó:kon, | when they lay down, |
| cokfí:kon shompántoho:limpatš. | they played with Rabbit, so it is said. |
| Má:mo:sin, | Thereupon, |
| cokfí:kok hotahán tàmmit ayókpahalpí:stoho:limpatš. | it is said that Rabbit was lying in the middle sufficiently happy. |
| Akkámmit tàmmo:sin, | He was just lying so, |
| ittįhalátkok shompá:nit, | and they grabbed him together playing with him, |
| acón stałłá:cok, | having taken him outside, |
| himá:k sbakóhlá:hih bànnok stí:sa:sin, | now they were in the process of trying to throw him, |
| cokfí:kok yawópkat yawópkok cofótli:k, | and when Rabbit, excessively frightened, jumped, |
| hohalátkahónka:sin, | they were holding on to him so tightly |
| atabifá afakcón socáffok, | that he slipped out of the skin of his back, |
| walí:kak nakáłtoho:limpatš. | ran off, and disappeared, so it is said. |

**Epilogue**

| | |
|---|---|
| Mó:tohok, | Then afterwards, |
| á:yatoho:š. | he went about. |
| Mó:tohon, | Then afterwards, |
| a:ti:pacobók afánkan, | he met Great-One-Who-Eats-Human-Beings, |
| ittinna:ɬí:katoho:š. | and they spoke to one another. |
| Mahmin, | Right then, |
| a:ti:pacobák ónkak, | Great-One-Who-Eats-Human-Beings spoke, |
| "Naksámmin cįholikfák cipa:íksó?" | "Why do you have no shirt on your back?" |
| ka:toho:limpatš. | he said, so it is reported. |
| Ká:han, | He said it, |
| Cokfík ónkak, | and Rabbit spoke: |
| "Iltóhnolik ó:š," ká:toho:limpatš. | "It is the case that I am working," he said, so it is reported. |
| Tayyihák ąhasaykáhcok ómmo:š. | It is the case that my women are many. |
| Acayókpat acayókpš," ká:toho:limpatš. | I am very happy," he said, so it is reported. |
| Mántik a:ti:pacobák iyyínkotoho:limpatš. | But it is said that Great-One-Who-Eats Human-Beings did not believe him. |

*Textual emendations*:

| | | |
|---|---|---|
| Line 6 | iñgahabạ´ ñgotos | ínká:hį bánkoto:š |
| Line 14 | ō´itaigiha | ocotaykihák |
| Line 20 | istilalē´ ts | sti:laiihc |
| Line 34 | matō´honatōs | mattóhnoto:š |
| Line 66 | nas hạmholit | mashamóhlit |
| Line 72 | mama´xpo | mamáhpok |
| Line 86 | bạlgaifō´gun | bálkáhi:fó:kon |
| Line 88 | ta´ minlahōs | tàmmillaho:š |
| Line 111 | isbạka´ le bạ´nok | sbakóhlá:hih bànnok |
| Line 112 | yawō´pgo | yawópkok |

*Textual commentary*:

Line 16 This line provokes laughter among listeners, for it reflects the role of Rabbit as one who openly violates the norms of society. Although the exchange of women for fire is part of the plot skeleton of this narrative, Langley's version emphasizes Rabbit's sexual voracity, in contrast to a version recorded by Bel Abbey (Kimball 1993a), which subordinates it to other elements.

Line 36 Rabbit's statement is considered quite shocking, and the language is blunt. The use of the verb *apoɬó:kan* 'to have sexual intercourse with someone (singular object)' with a plural object (*tayyí imaníhtaha óhyan* 'all the young women') implies that he will have sexual intercourse in sequence with the women, leaving one and going on to the next.

Lines 42–46 The length of this sentence, consisting of five lines, is an indication that this is an important point in the narrative. Rabbit sailed over the ocean on a rotten log; however, he returned by swimming. His swimming over the ocean is one of the climactic points. The statement that Rabbit threw off his shirt implies that he transformed himself from his human form into his animal form; in this version, the same transformation occurs at the second climax. The use of a rotten log as Rabbit's vessel is a good descriptive element. It is based on the observation that rabbits in nature, when hunted by dogs during the spring floods, will leap onto a rotten log floating by (rotten logs being hollow, and thus better floating) and thus escape the hunters.

Lines 51–63 The increasing lengths of the lines as this scene draws to a close indicates the importance of what is told here to the plot of the story. The land across the ocean is sketched by the mention of the forest that reaches down to the ocean. Dramatic tension is heightened by Rabbit reaching the ocean carrying the fire and stopping, even though others are in pursuit of him.

Lines 55–63 These lines contain a very finely wrought parallel structure: 'he carried it' of line 58 is paralleled by 'he ran with it' in line 54, repeated again as 'he really carried it' in line 60, and paralleled by 'he went and stood with it' in line 62. The 'Forest' in line 59 is balanced by 'ocean' in line 61.

Lines 64–76 This scene also is marked as important by the lengths of the lines. The most important part of the scene is that in which Rabbit rubs the back of his head with pine resin, although at the time why he does so is not stated. The reason for his action becomes clear in the second half of the scene, in which Rabbit, having grown tired holding the fire up above the water with his hand, strikes it to the back of his head, where the ignited pine resin will keep it burning until he returns to the other side of the ocean.

Line 88 Rabbit's statement here is another expression of his hypersexuality. Again, Langley seems to dwell on this feature of Rabbit's personality with interest, although the following scene will prove that Langley's interest is not unaffected by traditional mores.

Lines 93–115 The very long lengths of these sentences indicate that, to Langley, this was the main climax of the tale. As far as it can be determined, it is entirely of his creation; not even a hint of this scene can be found in the version of this tale told by Bel Abbey, which maintains all the other plot elements. Within this scene, Rabbit receives his comeuppance for his hubris In this instance, his hubris is of a sexual nature, manifested in his ready acceptance of the suggestion that all of the women would want him just as much as he wanted them. Hubris, as mentioned above, is considered by the Koasati to be a vice, and the comeuppance of a character with hubris is the main topic of those traditional narratives told with frequency at the present time. Also, the punishment for hubris is typically in character with the nature of the offence. The revolt of the women, who heretofore have been reified as goods to be given to Rabbit for his services, is much more typical of Koasati culture than Langley's patriarchal fantasies. The older Indians report that, in the 1930s, a woman whose husband took a secondary wife was so incensed that she beat the living daylights out of him. In this scene, Langley almost revels in the tables being turned on Rabbit—a violent reassertion of the norms of his culture in contrast to the patriarchal situation depicted in the previous scenes of the tale. The scene is quite descriptive; however, the sexual goings on are hinted at, rather than made explicit. The part at the end in which Rabbit slips out of his skin, transforming himself from human to animal, is very well handled. Listeners find this scene very funny, with the humor lying in the deflation of Rabbit's sexual hubris.

Lines 116–29 This epilogue is the weakest part of the narrative; in my experience, listeners preferred to have the tale end with the last line of the eighth scene. The epilogue violates the semantic standard for a well-formed tale by reintroducing Great-One-Who-Eats-Human-Beings, who dived into the ocean and disappeared (or drowned) in lines 17–19. The only connection with the rest of the tale is the lack of a shirt (or skin) on Rabbit's back, it having been stripped from him by the women. The only possible reason that Langley added this epilogue to the narrative was to show that Rabbit never learns from experience—that he is still full of hubris. Like the typical braggart and liar, as soon as he leaves the scene of his humiliation, Rabbit returns to his old self.

## RABBIT TRICKS GREAT-ONE-WHO-EATS-HUMAN-BEINGS
narrated by Selin Williams

The narrative *Rabbit Tricks Great-One-Who-Eats-Human-Beings* was taken by dictation in Koasati by John R. Swanton in 1910. He assigned it number seventeen in his manuscript "Koasati Texts, Second Series" (Swanton 1910) and later published a translation based on the interlinear glosses in this manuscript (Swanton 1929:207–8). It is notable that in the published version he deleted the lines in scene 3 in which Rabbit tells that his testicles will pop. Such deletions, and the translation in other narratives of salacious matter into Latin, were a concession to standards of decency set by the Post Office based on the Hicklin Rule and required of scientific publications of the period. A new translation of this narrative, presented without the Koasati text, has also been published (Kimball 1995).

Selin Williams, whose Koasati name is not remembered, was the mother of *Sacowáyhki* (Jackson Langley) by Joe Langley of the *Kowí ayiksá*. Her family was among the first of the Koasati to settle in southwest Louisiana in the 1860s and 1870s. Her sister was married to the Koasati *mikkó*, John Abbey, and her sister-in-law *Sokí* was a well-known traditional doctor. Selin Williams had a wide knowledge of traditional tales; in fact the vast majority of the Origin Tales found in chapter 2 were told by her.

### Scene 1: Rabbit Encounters Great-One-Who-Eats-Human-Beings

| | |
|---|---|
| A:ti:pacobá:kok iltohnóhcok cafhayó á:tatohon,<br>cokfók imóhłok intóhnofon. | Great-One-Who-Eats-Human-Beings was continuing to work in the field,<br>when Rabbit arrived over there to where he was working. |
| Cokfík ónkak,<br>"Na:son iltocíhnó?" ká:toho:limpatš. | Rabbit spoke:<br>"What are you working at?" he said, so they say. |
| Máhmin,<br>a:ti:pacobák ónkak,<br>"Palancobón acíhlila:š,"<br>ká:toho:limpatš. | Then,<br>Great-One-Who-Eats-Human-Beings spoke.<br>"I intend to plant string beans," he said,<br>so it is reported. |

### Scene 2: Rabbit Tricks the Wife of Great-One-Who-Eats-Human Beings

| | |
|---|---|
| Máhmin,<br>cokfík ałí:yak.<br>a:ti:pacobá halkifá óhłok,<br>ónkak,<br>"Palancobán ąhólcimpa:š," káhhan,<br>a:ti:pacobá halkík ónkak,<br>"Yáp palancobá acíhhílilahok ómmitš," káhhan,<br>"Mántik,<br>'Cįhó:łilaho:š," ká:ha:š,"<br>káhhan,<br>halkík iyyínkotoho:limpatš. | Then,<br>Rabbit went off,<br>and arriving at the house of the wife of Great-One-Who-Eats-Human-Beings,<br>he spoke.<br>"Your husband said that you should cook string beans for me by boiling,"<br>he said,<br>and the wife of Great-One-Who-Eats-Human-Beings spoke.<br>"But it is the case that we will be planting these string beans," she said.<br>"But,<br>'She will cook them for you by boiling,' he said," he said,<br>and they say that the wife did not believe him. |
| Máhmin,<br>Cokfik ónkak,<br>"Mó:li:p,<br>matimasilhá:cilin," káhhan,<br>ónkak,<br>"Ehę́," káhhan,<br>cokfik oshaccáhlok,<br>"Iská:son?" kahhan,<br>a:ti:pacobák ónkak,<br>"Ehę́," ká:toho:limpatš. | Then,<br>Rabbit spoke.<br>"Well,<br>I shall call and ask him," he said,<br>and she spoke.<br>"Yes," she said,<br>and Rabbit going and standing called,<br>"Did you say so?" and Great-One-Who-Eats-Human-Beings spoke.<br>"Indeed," he said, so it is reported. |

### Scene 3: Rabbit Pretends to Permit Great-One-Who-Eats-Human-Beings to Kill Him

| | |
|---|---|
| Mó:tohon, | Afterwards, |
| a:ti:pacobá:kok íhlok ónkak, | Great-One-Who-Eats-Human-Beings arrived and spoke. |
| "Palaná amanóshacǫ," káhhan, | "You have devoured my beans!" he said, |
| Cokfik ónkak, | and Rabbit spoke. |
| "Ahcihǫ:páˀsi?" ká:toho:limpatš. | "Are you really angry with me?" he said, so it is reported. |
| "Taybí cobá pa:balláhkalin, | "I shall lie down on a large box, |
| cakáɬkat cattakoyófš!" | and you chop and cut me in two!" |
| ká:toho:limpatš. | he said, so it is reported. |
| Máhmok, | Right then, |
| pa:balláhkan, | he lay down, |
| cakáɬkatohok, | and the other chopped at him, |
| cokfík cofótlin, | and he jumped away, |
| taybí pilahón cakáɬkat | and the other chopped against the box, |
| alwáhtoho:limpatš. | and destroyed it, so it is said. |
| Má:mo:sin, | Thereupon, |
| mán cokfík ónkak, | again Rabbit spoke. |
| "Mó:li:p, talí cobafón cokkó:lifa | "Well, I shall lie over on a large stone, over where it sits, |
| pa:balláhkalin, | |
| cakáɬkat cattakoyófš!" káhhan. | and you chop and cut me in two!" he said. |
| Má:mo:sin, | Thereupon, |
| cokfí:kok talifón ohpa:balláhkan, | Rabbit went over to a large stone and lay on it, |
| cakáɬkatohok, | and the other chopped at him, |
| cokfík incofótlin, | and he jumped away, |
| talí pilahón cakáɬkat | and the other chopped against the stone, |
| cafí onalwáhtoho:limpatš. | and destroyed the axe on it, so it is said. |
| "Á:tok caikbóhc," káhhok, | "No one can kill me," he said, |
| "Má:mik, í:san aconokbáhlok, | "unless, closing me in the house, |
| aconóstin, | and burning me, |
| cattaíllilaho:š," ká:toho:limpatš. | I shall die in the fire," he said, so it is reported. |
| "Cálli:p ónkalaho:š. | "It will make a noise as I die. |
| Ná:sok tokóhka mók, | Something also will pop, |
| cállin ónkalaho:š. | it will make a noise as I die |
| Cahiɬihcík ónkalaho:š," | My testicles will make a noise," |
| ká:toho:limpatš. | he said, so it is reported. |

| | |
|---|---|
| Máhmok, | Then, |
| ishayó ayahí nó:ta hóhcat, | in the house, he dug underneath the bedstead, |
| hopáhkin ohtachalíhkok | he went and got out far away, |
| á:tatoho:limpatš. | and stayed there, so it is said. |
| Akkammíhcok á:tatohon, | The other went on doing it, |
| onokbáhlok, | having shut it up, |
| onó:titoho:limpatš. | it is said he set it on fire. |
| Ma:fő:kap, | Right then, |
| walí:kat toppón ohtachalí:kat íhlok, | he ran and from far away he went and came out and arriving, |
| "Hó:!" ká:toho:limpatš. | "Ho!" he said, so it is reported. |
| "Ná:sok caíkbo:š. | "Nothing can kill me. |
| Pí:la ittimóklatílkaskš!" káhhan. | Let us become friends with each other!" he said, |
| A:ti:pacobá:kok imóklatoho:limpatš. | And it is said that Great-One-Who-Eats Human-Beings became friends with him. |

**Scene 4: Rabbit and Great-One-Who-Eats-Human-Beings Go Wandering**

| | |
|---|---|
| Má:mo:sin, | Thereupon, |
| a:yá:citoho:limpatš. | the two of them were going about, so it is said. |
| Máhmin, | Then, |
| ałłá:citohon, | as the two of them were going, |
| "Ittó pa:kawáłkok na:hóhc. | "There is a tree split by lightning. |
| Má:fon ohtinnó:cilaho:š," ká:hato:š. | We will sleep there," Rabbit said. |
| Mó:tohok, | Then afterwards, |
| ołá:ci:fó:kon, | when they arrived there, |
| ónkak, | he spoke. |
| "Ittón hasáyhkon wíhhílok, | "Having looked for a lot of wood, |
| innó:cilaho:š," ká:hato:š. | we will sleep," he said. |
| Má:mok, | Then, |
| ittó hápka tammá:hoscok haccá:lin, | an almost fallen dead tree stood there, |
| nikóhkat haccá:tohok, | it stood there shaking, |
| má ayakhá óhtin, | and he thought that near to that, |
| balláskato:š á:lok, | having kindled a fire, the two of them would lie down, |
| óhtin. | and he kindled a fire. |
| Mó:tohon, | Then afterwards, |
| nó:ci:fó:k, | while the other slept, |
| tołkaybí íkba kayápkat á:lok, | he thought to pick up some hot coals, |
| pa:tihípkok, | and pouring them out on him, |
| ibisnók sámmoscin póyhascon | he himself poured out for himself |

ilatihípkok,
falánkok á:tatoho:limpatš.

Mó:tohon,
mán nihtán ałłá:citohok.
"Hahci tontáfkok tàmmo:š," ká:hato:š
cokfik.
"Món ónłalaho:š," ká:haton.
O:łáhcin,
hahcosí iskónnascok tàmmitohon.
O:łáhcin,
cokfi:kok cofótlit tontafátlit ohhaccáhlok,
"Isná:łi man," káhhan,
a:ti:pacobá:kok matcofótlit
ithaccá:lin,
cokfi:kok łóykat matcofó:tlit
ithaccá:li:p,
hahcí stittakoyófkok,
a:ti:pacobák tałá má:lon
haccá:lin,
stoktá:yat
snakáłtoho:limpatš.
Má:mo:sin,
okicobá tałá pilahón ałí:yato:š.

a little bit on some cold ones,
and having risen from sleep,
it is said that he stayed on.
Then afterwards,
the next day the two of them went on.
"There is a river for jumping back and
forth across there," Rabbit said.
"Also, we will arrive there," he said.
On arriving there,
there was a narrow little creek.
On their arriving there,
Rabbit went and jumped across it.
"You also!" he said,
and Great-One-Who-Eats-Human-Beings
came jumping and stood there,
and when Rabbit came jumping back,
the river was cut in half,
and Great-One-Who-Eats-Human-
Beings stood only
on the other side,
and it floated off with him and
disappeared with him.
Afterwards,
it took him to the other side of the ocean.

*Textual emendations*:

| | | |
|---|---|---|
| Line 32 | ạ́ntcihṓnpa´asi | anciho̜:pá<sup></sup>ʔsí |
| Line 39 | ạliwa´tohō´limpats | alwáhtoho:limpatš |
| Line 52 | ạtconastē´ | aconóstin |
| Line 67 | tcaikobo´ | caíkbo:š |
| Line 68 | pēlot itimokạlạtkilks | pí:la ittimóklatílkaskš |
| Line 74 | na´ hats | na:hóhc |
| Line 79 | wehe´ lo | wíhhílok |
| Line 95 | gaxga´ hatōs | ká:hato:š |
| Line 98 | isku´ nastcu | iskónnascok |

*Textual commentary*:

Lines 1–27 The motif of a trickster tricking a being's wife (and thus the being itself) is widespread in the Southeast. Swanton (1929:254) gives a Natchez example where the Trickster is Turkey and the foil is Wildcat. Note that in this tale Great-One-Who-Eats-Human-Beings has no discernable cannibalistic characteristics and acts merely as a foil for Rabbit. This shows the transition from the cannibal monster to the bumbling Elephant.

Lines 18–27 Here, Great-One-Who-Eats-Human-Beings thinks that Rabbit has told his wife that he was planting string beans and that she did not know it, so he calls back to confirm it, not realizing that Rabbit has said that he said that she should cook them for Rabbit to eat.

Lines 54–57 *"Cálli:p ónkalaho:š. / Ná:sok tokóhka mók, / cállin ónkalaho:š. / Cahiłihcík ónkalaho:š," ká:toho:limpatš.* "'It will make a noise as I die. / Something also will pop, / it will make a noise as I die. / My testicles will make a noise," he said, so it is reported'. These lines, which listeners perceive as among the most amusing in the narrative, were deleted from Swanton (1929:207–8). Because of then-current Post Office standards, references to sex in the Southeastern narratives were either edited out completely, as in this instance, or, if they comprised too much of the narrative, translated into Latin. Koasati listeners perceive these lines not as sexual, but as droll.

Lines 87–92 This part of the scene, which is not completely clear, can be understood by comparison with similar scenes in other Southeastern narratives. Here, Rabbit and Great-One-Who-Eats-Human-Beings are camping in a place where Rabbit says something comes and pours hot coals on sleeping travelers. When Great-One-Who-Eats-Human-Beings goes to sleep, Rabbit pours some cold ashes on himself and hot ashes on Great-One-Who-Eats-Human-Beings, so that when he wakes up, he will think the same thing happened to Rabbit.

Lines 93–107 This part of the scene, the tricking of Great-One-Who-Eats-Human-Beings over the ocean, appears in other Southeastern stories and in later Koasati recordings as the final element of the narrative *Rabbit Switches Dung with Great-One-Who-Eats-Human-Beings*. The various episodes of Rabbit as trickster seem to have some degree of independent existence, and can be crafted together by the narrator in any way that she or he thinks feasible.

## RABBIT SWITCHES DUNG WITH GREAT-ONE-WHO-EATS-HUMAN-BEINGS
narrated by *Sacowáyhki*

This narrative, recorded in Koasati by John R. Swanton (1930), has never before been published. The dung-switching motif is found across the Southeast. Often, it occurs as part of a tale at the end of which Great-One-Who-Eats-Human-Beings is tricked over the ocean. This tale explains why at present-day Elephant (Great-One-Who-Eats-Human-Beings) is found only on the other side of the ocean and, metaphorically, why it no longer eats people, since by switching its dung from bones to grass, Rabbit made it into a plant eater.

### Scene 1: Rabbit Encounters Great-One-Who-Eats-Human-Beings

| | |
|---|---|
| Cokfín a:ti:pacobá ittafánkatoho:limpatš. | It is said that Rabbit and Great-One-Who Eats-Human-Beings met each other. |
| Máhmin, | Right then, |
| cokfík ónkak, | Rabbit spoke. |

"Ná:son ispáhcotohon?"
ká:toho:limpatš,
a:ti:pacobá imasilhá:cit.

"What do you usually eat?"
he said, so it is reported,
asking Great-One-Who-Eats-Human-Beings.

Máhmin,
a:ti:pacobák ónkak,
"Á:tį í:palíhco:š," ká:toho:limpatš.

And then,
Great-One-Who-Eats-Human-Beings spoke.
"I usually eat people," he said,
so it is reported.

Máhmin,
cokfík yínkotoho:limpatš.
Máhmik,
"Howó! Cikpóhc," ká:toho:limpatš.

Then,
Rabbit didn't believe it.
Then,
"No way! You can't eat them," he said,
so they say.

Máhmin,
"Anók ómmi mók á:tį í:palíhco:š,"
káhhan,
a:ti:pacobák iyyínkotoho:limpatš.

Then,
"I also am one who usually eats people,"
he said,
and Great-One-Who-Eats-Human-Beings did not believe him.

## Scene 2: Rabbit and Great-One-Who-Eats-Human-Beings Have a Defecation Contest

Máhmin,
ittinna:łí:kat stáswan,
má:mik,
"Hoppó:lat ilhicáskš!"
ká:toho:limpatš
cokfík.
Máhmin,
cokfík ónkak,
"Anáp hoppó:lali:p,
atcofkoninannáhco:š," káhhan,
stáswan,
"Mó:li:p, hoppó:lat ilhicáskš!"
káhhan.
Hoppá:lá:hi:fó:kon,
cokfík ónkak,
"Haytanátkat misi:lįh!"
Máhmo:sin,
ittá:sat hoppó:lat cikkí:katoho:limpatš.

Then,
the two of them stayed talking together,
and then,
"Let us try defecating!"
Rabbit said,
so it is reported.
Then,
Rabbit spoke,
"As for me, when I defecate,
it is nothing but human bones," he said,
and the two stayed together,
and the other said, "Well, let us try defecating!"
When they were about to defecate,
Rabbit spoke.
"Turn around and keep your eyes closed!"
Thereupon,
together the two of them sat defecating,
so it is said.

### Scene 3: Rabbit Switches Dung

| | |
|---|---|
| Mahmok, | Then, |
| fáyhlin, | as they quit, |
| "Híc! Ilhicáskš!" ká:toho:limpatš | "Now! Let us see!" said Rabbit, |
| cokfík. | so it is reported. |
| Illaykí matittacikkí:litoho:limpatš; | His dung lay in a heap on the ground, it is said; |
| pahinannáscok. | it was nothing but grass. |
| O:tamátlit ibisnók, | He himself switched it, |
| a:ti:pacobá illayką matpíhlok | and taking up Great-One-Who-Eats-Human-Beings's dung, |
| cikkí:toho:limpatš. | laid it down, so it is said. |
| Má:mo:sin, | Thereupon, |
| hohí:catoho:limpatš. | the two of them looked, so they say. |
| Mó:tohon, | Then, |
| hí:catohon, | they looked, |
| cokfí hoppó:litohofa, | and in the place where Rabbit had defecated, |
| nascofkoník cikkí:kan, | a heap of bones lay, |
| máhmin, | then, |
| a:ti:pacobá hoppó:litohofa, | in the place where Great-One-Who Eats-Human-Beings defecated, |
| pahí laykík cikkí:katoho:limpatš. | it is said that a heap of grass-dung lay. |

### Scene 4: Rabbit Angers Great-One-Who-Eats-Human-Beings

| | |
|---|---|
| Má:min, | Then, |
| cokfík ílbin stittibóklok, | Rabbit clapped his hands, |
| afa:lí:cit noksipá:citoho:limpatš. | laughed at him, and angered him, so they say. |
| Afa:lí:cit fáykon, | He did not quit laughing at him, |
| a:ti:pacobák noksíhpok, | and Great-One-Who-Eats-Human-Beings having become angry, |
| cokfí í:bih bànnatoho:limpatš. | he tried to kill him, so it is said. |

### Scene 5: Rabbit Tricks Great-One-Who-Eats-Human-Beings

| | |
|---|---|
| Má:min, | Then, |
| cokfík immałátlok, | Rabbit, being afraid of him, |
| įholástoho:limpatš. | lied to him, so they say. |
| "Ná:sik scincó:bak hocí:bá:š," ká:toho:limpatš. | "Something larger than you wants to kill you," he said, so it is reported. |
| Má:min, | Then, |
| "Acihiccá:cilá:š," káhhan. | "I will keep watch over you," he said. |

| | |
|---|---|
| Má:min, | Then, |
| "Cinó:ci:p, | "When you fall asleep, |
| okí láhpon ohcipa:tihípkalahǫ," | it will come and pour hot water |
| ká:toho:limpatš cokfík. | on you," said Rabbit, so it is reported. |
| Mó:tohok, | Then, |
| ibisná:lok okí ikbáhcon stí:latok, | he himself brought hot water, |
| nó:ci:fo:k, | and when he fell asleep, |
| matpa:tihípkok, | poured it on him, |
| walí:katoho:limpatš. | and ran away, so it is said. |

## Scene 6: Rabbit Tricks Great-One-Who-Eats-Human-Beings Again

| | |
|---|---|
| Má:mok, | Then, |
| "Cokfík hiná:p acón snó:ci:má:š, | "Rabbit must now sleep outside," |
| ká:toho:limpatš. | he said, so it is reported. |
| "Taybón naholí; | "I shall make a box, |
| hókfit nó:ci:š," ká:toho:limpatš. | get in it and sleep," he said, so they say. |
| Mó:tohok, | Then, |
| taybón náhhok, | having made the box, |
| okí pá:na ohpíɬkan, | he went and put it at the water's edge |
| tamó:ka:fó:k, | and when it was night, |
| a:ti:pacobák hókfon, | Great-One-Who-Eats-Human-Beings<br>was inside, |
| stonacástoho:limpatš. | and he [Rabbit] sealed it up,<br>so it is said. |
| Mó:tohok, | Then, |
| nó:ci:fó:kon, | when he was sleeping, |
| okifón masto:wapíhlok, | he threw it and him into the water, |
| walí:kat nakáɬtoho:limpatš. | and ran off and disappeared, so it is said. |

## Epilogue

| | |
|---|---|
| Ittohayó má:łon cokkó:lit, | He dwelt only in the forest, |
| maɬátlit, | he was afraid, |
| ittiɬík misípkot, | he did not close his eyes, |
| Ittiɬí įhó:patoho:limpatš. | and it is said that his eyes hurt. |

*Textual commentary*:

Lines 6–15  In this narrative, Great-One-Who-Eats-Human-Beings is still a cannibal, but his wits are not a match for Rabbit's.

Line 28  *"Haytántkat misí:iįh!"* ""Turn around and keep your eyes closed!"" By foolishly trusting Rabbit and doing what he says, Great-One-Who-Eats-Human-Beings makes it easy for Rabbit to trick him.

Lines 48–53 From this point on, this particular narrative varies from the other Koasati versions recorded and from those of other Southeastern groups. Martin Abbey mentioned that Great-One-Who-Eats-Human-Beings said, when he saw the switched dung, "I never shat like that before," and such a reaction is recorded in other Southeastern versions of this tale. In other versions, the episode of the translation of Great-One-Who-Eats-Human-Beings overseas follows; here, there are a couple of final tricks and the fear of Rabbit for Great-One-Who-Eats-Human-Beings is given as the reason why rabbits are so wild and almost never close their eyes.

## RABBIT AND GREAT-ONE-WHO-EATS-HUMAN-BEINGS HAVE A DUNG CONTEST

narrated by Bel Abbey

I recorded this narrative on tape in 1981. It is clearly related to the tale "Rabbit Switches Dung with Great One Who Eats Human Beings," but its focus is not on Rabbit tricking Great One Who Eats Human Beings, but rather on Rabbit's hubris. Rabbit suggests the dung contest because he doesn't really believe that Great-One-Who-Eats-Human-Beings is really the monster that he says he is, only to find out that he indeed is.

Bel Abbey was one of the premier storytellers of the last half of the twentieth century, who not only told stories well, but also encouraged their learning and preservation. On his father's side he was the grandson of *Sacikílli*, who was the Koasati *mikkó* for most of his young adult years. On his mother's side he was the grandson of the last of the traditional weatherworkers. He had an encyclopedic knowledge of traditional Koasati culture (*athómma imolpinó*), and was the last organizer of the *O:lanwí* festival (*o:lanwí stįhiná:ta*), which used to be celebrated between Christmas and New Year's.

This tale is told for its humor. Mr. Abbey's daughter and grandchildren were listening while the tale was being recorded, and they laughed in several places. The blunt language used by the characters in the narrative is considered to be quite funny; the introduction of generally taboo subjects such as sex, death, or excretion into a traditional narrative makes a narrative humorous.

### Introduction

| | |
|---|---|
| Mó:lip, | Well, |
| hacimmánkalá. | I will tell you all, |
| ná:hon, | well, |
| a:ti:pacobák cokfík stóklok | Rabbit and Great-One-Who-Eats-Human-Beings |
| ittafánkat ittima:ɬí:katoho:limp hacimmánkalá | I will tell you all how they met and spoke together |

## Prologue: Why Rabbit Hates Great-One-Who-Eats-Human-Beings

| | |
|---|---|
| Kántik cokfík cokǐ:boscómmok, | But Rabbit seems to have been small, |
| yomáhlit palámmot a:tipacobá. | going about with Great-One-Who-Eats-Human-Beings; |
| immałátlik ałí:yatoho:p, | he continued to be afraid of him; |
| immałátlik ałí:yat ómmátton, | after he was afraid of him, |
| A:ti:pacobák óntit á:yatoho:p, | Great-One-Who-Eats-Human-Beings came, going about, but he was frightened to meet him, so they say. |
| kántikap afánka immałatlá:hostoho:limpáhcok. | |
| Cokfík cokí:bosco:lik immałátlik. | Because Rabbit was small he was afraid of him. |
| Kántik bánkotoho:limpáhcok. | Therefore he hated him, so they say. |
| Cokfík a:ti:pacobá oholimpá imanó:lá:hi bánk. | Rabbit does not want to eat the food of Great-One-Who-Eats-Human-Beings |

## Scene 1: Rabbit Encounters Great-One-Who-Eats-Human-Beings

| | |
|---|---|
| Má:mo:sin, | Thereupon, |
| cokfók ałí:yatohok afą́hkok a:ti:pacobá. | Rabbit, going somewhere, met Great-One-Who-Eats-Human-Beings. |
| Má:mo:sin, | Thereupon, |
| "Naksofón ałcíˀyá?" ká:hatoho:limpáhcok a:ti:pacobá imasilhá:ci:k. | "Where are you going?" he said, asking Great-One-Who-Eats-Human-Beings. |
| A:ti:pacobák ónkak, | Great-One-Who-Eats-Human-Beings spoke. |
| "Ałí:yali:s yá:fon pilahón | "I am going towards that place, |
| ałí:yali:s yá:fon," káhhan, | I am going there," he said. |
| Má:mo:sin cokfík, | Thereupon, |
| "Anómmą. Anók ałí:yali:s má:fon," káhhan. | Rabbit said, "Me, too. I am going over there." |
| Kántik ónkak cokfík immánkat įholá:sit, | But Rabbit spoke, telling him a lie, |
| "Anó óntilitohofáp ną:si íksóhc. | "As for me, where I come from nothing exists. |
| Ǒ:hya anó:lit í:palíhcok óm," ká:hatoho:limpáhcok cokfík. | I have eaten it all up," Rabbit said, so they say. |
| Má:mo:sin, | Thereupon, |
| a:ti:pacobák ónkak, | Great-One-Who-Eats-Human-Beings spoke. |
| "Ó:! Anók óntilitohofap ná:sok iksóhc malmám. | "Oh! Where I come from nothing exists likewise. |
| Óhya anó:lilik í:lalíhcok óm," káhhan. | I have come eating it all up," he said. |

### Scene 2: Rabbit and Great-One-Who-Eats-Human-Beings Have a Dung Contest

| | |
|---|---|
| Má:mo:sin, | Thereupon, |
| mó:li:p, | well, |
| "Ittáshílik, | "Together, |
| yá:fon oscokkóhcin, | you go and sit over there, |
| anók yá:fa scokkó:lilin, | and I shall sit there, |
| holippo:lásk máp!" ká:hatoho:li | and let's shit!" he said, |
| mpáhcok. | so they say. |
| Má:mo:sin, | Thereupon, |
| "Hoppó:latískan hí:calą," ká:hatoho:li- | "I intend to see you shit," he said, |
| mpáhcok. | so they say. |
| Má:mo:sin, | Thereupon, |
| "Éhę! Isnók hocippó:lan ilhicásk máp! | "Yes! Let's see *you* shit! |
| Hoppó:lalin ilhicásk! | Let's see me shit! |
| Isnók yá:fa hocippó:lan, | *You* shit there, |
| yá:fon hoppó:lalin ilhicásk má:min," | and I shall shit over there, and let us |
| káhhan. | see, then!" he said. |
| A:ti:pacobák yá:fa ałí:yatohok, | Great-One-Who-Eats-Human-Beings went |
| | there; |
| ohcokkóhlok hoppóhlan, | he went and sat and shat. |
| cokfík yá:fa stałí:yatohok, | Rabbit went there, |
| tabakcospók cokkó:tohon, | where a stump stood, |
| pá:na pa:cokkóhlok, | and sat on top of it, |
| pa:hoppó:lan. | and shat on top of it. |

### Scene 3: The Results of the Dung Contest

| | |
|---|---|
| Má:mo:sin, | Thereupon, |
| hoppó:lat fayáhlin, | they finished shitting. |
| "Hiná:p mó ilhicásk!" káhhan. | "Let's see then!" he said. |
| "Hiná:p mó ilhicásk! Anáp fáylil" káhhan. | "Let's see, then! I am finished." |
| "Anók fáylil. Mó:li:p ilhicásk!" káhhan. | "As for me, I am finished. Well, let's see!" |
| | he said. |
| A:ti:pacobák ałí:yatoho:limpáhcok, | Great-One-Who-Eats-Human-Beings went, |
| | so they say, |
| cokfik hoppó:lato ohhí:cá:hi, | to see how Rabbit had shat, |
| ohhí:catohon, | he went to see it, |
| tonohtó:kost okhocakkǒ:scon | and small green round things, |
| pa:cikkí:katoho:limpáhcok | it is said were laid on top of it, |
| talibó:lit cassí má:mik tabakcospí | he made something like corn on top |
| pá:na. | of the stump. |

| | |
|---|---|
| Má:mo:sin, | Thereupon, |
| cokfík ałí:yatohok, | Rabbit went; |
| a:ti:pacobák hoppó:lato ohhí:catohon, | he went to see how Great-One-Who-Eats-Human-Beings had shat; |
| ná:si í:patohok | what he had eaten was somehow frightening; |
| ná:si małátka má:mit | |
| ná:si pahí má:mit | it was something like grass [in appearance]; |
| cofkoní má:mit | but it was something like bones |
| ná:si:pato má:min | which was that which he had eaten, |
| hoppó:latohon híhcok | and having seen what he had shat, |
| immałáttoho:limpáhcok cokfík. | Rabbit was afraid of him, so they say. |

**Scene 4: Rabbit is Caught in a Lie**

| | |
|---|---|
| Má:mo:sin, | Thereupon, |
| "Anóyok óntilifap ná:sok íksóhc, | "But as for me, where I come from, nothing exists; |
| ná:síksóhc katík óm," ká:hatoho:limpáhcok cokfík małátlik, | it is the case that nothing exists," frightened Rabbit said, so they say, |
| Akkántik, | But this being so, |
| "Áłłalá:híhcon óm. | "I intend to go there. |
| Łopótlilok," káhhok a:ti:pacobák. | I will pass through," said Great-One-Who-Eats-Human-Beings. |
| Alí:yatoho:limpáhcok łopótlok, | It is said that he went passing through, |
| kántik, | but this being so, |
| immałátlik, | he [Rabbit] was afraid, |
| ó:łá:hi bánko ónkayon | and even though he did not want him to go there |
| í:latoho:limpáhcok. | he arrived, so it is said. |
| Immałátlá:hostoho:limpáhcok cokfík a:ti:pacobá. | Rabbit was really frightened of Great-One-Who-Eats-Human-Beings. |
| Kántik | But this being so, |
| hoppó:latohofap | where he had defecated, |
| pahí okcákkonánnan hoppó:lat cikkí:tohon, | shitting he had laid down nothing but green grass. |
| Má:mok, | Thus, |
| a:ti:pacobák iyyínkotoho:limpáhcok. | Great-One-Who-Eats-Human-Beings did not believe him, so it is said. |
| Mǫ́! Kámmo:sin sobáylil. | Enough! Just so much is what I know. |
| Tafhiyám! | Finis! |

*Textual commentary:*

Lines 25–26 No motivation is given for Rabbit's outrageous lie here. The prologue states that Rabbit hates Great-One-Who-Eats-Human-Beings because he is afraid of him; perhaps Rabbit is trying here to frighten Great-One-Who-Eats-Human-Beings.

Line 36 *holippo:lásk máp!* 'Let's shit!' The Koasati verb *hoppó:lan* is equivalent in social sensibility to the English verb 'shit'. It is both graphic and not used normally in polite everyday speech. Thus, its sudden introduction, in a form that never, ever would be used in public (c.f. "let's shit!" in English) creates a sudden shift in tone and contrast which strikes the Koasati ear as being very humorous.

Scatological humor in the oral literature of the Southeast has rarely been discussed, although it seems to have been widespread. Natchez oral literature as recorded by Haas (1936–38) is particularly rich in humorous incidents involving feces, diarrhea, and defecation.

Lines 58–60 This is an accurate description of what natural rabbit dung looks like. The plural forms of the adjectives *tonóhkin* (*tonohtó:k-)* 'be round' and *okhocákkon* (*okhocákko-*) 'be green' are linguistically interesting because of the infixed reduplication (see Kimball 1988:431–42)

Line 59 *pa:cikkí:katoho:limpáhcok* 'it is said were laid on top of it'. Positional verbs in Koasati are marked for the shape of the object. Thus the verb pair *cokkó:lin/cikkí:kan*, which usually mean 'to sit (singular/dual) of animate objects' here means 'to lie (singular/plural) of globular objects'.

Lines 64–69 Rabbit tries to see the dung of Great-One-Who-Eats-Human-Beings as grass, but it is really slivers of human bone. Great-One-Who-Eats-Human-Beings really is the monster who he says he is, which suggests that this story is from the earlier tradition, before Great-One-Who-Eats-Human-Beings became a more comic figure.

Line 72 The form *anóyok* is quite interesting. It is composed of the pronoun *anó* 'I', verbalized with *-o-* 'to be,' followed by *-y-* 'contrary to expectation' and *-ok* 'same subject plus focus'. The line in which it occurs literally means: 'But on the contrary (despite what you observe) it is in the place where I come from that nothing exists'. Rabbit here is truly living up to his name *Cokfí Holá:si* 'Rabbit, the Liar'. Like many another liar, having been caught in a lie, he continues to lie, until the one to whom he lies goes to verify the liar's claims for himself. Rabbit never learns.

Line 89 *Tafhiyám!* 'Finis!' This interjection is the stereotypical ending of a traditional narrative, after which the teller of the tale is obliged to spit. If this was not done, the teller was supposed to grow a hump on his or her back. This interjection, which has no other meaning in Koasati, may be connected with the Creek word *tofkayankis* 'I have spit'.

## RABBIT TRICKS GREAT-ONE-WHO-EATS-HUMAN-BEINGS OVERSEAS
narrated by Bel Abbey

I recorded this narrative on tape in 1981, immediately after recording *Rabbit and Great-One-Who-Eats-Human-Beings Have a Dung Contest.* Unusually, Mr. Abbey started with no prologue or introduction. Rather, the tale begins immediately after the introductory conjunction *má:mo:sin* 'thereupon; and then'. This seems to be a feature of narrative performance. When the tales come one right after the other, especially if they are linked by character or theme, the storyteller can dispense with introductory matter, and start directly in on the tale.

This tale is similar to the final scene of Selin William's *Rabbit Tricks Great-One-Who-Eats-Human-Beings* above. Also, as mentioned above, the various scenes that make up traditional narratives (and tales of Rabbit in particular) can have an independent existence, as here, or can be combined into larger narratives. The Koasati storyteller is allowed considerable freedom to express her or his creativity, and to "take" from the communal repertoire those tales that she or he likes the best. As a result, there is no canonical version of any particular tale, although there are commonly known occurrences that listeners will expect to hear in any specific tale.

### Scene 1: Rabbit Lures Great-One-Who-Eats-Human-Beings to the River

| | |
|---|---|
| Má:mo:sin, | Thereupon, |
| a:ti:pacobák ohłopótlá:hi:fó:kon | as Great-One-Who-Eats-Human-Beings was about to pass by, |
| įholástoho:limpáhcok cokfík. | Rabbit lied to him, so it is said. |
| Įholá:sit fáykotoho:limpáhcok, | He never quit lying to him; |
| bánkóhcómmok | he hated him; |
| yá:li á:tá:hi bánkóhcóm. | he did not want him to live here. |
| Má:mo:sok, | Thereupon, |
| "Anłí:yásk má:min, | "Let's go, then, |
| yá:fon acacákhískan," káhhan. | You come with me over there," he said. |
| "Yá:fon ná:hok oholimpá ká:nok," káhhan. | "Over there is some good food," he said. |
| Ittacákkit ałłá:citoho:limpáhcok. | The two of them went off together, so it is said. |
| | |
| Má:mo:sin, | Thereupon, |
| hahcifá ołáhcin, | having arrived at a river, |
| hahcí cobafá ołáhcin, | having arrived at a big river, |
| má:mo:sin, | thereupon, |
| apatahá áswatohon. | the two of them were there alongside it. |

### Scene 2: Rabbit Suggests a Jumping Contest

| | |
|---|---|
| Pahí okhocákko:si í:pan, | He [Rabbit] ate the fresh green grass, |
| a:ti:pacobák imanó:lá:hi bánko:fó:kon, | but when Great-One-Who-Eats-Human-Beings did not want to eat it, |
| hahcifá ołáhcin, | they went over to the river. |
| "Cofótlit talabanápka:p ihá:nifok, | "One can jump across to the land [on the other side], |
| łóykat łopótli:fó:k . . . ," | and when one jumps back . . ." |
| "Yáncíkkóhc," káhat imilakasá:motoho:li-mpáhcok. | "You can't do it," he said, as he [Great-One-Who-Eats-Human-Beings] felt hubris towards him, so they say. |
| Cofótlit talabanápka:fó:k, | When he [Rabbit] jumped across, |
| "Cofótlit yáncíkkóhc," ká:hat | "You can't do it," he said, |
| łóykat talabanápkan. | and came back across. |
| Má:mo:sin | Thereupon, |
| a:ti:pacobák ónka:k, | Great-One-Who-Eats-Human-Beings spoke. |
| "Anáp akkántákkóhc. | "As for me, I cannot do it. |
| Casánkǫ. | I am unable. |
| caco:báhcok cofotlilá:hik," ká:hayon, | I am too big to jump," he said, but on the contrary, |
| "Ittima:yá:cílkásk!" ká:hat áswáhpin. | "Let's have a contest!" he [Rabbit] said, since they were there. |

### Scene 3: Rabbit Tricks Great-One-Who-Eats-Human-Beings

| | |
|---|---|
| Má:mo:sin, | Thereupon, |
| a:ti:pacobá bánkok ónkat cokfík. | it was the case that Rabbit hated Great-One-Who-Eats-Human-Beings. |
| Má:mosin, | Thereupon, |
| cokfík cofótlitohok, | Rabbit jumped over, |
| "Táhmok yám! | "Land like this! |
| Isnók yám matcofótl!" káhhan | You jump like this!" he said. |
| A:ti:pacobák ónka:k | Great-One-Who-Eats-Human-Beings spoke. |
| "Casánkóhc," ka:háhpok | "I can't," he just said, |
| a:ti:pacobá mók cofóttoho:limpáhcok. | but then Great-One-Who-Eats-Human-Beings also jumped, so it is said. |
| Cofótlit, | He jumped, |
| cofótli:fó:kon, | and when he jumped, |
| ohto:támmá:hi:fó:kon, | when he came and almost landed in the water, |
| cokfík okí tałán ohtámmíhcónkatohok. | and it is the case that Rabbit landed back on the other side of the river. |

### Scene 4: Rabbit Sends Great-One-Who-Eats-Human-Beings Overseas

| | |
|---|---|
| Kámmin, | On doing so, |
| "O:páth! O:path!" ká:hatoho:limpáhcok cokfík | "Water, be wide! Water, be wide!" Rabbit said, so they say. |
| Okík immáyt páthak óhya, | The water all became wider, |
| a:ti:pacobák o:łopótlit łóykat łopótko-nánnampak. | it is said that Great-One-Who-Eats-Human-Beings could not ford back. |
| Má:mo:sin, | Thereupon, |
| cofótlit ohtáhmok a:ti:pacobák, | Great-One-Who-Eats-Human-Beings, |
| cofótli:fó:k tałán ohtámmit ommá:ton, | having jumped, and gone and landed, |
| cofótli:fo:kap, | when he jumped, and after he landed |
| ihá:nik stimakoláfkan, | on the other side, |
| sto:paká:lok | when he jumped, |
| stałí:yatohok | the land calved off with him, |
| stałį:yat | it carried him. |
| | it really took him. |
| okí tałán ohtatipáskatohok ómmok, | it seems he was separated on the other side of the ocean, |
| yá:li iksóhcómmimpáhcok a:ti:pacobák. | and Great-Ones-Who-Eat-Human-Beings/Elephants do not exist here, so it is said. |
| Okí tałán ostonafáytoho:limpáhcok | On the other side of the ocean he stayed and never came back, so they say. |
| Cokfík ómmok | It seems to have been Rabbit, |
| o:łopotlíhcin, | having made him cross the water, |
| stonafáytoho:limpáhcok. | made him not to come back again. |
| Má:min, | Thus, |
| cokfík ima:yá:citoho:limpáhcok a:ti:pacobá. | Rabbit defeated Great-One-Who-Eats-Human-Beings |
| Kámmo:sin sobáylil. | Just so much is what I know. |
| Tafhiyám! | Finis! |

*Textual comments*:

Lines 1–6 Rabbit's motivation for trying to get rid of Great-One-Who-Eats-Human-Beings is here set out. Great-One-Who-Eats-Human-Beings is still a monster, and Rabbit would like to get him out of the way.

Line 22 "*Yáncíkkóhc,*" *káhat imilakasá:motoho:limpáhcok.* '"You can't do it," he said, as he [Great-One-Who-Eats-Human-Beings] felt hubris towards him, so they say'. Once a narrator tags a character with the characteristic of hubris, the listener can be sure that something bad will happen to that character as a result.

Line 46 *O:páth!* 'Water, be wide!' This is a very interesting linguistic form. Usually the verb *o:páthan* 'to be wide water' is impersonal. Here it is given a second person singular imperative form, as Rabbit uses his supernatural powers to change the river into a sea.

Lines 49–58 These lines form the climax of the story, based on the number of phrases linked together without a phrase-terminal marker.

Line 58 *yá:li iksóhcómmimpáhcok a:ti:pacobák* 'and Great-Ones-Who-Eats-Human Beings/ Elephants do not exist here, so it is said'. To Mr. Abbey and to most modern Koasati, Great-One-Who-Eats-Human-Beings is visualized as an elephant, rather than as a bipedal being with a nose in the form of an elephant's trunk. As a result, this narrative has the features of an origin tale, in that it explains why elephants are only found on the other side of the Atlantic Ocean.

## RABBIT AND BOX TURTLE RUN A RACE
narrated by Martin Abbey

I recorded this narrative on tape in November, 1981. Martin Abbey (1897–1991) was the last *mikkó* of the Koasati, having been elected to that position after the death of the previous *mikkó,* his father, Jefferson Abbey in 1952. In the mid-1970s, he gave up whatever political power he may have had so that the tribe could organize according to Bureau of Indian Affairs rules and be officially recognized as an Indian tribe by the federal government, which it finally was in 1975. By the time that this tale was recorded, Abbey was quite deaf, and the tale was elicited from him by asking him in writing to tell it. In addition he told a version of *Great Blue Heron and Hummingbird Race* and mentioned that he knew *Rabbit Switches Dung with Great-One-Who-Eats-Human-Beings*, but was unwilling to tell it to an outsider because of its scatological content. A notable feature of Abbey's storytelling style is the use of expressive gestures and interjections; their presence is noted in the commentary that follows. In addition, he adapted English words as Koasati verbs in this narrative, for reasons that are not entirely clear.

This narrative belongs to the innovative tradition, in which the character Rabbit replaces that of Wolf in the conservative tradition (see *Wolf and Box Turtle Run a Race* in chapter 4). The replacement of Wolf by Rabbit is partly due to Rabbit's widespread appearance in other Koasati traditional narratives and partly due to influence from the European fable *The Tortoise and the Hare.* Nonetheless, as far as content is concerned, the Koasati narrative that is closest to *The Tortoise and the Hare* is not this one, but rather *Great Blue Heron and Hummingbird Race.*

### Scene 1: The Race Is Set

| | |
|---|---|
| Cokfík sattapolón | It is said that Rabbit and Box Turtle |
| ittimmá:yatoho:limpáhcok. | ran a race. |
| "Copoksí ostá:ka ittimmá:yatilkásk!" | "Let us race over four mountains!" |
| ká:hatoho:limpáhcok cokfík. | Rabbit said, so they say. |

Má:mo:sin,
sattapolók, "Mó:tik!" ká:toh.
Sattapolók palhíkkopalamó:líhco:lisk,
iliyímmitoh immá:yá:hih,
pí:la yámmo:sin ałí:yaskan.
"Copoksí ostá:kan, ostá:ka:fó:k,
immá:yan akkáhcotok," ká:toh.

Thereupon,
Box Turtle said, "Okay."
Because Box Turtle was extremely slow,
Rabbit was overconfident that he would beat him;
as he could go only just so.
"Over four mountains; when it is the fourth one,
so one wins," he said.

**Scene 2: The Race Begins**

Mó:tohon,
má:mo:sin,
imittahó:ban,
ałłá:citohot tółkoh.
Cokfík cofótlitohmá:łok bikkón,
bikkón áłłatohoyok,
copoksí stałí:ya:fó:kap,
sattapolók yá:fon
osto:tanáttoho:limpáhcok yámmit.

Then afterwards,
thereupon,
they got ready,
and the two went off running.
Rabbit just jumped away first,
even though he went first,
when he reached the mountain,
Box Turtle over there was so going down the other side, so they say.

**Scene 3: Box Turtle Wins at the Second Mountain**

Má:mo:sin,
cokfík mán walí:kat walí:kat,
łopóttohot o:tanátli:p,
łopótlok ałí:ya:fó:k,
stałi:yak,
sattapolók osto:tanáttoho:limpak
mán himá:ya mán.

Thereupon,
Rabbit again ran and ran,
and when he passed him going down the slope,
when he went and passed him,
and reached it [the next mountain],
it is said that Box Turtle again,
going down the other side.

**Scene 4: Box Turtle Wins at the Third Mountain**

Má:mo:sin,
hí:cat łopótlok,
mán walí:ka:k,
walí:ka:k,
himá:ya mán copoksí
ohtałabanápka:fó:kap,
sattapolók mán yá:fon
ó:łatoho:limpahcok.

Thereupon,
seeing him he passed him,
and again when he ran,
when he ran,
once again when he was passing over the top of the mountain,
Box Turtle again had arrived there, so it is said.

### Scene 5: Box Turtle Wins the Race

| | |
|---|---|
| Má:mo:sin, | Thereupon, |
| mán hí:cat łopótlok, | again he saw him and passed him, |
| ałí:yat copoksí stóhyafon, | and he went to the last mountain, |
| mó:tohon, | then afterwards, |
| ohtałabanpkafa, | at the place of going and crossing over, |
| sattapolók bikkón ó:łat | Box Turtle had arrived first and |
| ohcokkó:toho:limpáhcok yá:fa, | gone and sat there, so it is said, |
| cokfík obá:lon ó:łatoh. | and Rabbit arrived behind. |
| Sattapolók immá:yatoh. | Box Turtle won. |

### Scene 6: Box Turtle Is Broken and Repaired

| | |
|---|---|
| Má:mo:sin, | Thereupon, |
| sattapolók immá:yatohon, | Box Turtle had won; |
| immá:yatohon, | he had won, |
| impalátkak, | and Rabbit grew cross, |
| bástkat apí:toho:limpáhcok. | and he busted him up and threw him away, it is said. |
| Má:mo:sok, | Thereupon, |
| bástkat apí:lin, | he busted him up and threw him away, |
| itcokkó:tohok | and he sat there: |
| itcokkó:tohok, | and he sat there, |
| má:fon itcokko:lí. | there he was sitting. |
| Cokbaník ołá:ci:fó:kon, | When some ants arrived, |
| immánkatoh. | he told them something. |
| Imalíkcilahon immánkatoh. | He told them to doctor him. |
| Imalíkcilahon immą́hkok, | Having told them to doctor him, |
| "Nihasí amí:pat acapackatók!" | "Eat some of my fat and patch me up!" |
| ká:toho:limpáhcok. | he said, so they say. |
| Má:mo:sin, | Thereupon, |
| cokbaní:kok akkammí:cit, | the ants did so, |
| apáckat anóstohon, | they completely patched him up, |
| pá:nak yámmifak, | and his top side is like so; |
| sattapoló afakcó yámmi:k, | Box Turtle's shell is like so; |
| yámmit na:hóhcónkon, | so is how they made it: |
| stinkánkat akkámmik, | they canned him like so, |
| cokbaník acó:tohon ómmimpáhcok. | It is the case that the ants sewed him, so it is said. |
| | |
| Móh! Stanó:k. | Enough! It is finished. |

*Textual commentary*:

Lines 5–6 *Sattapolók palhíkkopalamó:líhco:lisk, / iliyímmitoh immá:yá:hih* 'because Box Turtle was extremely slow, / Rabbit was overconfident that he would beat him'. Rabbit is here being set up for a fall; because of his hubris, Rabbit is going to suffer again.

Lines 16–17 *copoksí stałí:ya:fó:kap, / sattapolók yá:fon osto:tanáttoho:limpáhcok yámmit* 'when he reached the mountain / Box Turtle over there was so going down the other side, so they say'. The exact visual image is this: as soon as Rabbit reaches the top of the mountain, he sees Box Turtle already on the way down the other side. This narrative contains several uses of the rare verb *sto:tanátlin* 'to descend a slope'. This verb has gone out of use due to the extremely flat nature of the terrain in which the Koasati have lived for over the past century.

A notable feature of this narrative is that the way in which Box Turtle moves faster than Rabbit is not explained, it is just a given. In *Wolf and Box Turtle Run a Race*, Box Turtle wins by trickery, and Mr. Abbey may be simply assuming that his audience knows that trickery is being used here.

Line 36 *ohtałabanápkafa* 'at the place of going and crossing over'. This is a circumlocution for 'finish line'.

Line 45 *bástkat apí:toho:limpáhcok* 'and he busted him up and threw him away, it is said'. Here, an English word, *bust*, has been adapted as a Koasati verb, *bástkan*, with the meaning of 'to bust something up'. The standard Koasati verb would be *bosótlin*, which is the word used in other recorded versions of this narrative. The reason for Mr. Abbey's use of English in this scene is unclear. However, in other nonliterary narratives, he used many English loan words, and apparently the reason was that his purpose in telling all his narratives was to communicate his ideas and I had, at that time, only an imperfect command of Koasati. Therefore, in order to make himself clear, Mr. Abbey would use English. For the Koasati, the primary purpose of language is communication, and anything that facilitates communication is proper. At this point, Mr. Abbey picked up a stick and struck it repeatedly against the floor to indicate how Rabbit smashed Box Turtle up.

Lines 48–50 *itcokkó:tohok / itcokkó:tohok / má:fon itcokko:lí* 'and he sat there, / and he sat there, / there he was sitting'. Here, standard English would require a translation something like 'and he lay there, / and he lay there, / there he was lying'. However, in Koasati, the verb 'to lie,' *ballákan*, requires that its subject be of a roughly cylindrical shape. Since turtles (even broken ones) are roughly globular in shape, the verb *cokkó:lin* 'to sit' is used, as it covers the concept of 'to lie' for globular objects. The final verb, *itcokko:lí*, is an aorist form; by its use the narrator indicates that Box Turtle lay in an injured state for an indeterminately long time before the ants came to his rescue.

Line 55 *"Nihasí amí:pat acapackatók!"* "'Eat some of my fat and patch me up!'" Another English verb has been adapted here, *patch*, in place of the Koasati verb *apáckan* 'to patch something up'. The English verb is naturalized in Koasati in the specialized verb *ittapáckan* 'to make a patchwork quilt' and its derivative *tapácka* 'quilt'.

Line 60 *sattapoló afakcó yámmi:k* 'Box Turtle's shell is like so'. Here, Mr. Abbey made gestures with this fingers to indicate the roughly hexagonal patches that are found on the backs of box turtles.

Line 62 *stinkánkat akkámmik* 'they canned him like so'. This is the English word *can*, adapted as *stinkánkan* 'to can something for someone with something'. As can be seen from this example, and the others above, it is rather difficult to extract the English root from the matrix of Koasati morphology. If Mr. Abbey believed that by using English he was making his narrative more comprehensible, he was mistaken.

## HOW RABBIT MADE THE WATER RUN CROOKED

narrated by *Sacowáyhki*

This narrative was recorded by Mary R. Haas in 1939. John R. Swanton had collected a version of this tale in 1910 and published a translation based on his interlinear glosses under the title *Rabbit and the River* (1929:204–5). However, unlike Haas's version, Swanton's is conflated with some scenes from other Rabbit stories and is not a coherent whole,. For that reason, and for its transcriptional accuracy, Haas's version has been chosen here.

The setting for this narrative is the mythological time of the animal-humans (see discussion in chapter 2), and the other participant in the narrative is the unnamed and nebulous Water Carrier, clearly one of the ancient and almost forgotten powers that created the world. This tale shows Rabbit in the character of a creative trickster, making the world the way he wants it, rather than the way it has been ordained.

### Scene 1: Rabbit Begs Water from the Water Carrier

| Koasati | English |
|---|---|
| Cokfį́ á:ton stóklot a:yá:cin, | Rabbit and someone were going about, |
| á:tik okón stí:sin, | and the being was carrying water, |
| cokfík acákkit á:yak ónka:k, | and Rabbit, following him about, spoke. |
| "Anók sti:silá:š okį́," | "I want to carry the water," he said, |
| ká:hatoho:limpatš. | so they say. |
| Má:miyon, | But then, |
| á:tik ónka:k, | the being spoke. |
| "Mánko:š!" ká:hatoho:limpatš. | "By no means!" he said, so it is reported. |
| Cokfík ónkak, | Rabbit spoke. |
| "Anók scimí:silá:š," ká:hatoho:limpa:š. | "I want to carry it for you," he said, so they say. |

Ma:min,
  cokfík cilítkat cilítkatoho:limpa:š.

Then,
  Rabbit pleaded and pleaded with him,
  so it is said.

Má:miyon,
  á:tik stįhíkkotoho:limpatš.

But then,
  it is said the being would not give it to him.

### Scene 2: Rabbit Steals the Water and Spills It

Mó:tohon,
  cokfík okį́ stimíhsok,
    stiwwalí:katoho:limpatš.
Máhmok,
  okį́ óhyą tihí:kat swalí:kat,
    óhyą tintibí:citoho:limpatš.
Má:miskan,
  hahcík lamathíkkóhcómmimpatš.
Cokfík alwáhtohon ómmimpatš.

Thereupon,
  Rabbit took the water from him,
    and ran from him with it, so it is said.
At that,
  he spilled all the water as he ran with it,
    and he made it all crooked, so it is said.
Because he did so,
  rivers are not straight, so they say.
It is said that it is the case that Rabbit ruined them.

Cokfínkołá.

Rabbit is wicked!

Mó:š.

Enough.

*Textual commentary*:

Line 1 *Cokfį́ á:ton stóklot a:yá:cin* 'Rabbit and someone were going about'. Although the word *á:ti* usually means 'human being', the one who carries the water is clearly not human. Note also in the tale *The Contest of Heat and Cold* (in chapter 5) that both nonhuman protagonists are called *á:ti*.

Lines 14–23 This scene incorporates the elements of an origin tale in that it explains why rivers twist and do not flow straight. The only major difference between this and a typical origin tale is that Rabbit is responsible for how this feature of the world came to be. The theme of the Trickster making rivers run crooked is found throughout North America.

Line 23 *Cokfínkołá* 'Rabbit is wicked!' This interjection, which can also be translated 'Wicked Rabbit!' seems to be a comment upon Rabbit's actions by the narrator. Because of the ambivalent attitude of the Koasati toward Rabbit, half-shocked and half-admiring, this interjection may actually be interpreted as praise, as in the phrase *cokfík cokfí* 'Rabbit is Rabbit,' i.e., 'Rabbit is really behaving like he usually does'.

# RABBIT AND DEER SWAP FEET

narrated by *Sacowáyhki*

This narrative was recorded by Mary R. Haas in 1939. Swanton did not record any version of it, nor is a similar narrative recorded for any other Southeastern groups. This particular tale has the theme of "the trickster tricked," which seems to have been a favorite of *Sacowáyhki's* mother, Selin Williams. At times, the audience seems to appreciate tales in which Rabbit does not just receive a comeuppance for his hubris, but ones in which he, the consummate trickster, is himself the victim of a trick, as in this narrative.

## Scene 1: Rabbit and Deer Compare Feet

| | |
|---|---|
| Cokfón icón ittinna:ɬí:katoho:limpatš. | It is said that Rabbit and Deer were speaking to each other. |
| Máhmin, | Then, |
| icók ónka:k, | Deer spoke. |
| "Cayyík stalí:ya ká:not ka:nóhco:š," | "My feet are really good to carry," |
| káhhan. | he said. |
| Cokfík ónka:k, | Rabbit spoke. |
| "Anók cayyík malmá:š," | "My feet are just the same," he said, |
| ká:hatoho:limpatš. | so they say. |
| Mahmin, | Then, |
| mantik, | but, |
| icók cokfí iyyí imbànnat | it is said that Deer really wanted |
| imbànnatoho:limpatš. | Rabbit's feet from him. |

## Scene 2: Deer Wants to Trade Feet

| | |
|---|---|
| Máhmin, | Then, |
| cokfík ónka:k, | Rabbit spoke. |
| "Anók malmá:š; cayyík stalí:ya | "I am just the same; it is good to carry |
| ká:nok," káhhan. | my feet," he said. |
| Icók ónka:k, | Deer spoke. |
| "Ittimo:tamáthíláskš!" | "Let us trade them!" he said, |
| ká:hatoho:limpatš. | so it is reported. |
| Má:miyon, | But then, |
| cokfík ónka:k, | Rabbit spoke. |
| "Cayyį́ cayyíhš," ká:hatoho:limpatš. | "I treasure my feet," he said, so they say. |
| Máhmin, | Then, |
| icók ónka:k, | Deer spoke. |

"Cayyí nó:tak lopósti:son óhmin,
ká:not kanóhco:š,"
ká:hatoho:limpatš.
"Kasátkatik lǫ́kbasco:š," káhhan.

"The soles of my feet are just so soft,
and they are really good," he said,
so it is reported.
"Be the weather cold, or very warm,"
he said.

**Scene 3: Rabbit and Deer Trade Feet**

Stáswan,
ittimo:tamatlí:cit híhcan,
cokfík bánkotoho:limpatš.

The two of them stayed together,
and they tested trading them,
and it is said that Rabbit did not like
doing so.

Máhmin,
icók ónka:k,
ittįháɬɬit ilhí:cáskš!" káhhan,

cokfík háɬɬit hí:catoho:limpats
icó iwwilǫ́.

Then,
Deer spoke,
"Let us try putting on each other's shoes!"
he said,
and Rabbit tried putting on
Deer's shoes.

**Scene 4: Deer Steals Rabbit's Feet**

Icók ónka:k,
"Scimalí:lo:š," ká:hatoho:limpatš.

Deer spoke.
"They are appropriate for you," he said,
so they say.

Máhmin,
icók cokfí iwwiló įháhɬok,

stiwwalí:kat snakáɬtoho:limpatš.

Then,
having put on Rabbit's shoes against
his wishes,
he ran away with them and disappeared
with them.

Ká:mo:š.

The end.

*Textual commentary*:

Lines 1–9 The first scene sets up the premise of the narrative, that Rabbit has feet that Deer would prefer to have. The premise is almost identical to that in *Turkey and Owl Swap Calls* and very similar to that in *How Opossum Got a Bare Tail*, both in chapter 2.

Line 17 *"Cayyį́ cayyíhš"* '"I treasure my feet"'. This pun is used for humorous effect, since puns are one of the basic ingredients of Koasati humor.

Lines 30–31 *Icók ónka:k, / "Scimalí:lo:š," ká:hatoho:limpatš* 'Deer spoke. / "They are appropriate for you," he said, so they say'. These words are almost identical to those of Turkey in speaking to Owl after they had exchanged calls. It is very likely that the latter tale, which is a common Southeastern narrative, has had a strong structural effect on this tale, which is exclusively Koasati.

Line 33 *icók cokfí iwwiló įháhłok* 'having put on Rabbit's shoes against his wishes'. The fact that Deer is putting on Rabbit's shoes against his wishes is signaled linguistically by the use of a dative prefix to express a malefactive, that is, an action done to the detriment of someone. The dative, which usually expresses a benefactive, that is, an action done for the benefit of someone, may, under the proper semantic conditions, as here, have a negative meaning.

## THE BUNGLING HOST
narrated by Bel Abbey

This was the first Koasati text that I obtained, in the fall of 1977, as a member of a class in field methods in linguistics at Tulane University. It was a narrative that was readily volunteered, and it was one that Abbey knew well, liked, and enjoyed telling. This is reflected throughout the narrative by the expert use of stylistic devices, such as parallelism, description, and quoted speech. Furthermore in the sixth scene (lines 71–102), irony is used in the repeated duplicitous speech of Vulture.

Swanton obtained a much abbreviated version from Selin Williams in 1910, a translation of which he published under this same title (1929:210–11). Swanton's (1924:47–48) publication of a few lines of this text in his article "The Muskhogean Connection of the Natchez Language" is historically the first publication of Koasati text material.

### Scene 1: Bear Invites Rabbit to Dinner

| | |
|---|---|
| Nitáp a:táhcotohok, | Now, Bear used to dwell somewhere, |
| cokfík ittimbiní:litoho:limpáhcok. | and he and Rabbit used to visit each other, so it is said. |
| Má:mo:sin, | Thereupon, |
| "Ambiní:lįh!" ka:háhcotohon, | "Visit me later!" he said; |
| "Ambiní:lįh!" ka:háhcotohon cokfį. | "Visit me later!" he said to Rabbit. |
| Má:mo:sin, | Thereupon, |
| "Cimbiní:lilá:hiton," káhcok cokfík nitá. | "I was about to visit you," said Rabbit to Bear. |

### Scene 2: Bear Feeds Rabbit with Himself

| | |
|---|---|
| Má:mo:sin, | Thereupon, |
| imbiní:lá:hik ó:łan, | he went over there to visit him, |
| cikkí:kat ómmá:ton, | and after the two of them were sitting, |
| ná:son ínkat í:pat í:pá:hik imíksoton, | he had nothing to give to him to eat; |
| "Ná:son ínkat í:palaháʔwá" á:lok, | "What *am* I going to feed him?" |
| sobbáylok á:tatohok. | he thought, and then he knew. |

Ná:hok, nitak ni:háhco:liskan,
ikfí:kon mathalátkok,
aksalí matíhsok,
matkoyóffok,
illibátlok,
ínkat í:patoho:limpáhcok cokfį.
Má:mo:sin,
cokfík hí:cat cokkŏ::toho:limpáhcok.

Well, because Bear was fat,
he pulled out his stomach,
and picking up a knife,
and cutting off a piece,
cooked it,
and fed Rabbit with it, so it is said.
Thereupon,
Rabbit really sat and watched, so it is said.

**Scene 3: Rabbit Invites Bear to Dinner**

Má:mo:sok,
imbiní:láhpok łóykaton,
"Isnók amó:łąh!" ká:haton,
"Isnók amó:łąh!" ká:haton,
niták ałí:yatoho:limpáhcok
imbiní:lit cokfí.
Ná:hon, cokfík imó:łan,
cokkó:t ómmá:tok—
Akkáp nitá imí:sap ittó:bihayot ómmi:k,
ittó:bihayo cikkí:kat áswat,
áswat ómmá:ton,
cokfi imó:łaton.
Cokfík pahí scokkó:lo:sihayó
cokkó:tohon, má á:tahayotoho:limpáhcok.
Má:fon cikkí:katohon.

Thereupon,
having merely just visited him, he returned home.
"You too go over to my place later!" he said.
"You too go over to my place later!" he said.
and Bear went to visit Rabbit,
so it is said.
Well, he went over to visit Rabbit,
and after he sat down—
Now, Bear's house was the inside of a hollow tree;
the two of them sat dwelling in the hollow tree,
and after the two of them dwelt there,
he went over to Rabbit's dwelling place.
Rabbit dwelt within a little grass dwelling;
within that was his dwelling, so it is said.
Over there the two of them sat.

**Scene 4: Rabbit Injures Himself Imitating Bear**

Cokfík ónkak,
"Cokkó:citik! Libátlili má!" káhhan,
áswat ómmá:ton.
Ibisnók akkammí:cit hi:ca:fó:k,
aksalí matí:sit matacakoyóffitohon,
ikfí koyóffitoho:limpáhcok.
Ibisnáp sówwit solotkáhcotoho:litá:łok,
ilikoyóffit ilįho:páhcok,
"Amawíc!
Amawíc!
Amawicilkón càban!" káhhan.

Rabbit spoke:
"Please sit down! I shall cook!" he said,
and, after the two of them stayed there.
He himself did what he had seen;
he picked up a knife and cut out a piece,
he cut his stomach, so it is said.
Now, he himself being scrawny and lean,
he injured himself cutting himself,
"Help me!
"Help me!
I need help!" he said.

| | |
|---|---|
| Niták walí:katon, | Bear ran over. |
| "Naksámmik?" | "What is it?" |
| "Anók ąhó:p. | "I am injured. |
| Ilikóyffilíhcónka:s," káhhan. | It is the case that I have cut myself," he said. |
| Má:mo:sin, | Thereupon, |
| "Alikcón wíhlilą́, mó:li:p," káhhok, | "I intend to look for a doctor then," Bear said, |
| achalí:kok walí:katoho:limpáhcok niták. | and it is said that he ran out. |
| Ittatàmmin, | The other lay on the ground; |
| koyóffok ikfį́. | he had cut his stomach. |

## Scene 5: Bear Encounters Vulture

| | |
|---|---|
| Má:mo:sin, | Thereupon, |
| walí:kat ómma:tok, | after he had run a ways, |
| pa:cokkó:tohon híhcokš. | he caught sight of one sitting on a branch. |
| Saykík pa:cokkó:tohon híhcok, | He caught sight of Vulture sitting on a branch, |
| imasilhá:citoho:limpak. | and he asked questions of him, so it is said. |
| Má:mo:sin, | Thereupon, |
| "Amawicilkón cabàn," ká:hat ómmá:ton, | after he said, "I need help." |
| "Ná:son cibànnok ómmi:k?" | "What is it that you want?" |
| "Alikcón wíhlili:s." | "I am looking for a doctor." |
| "Naksán awicilkán hí:cá:hik cibáˀná?" | "Why do you want to look for help?" |
| "Cokfík amoklák ho:páhcon ónkah," káhhan, | "It is the case that my friend Rabbit is injured," he said. |
| "Cokfík įho:páhcon ónkan, | "It is the case that Rabbit is injured, |
| koyofkáhcon ónkan," káhhan. | it is the case that he has suffered a knife wound," he said. |
| "Stammą́híska:p, | "If you tell me about it, I will perhaps |
| cimawí:cillahomá:mik, | help you, and it is the case that I will |
| imalíkcillaho katík óm," káhhan. | doctor him," he said. |

## Scene 6: Vulture "Doctors" Rabbit

| | |
|---|---|
| Ołá:cit ómmá:ton, | After they arrived over there, |
| má:mosin, | thereupon, |
| "Naksofón táˀmí?" káhhan. | "Where is he lying?" he said. |
| "Yín tàm," káhhan. | "He lies over here," he said. |
| Má:mo:sin, | Thereupon, |
| "Ná:son sammi:císká? | "What are you doing? |

| | |
|---|---|
| Ná:son cibáˀná?" káhhan. | What do you want?" he said. |
| "Imí:sa stimaholihtá:cimá:mik, | "Fence in his house perhaps! |
| stimatanahlí:ci:p mo:lihalpí:s," káhhan. | Would that it be encircled!" he said. |
| "Tá:la hísson wíhlok, | "Look for palmetto leaves; |
| óhya stimaholihtá:cit isá:cit | fence it all in and make |
| stimatanatlíhcok!" | a house encircling it!" |
| "Mǫ́, hiná:p! | "Enough now! |
| Achalí:k! | Go out! |
| Acicákkik imalíkcilá:hihcon óm," | He will follow you upon my doctoring |
| káhhan. | him," he said. |
| Má:mo:sin, ná:hok, | Thereupon, well, |
| saykí:kok cokfí yahlí:citoho:limpáhcok. | Vulture made Rabbit cry out, so it is said. |
| Cokfí yahlí:ci:fó:kon, | When Rabbit cried out, |
| niták, "Sámmin ónká?" ká:toho:limpak. | Bear said, "Why is he making a sound?" |
| "Inko:š. Ahissí ambánkon ónk," káhhan. | "It is nothing. He does not want the medicine from me," he said. |
| Má:mo:sin, | Thereupon, |
| "Sámmin bánkon óˀmi?" káhhan. | "Why is it that he doesn't want it?" he said. |
| "Ahissí ínkalá:hik ambánkon ónkan, | "It is the case that he doesn't want me to give him my medicine, |
| naksá:kak," káhhan. | and he made noise," he said. |
| Má:mo:sin, | Thereupon, |
| "Ná:son cibáˀná man?" káhhan. | "What else do you need?" he said. |
| Má:min, | Then, |
| "Inkǫ. | "Nothing. |
| Imalíkcit fáylilá:hin óm. | I am about to finish doctoring him. |
| Ka:nóhco:liyon hiná:p. | But now he is good. |
| Hiná:p ka:nóhco:lin ónk," ká:hok, | Now it is the case that he is good," he said, |
| wáykat abá | and he flew up |
| ittó insá:wa ohpa:cokkó:lin. | into the branches of a tree and perched on one. |

**Scene 7: Bear Assaults Vulture**

| | |
|---|---|
| Má:mosin, | Thereupon, |
| niták cokhalí:kat hí:cat ómmá:ton, | after Bear went in and saw it, |
| cokfí óhya í:pat anó:lok, | that he had eaten Rabbit all up, |
| ipón í:pat anó:lok, | that he had eaten up his flesh, |
| cofkoninánnan cikkí:tohon, | that he had thrown down nothing but bones, |

| | |
|---|---|
| niták noksí:pahónka:sik, | Bear became extremely angry; |
| aksalí ilasá:citohok íhsok, | he took out the knife that he carried, |
| sbakóhlit saykí pilahón. | and he threw it overhand at Vulture. |
| Sbakóhlit ómmá:tok, | After he threw it at him, |
| ibisá:ni matacasáhlin, | it went through his beak; |
| ibisá:ni įłobóffin, | it pierced his beak; |
| ibisá:ni matacasáhlin | it went through his beak, |
| í:sit, | and he took it; |
| aksalį́ í:sit | he took the knife and threw it away, |
| matapí:litoho:limpáhcok. | so it is said. |

**Scene 8: The Result of Bear's Action**

| | |
|---|---|
| I:bilahotok, | He would have killed him; |
| immáttok, | he missed, |
| ibisá:ni łobóffitoho:limpáhcok. | and it is said that he pierced his beak. |
| Má:mo:sin, | Thereupon, |
| ibisá:ni łobófkak, | he was pierce-beaked; |
| niták įłobóffit ómmin, | it is the case that Bear pierced it on him, |
| ímmot stá:yat stonafáyt ómmok, | it seems he carried it as his possession unceasingly; |
| ímmot syomáhlinánnampáhcok. | it is said that they carried it all the time. |
| Kámmisk, | Just like that, |
| fó:sik naksántik ibisá:ni łobófka. | any kind of bird is pierce-beaked. |
| Kámmin, | Just so, |
| įłobófkat ómmimpáhcok. | it is said that they are pierced. |
| Ká:mo:s. | The end. |
| Tafhiyám! | Finis! |

*Textual commentary*:

Lines 4–7 This is a good example of the use of stylistic parallelism, with line 3 giving a statement, line 4 a repetition with addition, and line 7 a restatement.

Lines 8–19 The use of six lines to compose only two sentences indicates that this scene is an important part of the narrative. Abbey identifies himself with the character Bear, and reveals to the listeners how Bear reasoned what to feed Rabbit. Lines 14–19, containing a vivid description of Bear's actions, is stylistically good, according to native criteria.

Lines 29–41 These lines are an interpolation of material that Abbey felt was germane to the narrative. They describe in turn Bear's home and Rabbit's home, both of which are the naturalistic dens of real bears or rabbits. The description provides the listener with a vivid location in which the action takes place.

Lines 39–46 The actions of Rabbit here result from hubris, in this case his belief that he can do anything that anyone else can do. Bear has the magic power to provide food from his own flesh without injuring himself, but Rabbit does not, and, in imitating Bear, he does injure himself.

Lines 61–70 These lines are a good example of dialogue carrying the narrative of a tale. Generally, when speech is quoted, the quoted speech is introduced by the verb *ónkak* and followed by the verb *ká:han* 'to say', which carries person, tense, and aspectual information. However, in literary narrative, frequently *ónkak* and its subject are deleted, and here *ká:han* and its associated elements are also deleted so that the speech of each character follows the other, almost as if one were overhearing natural conversation.

In earlier years, when Koasati mythology still formed a coherent system, it seems that Vulture was considered to be the doctor among the various theriomorphic characters. In a story provided to Swanton (1929:189) by Selin Williams (1841–1917), Vulture acts as a true doctor, not the sham doctor that he is in this narrative.

Lines 78–81 Encircling the place where Rabbit is lying with a woven fence of palmetto leaves may reflect the practice of traditional Indian doctors, who were very possessive of their medicines, songs, and rituals. The secrecy of the doctor being expected, the listener does not realize that Vulture is having Rabbit hidden away for a more sinister reason.

Lines 85–93 There is a double meaning to the words that Vulture uses. Bear understands that Rabbit is crying out because he does not like the taste of the medicine that Vulture is giving him. Vulture very cynically refers to his true actions, which are tearing Rabbit apart and eating him, as "his medicine."

Lines 96–102 In this sentence, marked by its length as an important segment of the scene, Vulture's words again have double meanings. To Bear (and the listener), when Vulture says that Rabbit is good, he understands that Rabbit is now healthy again. In fact, Vulture is cynically mocking Bear, for he means that Rabbit is tasty.

Lines 103–10 This series of lines forms the climax of the narrative, when Bear realizes how he has been tricked by Vulture, and that, as a result, his friend Rabbit has been killed. Lines 104–7 are a good example of the use of parallelism to increase dramatic tension.

Lines 111–15 This, the subsidiary climax of the scene, shows the result of Bear's action. Rather than killing Vulture by throwing his knife, as he intended, he only pierced Vulture's beak. It is then left unstated, but understood, that Vulture escaped with his life.

Lines 116–28 This final scene sums up, in its first sentence, the intentions of Bear and the actual results of his actions, then goes on to state that magically, because Bear pierced Vulture's beak, the beaks of all birds are pierced in the same way. In the end, this take has cautioned the listener against hubris, such as Rabbit's, and against blind trust, such as Bear's, and explained a feature of the natural world.

## VULTURE "CURES" RABBIT
narrated by Martha John

I recorded this narrative on tape in September 1992. At once one can see that this tale is almost identical to the final portion of *The Bungling Host* as narrated above by Bel Abbey. Nonetheless, Miss John treats it as an independent story; in fact, the character Bear does not occur in it at all. This is an example of how Koasati storytelling is a creative art, rather than the rote repetition of a fixed and unvarying narrative. There are four scenes in this tale which, like most of the narratives told by Miss John, can be divided into two sections.

Martha John was a first cousin of Bel Abbey on her mother's side. They had lived together as children during his mother's widowhood, and remained close throughout their lives. John had a reputation as a very strict and upright person, and some people were quite afraid of her, as she was unwilling to suffer fools lightly. John never married, first by necessity, as her desired marriage partner was forbidden to her by rules of clan exogamy, and second by personal choice, as she came to realize the freedom that an unmarried woman was able to enjoy. She raised her two youngest half-siblings from her widowed mother's levirate remarriage after her mother's early death, and was able to enjoy child-rearing without the complications of husband or childbirth. She was the equal of Bel Abbey in knowledge of traditional narratives, knowing several that escaped Swanton's notice, her version of the origin of corn (Chapter 2) being among them.

Miss John found this tale to be highly amusing, and after the final sentence, but before the apotropaic interjection *tafhiyam*, she could not restrain her laughter. Koasati humor, and what the Koasati find humorous, is somewhat different than what is conceived of as humorous in European society. The duplicity of Vulture, and the ironical double-meaning of his words to the spectators, are the elements that make this narrative humorous to the Koasati listener. There are untranslatable linguistic features that add to the irony. Vulture almost exclusively uses the phrase-terminal marker *-:š,* which was the linguistic property of persons who were considered to be of high social status, such as doctors, prophets, and political leaders. In addition, like a true doctor, he uses rare words and syntactic constructions. All this helps him deceive those who listen to him, and intensifies the contrast between what is real and what is expected, which contrast informs much of Koasati humor.

## Prologue

| | |
|---|---|
| Má:mik, cimmánkalą cokfa:łihilkón anók. | Well, then, I shall tell you a Rabbit Story. |
| Ná:hok, | Well, |
| cokfî saykí stóklot áswatoho:limpáhcok. | it is said that Rabbit and Vulture used to exist. |

## Scene 1: Rabbit Falls Ill and None Can Cure Him

| | |
|---|---|
| Mó:tohon, | Then, |
| cokfík a:táhcok hóhpan, | Rabbit was continuing to be ill, |
| í:san. | |
| Má:mo:sin, | Thereupon, |
| ná:hok, | well, |
| ná:si małátli caffákan, | One of the wild animals, |
| naksó:n sattá immąhkan, | somewhere told Turtle |
| íhlok i:timalíkci:k, | and he arrived and came to doctor him |
| įfáykon, | but he did not cure him, |
| Wíhlit, wihlit, ná:si onapá iwwíhlit, | They looked and looked and looked for domestic animals |
| małáhli óhya caffák ŏ:hyask | for one and all of the wild animals, |
| ná:ho máhco:t | such as what there were, |
| sattá máhco:t | such as Turtle, |
| konó máhco:t | such as Raccoon, |
| ná:ho:t | well, |
| óhya nasmałáhlok hacca:lí | all the wild animals that there were |
| fó:si máhco:t | such as the birds |
| óhya alikcí | all the doctors |
| óhya wíhlin, | they looked for them all, |
| ná:ho:t | well, |
| imasilhá:cit wíhlin, | they looked for and asked for them all, |
| imalpí:sat tàmmin cokfík. | and Rabbit lay there feeling poorly. |

## Scene 2: Vulture is Asked to Treat Rabbit

| | |
|---|---|
| Má:mo:sin, | Thereupon, |
| sánkon í:san a:táhpin, | They were continuing to be unable to do anything, and he [Rabbit] merely continued, |
| ná:hok, | well, |
| saykį ohhí:can, | they went and saw Vulture, |
| saykí híhcok imasilháhcin, | and having seen Vulture, they asked him, |
| "Alikcíská?" káhco:lik, | "Are you a doctor?" they said. |
| "An'alikcilíhco:lik katík óm," káhhan. | "It is the case that I, I am a doctor," he said. |

### Scene 3: Vulture Comes to Treat Rabbit

Má:mo:sin,
stilmá:katohok,
stiláhcin,
saykí:kok íhlok,
incokhalí:kok,
ná:hon,
"Í:sa óhya okbá:ho:š!" káhhan,
í:sa óhya okbáhlin.
Má:mo:sok,
acá í:satoho:limpáhcok
nasmałáhli ŏ:hyak í:sat
óhyak ittimatanátlik acáp.
Ná:hok,
saykí:kok cokfi hó:pa:kon imalíkcit .

Thereupon,
They brought him,
and arrived with him.
Vulture having arrived,
he went in with him,
well,
"Close ye up the entire house," he said,
and they closed up the whole house.
Thereupon,
it is said that they stayed outside,
every one of the animals stayed,
they all were in a circle outside.
Well,
Vulture doctored the sick Rabbit.

### Scene 4: Vulture "Treats" Rabbit

Má:mo:sok,
í:pa:fó:kon ónkat,
"Yǎy!" ká:ha:p,
"Sammi:ciskan ónká?" ká:hat
matasilhá:cin,
"Ínko:š, pilá:kalih ó:š," ká:hat,
"Spilá:kalih ónkš," ká:hat,
cakáłkat í:pat,
cakáłkat í:pat stałi:yáhpok,
íhbon ómmiton mók.
saykók nakáłłan,
"Sáhmí?"
"Hiná:p kánt ałí:yá:hi:yon ó:š.
Ka:nóhco:lá:hi:yon ó:š hiná:p.
Ká:not ka:nóhcok ałi:yá:hi:yon ó:š," ká:hat,
í:pak,
í:pak anóhlok,
cofkoninánnan balláhlok,
ná:hon,
"Hiná:p ká:not halpí:sa:yon ó:š.
Na:santiyáphó:š!" káhhan,
ohintiyáplin,

Thereupon,
as he [Vulture] was eating him, he [Rabbit] made a noise,
"OUCH!" he said,
"What are you doing that he makes a noise?"
they said asking him.
"Naught! I am making the physic."
He maketh noise through the physic," he said,
and he tore him apart with his beak and ate him,
he merely continued to tear him apart and eat him,
it is the case he killed him,
and when he was ready to go,
"How is he?"
"But now he is just this way:
but now he is quite good,
but he is extremely good," he said.
He ate him,
he ate him up,
he laid down nothing but bones.
well,
"But now he is sufficiently good.
Open ye it for me!" he said,
and they opened it,

| | |
|---|---|
| wáykok nakáłtoho:limpáhcok saykík. | and it is said Vulture flew off and disappeared. |
| Má:min, | Then, |
| cokfí cofkoninánnat tàmmitoho:limpáhcok. | there were nothing but Rabbit bones lying there. |
| Kámmi mók įfáylik ómmit. | That is how he cured him! |
| Tafhiyám! | Finis! |

*Textual comments*:

Line 32 *"An'alikcilíhco:lik katík óm," káhhan* '"It is the case that I, I am a doctor," he said'. The final vowel of the pronoun *anó*, is elided. This pronoun is used here as an emphatic subject complement to the first person singular subject suffix *-li*. Elision like this is unusual in normal speech, and is the first indication that Vulture speaks very differently than other people.

Line 39 *"Í:sa óhya okbá:ho:š!" káhhan* '"Close ye up the entire house" he said'. Vulture here starts using elite speech, which he continues to do for the rest of the narrative. By using this highly marked form of speech, which among the Koasati was used only by persons of high political or ritual status, Vulture is indicating that he is an aristocrat. The common speech form of *okbá:ho:š* is *okbá:hól*.

Line 49 *"Yǎy!" ká:ha:p* '"OUCH!" he said'. This interjection was uttered more loudly and more sharply than the rest of the words around it.

Lines 51–52 *"Ínko:š, pilá:kalih ó:š," ká:hat, / "Spilá:kalih ónkš," ká:hat* '"Naught! I am making the physic." / He maketh noise through the physic," he said'. Here archaic English is used to translate Vulture's combination of elite speech and rare vocabulary and syntax, which he uses to confuse the listeners with his erudition. As Miss John reported having seen traditional doctors practice when she was a girl, before the abandonment of Koasati religion, the behavior she ascribes to Vulture may well reflect the actual attitude of the traditional doctor.

The phrase *Ínko:š, pilá:kalih ó:š* would be rendered in the common speech as *Ínkǫ, ahissí stiltohnolíhcok óm* 'Nothing. I am using medicine', and *Spilá:kalih ónkš* would be rendered *Stiltóhnolin ónk* 'I am using it and he is making noise'. The verb *pilá:kan* is a rare word meaning 'to prepare or to use medicine', while *-h* is a connective suffix of rare occurrence.

Line 53 *cakáłkat í:pat* 'and he tore him apart with his beak and ate him'. The verb *cakáłkan* usually means 'to chop once'. Here it is metaphorically extended to Vulture's tearing Rabbit apart with his beak.

Lines 59–60; 65 As in *The Bungling Host* above, Vulture makes an ironic pun on two meanings of the verb *ká:non*. Vulture's hearers understand it in the meaning of 'to be well' but he himself is using it in the meaning of 'to be tasty'.

# 2

# Origin Tales

Origin tales comprise a large group of Koasati traditional narratives. Their principal purpose is to explain how some feature of the natural universe came into being. This explanatory purpose can be DIRECT, that is, the entire thrust of the tale, or OBLIQUE, that is, an appendage to the tale. Origin tales can additionally be divided into two groups, depending on the style of the narrative. The larger group consists of serious narratives, in which the action, no matter how strange, is taken seriously by narrator and listener. The other group consists of humorous narratives, in which the situations are intended to provoke laughter in the audience. The origin tales included in this chapter may be classified as follows:

| | SERIOUS | HUMOROUS |
|---|---|---|
| DIRECT | *The Origin of the Koasati*<br>*The Origin of Orion's Stars*<br>*The Origin of the Pleiades*<br>*The Origin of Deer*<br>*The Origin of Illness*<br>*Corn Woman*<br>*The Origin of Corn*<br>*The Origin of Deciduous Trees* | *The Origin of Opossum's Tail*<br>*The Origin of Owl's Call* |
| OBLIQUE | *The Thunderer and the Man*<br>*The Origin of Deer* | *The Creation of Crow*<br>*How Bat Received His Wings* |

As can be seen in the table, a tale may be placed in two categories at the same time. *The Origin of Deer*, for example, is SERIOUS and DIRECT in its main focus on the origin of deer in the world, and SERIOUS and OBLIQUE in its explanation of why flying squirrels seem to like things made of horn.

Oblique explanations have had a tendency to spread out from this subcategory of tales and become attached to tales of other subcategories. For example, in the Rabbit story *Rabbit Tricks Great-One-Who-Eats-Human-Beings,* an OBLIQUE statement indicates that this is the reason that elephants (which share the term *a:tipacobá* with Great-One-Who-Eats-Human-Beings) live only overseas. Likewise, in the Rabbit story *The Bungling Host*, the fact that the beaks of birds are pierced is explained, as is the peculiar nature of Box Turtle's shell in the tale *Wolf and Box Turtle Run Race.*

A striking stylistic parallel can be seen between these tales and Rudyard Kipling's "Just So" stories. Both explain the occurrence of features in the natural world in a way that is unscientific, but psychologically satisfying. Both use droll humor on occasion, and both do not require the intervention of a deity.

The most interesting feature about Koasati origin tales is that even in the most serious of these tales there are no deities. There are, of course, supernatural beings and supernatural happenings, but they occur without divine intervention—there are no gods per se. In two tales collected in 1910 and included here, *The Origin of Illness* and, especially, *The Origin of Deer*, one can infer the presence of a mysterious, unnamed, powerful being, linguistically suggested by the use of the distributive prefix in its function of marking an indefinite actor. Perhaps this is a hint at the being anciently known as *Hifoshilkimí:si* 'The Owner of Breath', and *lmililliksó* 'His-Death-Does-Not-Exist'. However, this cannot be determined at the present time, since the former title has been forgotten, and the latter has become applied to the Christian God.

In these origin tales, one can discern the outline of the world in myth. At some ancient point in time, the only beings in the world were the animals, who were intelligent, speaking beings that combined human personalities with the essentials of their animal natures. At a later date, humans emerged from the earth and coexisted for a time with the earlier animal-humans, who are understood as having the power to transform themselves from animal to human form. Finally, the animal-humans mysteriously disappeared, with the major exception of Rabbit; he, and the tales concerning him, appeared in the first chapter.

## THE ORIGIN OF THE KOASATI
narrated by *Pahá:ca*

This short and fragmentary text is the only one that speaks to the aboriginal ideas as to the origin of the Indians. *Pahá:ca*, known in English as George Henry, was a Koasati who had never left Texas. He was originally from the Colita village near Shepherd, Texas, but early on he married to an Alabama woman, *Sihomáhki*, and moved to the Alabama village near Livingston, Texas. One of his daughters married into the Koasati of Louisiana, and his descendants dwell there to this day. *Pahá:ca* himself visited the Koasati settlement in Louisiana. He happened to be there in 1908 and was photographed by Mark Raymond Harrington, who was visiting the Indians of Louisiana at the behest of George Heye, founder of the Heye Museum in New York. Swanton recorded this unnumbered text from Henry in 1910. Despite its brevity, the text can be divided into four scenes. The last scene, consisting of one line, seems dubious; however, it is likely that the tale contained more information about *o:lacó:ba* 'Abandoned Town'.

All of the Southeastern Indians believed that they had emerged from the earth at some point in time. The motif of emergence occurs elsewhere in North America, although it is best known from the Hopi and Puebloan groups of the American Southwest. It is of interest that the tale portrays the Indians as already practicing agriculture at the time of their emergence.

Archaeological evidence indicates that certain cultigens were cultivated in the Southeast by the beginning of the Christian era, about the time of the breakup of the ancestral Muskogean language. Thus the Koasati had no traditions of any lifeway that did not include agriculture.

### Scene 1: The Emergence

Askahká yá ihá:ni,
yá tallá:kan,
yá hasi cokkó:li:k,
pontokkó:lin onalokbá:ci:fó:kon,
pahik olfá.

They emerged onto this earth,
this outspread land,
and when this sun was in the sky,
at noon, when there was heat all over,
the grasses sprouted.

### Scene 2: The Planting

Má:mo:sok,
ná:so:t ohacíhlik ałí:yan,
hasí námpo:fó:kon,
ná:sotohok hóktitoho:limpats.

Thereupon,
they began to plant all kinds of things,
and when just so many months had passed,
it is said that that which was there was ripe.

### Scene 3: The Wandering

Má:mo:sok,
aláhkak ihá:ni mí:to:t cikkí:kat,
yomáhlitohok
albiná:cit
má:mit,
ó:lafok hotallá:to:š.

Thereupon,
the others who dwelt in some kind of different land,
they were wandering;
they made camps,
and then,
a town was built.

### Scene 4: The Building of the Old Town

O:lacó:ba ithotalláhlok.

They came and built the abandoned town.

*Textual emendations*:

The following emendations of Swanton's Koasati text have been made:

| | | |
|---|---|---|
| Line 7 | ohatcī´ hīle´ | ohacíhlik |
| Line 11 | mē´ntot | mí:to:t |
| Line 16 | īlhotạlā´ ’ok | ithotalláhlok |

*Textual commentary*:

Line 1 *askahká yá ihá:ni* ‘they emerged onto this earth’. This emergence legend can be compared to the fragment of a Choctaw origin myth recorded by Nicklas (1974:218):

| Maškoki oš tikba | The Creek first |
|---|---|
| Nanih Wáyya a:koccatto:k. | emerged at Wayya Mound, |
| Cilákki oš a:toklą̨nt | the Cherokee second |
| Nanih Wáyya a:koccatto:k. | emerged at Wayya Mound, |
| Cikša oš a:tócci:nat | the Chickasaw third |
| Nanih Wáyya a:koccatto:k. | emerged at Wayya Mound, |
| Cahta oš onta:yóštah mą | the Choctaw fourth there |
| Nanih Wáyya yammą | at that Wayya Mound |
| ištáyyo:pi a:koccatto:k. | they emerged last. |

Line 16 *O:lacó:ba ithotalláhlok* ‘They came and built the abandoned town’. This verse is literally translated ‘their having come and built the abandoned town, they’. The final verb of the verse is in a form that presupposes a following sentence having the same subject as the previous one and occurring shortly afterward in time. This linguistic evidence suggests that Swanton did not record this tale completely, but rather was forced to end recording it before the speaker was through telling it. The reversal of logical order in this sentence (the town was not abandoned when they built it) is an example of the figure of speech called hysteron proteron.

## THE ORIGIN OF CROW

narrated by Selin Williams

This narrative was recorded by John R. Swanton in 1910 from dictation. He gave it the number twenty-three in his “Koasati Texts, Second Series,” and published an English translation based on his interlinear glosses in *Myths and Tales of the Southeastern Indians* (Swanton 1929:181) under the title *The Story of Crow*.

This tale is a good example of the type in which the feature explained in the tale is subsidiary to the principal action. This narrative, which does not appear particularly amusing to the non-Koasati reader, is, nonetheless, considered by the Koasati to be quite humorous. The humor is perceived initially in the dysfunctional social relations of the human characters and, finally, in the scene of Crow’s creation, by the interpolation of a taboo subject.

The interrelationship of the humans involved is highly dysfunctional by Koasati standards. It is a family in which there are no women, the father does not provide properly for his sons, and the boys regard their father with suspicion and (later justified) distrust. This is almost the opposite of the ideal situation in traditional Koasati society, in which the relationship between father and children is close and friendly, and where maternal uncles and paternal aunts are more likely to discipline children than are their parents. In addition, a family that has lost the mother does not long remain without a female member—an aunt or grandmother will step in during the period of mourning, and the remarriage of the widower is expected. A woman was essential to the running of the household; it was difficult for a man to live alone. Thus, the basic premise of this tale is absurd to the Koasati in a way that is not easily appreciated by someone living in modern Western society.

There are three subjects that are taboo in ordinary social communication among the Koasati: sex, death, and excretion. However, because of the psychological power of these taboo subjects, the shock of their use in a narrative provokes a strong humorous reaction. In *The Creation of Crow*, this kind of humor is provoked by the transformation of the father into Crow by sawing a bowstring across his anus. The reaction of Bel Abbey, who had never before heard this tale, is indicative of the intensely humorous reaction of a typical Koasati listener to the use of taboo subjects. Not only did he find the story amusing, but, for years afterward, he would start to laugh when he thought about the transformation scene.

### Scene 1: The Mystery of the Meat

| | |
|---|---|
| A:ti ocoskí tókloscok á:tatohok, | There once was a man with only two sons, |
| ilanawíhlit áɬɬa:k, | and when he went hunting, |
| icó í:bi:k, | when he killed a deer, |
| lopí má:ɬon stimí:lan, | he brought them back only the liver, |
| áswatohon. | and so the two of them dwelt. |
| Atlawístak ónkak, | The children spoke, |
| "Kontá:tak a:nipón naksammi:cíhcok | "What is it that our father does with the |
| ommóʔlí?" káhhok, | meat?" they said. |
| "Himá:yan áɬɬa:p, | "Now, when he goes, |
| aconóhhilok ilhí:cáska:š!" ká:haton. | let us sneak up on him and watch him |
| | then!" they said. |
| Intá:ta:kok áɬɬan, | Their father went off, |
| obá:li má:kok, | and behind him those two, |
| má ocoskí:kok aɬɬá:citok. | those his sons, went off. |
| Má:mok, | Then, |
| a:yá:citohon, | the two of them went, |
| intá:ta:kok icón í:bok, | and their father having killed a deer, |
| stóntit stá:yatohon, | carried it and brought it, |
| hohíhcok, | and the two of them saw him, |
| illónkat hikkį́:tohon, | the two stood in hiding, |
| icó:kon, | and as for the deer— |
| okfá cobáhcok tallá:káhcok | there was a large lake lying there |
| ómmitohon, | and again he stood with it |
| món pá:na shaccá:lok, | at the edge, |
| impáhkatohon, | and he called out to someone, |
| tayyihók itachalí:kan. | and a woman came out. |

### Scene 2: The Boys Kill the Bullfrog Woman

| | |
|---|---|
| Món ómmitohok impíɬkok, | It was for that one that he put it down, |
| ɬóykan, | and returned, |
| ocoskí:kok hí:cat, | and his sons saw it, |
| ɬoyóhkat oɬáhcok, | and when they went back, |
| áswatohon, | the two of them stayed there, |
| intá:ta:kok lopí má:ɬon stimóɬto:š. | and their father took them only the liver. |
| Kántik, | But this being so, |
| na:síkkok áswato:š. | the two of them said nothing. |
| "Himá:ko:š!" á:lot áswatohok. | "Wait!" they kept on thinking. |
| Mán intá:tak ilanawíhlik áɬɬan, | Again their father went off to hunt, |
| ocoskí:kok tóɬkat okfafá:kon, | and his sons ran to the lake, and arriving there |
| oɬáhcok ohimpáhkan, | went and called out to her, |
| tayyihá:kok achalí:kan, | and the woman came out, |
| ɬá:hit í:bitohon, | and they shot and killed her; |
| hanonók ómmitohon. | she was a Bullfrog. |

### Scene 3: The Father Threatens the Boys

| | |
|---|---|
| Ɬoyóhkat oɬáhcok, | Having gone back, |
| áswatohon. | the two of them stayed there. |
| Intá:ta:kok íhlok, | Their father arrived, |
| "Ná:sok sąhaci:cí:š!' ká:halibá:no:š. | "I always told you 'Do not then do something!" |
| Ná:son sąhací:cin," ká:hatoho:limpatš. | You have done something," he said, it is reported. |
| Ká:ha:p, | When he said this, |
| ocóski:kok na:sikkóhcok áswatoho:limpatš. | his two sons kept on not saying anything, so it is said. |
| Máhmok, | At that, |
| intá:tak ónkak, | their father spoke. |
| "Haciná:niho:líhc ómmo:š. | "It seems that one can assume you are men. |
| Má:ko:k hoɬón haciwwíhlilá:š," ká:hato:š. | I shall look for some enemies for you," he said. |
| Káhhok, | Having said that, |
| wíhlok aɬí:yato:š. | he went looking for them. |

## Scene 4: The Boys Develop a Weapon

Máhmin,
atlawísta:kok łakón hasáyhkan ná:hot anóslok.
Má:mo:sok,
fohó:t,
foyobaskó:t,
haskinón,
fohcokbó:t,
foholá:no:t,
ǫ̆:hya ná:si inłakí:san wíhlit,
stilá:cit onokbáhlit anóslok,
ibisnók lónká:hi:k,
ihanhayó hóhcat anóslok,
áswatohok.

Then,
the children made up a lot of arrows.
Thereupon,
bees,
wasps,
bumblebees,
hornets,
and yellow jackets,
they looked for each and every stinged thing,
and brought them and closed them up,
and when they themselves were about to hide,
they dug out a place in the ground,
and the two of them stayed there.

## Scene 5: The Weapon Is Used

Mó:tohon,
intá:ta:kok á:tikon hasă:ykáhcon ilapíhlit stóntitoho:limpatš.
Mó:tohok,
stíhlan,
má:kon ná:si inłakí:sa:kon intíwwit
stittabakóhlit anóslok,
lónkato:š.
Máhmin,
wononohká:cáhpok,
fáyhlin,
askáhkok mathí:catohon,
á:ti íllik ittalǫ̆:catoho:limpatš.

Then,
their father was coming, leading very many men.
Then,
his having brought them,
they opened those, the stinged things, against them,
and having completely thrown them against the ground,
they hid.
Right then,
there was merely a humming noise,
and, it having stopped,
they came out and looked around,
and the ground was black with dead men, it is said.

### Scene 6: The Father Is Transformed into Crow

Má:min,
atlawísta:kok ónka:k,
"Kontá:ta:kok naksó:n tàmmo:š,"
káhhok,
wíhlit a:yá:citohon.

Tàmmitohon híhcok,
"Cikostinkóhcommo:š," káhhok,
bihí acitiká má:lok iccommí
ittaksahlí:cit
apíhlok,
"Lakcá akkáscon ací:yalaho:š,"
káhhok,
fayáhli:k,
lakcá:kok falą́hkok,
"Há! Há! Há!" ká:hat
aɬí:yatohok.
Mó:limpats lakcák.

Then,
the children spoke.
"Our father is lying somewhere,"
they said,
and the two of them went about looking for him.
On seeing where he was lying,
"You seem to be unwise," they said,
and they rubbed his own bow string
across his anus and having thrown it away,
"As Crow you will go about,"
they said,
and leaving off,
Crow having got up,
"Caw! Caw! Caw!" he said
and went off.
Crow is that one, so it is said.

*Textual emendations:*

The following emendations of Swanton's Koasati text have been made:

| | | |
|---|---|---|
| Line 7 | nąks mē´ djitc ōk omō´ ole | naksammi:cíhcok ommóʔlí |
| Line 38 | hą´ nonomitu´n | hanonók ómmitohon |
| Line 66 | asē+ gaxtcun | hasă:ykáhcon |
| Line 84 | ō´gostcun atcē´ yelos | akkascon ací:yalaho:š |

*Textual commentary:*

Line 9 *aconóhhílok ilhi:cásksa:š!* This phrase, which in common speech would be *aconóhhílok ilhi:cáskąh*, shows the power of syntactic constructions in contrast to using distinct lexical items to affect meaning in Koasati. Here, with the first verb marked for first person subject and switch reference, it means 'let us sneak up on him and watch him then!' If the connective suffix *-t* had been used with the first verb (note that this suffix cannot occur with subject affixes), it would have produced *aconólit ilhi:cáskąh*, meaning 'let us try sneaking up on him!' What is handled lexically in English with the two verbs *see* and *try* is handled syntactically in Koasati.

Line 20 *pá:na.* This postposition usually means 'on top of', but when used to modify a word referring to a body of water, it has the idiomatic meaning 'at the edge of'.

Line 23 *tayyihók i:tachalí:kan* 'and a woman came exiting [the water]'.
Line 36 *tayyihá:kok achalí:kan* 'and the woman exited [the water]'.
These two verses are examples of one of the most vexing semantic features of Koasati, the use of a marked nominal plural in a context where the actual noun must be singular. In these two lines, it is particularly noticeable, since the verb *achalí:kan* 'to come out' takes a singular subject only; its plural form is *askáhkan*. Number concord between a plural noun and a plural verb is rarely, if ever, violated in this language. Nonetheless, a plural noun in a singular context occurs with some regularity; other instances may be found in the tale *The Two Winds*, below. It seems in this case, and perhaps in most cases, that the plural is used in this construction when the subject is one of a possible group. Here, the woman is a "Bullfrog"; clearly she is not the only bullfrog, and perhaps not the only Bullfrog Woman. Therefore, the first phrase, *tayyihók i:tachalí:kan*, can be literally translated as 'and one of a number of women came exiting [the water]' and the second, *tayyihá:kok achalí:kan*, as 'and that one of the women came out'. This would also explain the appearance of the article suffix *-:ka-* on the second noun, since the boys would want to kill only this one particular Bullfrog Woman.

Line 38 *hanonók ómmitohon* 'she was a Bullfrog'. This is the only mention in Koasati literature of a Bullfrog Woman; the only similar character in the literatures of the Southeastern Indians is Old Toad Woman of the Tunica (Haas 1950:84–85), whose function is very different. Bullfrog Woman seems not to be an animal-human, but rather an unfriendly supernatural, as attested by her enticement of the boys' father to give her the meat that he should have given to them.

Line 76 *á:ti íllik ittalǫ̂catoho:limpatš* 'and the ground was black with dead men, it is said'. In the reverse of the linguistic situation in lines 23 and 36, here, a singular noun is used in a plural context. The word *á:ti ílli* usually means 'dead person'; the plural is *áti hápka*. However, in Koasati, even when a plural noun is possible, a singular noun may be used, since plurality is obligatorily marked only on those verbs that have special plural forms.

This verse preserves an interesting expression from the vocabulary of war, 'for the ground to be black with the dead'. Since the Koasati abandoned armed conflict in the 1840s, such terms have been forgotten in other contexts.

Line 83 *bihí acitiká má:lok iccommí ittaksahlí:cit* 'and they rubbed his own bow string across his anus'. This incongruous action by the boys and the subsequent transformation of their father into Crow are considered extremely funny by Koasati listeners. As mentioned above, the sudden interpolation of a taboo subject in a narrative tends to provoke laughter, even in the most straightlaced listener. This final, blatantly humorous section, in connection with the absurd relations apparent between the family members, emphasizes to the Koasati audience that the entire tale is meant to be amusing.

## THE ORIGIN OF THE STARS IN THE SWORD AND BELT OF ORION

narrated by Selin Williams

This tale was recorded by John R. Swanton in 1910 and given the number twenty-eight. He published a translation (Swanton 1929:166) under the title *The Stars-in-a-Row*; he was unaware at that time as to what constellation the Koasati term referred. This narrative and the following are the only two astronomical myths recorded in Koasati, although Paz-Taylor (1937:31) records in English a tale about the origin of the spots on the moon. Almost certainly, there were tales to accompany other constellations, such as *hociłpiłá* 'the canoe stars' (Ursa Major), *hociłsawittiłí* 'the racoon's-eyes stars' (Castor and Pollux), and *hociłtaybí* 'the box stars' (Pegasus); however, none are now remembered. Swanton (1929:138–39) has preserved the Alabama tale that accompanies Ursa Major, and it is not unlikely that the Koasati tale was similar. The night sky was looked upon with fear by the Koasati as the dwelling place of evil supernaturals who would ride to earth on bright meteors, or fireballs. The stars themselves were believed capable of causing death to one who looked on them unprotected.

### Scene 1: Three Men Go Off

| | |
|---|---|
| A:tok fohó incáklit amá:katoho:limpatš. | It is said that some people went off to get honey. |
| Toccí:nan, | They were three in number, |
| caffá:kat cá:fon í:sin, | one took an ax, |
| caffá:kat icó hisá:kon ciní:kan, | one wore a deerskin robe on his back, |
| caffá:kat folón í:sin, | and one took a spoon, |
| amá:katoho:limpatš. | and it is said that they went off. |

### Scene 2: They Are Lost and Become Stars

| | |
|---|---|
| Má:mik, | And then, |
| ilhóhsok, | having got lost, |
| yomáhlit ikló:cot | they went about and did not return, |
| stonafáytohok. | they stayed away. |
| Mók ómmimpatš hociłí bayátlik í:sak. | It is said that that is what the Row Stars (the sword and belt of Orion) are. |

*Textual emendations*:

| | | |
|---|---|---|
| Line 4 | tcạfa´ gan | caff:kat |
| Line 9 | ikla´ djit | iklá:cot |

*Textual commentary*:

Lines 1–5 These lines indicate that the three persons represent the three stars in the belt of Orion, and the ax, the deerskin robe, and the spoon represent the three stars in the sword of Orion.

Line 10 *stonafáytohok* 'they stayed away'. Martha John, listening to this tale, remarked that she hoped that they would never come back, reflecting the fear that evil celestial forces inspire even to this day among the Koasati. This makes the investigation of constellation and star names and of astronomical myths very difficult, since many people have avoided finding out about the night sky because of their fears.

Line 11 *Mók ómmimpatš hociłí bayátlik í:sak* 'It is said that that is what the Row Stars (the sword and belt of Orion) are'. Literally, this means 'The Row Stars sit, and that is what is said that they are'. All celestial objects are said 'to sit' (sg. *cokkó:lin*, dual *cikkí:kan*, pl. *í:san*) in the sky, rather than 'be out,' as in English.

## THE ORIGIN OF THE PLEIADES
narrated by Selin Williams

This narrative was recorded by John R. Swanton in 1910, who gave it the number twenty-nine. He published a translation (Swanton 1929:166) under the title *The Pleiades*. As in the previous tale, the stars were considered to be people originally; that this was the case for all stars is confirmed by Paz-Taylor (1937:32) and by the short tale *The Star Husbands* (Swanton 1929:166–67). The second scene of the narrative is important because it suggests that planting (and the first month of the ancient lunar calendar *na:sacíhli hasí* 'Planting Month') was tied to the disappearance of the Pleiades in the east at sunrise during the spring. Without such an astronomically fixed date, the old lunar calendar of thirteen months would have fallen out of coordination with the seasons, since there are twelve lunar months and eleven days in a solar year. Maintaining coordination was important, since the old months bore names descriptive of natural occurrences that are fixed in respect to the solar year (e.g., *bakcó hókti hasí* 'Blackberry Ripening Month').

### Scene 1: Who the Pleiades Are

| | |
|---|---|
| Hociłí lokkó:li mók ómmi:k, | Also, as for the Standing Stars (Pleiades), |
| yómahka stinká:not, | they liked to wander; |
| bítka má:łi stinká:not yomáhlit. | they wandered liking only to dance. |
| A:ti imayyí:hok ómmǫ. | They seem to have been lazy people. |
| Bítka má:łon bànnat yomáhlit. | They went about wanting only to dance. |

### Scene 2: What the Pleiades Do

Ohayyí ó:ła:fó:kon,
palaná abiłhilká má:łon acíhlit,
hoktí:cit í:pak.
Lókbat anó:ka:p,
wasátkatoho:limpatš.

When summer was about to arrive,
they only planted pole beans,
and ripened them and ate them.
When the weather got warm,
it is said that they disappeared.

Mók ómmimpatš hociłí lokkó:lik.

It is said that that is what the Pleiades are.

*Textual emendations*:

| | | |
|---|---|---|
| Line 2 | istimkanat | stinká:not |
| Line 4 | ati maye'huk ko'm | á:ti imayyí:hok ómmǫ |

*Textual commentary*:

Lines 1–5 This description of the people who form the Pleiades is unique among those recorded for Southeastern Indian peoples. The Shawnee (Clifton 1984:2) depicted the Pleiades as siblings, and the Natchez (Swanton 1929:242) as medicine men.

Lines 9–10 These lines have two meanings. The first is literal, meaning that the beings who form the Pleiades go away somewhere in warm weather. The second is astronomical, meaning that when the weather is warm in the spring the constellation is not to be found in the night sky.

## THE THUNDERER AND THE MAN
narrated by Selin Williams

This narrative was recorded by John R. Swanton in 1910 and given the number forty-three. He published a translation (Swanton 1929:184) under the title *Thunder and Laigatonōhona*; the last word is a corruption of the Koasati word *laykitonó:no* 'scarab beetle', who is actually only a minor character in the story.

Though very interesting, this tale is also very difficult. Because the original text was taken down by dictation, Selin Williams compressed the history as much as possible, perhaps due to fatigue on her part. Originally, the narrative seems to have consisted of six scenes, with a prologue and an epilogue. However, in this case the prologue and epilogue are reduced to single sentences and four of the original scenes were compressed into two. Scene 2 is comprised of two parts: in the first, the man encounters Iron Woman and, in the second, she cures his burns. Scene 3 conflates the advice of Iron Woman, which predicts what the man should do when he returns to challenge the Thunderer, with what actually happens when he returns.

Linguistically, too, the text is difficult, for it is full of obsolete words and concepts, and in several places (noted below), the Koasati text as written by Swanton is difficult to interpret.

### Prologue

| | |
|---|---|
| Winíhkok á:ton ittabáhlok, | It is said that the Thunderer and human beings placed bets with one another; |
| hassapolóhkon ittįhóccatoho:limpatš. | they used to shoot against each other at the chunkey roller. |

### Scene 1: A Man Bets His Wife and Loses Her

| | |
|---|---|
| Máhmok, | Then, |
| stáswan, | there were two people dwelling with him [the Thunderer], |
| winíhkak įháplit stanó:lit, | and the Thunderer won completely from him, |
| halkí má:lon abáhlin, | and he [the man] bet his own wife, |
| ittįhóccat įhápliyon, | and though they shot against each other |
| ínká:hik bánkot imiyyí:hon, | and he [Thunderer] won, he [the man] did not want to give her to him, |
| winíhkak tikbón stompófkat | he treasured her against him, and the Thunderer blew fire on him |
| óhya libátlin. | and burned him all over. |

### Scene 2: The Man Encounters Iron Woman

| | |
|---|---|
| Iwwalí:kak, | He [the man] ran from him, |
| hahcín apotó:kat á:yatohon, | and while he was going along a river |
| oconók camahká:cin há:lot ałí:yatohon, | he went hearing the sound of metal ringing; |
| Oconá Tayyók ónkatohok á:tatohon. | it was Iron Woman who was making the sound. |
| Ohłan, | As he arrived over there, |
| Oconá Tayyík ónkak, | Iron Woman spoke. |
| "Pátkafa acokkó:š!" káhhan, | "Sit beside the bed!" she said, |
| ká:hayon, | but even though she said so, |
| "Mánko:š! Capasá:kahonkáhcon ó:š," káhhan. | "By no means! It is the case that I am filthy," he said. |
| Stałí:yak, | She took him, |
| okifá ohto:píłkan, | and went and put him into the water, |
| łałlawístak hó:ti óhya imí:pat įfáytoho:limpatš. | and the minnows ate all the sores from him, and cured him, so it is said. |

### Scene 3: Iron Woman Advises the Man

Máhmin,
Oconá Tayyík ónkak,
"Isnók imatobá:táskalahon ónkali:š,"
káhhok,
łakón innáhhok,
mattóhnon,
ałí:yatoho:limpatš.
Oconá Tayyík ónkak,
"Ołci:fó:kon,
winíhkak ónkak,
'Kosná:lok ittįhiná:tak holiccaskš!'
ká:laho:š.
Ma:fó:kon,
"Łakí mók ąhokánkóhcon ó:š,"
íska:laho:š.
Máhmin,
'Watolák cikkí:lo:š.
Mók cimonáłłin,' ká:halaho:š.
Ká:há:pin,
ímmo má:lon ohpíhlin
ittįhóccąh!"

And then,
Iron Woman spoke.
"I intend that you indeed will win
her back," she said,
and having made arrows for him,
she sent him off,
and it is said that he went.
Iron Woman had spoken.
"When you arrive there,
the Thunderer will speak.
'Let us by ourselves shoot, leading
against each other!' he will say.
And then,
You are to say, 'It is the case that my
arrows also are no good for me.'
And then,
'Whooping Crane keeps some indeed.
He will also loan them to you,' he will say.
Upon his saying this,
go over and take his very own ones
[arrows], then shoot against each other!"

### Scene 4: The Man Defeats the Thunderer

A:tik mán winíhkan óhya įháplit,
halkí:kon stimałáhkan.
Winíhkok iyyí:hohónka:sin,
á:tik tikbón stompófkat libátlit
wali:lí:cok łóhlit ompófkan,
łóhlin ihá:ni sokókbi ostá:kan
atanátkat.
Libá:ka:k,
cofkonó:tohok ittapáłkat ciłátlin,
laykitonó:nok sítkat pa:tallá:litohok.

Mók ómmipatš, pa:lokkó:li.

The man again won each and every thing
from him,
and got his wife from him by guile.
The Thunderer really treasured her,
and the man blew fire upon him and
burned him;
he made him run and chased him and
blew on him,
and he chased him around the four
corners of the world.
When he was burned up,
those that were his bones splintered and fell,
and Dung Beetle gathered them and placed
them upon his back.

This is what it is said that the standing things
on his back are.

## Epilogue

| | |
|---|---|
| Má:min,<br>winíhkak hasachalí:kan áłłat<br>nakátoho:limpatš. | And then,<br>the Thunderer went into the east and<br>disappeared, so it is said. |
| Kámmo:š. | It is finished. |

*Textual emendations*:

| | | |
|---|---|---|
| Line 7 | itihō´ tca | ittįhóccat |
| Line 8 | iñgabạ´'ñgut | ínká:hik bánkot |
| Line 11 | yūwalē´ gak | iwwalí:kak |
| Line 19 | tcạpạsạkaho´ ñgas tconōs | capas:kahonkáhcon ó:š |
| Line 33 | kusna´ yok | kosná:lok |
| Line 33 | i´ tinạtạk | ittįhiná:tak |
| Line 33 | holē´ tcatc | holiccáskš |
| Line 40 | ōxpahi´ lin | ohpíhlin |
| Line 41 | itihō´ tca | ittįhoccąh |
| Line 49 | ki´ łatlin | ciłátlin |
| Line 50 | laigatonō´ honōk | laykitonó:nok |
| Line 53 | hạsētchạlē´ gan | hasachalí:kan |

*Textual commentary*:

Line 2 *hassapolóhkon ittįhóccatoho:limpatš* 'they used to shoot against each other at the chunkey roller'. Even in 1910, when this text was collected, the Koasati version of chunkey had almost gone out of memory; today it is completely forgotten. The game was played by rolling a disk of elm wood (the *hassapolóhki*) along a flat stretch of ground. Then the players shot their arrows at the point at which they thought the disk would come to rest, and the person whose arrows struck nearest the spot where the disk came to rest won the game. A fact that is tacitly understood in this narrative is that the arrows of the Thunderer are lightning bolts; *winihka įłakí* 'the Thunderer's arrows' is a still-common idiom for 'thunderbolt'.

Lines 9–10 *winíhkak tikbón stompófkat / óhya libátlin* 'and the Thunderer blew fire on him / and burned him all over'. The Thunderer had the power to blow fire on things. That this power resided in his arrows, the thunderbolts, is made clear in line 34, where the man has control of the thunderbolts and uses their power to burn the Thunderer.

Line 14 passim *Oconá Tayyí* 'Iron Woman'. This figure has been lost to the present-day Koasati. A similar mythological figure is found in the narratives of the Tunica, an Indian group of Louisiana who had long-standing contacts with the Koasati well into the middle of the twentieth century. This is the Stone Witch, called in Tunica *tíšlina*, described by Sesostrie Youchigant as follows:

> *tíšlinăhc, ˀóninahpókatɛ́nì. hínahkuškăn, šíhkalɛ́nì. ˀóninayánakatɛ́nì. ˀónisamátihc, sisakukatɛ́nì. póluntˀɛˀílĭn, yúkatĭhc, tíšlinăhc, hátikăn, yákatikˀahcáni.*
>
> The Stone Witch looked like a person. Nevertheless, she was (made of) stone. She talked like a person. After cooking people, she would eat them. In two thousand years, the Stone Witch will come back again. [Haas 1950:167]

In the *Thunderer Myth* (Haas 1950:25–43), a commander has bet his relatives and lost them and goes off to die. He comes to the house of the Stone Witch, who offers him hospitality, including an invitation for him to lie down on her bed. However, unlike in the Koasati narrative, the Stone Witch turns on the man and he has to fight to escape her and is only saved from her when others offer two orphan girls in his place. Indeed, the fact that Iron Woman is not a creature of flesh ("he went hearing the sound of metal ringing; / it was Iron Woman who was making the sound") coupled with the similarities in the onsets of the two narratives suggests the possibility that *The Thunderer and the Man* was adapted from a Tunica tradition. Another similarity between the mythology of the Tunica and the Koasati is found in the character Clawed Witch (Haas 1950:79–81)—Tunica *tínikówi*, Koasati *copoktaykí* (see chapter 4). During a reading of the present narrative to Martha John, the suggestion was made that Iron Woman might perhaps be *copoktaykí*.

Lines 22–23 *łałlawístak hó:ti óhya imí:pat / įfáytoho:limpatš* 'and the minnows ate all the sores from him, / and cured him, so it is said'. This may reflect an actual medical practice, using fish to consume dead and dying flesh, leaving only healthy tissue behind. It is paralleled by the modern American use of maggots to cleanse severe wounds.

Line 33 *"Kosá:lok ittįhinátak holiccáskš"* '"Let us by ourselves shoot, leading against each other!"' The Koasati is here hopelessly obscure, which is regrettable as this is the beginning of the crux of the story. The implication of this phrase is that the man and Thunderer are two of several players of the chunkey game, and that they are to start playing before the others.

Lines 34–41 Although these lines were recorded relatively accurately, the action they depict is so compressed as to hinder comprehension seriously. A plausible reconstruction of the action is that Whooping Crane is the keeper of all of the arrows to be used in the game, and that the man goes to Whooping Crane, out of sight of Thunderer, and exchanges the arrows that Iron Woman made for him with Thunderer's arrows, thus acquiring his power. The phrase *ímmo má:lon ohpíhlin* 'go over and take his very own ones' implies that the man can get his hands on Thunderer's arrows as they were not in his personal possession.

Line 43 *halkí:kon stamałáhkan* 'he got his wife from him by guile'. This expression confirms the supposition that the man tricked the Thunderer into surrendering his powers to him. The verb *stimałáhkan* is used to describe various actions, such as Comanche horse stealing and crows distracting and stealing prey from hawks, and can mean 'to steal in a raid', 'to loot', or 'to get something away from someone by trickery'. Most recently, it is used for someone who gets something away from other people by eliciting their sympathy.

Line 47 *ɬóhlin ihá:ni sokokbí ostá:kan atanatkát* 'he chased him around the four corners of the world'. It is tempting to see European influence in this phrase; however, precontact Koasati cosmology is so poorly known that the idea of world corners could well be indigenous. The aboriginal house, from which analogies to the sky and earth could have been drawn, was a rectangular structure with corners (*sokokbí*).

Line 50 *sítkat*. This now obsolete verb was used in the sense of 'to pick', as with flowers or fruits. Here, however, it seems to be used in the sense of 'to gather together', which would be modern *ittanáhlin*.

Line 53 *winíhkak hasachalí:kan áɬɬat nakáɬtoho:limpatš* 'the Thunderer went into the east and disappeared, so it is said'. This ending, which is atypical of the endings of Koasati traditional tales, recalls the endings of Natchez Winter Stories (Haas p.c., 1986), in which, at the end, the characters always go west—as, for example, the narrative entitled *The Opossum and the Woodpecker*, which ends *caWcahą kʷaLnelu·ya ho·ca·ka·šuhtį* 'the Woodpecker went towards the west, so it is said'.

## THE ORIGIN OF DEER

narrated by Selin Williams

Recorded by John R. Swanton in 1910, this tale was assigned the number thirty-seven. However, the translation he published (Swanton 1929:186) under the title *The Great Deer* is a conflation of this narrative and *The Contest of the Elf, Human, Panther, and Wildcat* (see chapter 4). This indicates that Swanton prepared his translations of the Koasati texts from his field notes, which were on loose sheets, rather than from his typescript. Apparently, he got his sheets of notes mixed up when he was preparing the manuscript. This narrative is one of the few that suggest the presence of an indefinite controlling power in the time of the animal-humans. The one who kept the first deer in the world is never named, although Swanton, in a note, calls him (or her) the "owner." This seems to be a reference to *Hifoshilkimí:si* 'Owner of Breath', the remote, ill-defined creator, who seems to have had little importance in Koasati mythology. This being can be compared to the Prime Mover of the Deists, since he or she has little function other than to distribute items of creation and does not interfere in the affairs of the world.

### Scene 1: The One Deer in the World Is Lost

| | |
|---|---|
| Icók caffą́:kascon hopiɬkáhcotohon, | One lone deer used to be kept, |
| cahabiloskó fó:sok ahiccá:cik | and the bird, Swallow, watched him from a perch, |
| pa:cokkó:lin, stáytoho:limpatš. | and used to go about with him. |
| Stá:yatohok fó:sik, | The bird went about with him, |
| nóhcin, | but having fallen asleep, |
| icók nakáɬtoho:limpatš. | it is said Deer disappeared. |

### Scene 2: The Search for Deer

Má:mo:sin,
palón hosobaylí:cin,
naksó:n ahhí:cat ballá:kat á:tat,
ónkak,
"Oko:mahlifón,
okhotahán
ittók spa:tallá:kafon
icóp átš." ká:toho:limpatš.

Thereupon,
Flying Squirrel was informed,
everywhere he looked and stayed lying,
and he spoke.
"To the south,
in the midst of the sea,
over in an oak grove,
there Deer is," he said,
so it is reported.

### Scene 3: Deer Is Called Back

Mó:tohon,
matohahopayí:cin,
máhmin,
í:lá:hi:fó:kon icók,
á:to:t,
a:tilhiciksó:t,
kowó:t,
ifó:t,
wasó:t
má:łon ohínkato:š.

Then,
he was called from afar by means of telepathy,
at that,
when Deer was about to arrive,
to humans,
to elves,
to panthers,
to dogs,
and to wolves,
to them alone he was given.

### Scene 4: Deer Is Transformed from One to Many

Má:mok,
híssin tíhkat,
tíhkat,
tíhkat,
óhya apísli:fó:k,
icók hacó:tohok hátkat hátkan,
amá:kat ístoho:limpatš.
Má:mo:sin,
icók hasáykatoho:limpatš.
Icó hísso:tok ómmimpatš.
Má:min,
paló lapí má:łon ohínkato:š.
Kámmisk,
naslapí má:łon alostíhcommimpatš.

Then,
they plucked his hair,
and plucked it,
and plucked it,
and threw it all about,
and that which was Deer's tail was very white,
it is said they went taking it.
Thereupon,
it is said that deer became many.
It is said that they are Deer's former hair.
Then,
they gave Flying Squirrel only the horn.
Just like that,
it is said he likes only things of horn.

*Textual emendations:*

| | | |
|---|---|---|
| Line 18 | ilai´ yefō̃´ gon | í:lá:hi:fó:kon |
| Line 24 | ma´ łun pạlo´n ohi´ ñgatōs | má:łon ohínkato:š |
| Line 34 | hisō´ to-o´ mimpats | hísso:tok ómmimpatš |
| Line 37 | a´ mis | kámmisk |
| Line 38 | gạłitco´ mimpats | alostihcómmimpatš |

*Textual commentary*:

Line 1 *hopiłkáhcotohon* 'he used to be kept'. Here, the distributive prefix *ho-/-oh* is used to indicate an indefinite subject. Even though the verb here is active, it is translated as an English passive, since English, unlike Koasati, cannot delete an agent without changing the voice of the verb. The use of this prefix indicates that the narrator does not know, or is unwilling to reveal, anything about the one performing the action, only that an actor existed.

Line 13 *ittók spa:tallá:kafon* 'over in an oak grove'. Swanton glosses the word *ittó* here as 'oak', although it usually means 'tree'. Nonetheless, the concepts of 'tree' and 'oak' are closely connected in Koasati—note *ittó hómma* 'red oak', lit. 'red tree', and *ittó hiná:ba* 'live oak', lit. 'hard tree'. It is possible that the original meaning of *ittó* in Koasati was 'oak' and was later extended to mean 'tree', just as *hałbí* once meant 'pine bark' and was later extended to mean 'bark of any tree'.

Line 16 *matohahopayí:cin* 'he was called from afar by means of telepathy'. Telepathic powers were ascribed to a class of ritual specialists known as *hopá:yi*, and called "prophets" in English. These people, who received their powers from *Imilillíkso* in dreams, were able to find lost people or objects, to call game animals for hunters, work magic against enemies, and foretell the future. Note that this verb refers primarily to these ritual specialists. The term used for average people calling by telepathy is *matilahallá:kan*.

Line 20 *a:tilhiciksó:t* 'to elves'. The Koasati translate the term *a:tilhiciksó* as *elf* in English, although the literal translation is 'invisible person'. In literature, elves are beings who are neutral or friendly towards humans. In Koasati folklore, however, elves are dangerous, at least with regard to the fact that seeing one presages the death of a close relative. Elves live in trees. Their presence is indicated by smooth bare patches on a tree's trunk or by mistletoe (*a:tilhiciksó imittó* 'the elves' tree') growing on its branches.

Line 24 *má:łon ohínkato:š* 'to them alone he was given'. In Swanton's text, the word *palón* 'flying squirrel (accusative case)' is inserted. This seems to have resulted from a slip of the tongue by Williams, anticipating the end of the tale where Flying Squirrel reappears.

# THE ORIGIN OF ILLNESS

narrated by Selin Williams

This text was recorded by John R. Swanton in 1910, who gave it the number forty-one. He published a translation of this tale under the title *Sickness* (Swanton 1929:169). This narrative is set in the time of the animal-humans. Here, as in *The Origin of Deer*, the existence of the mysterious motivating power is hinted at by the use of the indefinite agent prefix. Woodcock, a character that appears nowhere else in Koasati literature, is here the type of hubristic character often found in these tales. This type is a being who has an inflated idea of his abilities, and who then acts on this self-estimation, eventually coming to a bad or foolish end. In current Koasati storytelling, Rabbit is the character who displays this consummate hubris.

## Scene 1: An Attempt to Eliminate Illness

| | |
|---|---|
| Nasholpák yá:li íksolahon hobànnok, | It was desired that Illness should no longer exist here, |
| holpán í:sit | and taking the illnesses, |
| óhyan anóslok, | finishing them up, |
| cokbón áɬɬit shaca:lí:cok, | and having put them into a vessel and stood it up; |
| "Naksók abá pilahá ó:š; | "Whosoever is from beyond the |
| Fáyhó:š!" ká:hayon, | sky; dispose of them," they said, |
| ná:si óhyan howíhlin, | but contrary to expectation, though all were sought, |
| ná:si wáykak óhyan stilá:citik, | even though all things that flew were brought, |
| sánkon. | they were unable to do it. |

## Scene 2: Woodcock Persuades Them to Try

| | |
|---|---|
| Picokcók ónkak, | Woodcock spoke, |
| "Anók ómmi:p" káhhok, | "As for me," he said, |
| "Abá pilahá amáɬɬat." | "I can go beyond the sky." |
| Abá hokkí:taha áɬɬat nakáɬtohok, | He went and disappeared into the zenith, |
| ɬóykat í:la:k, | and when he returned, |
| "Anáp yintákkon," ká:toho:limpatš. | "As for me, I don't believe it," one said, so it is reported. |

**Scene 3: They Give Him the Illnesses**

| | |
|---|---|
| Má:mo:sin, | Nevertheless, |
| ohiyyímmok, | they believed him, |
| cokbá:kon stohínkan, | and they gave him the vessel, |
| stáɬɬat, | and he took it, |
| abá pilahón áɬɬat nakáɬtohok. | and he went into the sky and disappeared. |

**Scene 4: Woodcock Fails**

| | |
|---|---|
| Ihokí:con, | Soon, |
| sɬóyhkok, | he brought it back; |
| stóntik stí:sihónka:sin, | he brought it holding it tightly, |
| stittatámmit, | but it fell from his grasp, |
| sbosótlit, | and it shattered, |
| holpák óhyan aboyótlok. | and the illnesses all scattered. |
| | |
| Mók ómmimpatš holpák ohyá:ci:k. | Such is what is said how illnesses occur all over. |

*Textual emendation*:

| | | |
|---|---|---|
| Line 1 | eksulan | íksolahon |

*Textual commentary*:

Line 1 *hobánnok* 'it was desired'. Here, and elsewhere in this tale, the distributive prefix *ho-*/ *-oh* is used to indicate an indefinite actor. As in *The Origin of Deer*, this indefinite actor may be identified with *Hifoshilkimí:si*. That omniscience is not an attribute of this being is shown both here, when he or she believes Woodcock's false claims, and in *The Origin of Deer*, when he or she does not know where the lost Deer is to be found.

Line 5 *naksók abá pilahá ó:š* 'whosoever is from beyond the sky'. This sentence could also be translated as an imperative: "Someone be towards the sky!" It would then be a command to one of the flying beings to go beyond the sky. Note that *abá*, which usually means 'up' or 'Heaven', here has the older meaning 'sky'. *Pilahá* can mean both 'toward' and 'from', depending on context. Here it seems to mean 'beyond'.

Line 12 *Abá pilaha amáɬɬat* 'I can go beyond the sky'. Here, the verb *áɬɬan*, which usually means 'intends to go', is used in an unusual way as a stative verb meaning 'to be able to go', or 'to habitually go'. The fact that Woodcock is the bird chosen is probably due to the fact that the actual bird is noted for its nocturnal displays high over fields and pastures.

Line 15 *Anáp yíntákkon* 'As for me, I don't believe it'. This statement by an anonymous animal-human about Woodcock's claims presages for the audience that Woodcock is going to fail. This gives a tragic aura to the proceedings, since it offers a moment in which the error is foreseen and could have been avoided. The form *yíntakkǫ* is fairly unusual because it denotes an absolute assertion 'I do not believe it by any means'. The more usual form is *incayínkǫ* 'I don't believe it (but I am leaving room for doubt)'.

## CORN WOMAN

narrated by Selin Williams

This narrative was taken down by dictation by John R. Swanton in 1910; he gave it the number forty-seven, and published a translation (1929:168). This is one of two different traditions found among the Koasati about the origin of corn. The tale following this one, The *Origin of Corn*, illustrates the other tradition. The being Corn Woman is found in the literatures of other Southeastern groups, such as the Creek and the Natchez; among the latter group, she is also tied to the origin of beans. This is the first narrative in the collection in which the stock character Orphan appears. Orphan, a character without social ties and displaying complete independence of action, was fascinating to the Koasati and appears repeatedly in various tales and even in a semihistorical narrative such as *The First Meeting of the Indians and The Europeans*. In a society that was organized as a system of reciprocal kin relationships (*ittimalahhilká*), Orphan offered a character who could be both pitied and envied.

### Scene 1: Corn Woman Is Rejected

| | |
|---|---|
| Tayyí sihnóhcok á:yatoho:limpatš. | It is said that an elderly woman was going about. |
| Ho:tinannáhcok, | She was covered with sores, |
| pasá:kascok, | and she seemed dirty, |
| ohimpalátka:sin. | and people were quite cross with her. |

### Scene 2: Corn Woman Is Accepted by Orphans

| | |
|---|---|
| A:yatohok, | She went about, |
| atlawístanannáhcok, | and there were nothing but children; |
| loká:caskok í:satohon. | there were orphans dwelling there. |
| Ohłan, | Having arrived over there, |
| atlawístak ayyihó:cihónkan, | and the children felt great pity for her, |
| cokkó:toho:limpatš. | and she sat down, so it is said. |
| "Koncokkǫ:li:š," káhhan. | "Continue to dwell with us!" they said. |

### Scene 3: Corn Woman Feeds the Orphans with Herself

| | |
|---|---|
| Má:mo:sin, | Thereupon, |
| tayyí síhnok ónkak, | the old woman spoke. |
| "Ná:son shopónhácíhcotohok | "Whatever you use to cook things with, |
| i:talloko:líhcok!" káhhan. | come and set it up for me!" she said. |
| I:tilloko:líhcin. | They came and set it up for her. |
| Má:mo:sin, | Thereupon, |
| ibisnók cassók a:yáhcok ómmitohok, | she herself was corn going about; |
| ilisahlí:cit intabáhlin | she scraped herself and made bread for them, |
| í:pat í:satoho:limpatš. | and they continued to eat it. |

### Scene 4: Corn Woman Is Transformed into Corn

| | |
|---|---|
| Mó:tohon, | Then, |
| ónkak, | she spoke, |
| "Cassík hiná:p hiná:bat hinábš," | "The corn is now quite hard," |
| káhhan. | she said. |
| "Pitáhkok acó:bok haccá:tohon, | "The old storage house standing there, |
| yón páslit anóslok, | clean it up, |
| onokbáhlok nocitóka:š!" káhhok. | close it, and go ye then to sleep!" she said. |
| "Anók hacimpicí mó:š," káhhok, | "I indeed am your mother," she said. |
| "Cassí hátką." | "White Corn." |
| Onkak, | And she spoke. |
| "Tabahálit háspalaho:š," ká:hatohon. | "You will make bread and eat," she said. |
| Tamóhkan, | Night fell, |
| hobálka:p, | and when they lay down, |
| pitáhkak kobohlí:cit | the storage house made noises |
| nakáłtohok. | and then was quiet. |
| Níhtan, | Day broke, |
| ohtohintiwáptohon, | and they all went to open it up, |
| cassík alotó:kat shaccá:toho:limpatš. | and it stood there full to the top with corn, so it is said. |

*Textual emendation*:

| | | |
|---|---|---|
| Line 14 | sṓ pon hą́ tcitcōtōk | shopónhácíhcotohok |

*Textual commentary*:

Line 2 *ho:tinannáhcok* 'she was covered with sores'. The actual appearance of Corn Woman was that of a human being with skin of corn kernels and hair of corn silk. However, to people who did not know corn, her kernel skin appeared to be sores of some kind.

Line 9 *atlawístak ayyihó:cihónkan* 'the children felt great pity for her'. Pity of humans for supernaturals is a powerful way of gaining the eventual support of that supernatural, as in the tale *Peregrine Falcon and Great Horned Owl* (Kimball 1989), in which the human protagonist's pity for Peregrine Falcon eventually led to him being granted the power to hunt successfully. This attitude is the exact opposite of that held by the Algonquian and Siouan peoples of the United States, who believed that supernatural power was obtained by eliciting the pity of supernatural powers. It is probably for this reason that the vision quest, which is intended to induce supernatural pity, is completely lacking in the Southeast.

Line 24 *pitáhkok* 'storage house'. The word *pitahká*, no longer known by Koasati speakers, is glossed 'corncrib' by Swanton (1929:168). However, it is a logical contradiction to have a corncrib before having corn. It is more likely, then, that the word referred to a storage house for gathered plant items.

Lines 27–30 *"Anók hacimpicí mó:š," káhhok, / "Cassí hátką." / ónkak, / "Tabahálit háspalaho:š," ká:hatohon* '"I indeed am your mother," she said. / "White Corn." / And she spoke. / "You will make bread and eat," she said'. Swanton's translation of these lines is quite different: "I am your mother. You can eat bread made out of white corn" (1929:168). However, this translation does violence to Koasati syntax. It is just possible that the noun phrase *cassí hátką* 'white corn' is in the variant of the accusative case. Nonetheless, there are no examples elsewhere of a syntactic object separated from the verb that modifies it by the word *ónkak*, which always introduces a new act of quoted speech. And the verb *tabáhlin* 'to make bread' is an intransitive verb. Thus, the phrase *cassí hátka*, which hangs between the two clear acts of quoted speech, refers to Corn Woman's name, "White Corn."

## THE ORIGIN OF CORN

narrated by Martha John

I recorded this narrative on tape in October, 1990. This narrative is of interest for its strong similarities to, yet striking differences from, the previous narrative, recorded by Swanton in 1910. It is clearly from a completely different tradition. Three features that the two narratives share are a little house, the character Orphan, and a being that produces corn. An additional notable feature that is common between the two traditions is that corn is produced in a revolting fashion. In *Corn Woman*, corn was produced from scraping what appeared to be open sores, and in this tale, corn is produced through vomiting. A repugnant origin for corn is a widespread theme in the Southeast. In Creek tradition, corn is produced from dirty feet (Swanton 1929:9); in Natchez tradition, corn is produced through defecation (Swanton 1929:230).

### Scene 1: The Orphan Is Closed Up

Athómmak ná:hok,
á:ti loká:casok á:tat,
stohibakłí:cit palámmo:tohon.
A:táhcotohok,
í:sasok haccá:tohon,
"Ohtaconokbálhól!" káhhan,
ohtonokbáhlit,
ohtonokbáhlitohon,
á:tatohok,
ná:sik hiłilihká:cin,

hiłilihká:cin
hohá:lotohomá:łok.

There were Indians,
and an orphan dwelt there,
and they all were excessively poor.
He used to dwell there,
and a little house stood there,
"Go and close ye me up in it," he said,
and they went and closed him up in it,
and having closed him up in it,
he stayed there,
and something made a sound of regurgitation;
they must have heard
the sound of regurgitation.

### Scene 2: Corn Is Produced

Akkó á:tik ahó:to:sit ómmá:tok,
cassí anámpok,
cassi óhyak,
óhya:pin,
óhyak,
óhyak ittaciłáttoho:limpáhcok.

Acá óhyan,
ná:hon,
akkó í:sasi haca:lí:cá:pin.

After that being had fully vomited,
it was corn again,
all kinds of corn,
almost all,
and it was all,
and all had fallen to the ground,
so it is said.
It was all outside,
it was there,
where they had built that little house.

### Epilogue

Kámmiskan,
ná:hok
cassík ómmi:k,
walóhlo:sin ishí:ca:p,
atholtó:tok ómmok.
Ná:ho yámmit,
"Hiłilí:cískat,
ná:hotiskat íspa:p,
íspahónka:si:p,
atholtó:tǫ," hokáhco:lik món.

Just like that,
well,
as for corn,
when you see it and it is very tender,
it seems to be former human vomit.
Well, it is so,
"If you cook it,
if you use it and eat it,
if you really eat it,
it is former human vomit," they also used to say.

*Textual commentary*:

Line 2 *á:ti loká:casok á:tat* 'and an orphan dwelt there'. One notable feature about this tradition is that it is Orphan that turns into Corn, rather than helping the one who becomes corn. When John was quizzed about whether she had ever heard about Corn Woman, she replied: *"Pí:la atloká:casok akkó í:sasi matonokbáhtohon, mók cassanáhkatoho:limpáhcok* 'Just that they closed up the orphan in that little house, and they say that he also turned into corn'." It is interesting that two such different traditions were maintained in a community as small as that of the Koasati.

Line 10 *násik hiłilihká:cin* 'and something made a sound of regurgitation'. The verb *hiłili:kácin* is one of a series of verbs that describe onomatopoetic sounds. It does not have an exact translation in English, since it can also be used to describe the crackle of fire or the burble of boiling water. The sound that this verb is meant to describe here is the rattling rustle of corn grains striking each other as they fell to the ground.

Line 24 *walóhlo:sin ishí:ca:p* 'when you see it and it is very tender'. This phrase indicates that unripe corn was considered to be the "true" corn. The Koasati performed the Green Corn Dance to celebrate the first corn of the year up until 1919, when, to all intents and purposes, they abandoned their traditional religion. The fact that green corn is whitish in color strengthens the possibility that the name of Corn Woman in the previous tale was "White Corn."

## HOW OPOSSUM GOT A BARE TAIL
narrated by *Sacowáyhki*

This text was recorded by John R. Swanton in 1910, who gave it the number thirteen and published a translation of it under the title *Opossum and Skunk* (Swanton 1929:200). This tale is a humorous one; in fact, the whole concept of an origin tale is played here for laughs. The theme of this narrative is the switching of body parts or attributes between animals—especially with one animal desiring that which belongs to another so much that he steals it by trickery—and it has proven quite durable and popular and is used again in *Turkey and Owl Swap Calls* and in several Rabbit stories, including *Rabbit and Deer Swap Feet* (chapter 1).

This narrative is abbreviated, as were a number of tales collected by Swanton, since the process of dictation was quite laborious for the narrator, *Sacowáyhki* (Jackson Langley). In this narrative, the final scene portrays as future events what would have been explicitly told had *Sacowáyhki* not felt the constraint of time. One can postulate that there were at least another two scenes—a fifth scene, in which Skunk took his revenge, and a sixth scene, in which Opossum realized what had been done.

### Scene 1: Opossum's and Skunk's Tails Compared

Sokhaták á:yatohon,
hacík wohǫ́ksit wohoksíhcotoho:li-
mpatš.
Má:min,
konók ómmi:k,
hacík łimihkóhcotoho:limpatš.

Opossum was going about,
and it is said that his tail was really
very furry.
Then,
as for Skunk,
his tail was smooth, so it is said.

### Scene 2: Opossum Mocks Skunk

Má:min,
sokhá hátkak hí:ca:k,
afalį́:citoho:limpatš.
Stacákkit,
obá:li stá:yat ónkak,

"Konó hací łó:fka!" ká:toho:limpatš.

"Anó cahací watalwatá:l!"
ká:toho:limpatš.

Then,
when Opossum saw him,
it is said that he laughed at him.
He followed after him;
he went along with him behind him
and spoke.
"Skunk's tail is UGSOME!" he said,
so they say.
"Me, my tail is SPLENDIFEROUS!" he said,
so they say.

### Scene 3: Skunk Is Angered

Ma:fó:kon,
konók noksí:patoho:limpatš.
Mántik,
ná:son sammí:cá:hik
sobáykotoho:limpatš.
Mó:tohok,
á:yáhpok,
"Są́hcok cihacį́ cįsáhlili:p mó:la:š,"
káhco:š.

At that point,
it is said that Skunk grew angry.
But,
it is said that
he did not know what to do.
Then,
he just went along,
"Would that somehow I could cut the
hair off your tail," he said.

### Scene 4: Skunk Plans Revenge

Mó:tohok,
imoklón wíhlit,
colotkón híhcok,
inna:łí:kak,
"Sokhatkák camánkš, 'hací łó:fka,'
káhco:š.

Then,
he looked for his friend,
and he caught sight of Cricket,
and he spoke to him,
"Opossum called me UGSOME-tail,"
he said.

| | |
|---|---|
| "Má:min, | "Then, |
| nó:ci:fó:kon, | when he sleeps, |
| ółcin, | you will go over there, |
| įsáhhílok, | we will come and scrape it off of him, |
| cahacifá amacásli:š!" | and you attach it then to my tail!" |
| "Má:min, | "And then, |
| sokhatkák falánka:k, | when Opossum wakes up, |
| afá:hilí:cá:š." | we will laugh at him." |
| "Ibisnók inkánkok, | "He himself will not like it, |
| icokhalbík icoktaká:lin, | his mouth will open, |
| nokhayó:lit stonafáylilaho:š." | and he will drool and stay that way." |

*Textual emendations*:

| | | |
|---|---|---|
| Line 2 | oho´ ñksit wo´ ksitcotoho´ limpats | wohóksit wohoksíhcotoho:limpatš |
| Line 18 | aya$^{n}$´ pō´ | á:yáhpok |
| Line 19 | tci$^{n}$sa´ halile mō le | cįsáhlili:p mó:lá:š |
| Line 34 | ibisna´ | ibisnók |
| Line 35 | stạnafai´ lilō s | stonafáylilaho:š |

*Textual commentary*:

Line 8 *afalį:citoho:limpatš* 'it is said that he laughed at him'. By ridiculing Skunk, Opossum has set himself up as the villain of the piece. Laughing at a person was considered socially unacceptable behavior and a sign that a person had a tendency toward hubris. Opossum is clearly overweeningly proud of his beautiful tail; he is thus setting himself up for his inevitable fall.

Lines 11 and 12 *łó:fka* and *watalwatá:l*. These two words, unknown to present-day speakers, are glossed by Swanton as "opossum language" (1929:200n.3). It is of interest that in Natchez traditional narrative, Opossum also has particular words used only by him (Haas p.c., 1988). The language of origin of these two words, if they are not simply nonsense vocables, may differ. The word *łó:fka* looks as if it could be from another Muskogean language, while *watalwata:l* looks similar to Natchez *wata·kup* 'long'. Although these words are unknown, the general meaning of *łó:fka* seems to be 'ugly', and of *watalwatá:l*, 'handsome'. They are translated respectively as "UGSOME" and "SPLENDIFEROUS" with the unusual English words and small capitals indicating their unique status.

Line 22 *colotkón híhcok* 'he caught sight of Cricket'. How Cricket is supposed to help Skunk is not made explicit in this narrative. However, he is the one who will probably scrape the hair off Opossum's tail with his serrated legs.

Lines 30–35 This section consists of a foretelling relating what would have occurred at the end of the tale in its full narrative form. This should be compared to *The Thunderer and the Man*, in which the same stylistic method is used to shorten the narrative. This concluding section explains not only how Opossum got a bare tail, but also why Opossum hangs his mouth open and drools (as when he plays dead).

## TURKEY AND OWL SWAP CALLS

narrated by *Sacowáyhki*

This narrative was collected by Mary R. Haas in 1936. A version of this tale was also collected by John R. Swanton in 1910 from the same narrator; a translation was published under the title *The Owl and the Turkey* (Swanton1929:198). Haas's version has been preferred over Swanton's because the tale is more complete. This particular tale falls into the category of "trade and trick," where one animal desires an attribute of another so much that he steals it from him by trickery. Again, as in the previous narrative, it seems that the main purpose of this tale is to inspire laughter.

### Scene 1: Owl and Turkey Compare Calls

| | |
|---|---|
| Opók fi:tón ittihíhcok, | Owl and Turkey having caught sight of each other, |
| ittinna:łí:katoho:limpatš. | spoke to each other, so it is reported. |
| Má:min, | Then, |
| fi:tók ónka:k, | Turkey spoke. |
| "Ná:si iskáhcoton olatíská?" káhhan. | "What do you say calling out?" he said. |
| Má:min, | Then, |
| ópak ónka:k, | Owl spoke, |
| "'Ká: lók lók!' ká:halíhcokš," káhhan. | "'Gobble gobble!' I say," he said. |
| Fi:tók ónka:k, | Turkey spoke, |
| "Anáp ó:lali:k, | "As for me, when I call, |
| 'Ŏ:::wa!' ká:halíhcokš," káhhan. | 'Whooo!' I say," he said. |

### Scene 2: Turkey Desires Owl's Call

| | |
|---|---|
| Stáswan, | The two of them stayed together, |
| fi:tók ónka:k, | and Turkey spoke. |
| "Olatilką́ ittimo:tamáthiláskš!" | "Let's trade calls!" |
| káhhan. | he said. |
| Opák ónka:k, | And Owl spoke, |
| "Mánko:š!" káhhan. | "By no means!" he said. |
| Fi:tók olatilką́ imbànnat | And Turkey really wanted his call from him, |
| imbánnatoho:limpatš. | so it is reported. |

Má:min,
opák ónka:k,
"Mánko:š!" ká:hatoho:limpatš.

Then,
Owl spoke.
"By no means!" he said, so they say.

**Scene 3: Owl and Turkey Trade Calls**

Má:min,
fi:tók ónkak,
"Ittimó:lat ilhí:cáskš!"
káhhatoho:limpatš.
"Ittimonáɬɬit ó:lat ilhí:cáskš!" káhhan.

Opak ónka:k,
"Mó:tiks," ká:hatoho:limpatš.
Má:mo:sin,
fi:tók ónka:k,
"O:lat híc!" káhhan.
Opák wáykat,
mă:::fon,
ittofón ohpa:cokkóhlok,

"Ŏ:::wa!" ká:hatoho:limpatš.
Máhmok,
ɬóykat í:lan,
fi:tók ónka:k,
"Scimalį́:lo:š," ká:toho:limpatš.

Then,
Turkey spoke.
"Let us try calling for each other!"
he said, so they say.
"Let us try trading calls with each other!"
he said.
And Owl spoke.
"Okay," he said, so they say.
Thereupon,
Turkey spoke,
"Try calling!" he said.
And Owl flew,
waaay over there,
over to a tree he went and perched
on a branch,
and "Whooo!" he said, so it is reported.
And then,
he came back,
and Turkey spoke.
"It is appropriate for you," he said,
so they say.

**Scene 4: Turkey Steals Owl's Call**

Máhmok,
fi:tók opá imolatilką́ stíhsok,
swalí:ka:k,
mă:::fon oshaccáhlok,
ó:la:k,
"Ká: lók lók lók,"
ká:hatoho:limpatš.
Ká:hat, ká:hat,
stiwwalí:kat snakáɬtoho:limpatš.
Má:mo:sin,
opák imacį́hbat imacíhbatoho:limpatš.

Then,
Turkey having taken Owl's call,
he ran with it,
waaay over there he went and stood,
and he called,
"Gobble, gobble, gobble!"
he said, they say.
He said it, and he said it,
and he ran with it and disappeared with it.
Thereupon,
it is said that Owl was very, very unhappy.

Ká:mo:š.

The end.

*Textual commentary*:

Line 8 *Ká lók lók!* 'Gobble gobble!'
Line 11 *Ǒ::wa!* 'Whooo!'
The use of onomatopoetic words in a story is intended to cause laughter; their use early on is a cue that this is a humorous story. There is an interesting relationship between onomatopoetic calls and verbs used to describe the calls. For example, 'to gobble' in Koasati is *kalóhkan* and 'to gobble on and on' is *kalohkóhkan*, both clearly related to *ká: lók lók.*

Line 38 *scimalį́:lo:š* 'it is appropriate for you'. The verb *alí:lǫ* is a defective verb that means 'to be good'. It lacks the moral connotations of *ká:non* 'to be good'. It frequently appears in interjections such as *alí:la mǫ́* 'thank you!' (lit. 'indeed good!') and *alí:la:sǫ* 'very good!' *Stimalí:lǫ*, which is compounded of this verb and the instrumental and dative prefixes, literally means, 'it is good for you because of it'.

## THE TWO WINDS
narrated by Bel Abbey

I recorded this narrative on tape in May, 1987. It differs slightly from the other tales in this chapter in that it lacks a plot per se and is of a more descriptive nature. Nonetheless, there is little difficulty in discovering in it the internal structure typical of traditional narrative. Some of the more interesting structural features of this narrative are the two asides. At natural breaks in the narrative, Mr. Abbey stopped and said that he was telling the tale because "this white person" (*yín thátka*) was interested. Since Abbey notes that he and others still believe in the Wind People, and the narrative was told out-of-doors, it seems likely that the asides were intended for the Winds, should they be listening, to indicate that, even though they were being spoken about, they were not being taken lightly.

### Scene 1: The Nature of the Winds

| | |
|---|---|
| Fáplik yomáhlit, | The winds go about, |
| ohayyí yámmi:p, | as in summer, |
| fáplik ilá:ci:k, | when the winds arrive, |
| ilá:cik yomáhli:fó:kon, | when they go about arriving, |
| fápli:fó:kon, | when it is windy, |
| athómmak ittimmánka:k, | the Indians speak to each other about them, |
| athómmak atlawísta immánka:fó:k, | when the Indians tell children, |
| fáplik akkánt | how it is said that the winds |
| akkáhcómmohalpi:sa-mpáhcok. | are supposed to be: |
| "Fáplik ná:nihok á:yan, | "A Wind Man goes about, |
| fáplik tayyihók a:yáhci," ká:hak, | and a Wind Woman goes about," they said, |
| imatlawísta immankáhcotohon. | telling it to their children. |

### Aside 1

| | |
|---|---|
| Yín thátka immánkali:sáyon, | That which I am telling this white person, |
| imalóstik, | he is interested in it; |
| bànnak a:táhcómmin, | it is the case that he is wanting it, |
| immánkalą́, | and I am telling him, |
| hacimmánkalą́. | and I am telling you all. |

### Scene 2: The Wind Man

| | |
|---|---|
| Himá:ya katík, | But now, |
| fáplik ná:nik ómmi:k, | as for the Wind Man, |
| sittainnahón í:sit stá:yat, | he takes and carries about a fire poker, |
| ittó sbókli:fók, | and when he strikes trees with it, |
| ittinsá:wan kawwí:cit, | he snaps branches, |
| ittó bóklit páłłit, | he strikes and splits trees, |
| ittó matapíslit, | he throws trees down, |
| cilaktó:cit, | he uproots trees, |
| tafíllit ałí:yatoho:limpáhcok. | and it is said he goes overturning them. |
| Fáplik ná:nok ómmi:p, | If it is the Wind Man, |
| kammí:cit, | he does so, |
| matapíslit, | he throws them down, |
| ittón alwáhlit, | he ruins trees, |
| na:salwáhlit, | he ruins things; |
| na:salwáhlipalámmok | if it is the case that one is going |
| a:yáhcómmi:p, | about really ruining things, |
| "Ná:nok ómmitoho:limpáhcok," | "It is a man, it is said," |
| ka:háhcok, ka:háhco:lik, | they say, they used to say, |
| atcó:bahak kommánka:k. | the old people, when they told it to us. |
| Kámmi:fó:kon, | When this occurred, |
| inkommałáhlá:hosco:lik, | we used to be very frightened of him, |
| kámmi:k í:lá:hi:p. | when such a one was about to arrive. |
| Mó:tohon, | Then, |
| "Sittainnahón í:sit stá:yat, | "He takes and carries about a fire poker, |
| sboklihcómmok ómmimpáhcok," | it is said that it is the case that he strikes |
| ka:háhco:lik. | things with it," they used to say. |
| Kámmi:fó:kon, | When this occurred, |
| ittó alwáhlit, | he ruined trees, |
| na:salwáhlit, | he ruined things, |
| nasbóklik alwáhlit stałí:ya:fó:kon, | he struck things and ruined them |
| ommíhcotohok. | when he carried it, and so it was. |

Kámmik,
alwáhli:k,
má:mok,
"Ná:no:lik ómmitohok," ka:háhco:lik.

"Na:nolíhcok ómmok," ká:hat
kommankáhco:lik.
Má:mok,
"Sittainnahón í:sit stá:yat
sboklíhcómmíhci.
Ná:si alwáhlik," ka:háhco:lik.

Thus,
when he ruined things,
then,
"One can deduce that it is the case
that it is a man," they used to say.
"One can deduce that it is perhaps a man,"
they used to say, telling it to us.
Then,
"He is taking and carrying and striking
things with a fire poker.
"He ruins things," they used to say.

**Aside 2**

Mó:tohon,
yín immánkali:sáyon,
imalóstik á:ta:s.
Immmankalíhcok óm.

Then,
that which I am telling this one here,
he keeps on being interested in it.
I am telling it to him.

**Scene 3: The Wind Woman**

Mó:tohon,
tayyihók ómmi:p,
sittainnahón stá:yatǫ ná:nihak katík,
tayyihók ómmi:p,
stá:yaton stayánkon,
stayánkon sta:yáhcómmok,

mók bóklit intoɬɬí:cit,
ittintoɬɬí:cit,
ittinsá:wa matapíslit
nasmatapíst alwáhlit.
"Ná:ni alwáhli yánkot,
alwáhlit ɬopóttoho:limpáhcok,"
hokáhcok.
Kámmiskan,
má tayyík ómmiton,
alwáhlit palánko:p,
alwáhlitik,
ná:ni alwáhlito yánkoton,
tayyihó:liskan.

Then,
if it is a woman;
even though a man carries a fire poker,
as for a woman,
she carries a stirring stick,
and she also strikes and cuts off
branches,
she cuts branches from trees,
she throws branches down,
she throws things down
and ruins them.
"She is not like a Ruiner Man,
she just damages and passes through,"
they say.
Just like that,
that one being a woman,
she does not ruin excessively,
although she does ruin,
she does not ruin like a man,
because one can deduce she is a
woman.

| | |
|---|---|
| Má:misk, | Because of this, |
| máp stayánkon mók sboklíhcómmok, | she also seems to strike with the stirring stick, |
| alwáhlit staka:no:fį́tíkkot | she ruins, and it is not too bad, |
| á:yat łopotlíhcómmok | it is said that it is the case that she |
| ómmitoho:limpáhcok. | seems to go and pass through. |
| Tayyiháp stakanofíhnalwáhkotǫ. | The Woman does not ruin severely. |

**Scene 4: How People React to the Winds**

| | |
|---|---|
| Kámmiskan, | Just like that, |
| ká:t ammankáhco:lik. | they used to say telling me. |
| Ihó:ca:p, | Long ago, |
| ká:t ohanna:łí:ka:fó:kon, | when they spoke to me, |
| kommałáhlá:hosco:lik katíkap, | we used to be afraid, |
| inkomałáhlik onáhcok, | we are still afraid of them, |
| mán fáplik á:ya:p, | and if a wind comes again, |
| fáplik acihbapalámmo:lik, | and one can deduce that it is a hard wind, |
| atlawísto:t, | such as children, |
| ná:si alwáhlit, | he or she ruins things, |
| ná:so:t alwáhlit ałi:yáhcok | he or she is going ruining things, |
| ómmin, | |
| immałátko:líhcok. | and he or she is something fearful. |
| Kámmiskan, | Just like that, |
| tayyí, ná:ni, sám áłłá:hik, | whichever is about to arrive, a Man or a Woman, |
| incamałatlíhcok anáp. | I am afraid of him or her. |
| Mǫ́. Ká:mo:s. | Enough. The end. |

*Textual commentary*:

Lines 9–10 *fáplik ná:nihok á:yan / fáplik tayyihók a:yáhci* 'a Wind Man goes about, / and a Wind Woman goes about'. Here, as in *The Creation of Crow*, the syntactic construction "plural for singular" is found. Both the nouns *ná:nihok* and *tayyihók* are marked plural, however, the verb *á:yan*, of which they are the subject, is marked singular. Once again, what is being suggested is a singular representative of a plurality. Although at any one time there is only one wind, that wind is one of a number of winds, each of which is separate. Thus, these lines could be translated more literally as "of the Wind Men, one will go about, and of the Wind Women, one will go about." Note also that, although 'wind' is the most usual translation of *fápli*, the term is also used in the meaning 'storm', as in *fápli cobá* 'great wind', used as a gloss to the word *hanafololó* 'tornado'. *Fápli cobá* is also the way that the English word "hurricane" is translated. It must therefore be kept in mind that this narrative could be about storms as well as winds. In addition, the word *fápli* is an agentive noun derived from the verb *fáplin* 'to blow as a wind', and literally means 'that which blows as a wind' or 'the one who blows as a wind'. The treatment of meteorological events as verbs in Koasati is very different from English, where most are treated as nouns.

Line 19 *sittainnahó* 'fire poker'. This instrument is a long, straight piece of fire-hardened wood used to stir the coals of a campfire to keep the fire burning. Since maintaining a fire is typically a man's job, the Wind Man is given the fire poker as his attribute. Both the Wind Man and the Wind Woman are assigned culturally appropriate objects as their attributes.

Line 32 *"Ná:nok ómmitoho:limpáhcok," ka:háhcok* '"It is a man, it is said," they say'. This is a rare instance of the verbal suffix string *-toho:limpáhcok*, typical of traditional narrative, occurring in quoted speech. The narrator here is trying to indicate that he is conveying traditional mythological knowledge about something that he considers to be fact by embedding the suffix string in a quoted sentence as if it were a piece of knowledge about traditional material culture.

Line 61 *stayánkon* 'a stirring stick'. The *stayánka* is an oar-shaped tool with a flat paddle on one end and a long handle on the other. It can be from three to four feet in length. It was traditionally a tool used by women in cooking and in the preparation of hides. As such, it is appropriate as an attribute of the Wind Woman.

Line 67 *ná:ni alwáhli yánkot* 'she is not like a Ruiner Man'. Here, Wind Man is called "Ruiner Man," since he damages so many things with his fire poker. Here begins a comparison of the powers of the two winds.

Lines 70–74 These lines indicate that the Wind Woman is a less destructive being than the Wind Man. The narrator does not make clear why she is less destructive, saying only *tayyihó:liskán* 'because it can be deduced that she is a woman'. It may only mean that the Wind Woman does less damage because, as a woman, she is physically less strong than a man, or it may indicate that there is some kind of sympathetic quality in femaleness that restrains the Wind Woman from doing all of the damage of which she is capable.

Lines 89–91 Here the lack of gender in Koasati third person reference makes for difficult translation in English. These lines are concerned with a single wind, but unlike written English, which might use "he" to denote the common gender, or spoken English, which might use "they," Koasati, which does not require pronominal adjuncts, gets by with a third person verb form with a singular subject tacitly present. Thus, the translation uses the awkward "he or she," since these lines are equally appropriate to describe the Wind Man and the Wind Woman.

Lines 92–94 *Kámmiskan, / tayyí, ná:ni, sám áłłá:hik, / incamałatlíhcok anáp* 'Just like that, / whichever is about to arrive, a Man or a Woman, / I am afraid of him or her.' One of the major stylistic requirements of traditional narrative of any sort is that the narrator not appear in the narrative except in prologues and epilogues, which contain framing information about the situation in which a narrative was told, its origin, and other incidental matters. In addition, as a rule, personal reaction to anything in a narrative is not permitted. Abbey here violates both of these strictures by placing himself in the narrative and reacting to its contents. Nonetheless, listeners to this narrative do not perceive this as a fault, but rather as something that gives the narrative added power. Because such personal interpolations are so rarely done, Abbey, who was sensitive to traditional narrative style, put in this section as a personal innovation. He used this particular innovation occasionally with care, and the result of the narrator appearing in the narrative and commenting on the action gives a novelistic feel.

## THE ORIGIN OF DECIDUOUS TREES (First Version)
narrated by Martha John

I recorded this narrative by dictation in October, 1982. At that time, Martha John was not comfortable with the use of a tape recorder, but preferred dictation so that she could set down a narrative "correctly." The difficulty with dictation is that it warps the structure of a narrative. For example, in dictation, lines are grouped in twos and threes, in contrast to the multiple-line groups found in texts recorded under more natural circumstances. On the other hand, more information is likely to be included in a dictated narrative, since the narrator has time to recall all the pertinent facts. Here, two versions of *Why Trees Lose Their Leaves* are included—the first for content and the second for style. This particular narrative has never been recorded before; the only similar tale found in the Southeast was recorded among the Cherokee (Mooney 1900:240). The basic plot of the narrative is that all the trees were the same at one time, and that they were living, speaking beings. Then, they were told not to sleep, and the trees that slept lost their leaves in the winter, while those who stayed awake did not lose their leaves.

### Scene 1: The Trees Speak to One Another

| | |
|---|---|
| Ihó:cap ittó óhya hi:báhkak ónkak, | Long ago, all the trees that were standing spoke. |
| "Hasno:cínnąh!" ká:hat, | "Do ye not sleep later on," they said. |
| "Haciknó:con níhtalǫ," ká:hat. | "You do not sleep it being just day," they said. |
| Mók ohayyí caffá:kan ónkatǫ. | Also, this means one summer/year. |
| Mó:tohon, | Then, |
| ittók í:satohok, | of the trees that were dwelling there, |
| aláhkok honó:cit níhta:fó:kon. | some fell asleep when it was day. |
| Mó:tohon, | Then, |
| mí:tak aláhkak í:sak iknó:cotohon. | others of the remainder there did not sleep. |

### Scene 2: The Trees Who Slept and the Trees Who Stayed Awake

Má:min,
nó:citohok ohayyí caffá:kan honó:cin,
ittó ishí:ca:p,
himá:ya yámmi:p honó:citohoyáhlok,
híssi óhyak incíłatlíhci.

And then,
the ones who slept for one summer,
and when you see trees,
nowadays the ones who occasionally
went to sleep, all their leaves fall
from them.

Má:min,
iknó:cotohok híssik incíłatkóhci.

And then,
the ones who did not sleep,
their leaves do not fall from them.

Holcifó iknó:cok:
ittohalokpó:t,
coyyó:t,
toló:t,
tolacobó:t,
tokoybohkó:t,
cowahlók ommihci.
Mók ohayyí caffá:lin,
iknó:cot níhtat ohayyí,
łafí híssik inna:hóhci.

The names of the sleepless ones are:
holly,
and pine,
and red bay,
and magnolia,
and gardenia,
and cedar.
Also it makes one summer,
they stayed awake during the summer,
and they have winter leaves.

Ká:mo:sin sobáylil.

Just so much is what I know.

*Textual commentary*:

Line 1 *ihó:cap ittó óhya hi:báhkak ónkak* 'long ago, all the trees that were standing spoke'. In Koasati mythology, trees were able to speak, not only to each other, but to human beings as well. Paz-Taylor (1937:20) records two fragments of medicine origin tales in which trees that produce medicines speak to humans to apprise them of their medical uses. Even today, when a tree creaks in a high wind, it is said to weep.

Line 4 *Mók ohayyí caffá:kan ónkatǫ* 'Also, this means one summer/year'. The word *ohayyí* can mean both 'summer' and 'year'. It seems unlikely that the deciduous trees slept for an entire year—an entire season seems more logical. If so, their loss of leaves in winter is their penalty for sleeping in summer.

Lines 18–22 The Koasati names of the trees that do not lose their leaves are followed by the suffix *-o:t*, which indicates that these terms form a list and that they are representative members of a larger class. Although the trees listed here are the principle ones that do not lose their leaves, there are others, such as the wax myrtle (*ittoikíllo*).

Line 26 *łafí híssik* 'winter leaves'. Plants that keep leaves or produce flowers in winter are considered unusual, and terminology such as *łafí híssi* 'winter leaves' and *łafí paká:li* 'winter flowers' is used in discussing them. There is, however, no corresponding terms such as 'summer leaves' or 'summer flowers', since, as Bel Abbey explained, leaves and flowers are normal in summer, so there is no need to single them out especially.

## THE ORIGIN OF DECIDUOUS TREES (Second Version)
narrated by Martha John

I recorded this version of the tale on tape in March, 1989. Seven years after she dictated the first version of this narrative, Martha John permitted the tape recording of the second version. It is interesting how the content of the two versions is almost identical, as is the sequencing of events: the conversation of the trees, the act of sleeping and its result, staying awake and its result, the address to the listener, and the fact that those trees that stayed awake keep their leaves in winter. Nonetheless, the two versions are stylistically quite different. The second version is much more typical of traditional narrative as a whole, with sentences comprising four or more verses, in contrast to the first version, where they consisted mostly of two or three.

### Scene 1: The Trees Speak to One Another and Some Sleep

| | |
|---|---|
| Ittó óhyak í:san, | All the trees were dwelling there, |
| "Ikhonó:colahǫ," ká:hon, | "They all will not sleep," they said, |
| ka:háhcot ómmotohon, | they seem to have said so, |
| "Hasno:cínnąh!" ká:hak, | "Do ye not sleep then!" they said, |
| ohayyí caffá:kan ónkatǫ. | and it meant one summer. |
| Tamó:ka, | Night, |
| tamó:ka caffá:kascómmiton, | it was the case it was only one night, |
| ohayyí caffá:kan ónkatǫ. | and it meant one summer. |
| Mó:tohon, | Then, |
| í:san, | they were there, |
| i:sáhcotohok honó:citǫ. | and those that were there went to sleep. |
| Aláhkak hono:ci:p, | Some when they slept, |
| honó:citohok ómmok, | they were perhaps sleeping, |
| łafó:łá:hį, | when it was about to be autumn, |
| híssi incиłátlik ómmimpáhcok. | it is said that their leaves were falling from them. |

### Scene 2: The Trees That Did Not Sleep

| | |
|---|---|
| Máhmin, | And then, |
| ikhono:cóhcotohok, | those who did not sleep, |
| híssi inciłatkóhcómmok. | it seems their leaves do not fall from them. |

Coyyík ómmi:k iknó:con,
mi:tácotohok ómmin,
híssi inciłátkon káhcómmíhcon.

As for the pine trees, they did not sleep,
and it is the case that there were others,
and in the same way their leaves do not
fall from them.

"Ittó hi:báhkan hashí:ca:p,
'Ikno:cóhcotohok híssi
inciłátkohá:wa,'
ashací:lolahǫ," hokáhco:lik.
"Kámmisk,
hosobáyhácilahǫ." hokáhco:lik.
Ikhonó:con,
mi:táhcotohok híssi
inciłatkóhco:limpáhcok.
Má:min,
łafí:p,
híssi hashí:cáhco:limpáhcok.

"If you look at the standing trees,
the ones who did not sleep do not
lose their leaves,
you can surmise," they used to say.
"Just like that,
you all will know them," they used to say.
They did not sleep,
those others that they say do not
lose their leaves.
Then,
when it is winter,
it is said that you see their leaves.

Kámmo:sin sobáylil.

Just so much is what I know.

Móh.

Enough!

*Textual commentary*:

Line 2 *ikhonó:colahǫ* 'they all will not sleep'. This form is a third person with the anomalous sequence of prefixes *ik-ho-* instead of the usually obligatory *oh-ik-*. See the commentary below.

Lines 7–8 *tamó:ka caffá:kascómmiton, / ohayyí cafá:kan ónkatǫ* 'it was the case it was only one night, / and it meant one summer'. Here, the "night" through which the trees were asked to stay awake is explicitly the season of summer, unlike the previous narrative in which the time reference is left vague. The trees are clearly still sleeping when autumn comes (in lines 12–15), and while they sleep they lose their leaves.

Line 17 *ikhonó:cotohok* 'those who did not sleep'
Line 27 *ikhonó:con* 'they did not sleep'
In these two examples, the verbs have the aberrant sequence *ik-ho*, as in the example in line 2. Occasionally, the affix *ho-/oh-*, which usually occurs outside agent, dative, and accusative prefixes, will be found bound close to the stem. This is most typical of adjectival words, such as *st-į-ho-ká:non* 'for them to like something', for expected **st-oh-in-ká:non*. There is a possibility that there is a meaning difference depending upon placement, with stem-bound *ho-/oh-* referring to a complete group and the *oh-/ho-* in normal position referring to a less inclusive grouping of subjects.

## HOW BAT RECEIVED HIS WINGS

narrated by Bertney Langley

I recorded this narrative on tape in May, 1992. It was a tale told by the late Bel Abbey; Langley learned it because it was a tale that he liked and identified with—it is the only tale that he feels competent to tell. Langley, born in 1951, is among the first generation of Koasati speakers who have an equally good command of English. Indeed, Langley's command of English vocabulary is, in fact, better than his Koasati vocabulary. In speech, if he cannot recall the Koasati word immediately, he will incorporate an English word. In addition, he uses the English pause word "uh" with almost equal frequency as the Koasati pause word *ná:hon*. In this narrative, at his request the three English words actually used and recorded have been replaced with their proper Koasati equivalents.

This tale has not previously been recorded among the Koasati, although a very similar narrative was recorded among the Cherokee (Mooney 1900:286–87). For the narrator, the origin features of this tale are not as important as the didactic ones, which he sees as an admonition not to disparage one who seems to be small and weak, for that person may yet have hidden valuable abilities.

### Prologue

| | |
|---|---|
| Ná:hǫ, | Well, |
| ihó:ca:kitton coficó:bak | long ago Old Uncle told me this; |
| ammankáhco:lik yón, | |
| ná:hǫ, | well, |
| cokfałihilkasón káhco:lik món. | he also used to tell this little story. |

### Scene 1: The Birds and Animals Prepare to Play Ball

| | |
|---|---|
| Ná:hok, | Well, |
| ittohayó ihó:ca:kittap, | in the forest long ago, |
| fó:si yáhco:t, | the ones who were like birds, |
| ipłó yáhco:t. | the ones who were like squirrels, |
| ná:si małáhli í:sa yámmi:p, | the ones who were animals, |
| ittanáhkat | they gathered together |
| ittį̨hopá:nitoho:limpak. | and played together, they say. |
| Pokkó tó:ka yáhcon, | It was like the ball game; |
| pokkó tó:lit ittimayá:cit | it is said that they kept on contesting |
| í:satoho:limpak. | with each other in the ball game. |
| Mó:tohon, | Then, |
| fó:si óhyak ittanáhkok, | the birds all gathered together; |
| ałakí óhyak ittanáhkok, | every kind gathered together, |
| alahká ittohayó nasmałáhlí:sa yámmi, | and the others, like the forest animals, |
| kowí yáhco:t, | the ones who were like panthers, |

nitá yáhco:t,
ittanáhkok,
ittįhopá:nitoho:limpáhcok.
Ittįhopá:nit
ittalokístotoho:limpáhcok.

the ones who were like bears,
having gathered together,
it is said that they played together.
They played together,
and it is said that they did not like
each other.

Ná:hok,
pokkó tó:kon káhcok himáka:kittap.
Kámmiskan,
óhyap fó:si yámmit ittanáhkok,
sámmit naksók hopá:ná:hį
imawí:cit ittimmánkat í:san,
"Tałá mán," hoká:h,
nasmałáhli í:sat naksámmit ittįhopá:ná:hik,
ittimawí:cit hopá:ná:hik,
itimmánkatik ísto:n.

Well,
the ball game was like that long ago.
This being so,
all who were like birds gathered,
they kept on talking to each other
about which ones might help them play.
The other side, as it is said,
the animals, how they might play,
how they might help each other,
they kept on telling each other.

## Scene 2: Bat Is Rejected by the Animals

A:tawí:ci:kap cokĭ::bo:sok
haccá:toho:limpak.
Ná:hok,
hallakók ómmǫ,
hiná:ya katík,
ma:fó:ka:kíttap,
falakcí imíksoscotohok.
Má:mo:sin,
nitá yámmit hocó:bafihnaskan,
hobánkotoho:limpak.
Máp cokí:bo:fíhnaskan
įhompá:ná:hi katík,
falakcík imíksoskan,
fó:sokkoskan mók.

It is said that a tiny one who wanted
to help them stood there.
Well,
it was Bat,
as he would be nowadays,
but in those times long ago,
he did not have wings.
Thereupon,
the ones such as Bear, because they
were big,
they did not want him, so they say.
Because that one was so small,
but even so he might play for them
[the birds],
even though he had no wings,
and also he was not a bird.

## Scene 3: Bat Is Accepted by the Birds

Ná:hok,
fó:si yámmí:sat,
"Kohompáncihalpí:skot,
cimíksoskan falakcík,"
ká:hatoho:limpak.

Well,
the ones who were like birds,
"You are unable to play for us.
You lack wings,"
they said.

Kámmiskan,
hallakík haccá:toho:li:yok,
sámmit sobáykok,
hopánka bànnatik,
"Anók hopánka cabànná::ho:s katík á:tok cahopaní:cih bánkǫ," ká:hat á:táhpin.
"Má hiná:p!" ká:hat i:sahpin,
fó:sik i:sáhpok stįhawá:lotoho:limpak.

But this being so,
Bat was standing there,
how he did not know,
but he wanted to play.
"I really want to play, but it is the case that no one will let me play," he merely said.
"Enough now!" they just said,
and it is said that the birds there had pity on him.

**Scene 4: The Birds Try to Figure Out How to Use Bat**

Má:mo:sok,
immánkatoho:limpak.
"Mó:li:p, ná:so:t cimawí:cílkan,
sammíhcot sobáyhhílin.
Ittimawíhcok,
akostiní:cih sobáyhili:fó:kon,
kǫhopáncihalpí:sa:p sobáyhílásk!"
káhhat amá:katon.
Mó:tohon,
"Ná:son sánco:lin," ká:p,
"Capálkipalámmik walí:kalik,"
ká:toho:limpak.
"Cacokí:bosco:liskan,
sántik walí:kalik ittałopótlillahǫ,"
ká:hayon,
"Mán nitá yámmit có:bafihnaskan,
hocipa:łiyápli:p,
ciillí:cimá:milahok."
Kámmisk,
akkámmit hobánkon.
Kámmiskan,
"Naksammíhcot ná:hotkílko:lik"
ká:toho:limpak.
"Falakcó:t cintalibó:hílit ómmǫ kosnók,
isnók wáykat ací:yaskan,"
ká:toho:limpak.
Má:mo:sin,
"Sammíhcok falakcí ná:hotílkahalpískǫ?"
á:lok í:sa:fó:kap,
caffák, fó:sik híhcok,

Thereupon,
it is said that they spoke to him.
"Well, we will help you in some way,
howsoever we know.
Helping each other,
we will think and when we know,
let us find out how you could play for us," they said going on.
Then,
"What is is that you can do?" they said.
"I run with excessive speed," he said,
so it is reported.
"Because I am small,
anyhow, I will run underneath them,"
he said,
but, "Also, because the ones like Bear
are so big, if they were to step on you,
they will perhaps fatally injure you."
This being so,
in such a way they did not want him.
This being so,
"How is it possible we cannot do something?" they said, so they say.
"Perhaps we can make wings for you,
and you too can go about flying,"
they said.
Thereupon,
"How can we not be able to make wings?"
they kept on thinking,
and one, a bird caught sight of it,

| | |
|---|---|
| yá:fon aykacabonóhkok | it is said that he saw a drum that |
| ittatàmmitohon hí:catoho:limpak. | was lying over there on the ground. |
| Má:mo:sin, | Thereupon, |
| "Yá:fa ishók! | "Take ye that! |
| Afakcó onapíhlok, | Taking off the skin, |
| onapíhhíliskan, | we can take it off, |
| alwahkáhco:liskan, | because it [the drum] is broken, |
| hobankóhcok ómmimá:m. | they perhaps do not want it. |
| Kámmiskan, | This being so, |
| ishók! | take ye it! |
| Sammi:cíhcot falakcó:t cintalibó:hílin | Take a look at how we make wings |
| híhcąh!" ká:toho:limpak. | for you!" they said, so it is reported. |
| Má:mo:sin, | Thereupon, |
| ittanáhkok óhyak fó:sip, | all the birds gathered together, |
| óhyak afakcó imí:sit, | they took all the skin from it, |
| óhya inkóyt anó:lok, | they cut it all up, |
| óhya impa:lapaffíhcok | they attached it all to him, |
| stimponná:cit anó:ka:p, | and when they finished teaching |
| sámmit wayhilkó:li, | him how to fly, |
| "Atwáyhískalahǫ," ka:hat, | "You will be a flier," they said, |
| ná:hon, | well, |
| á:tat lamátkin áłłá:hi:p, | if one were to go straight, |
| yámmit aláhkap, talokkó cobá yámmit, | as some did, like the eagle, |
| pálkin amá:katik | even though they went fast, |
| máp sánkotoho:limpak. | they could not thus win. |
| Sántik óhya hiná:p, | But, it was that they all now, |
| ná:hǫ, | well, |
| fó:so:t, fó:si yámmin, | those such as birds, |
| talibó:lá:hiskan sántik óhya, | because they had so made him, |
| hallakík yomahlíhcok, | bats going about |
| akkámmit á:tatoho:limpak. | so [*gestures*] continue to be, they say. |
| Yámmin sámmik sobáykot, | They [the birds] did not know how to do thus, |
| kámmin stá:táhpok, | so he just stayed with them, |
| stimpónnatoho:limpak. | and it is said that he learned everything. |

### Scene 5: Pregame Maneuvers

| | |
|---|---|
| Ná:hon, | Well, |
| hopánka mók hohá:lon. | they heard about the game. |
| Má:mo:sin, | Thereupon, |
| stimponná:cih stí:sáhpok, | having kept teaching him about it, |
| "Hiná:p, wáyka yámmit matcínka:p | "Now, if one who flies hands it off to you, |
| lamátkin ałcí:ya:p, | if you go straight, |
| naksofón ałcí:ya sobayą́:lo:siskan, | because they can figure out where you go, |

| | |
|---|---|
| ahacibatapká:cit má:lotik | they will strike the ball away from you, |
| sántik isnáp yánt ací:yafíhnaskan, | but if you go thus excessively, |
| łopótlok, | passing through, |
| kohtafá ohtółcihalpí:sok, | you can go and reach the goal, |
| konná:sok konką́” | and one of ours will give it [the point] to us,” |
| ká:hatoho:limpak. | they said, so they say. |
| Má:mo:sin, | Thereupon, |
| i:sáhpok ittanáhkok, | they merely stayed together, |
| “Mǫ́, hiná:p! | “Enough now! |
| Tó:hilá:hi mǫ́!” káhhan, | We are to play ball!” they said, |
| amá:katon. | and they all went. |
| Mó:tohon, | Then, |
| nitá yámmip óhyak ołá:citoho:limpak. | the ones who were like Bear all arrived. |
| Ohyak alpí:samá:mit hoco:báhco:liskan, | They all seemed mean, because they were big, |
| “Ná:sok onabókhílą́, | “We shall beat anyone, |
| óhya onabókhíltohoyáhlok,” ká:hat | we have always beaten them all,” |
| immánkatohon. | they said, telling it to them. |
| Mó:tohok, | Then, |
| ołáhcok í:san, | having arrived, they stayed there, |
| hopánka óhya ho:tíhnoskat | and because they counted the whole game, |
| ho:tíhnot i:sa:fó:kap, | when they kept on counting, |
| haccá:tohon má:fa í:sitoho:limpak. | one stood there, and it is said that he took it [the ball]. |
| Ná:hok, | Well, |
| “Hallakík hompá:ná:hik bànnaskat | “Bat wanted to play, |
| sánkot. | and he could not. |
| Kosnáp akó:sá:hik sánkoskan, | Because he could not be with us, |
| ishaciakoyókp. | we are glad for you. |
| Kosnáp ná:son | There is no way he could help us, |
| komawí:cihalpískosk, | |
| cokí:bofíhnaskan,” | because he is too small,” they |
| afa:lí:co:listoho:limpak. | laughed, so it is said. |
| Má:mo:sin, | Thereupon, |
| akkámmin, | this being so, |
| fó:si yámmi í:sa:p ná:son afa:kí:cot | the birds that were there in no way laughed, |
| pí:la, “Akkántik hiná:p | just “This being so, now he is our |
| komawí:cok óm,”káhhan. | helper,” they said. |

### Scene 6: The Ball Game Is Played

Ná:ho máp hiná:p má:fa stó:limpak.

Mó:tohon,
ałí:ya:fó:kon,
hiná:p pokkó tó:ka stáhłan,
himá:ka yámmit,
má nitá yámmit tółkat słopóhlit
immayá:cisk,
słopóhlit stí:sáhpitohok,

stanó:ka:sik ałí:ya:fó:kon,
fó:sik, "Hiná:p matcokhali:lí:cílkásk
hallakí:sáyon!" káhhan,
matcokhali:líhcok,
pokkó matinłopót í:sit wáykat
yámmit á:san,
hocákká:hik sánkon,
walí:katoho:lit słopóttoho:limpak.

Á:yat kammí:cit,
kammí:cit,
óhya, óhya słopóthlin,
nitá yámmit
honoksi:pá::hostoho:limpak.
Cákhíkko:p,
tabátká:hik sánko:p,
nokco:bá:cá:hik sánkon.
Kámmisk,
fó:si:sáyok í:sak
pokkó immayáhcin,
ostanó:katoho:limpak.
Mó:tohon,
ná:ho yámmi:p,
"Hiná:p ciná:sok óˀmí?
Naksán cifó:sok óˀmí?"
"Anó nasmałatlok ómmik á:talin,
wáyka casobáykotik,
pí:la anáp 'pokkó tó:lillahok,'
á:loli:sa:p,
stánkan yámmin,
acikkí:lilá:hik cabàn yámmin,

Well, thus, now it is said that they played
ball there.
Then,
when one went,
now having gone in the ball game,
the ones who were first,
because those like bear ran and passed
through with it and surpassed them,
they just kept on passing through
with it,
when they were about to win,
the birds said, "Now let us put Bat into
the game!"
and they put him in,
and passing by the ball, he took it and flew,
he was thus [*gestures*] with it,
and they could not catch up with him,
he ran and passed through with it,
they say.
He went about doing so,
and doing so,
and all, all he passed by with it,
and the ones like Bear were
exceedingly angry.
When they could not catch up with him,
when they could not catch him,
they could not stop him.
Just like that,
the birds that were there,
having surpassed them in ball,
went and won the game, it is said.
Then,
those [animals] that were there [said],
"Now what are you?
What kind of bird are you?"
"It is the case that *I* lived as an animal,
I did not know how to fly,
but I thought I could play
the ball game,
and they gave them thus to me,
I want to keep them on like this,

| | |
|---|---|
| falakcí hiná:p cabàn. | I want wings now. |
| Cikkíhtákąh!" ká:toho:limpak. | Let me keep them then!" he said. |

## Epilogue

| | |
|---|---|
| Kámmiskan, | Just like that, |
| hiná:p cofík ammánkan, | (now Uncle told me,) |
| yámmi píhtohok ónkǫ, | it is the case that he received them so, |
| hiná:p falakcí káhcok ómmǫ | now it is perhaps how the bat |
| hallakí. | got wings. |
| Kámmiskan, | Just like that, |
| hiná:yámmi:p á:tį atlawísto:t | nowadays when children are about, |
| hoyomáhlin, holawístastik, | even though they are small, |
| "Afa:hacikí:cot ałahkóhya | "You do not laugh at them, |
| naksámmit | I intend to play them, every kind |
| hopá:nilą́," ká:p, | how they are," one says. |
| "Įhopá:nit matasá:caskalahǫ," | "You will let them in to play," they |
| ka:háhco:lik. | habitually say. |
| Ká:mo:s. | It is done. |
| Tafhiyám! | Finis! |

*Textual commentary*:

Line 2 *coficó:bak* 'Old Uncle'. This is Langley's nickname for Bel Abbey, his maternal uncle.

Line 13 *pokkó tó:lit ittimayá:cit í:satoho:limpak* 'it is said that they kept on contesting with each other in the ball game'. The ball game in which the animals and birds compete is the stickball game played aboriginally and still today in the Southeast. There were two kinds of stickball games played by the Koasati—the men's game, and the men and women's game. The men's game was originally played between teams from different towns or different tribes, while the men and women's game was played within one town. The game that is to be played here is the men's game. Mr. Langley structures each team so that it forms a homogenous group—the birds against the animals. This is parallel to the actual game, in which one town would face another. Mr. Langley does not go into great detail as to how the game was played. Since the Koasati have not played stickball games for many years, he is unlikely to have witnessed even the Koasati men's and women's game, which was played occasionally until the 1950s. The Koasati men's and women's game is discussed in Taylor (1937:37–38); for a description of similar ball games among the Yuchi, see Speck (1909:86–89).

Line 23 *ittalokístotoho:limpáhcok* 'it is said that they did not like each other'. In tradition and practice, opposing teams did not like each other. Historically, playing a ball game was considered an alternative to war and much of the vocabulary of the ball game seems to have come from war: e.g., *imí:bin* 'to win a ball game', lit. 'to kill it on someone'; *į̨háplin* 'to win a ball game', lit. 'to make a war against someone'; and *ittacokcaná:kan* 'to play a ball game', lit. 'to quarrel together'.

Line 58 *fó:sik í:sáhpok stį̨hawá:lotoho:limpak* 'it is said that the birds there had pity on him'. Once again, having pity on someone grants the pitier power. By taking pity on this small creature and including him in their game, the Birds have set themselves up for eventual victory.

Lines 71–73 The comments of the Birds regarding Bat's running skills are both appropriate and drolly humorous. Here, too, the mention of death out of context is used to evoke laughter.

Line 85 *yá:fon aykacabonóhkok ittat'ammitohon hí:catoho:limpak* 'it is said that he saw a drum that was lying over there on the ground'. Koasati drums historically were made of a deerskin or other tanned animal hide stretched over the mouth of a pot; the word for drum, *aykacabonohká*, is related to the word for pot, *aykací*. In this instance, someone has dropped a drum and broken it, but the drumhead is still intact and the Birds will use it to make wings for Bat.

Line 114 At this point in the tale, the narrator makes swooping zig-zag gestures with his hand to show how Bat flies. At other places in the narrative where this hand gesture is repeated, it is noted in the translation.

Lines 138–39 This statement by the animals is full of hubris. Any being who expresses hubris in a Koasati tale is bound to come to a bad end. This speech is a stylistic device to let the audience know who the heroes of the story are. Lines 146–50 reinforce this conclusion, with the animals' airy dismissal of Bat's worth.

Lines 157–63 Mr. Langley increases dramatic tension in these lines by indicting that the animals are doing well in the game and are about to win. This increases the impact of Bat's participation, who, being put into the game, saves it for the birds. This entire section speaks to an apparently panhuman fantasy of the nobody coming out of nowhere, playing brilliantly, and winning the game for the home team.

Lines 183–84 *"Hiná:p ciná:sok óˀmí? / Naksán cifó:sok óˀmí?"* '"Now what are you? / "What kind of bird are you?"' These lines, spoken in tones of angry frustration, are intended to make the listener laugh.

Lines 192–202 The epilogue, which in other traditional narratives has the function of providing additional material outside of the main tale, is used here to give the moral of the story. This tale, at least for Mr. Langley, has passed from myth to fable.

# 3

# Monster Stories

Monster stories form a genre of traditional narrative that is rarely, if ever, told at present. The psychological need for monster stories seems to have arisen from the need to deal with the uncertainty of life, especially in the traditional economy, where men and women would go off in small groups to hunt or gather and, at times, never returned. Therefore, the forest was seen to be inhabited by a number of extremely unpleasant beings, most notably the Hankha (*hąkhá*), who ate children, Great-One-Who-Eats-Human-Beings, Eater-of-the-Living, the Great Lizard, and the Clawed Witches. Other less noxious forest inhabitants were Great-One-Lost-in-the-Woods, who merely caused people to lose their way, and the Invisible People, who dwelt in trees where mistletoe grew and who only became visible when death was imminent in a family.

The Indians of long ago perceived the natural world as containing two realms. The first was the celestial world, which was malevolent toward man, containing such unfriendly beings as the Thunderer, the Rainbow, the two Winds, the Milky Way (*Solopí įhíni* 'the Ghosts' Path'), and the deadly Stars. The second was the terrestrial world, which was benevolent, containing such helpful beings as the Trees, Corn, the Merpeople, Water, and the Sea Monster. A few of the celestial beings were benevolent, most notably, the Sun, the Moon, and Venus, and a few of the terrestrial beings were not, primarily the owls, most particularly the barred owl. Light and the things pertaining thereto were considered good and darkness and its inhabitants were considered evil. New light, such as the light of dawn or the light of a fire was considered particularly effective against evil supernatural beings. The various kinds of monsters fit into the ancient Indians' psychological interpretation of the universe; they were terrestrial evil beings whose strength was greatest in darkness.

The four monster stories included here each feature a different kind of monster. Nonetheless, all four have a broad general similarity: in each tale, there is a monster who eats people and there is a human being who encounters the monster and escapes from it with his or her life. In each tale, therefore, there is an affirmation of the power of human beings to overcome the horrors of the world, personified as a monster. As mentioned above, monster stories are now extremely uncommon. This seems to be due to the great changes in Koasati society that have taken place in the last century. The traditional hunting and gathering economy is only a memory, and people no longer go into the woods never to come out again. In addition, the collapse of traditional religion in the first two decades of the twentieth century and the widespread adoption of Christianity have changed the Indians' worldview drastically, so that the personification of the powers of nature survive only as superstitions. Being more secure economically, and no longer regarding the powers of nature with fear, the modern Indians lack the psychological need that monster stories used to fill.

As the need for these monster stories grew less, the monsters themselves either disappeared or took on new forms. For example, Great-One-Who-Eats-Human-Beings, who is pure monster in the tale translated below, in later tales grows less and less monstrous and, in fact, turns into a foil for Rabbit in a number of Rabbit stories (see chapter 1). The elephant of the Old World, which apparently had some physical similarities to the legendary Great-One-Who-Eats-Human-Beings, was given its name and now *A:ti:pacobá* is considered to be Elephant.

## THE OBSTACLE FLIGHT
narrated by Selin Williams

This narrative was collected by John R. Swanton in 1910, who assigned it the number twenty in his "Koasati Texts, Second Series." A translation based on his interlinear glosses was published in his collection of Southeastern narratives (Swanton 1929:183–84).

Although the basic theme of this narrative is the obstacle flight, that portion of the plot is actually downplayed here; rather, the focus is on Great-One-Who-Eats-Human-Beings. This is one of the few Koasati narratives in which Great-One-Who-Eats-Human-Beings acts purely as a monster. In most narratives, he is at least partially a buffoon who frequently falls victim to Rabbit's trickery.

*The Obstacle Flight* is composed of four scenes. Scenes 1 and 2 constitute the first half of the narrative and scenes 3 and 4 constitute the second. This division of a narrative into halves, each half composed of one or more pairs of scenes, is a structural feature typical of Koasati narrative.

### Scene 1: Great-One-Who-Eats-Human-Beings Kidnaps a Girl

| | |
|---|---|
| A:ti:pacobák tayyosón a:tinkoybóhlok, | Great-One-Who-Eats-Human-Beings kidnapped a girl from some people, |
| ikí cokkó:lifon ohpíłkok á:tato:š. | and he went and was keeping her at his mother's dwelling place. |

### Scene 2: He Asks for Her Flesh, but His Mother Deceives Him

| | |
|---|---|
| Mó:tohok, | Then, |
| a:ti:pacobá:kok naksó:n ałíyat ónkak, | Great-One-Who-Eats-Human-Beings spoke as he was going somewhere. |
| "Tayyosón tosáffok ąho:łi:š," káhhok | "Cut a piece out of the girl and cook it for me later by boiling!" he said, |
| nakáłłan. | and went off. |

Ikí:kok ibisná:li a:nipó má:lon tosáffok,
įhółtohon.
Ihlan,
ittintaláhlin,
í:payok ónkak,
"Tayyosín ónciyon ómmin?
Hiná:bat hiná:bš," ká:toho:limpatš.

His mother, having cut a piece from her very
own flesh, cooked it for him by boiling.
On his returning home,
she laid it out for him,
and, even though he ate it, he spoke,
"Is it the case that you have used the girl?
It is extremely tough," he said,
so it is reported.

Ká:han,
"Mó:liyok ó:š," ká:toho:limpats ikík.

He said it, and,
"It really and truly is hers," his mother said,
so it is reported.

### Scene 3: His Mother Aids the Girl's Escape

Mó:tohon,
mán nakáłła:fó:kok,
ónkak,
"Mán tosáffok ąhó:li:š!" káhhok
nakáłłan.
Ikik ónkak,
"Naslibátkon wíhlš!" ká:toho:limpatš.

Thereupon,
again, when he was going off,
he spoke.
"Cut a piece out of her again and then
cook it by boiling," he said,
and went off.
His mother spoke,
"Look for ripe fruits!" she said,
so it is reported.

"I:pa:k,
stimbakłí:cihcok ó:š.
Acinó:lilaho:š," káhhan.
Naslibátka wíhlit,
bakcó:t,
okwołó:t,
talakcó:t
ná:si óhya stí:lan.
"Hina:p anóhlok!
Híc walí:kš!" ká:toho:limpatš.
"Mó:tohon,
a:ti:pacobák cičóhli:k,
ónkalaho:š wononohká:ci:k.
Ma:fó:kon,
bakcón stimittabatáplok,
walí:hískalaho:š.
Má:mi:k,
nascobón łohlí:cit sta:yáhcok,
má:min,
anámpon cákka:si:fó:k,

"When he eats one,
it is the case he makes one thin.
He will devour you," she said.
She looked for ripe fruits,
such as blackberries,
such as dewberries,
such as watermelons,
she brought everything.
"Lo! Finish!
Now! Run!" she said, so it is reported.
"Thereupon,
when Great-One-Who-Eats-Human-Beings
chases you, he will make a roaring sound.
Thereupon,
having thrown the blackberries to the
ground, you will run.
Then,
he goes about causing something large to
chase one,
then,
again when he is about to catch up,

| | |
|---|---|
| tóklon stimittabataplit, | you throw the second thing against the ground, |
| walí:kat ałcí:yan. | and go running. |
| Mán cákki:fó:kon, | Again, when he is catching up, |
| okwołí stimittabatáplok!" | throw the dewberries against the ground!" |

**Scene 4: The Girl Returns Home**

| | |
|---|---|
| Kámmin, | In such a manner, |
| imí:safa ó:łá:hosin, | she came very close to her house, |
| tálwat ałí:yatohon, | and she began to sing, |
| intá:to:t ikó:t kámmik | and her father and her mother, |
| háhlok, | thus heard her. |
| "Híhà! | "Hot damn! |
| Tayyosík á:yatik | But it is the case that the girl is still going |
| ommíhcotohok óntiha:š!" káhhok, | about; one can hear her coming!" he said, |
| łakį píhlit afánkat | and picking up arrows, |
| mattółkatoho:limpatš. | they ran off to meet her, so it is said. |
| Má:mik, | Then, |
| ittafánka:fó:kap, | when they met, |
| a:ti:pacobák ná:si konotlí:con | it was the case that Great-One-Who-Eats- |
| słohlíhcon ómmitohon. | Human-Beings was chasing her with rolling things. |
| Ihlan, | On his arriving, |
| tayyosí intá:ta:kok łakį shóccat | the father of the girl shot at them with |
| imalwáhlit anóslin, | arrows, and he completely ruined them, |
| a:ti:pacobá mán łakį shóccat, | and again he shot arrows at Great-One-Who-Eats-Human-Beings, |
| ohłá:hi:fó:kon, | when he went and shot and hit him, |
| a:ti:pacobák ónkak, | Great-One-Who-Eats-Human-Beings spoke. |
| "Heyé! | "Hoo-whee! |
| skalapistá yók alpí:sa:š," | these mosquitoes are fierce," |
| ká:toho:limpatš. | he said, so it is reported. |
| A:tok í:bá:hį sobáykon, | [Since] no one knew how to kill him, |
| á:tatoho:limpatš. | it is said that he continued to exist. |

*Textual emendations*:

The following emendations of the Koasati text as written by Swanton have been made:

| | | |
|---|---|---|
| Line 4 | na´ ksot ałī´ yiya | naksó:n ałí:yat |
| Line 8 | ēhi´ lan | íhlan |
| Line 20 | wēłs | wíhlš |

| | | |
|---|---|---|
| Line 29 | i´ nahak | hiná:p |
| Line 36 | wale´ sgalahō´s | walí:hískalaho:š |
| Line 50 | taiyō´ sikiktok | tayyosík |
| Line 59 | sō´ tcat imalowa' halit | shóccat imalwáhlit |
| Line 60 | hoła´ hefō´ gon | ohłá:hi:fó:kon |
| Line 64 | ibisubai´ kon | í:bá:hį sobáykon |

*Textual commentary*:

Line 1 *a:ti:pacobá* 'Great-One-Who-Eats-Human-Beings'. At present, this character is visualized as an elephant; however, the original visualization seems to have been rather different. It is likely that Great-One-Who-Eats-Human-Beings was perceived much like a similar Chitimacha monster, the Long-Nosed Devil, *neka šiš kˀamin*. Swadesh describes this being as a "Devil of a certain kind having [a] long nose which it manipulates like an elephant's trunk, but unlike the elephant, it is a biped" (1950:48).

Line 2 *ikí* 'his mother'. The word *ikí* is a rarely used word that is applied only to a third person; other words for mother (*iskí; picí; má:ma*) are used for first and second persons and most third persons. *Ikí* is primarily used for the mother of a young child or an animal, as opposed to the other words, which are used only for humans and can refer also to the mother of an adult. The use of *ikí* here emphasizes that Great-One-Who-Eats-Human-Beings is not human.

Line 5 *ąhó:łi:š* 'cook it for me later by boiling!'. This linguistically interesting form shows the delayed imperative followed by phrase terminal marker that was typical of elite speech (see Kimball 1987b:30–38, 1990:158–61). The common speech form is *ąhó:łįh* for first delayed imperative, and *ąhó:łį:hah* for second delayed imperative.

Lines 6–7 and 19–44 Contrary to expectation, the mother of Great-One-Who-Eats-Human-Beings helps the girl, rather than her son. She has the function of wise woman and supernatural helper; the girl escapes because she follows her instructions exactly.

Line 11 *Tayyosín ónciyon ómmin?* 'Is it the case that you have used the girl?'. This is a very difficult sentence to translate because it is an example of a form of gapping not uncommon in colloquial Koasati, but nonexistent in English. In this kind of gapping, the verb in the question is omitted, leaving overt only the subject, the object, and the auxiliary verb *ómmin*. The hearer is expected to supply any one of several appropriate verbs. In this case, *tayyosín ónciyon ómmin* may stand for *tayyosín isna:hóhcok ónciyon ómmin* 'Is it the case that you have used the girl?', *tayyosín hołcíhcok ónciyon ómmin* 'Is it the case that you have cooked the girl by boiling?', or *tayyosín libatcíhcok ónciyon ómmin* 'Is it the case that you have cooked the girl?' The use of this construction, observed most frequently in quiet domestic contexts, lends a bizarre homeyness to the situation of a cannibal monster being served human flesh by his mother.

Line 20 *Naslibátkon wíhlš!* 'Look for ripe fruits!'. The gathering of the fruits prepares the girl for the obstacle flight. It is assumed that the fruits are given some magic power by the mother of Great-One-Who-Eats-Human-Beings.

Line 24–28 *Naslibátka wíhlit, / bakcó:t, / okwołó:t, / talakcó:t / ná:si óhya stí:lan* 'She looked for ripe fruits, / such as blackberries, / such as dewberries, / such as watermelons, / she brought everything'. Although only three kinds of fruits are mentioned, the suffix *-o:t* implies that other kinds of fruit were also gathered. Considering the fact that four is the ritual Koasati number, one would expect that four kinds of fruits be mentioned; however, both here and in lines 34–44, only three are mentioned.

Lines 31–44 This is the only description of the obstacle flight in the narrative. As Great-One-Who-Eats-Human-Beings comes after her, the girl throws down one of the fruits, which somehow restrains or distracts him. From similar narratives recorded for other Southeastern groups, it could be surmised that when she throws down the blackberries a blackberry bramble appears, and so forth.

Line 38 *nascobón łohlí:cit stayáhcok* 'he goes about causing something large to chase one'. Other Koasati and similar Southeastern tales indicate that Great-One-Who-Eats-Human-Beings chases his victims with four chunkey stones that roll after the victims and lead Great-One-Who-Eats-Human-Beings to them. According to Haas (1940), the Koasati chunkey stone (*hassapolohkí*) was a disk carved of elm wood; there is no stone available in the Gulf Coast areas of Louisiana and Texas where the Koasati have lived since 1795.

Lines 46–47 *imí:safa ó:łá:hosin, / tálwat ałí:yatohon* 'she came very close to her house / and she began to sing'. It is not stated what song the girl sang, but since song was always of a ritual or magical nature, it is clear that she was using other magical means to escape Great-One-Who-Eats-Human-Beings. Swanton (1929:20–21) published a Creek version of this tale that included the girl's song. It suggests that in the Koasati tale the girl is singing "I can reach my parents' house / before he catches me, / I think."

Line 49 *Híhà!* "Hot damn!" This is an almost untranslatable interjection. It is used to indicate great surprise or annoyance and is considered to be equivalent to English or French curse words. (It was explained to me that when one's car broke down an Indian would say *híhà* while a Cajun would say *fils d'putain!* 'son of a whore!'.) In this instance, it indicates great surprise at hearing the voice of the girl who had been presumed dead.

Lines 50–51 *Tayyosík á:yatik / ommíhcotohok óntiha:š!* 'But it is the case that the girl is still going about; / one can hear her coming!' The basic sense of these two lines is that 'the girl is still alive in spite of everything'.

Lines 57–58 *tayyosi intá:ta:kok łakį̨ shóccat / imalwáhlit anóslin* 'the father of the girl shot at them with arrows, / and he completely ruined them'. The father shoots at and destroys the chunkey stones of Great-One-Who-Eats-Human-Beings, thus making him unable to pursue the girl any further.

Lines 59–65 The man tries to slay Great-One-Who-Eats-Human-Beings, but is unable to do so. Although an individual can be saved from his clutches, it is beyond the capabilities of humankind to destroy him. It is Rabbit the trickster who has the power to transform Great-One-Who-Eats-Human-Beings into Elephant and exile him to the other side of the ocean.

Line 62 *heyé* 'Hoo-whee!' This is another basically untranslatable interjection. The English version is the interjection that would be used in the same context.

## EATER-OF-THE-LIVING

narrated by *Sacowáyhki*

This narrative was recorded by John R. Swanton in 1910, who assigned it the number three in his "Koasati Texts, Second Series." He published a translation based on his interlinear glosses (Swanton 1929:196–97). Swanton translated the name of this monster as 'Life-Eater', based on a misunderstanding of the Koasati word. The name of the monster, *okcayyaí:pa*, is a nominalization of the phrase *okcáyyan ipá* 'he customarily eats that which lives', and literally means 'one who eats that which lives'.

This short narrative is comprised of four scenes. The rhetorical patterning of this narrative is not as symmetrical as in most other cases. Although the narrative can be divided into two sections, the first section consists of the first three scenes and the second of the last scene. It is possible that there are only two scenes in this narrative, with the first three scenes being properly subsumed into one. However, the subdivision in the first section and the lack of subdivision in the second section are still obvious and lack explanation.

### Scene 1: A Man Encounters Eater-of-the-Living

| | |
|---|---|
| Okcayyaí:pok á:yatohon, | Eater-of-the-Living was going about, |
| á:tok ilanawihlíhcok á:yatohon, | and a man who was hunting was going about, |
| Okcayyaí:pok afánkatoholimpatš. | and it is said that Eater-of-the-Living met him. |

### Scene 2: The Man Tries to Evade Eater-of-the-Living

| | |
|---|---|
| Máhmin, | Then, |
| immaɬátlit immaɬáttoho:limpatš. | he [the man] was very very frightened of him, so it is said. |
| Máhmok, | At that, |
| athómmak aɬí:ya:p, | when the Indian went, |
| obá:lin Okcayyaí:pok | behind him Eater-of-the-Living |
| matacakkíhcotoho:limpatš. | followed at a distance, so it is said. |
| Má:min, | Then, |
| stá:yat iwwalí:kat nakáɬɬah bànnatik, | he went about with him, and although he ran and tried to lose him, |
| sánkotoho:limpatš. | it is said that he was unable to. |

### Scene 3: The Man Tricks Eater-of-the-Living

| | |
|---|---|
| Mó:tohon, | Thereupon, |
| stá:yatohon, | he went about with him, |
| cokfosón íhsok | taking up a young rabbit, |
| atohcifón hókfitohon, | he put it into his bandolier bag, |
| Okcayyaí:pak ifán immaɬátlit | and Eater-of-the-Living being very much |
| immaɬatlíhcotohon, | afraid of dogs, when it was dark, |
| tánka:fó:k á:tik immaɬátli:k, | as the man was afraid of him, |
| ifá imilayókcitoho:limpatš. | it is said that he imitated a dog. |
| Má:min, | Then, |
| himă::ɬko:sit wohwóhkatoho:limpatš. | it is said that he barked very softly. |
| Má:min, | Then, |
| Okcayyaí:pok ónkak, | Eater-of-the-Living made a sound, |
| ponhá:lot haccáhlok, | having stood listening, |
| "Máh!" ká:toho:limpatš. | "Hist!" he said, so it is reported. |
| Káhhan, | He said it, |
| mán să::mo:sin | and again, the other barked just a little, |
| wohwóhkatoho:limpatš. | so it is said. |
| Ma:fó:kon, | At that, |
| haccá:toho:limpatš. | it is said that he [Eater-of-the-Living] stood [still]. |
| Má:min, | Then, |
| cokfosí matí:sit hiccá:cin, | the other took out the little rabbit and showed it to him, |
| walí:kat nakáɬtoho:limpatš. | and he ran off and disappeared. |

**Scene 4: The Man Is Attacked at Night**

Má:min,
łóykat intikbá óltifa,
óhłok,
tamó:kan ittacokkǫ:toho:limpatš.
Mó:tohon,
tamó:ka:fó:kon,
nasholló:kok ółtoho:limpatš.
Ittón ká:noscon í:sit,
á:tin sbatáplá:hį,
athómmak tàmmitohon
alapí notón óhłok,
nasholló:kok batáplit í:bá:hik,
ittó famótkayon,
alapí imiyyí pilahón batáplin,
á:tik falánkok,
walí:kat,
okfá cobáhcok tallá:katohon,
ohto:cofótlit o:łopótlit,
mathí:ca:p,
má:kok łóhlit tałá,
ithaccá:toho:limpatš.
Má:mo:sin,
athómma:kok ná:son íkbot,
łóykat ółtoho:limpatš.

Then,
he returned to his camp fire,
on arriving there,
at night it is said he sat on the ground.
Thereupon,
when it was night,
the evil being arrived there, it is said.
It picked up a strong stick
in order to strike the man,
and the Indian was lying down,
and got under a forked stick,
and the evil being struck to kill him,
he waved the stick around in the air,
but he struck the legs of the forked stick,
and the man got up,
and he ran,
and there was a large lake lying there,
and he jumped into the water and forded it,
and when he looked back,
that one chased him to the other side,
and it is said that it came and stood there.
Thereupon,
the Indian did not kill any game,
and he returned home, so it is said.

*Textual emendations*:

The following emendations of the Koasati text as written by Swanton have been made:

| | | |
|---|---|---|
| Line 2 | hilanawe´letcok’ | ilanawíhlihcok |
| Line 16 | atō´xtcifan hō´kfitan | atohcifón hókfitohon |
| Line 21 | i´ma + tkō´sit | himă::łko:sit |
| Line 27 | sa´ + mosin | să::mo:sin |
| Line 34 | intikoba$^{3}$u´ltifa | intikbóltifa |
| Line 36 | itatcugo$^{n}$´ toolimpats | ittacokkǫ:toho:limpatš |
| Line 52 | ma´ + ko$^{3}$ ło´hele | má:kok łóhlit |

*Textual commentary*:

Line 1 *Okcayyaí:pa* 'Eater-of-the-Living'. This character is found only here in Koasati oral literature. Swanton (1929) notes no parallels with other Southeastern Indian characters. Eater-of-the-Living is another of the forest-dwelling monsters that lived on human flesh (when they could get it).

Lines 4–12 These lines set up the problem to be faced by the hunter: how to avoid Eater-of-the-Living. Although Eater-of-the-Living does not use any magic tracking devices as does Great-One-Who-Eats-Human-Beings, it is not possible for a human being to evade him so long as he is following.

Line 16 *atohcifón hókfitohon* 'he put it into his bandolier bag'. The bandolier bag, *atohcí*, was a bag on a long strap worn over the shoulder. It contained a hunter's bullets and provisions, and any other small, portable items that he needed.

Line 17 *Okcayyaí:pak ifón immałátlit immałatlíhcotohon* 'Eater-of-the-Living being very much afraid of dogs'. A hunter was frequently accompanied by his dog, although not always, as is the case in this story. It was believed that evil supernatural beings were afraid of dogs, and dogs had the power to deter them or drive them away. This power can also be noted in the tale, *The Clawed Witches*, below.

Line 25 *"Máh!" ká:toho:limpatš* '"Hist!" he said, so it is reported'. The word *máh* is the suppletive imperative of the verb *há:lon* 'to hear; listen', and, depending on context, it can also be translated 'Listen!'. Here, Eater-of the-Living is speaking to himself, as he thinks he is hearing a dog barking.

Lines 30–32 These lines seem to form the end of the first section of this narrative. One might suppose that, at this point, the narrative is complete, including, as it does, the encounter with Eater-of-the-Living, the dilemma, and the solution that drives the monster away. However, this is not the case.

Lines 37–39 *Mó:tohon, / tamó:ka:fó:kon, / nasholló:kok ółtoho:limpatš* 'Thereupon, / when it was night, / the evil being arrived there, it is said'. Although here and in the rest of the narrative Eater-of-the-Living is not mentioned by name, he is still the monster being spoken of. The suffix *-:ka* (in the nominative case, *-:kok*) attached to the noun *nashollo*, which here means 'supernaturally evil being', indicates that the noun to which it is attached is something that has been mentioned before in the narrative, and thus connects the two segments of the narrative. Note that Eater-of-the-Living, who was only able to follow the hunter during the day, attacks him at night. Like many other monsters, this one has its greatest power in the darkness.

Lines 41–53 These lines syntactically form a single long sentence, each line ending in a connective suffix or a switch-reference suffix that relates that line to the line following. Such long sentences have a stylistic use: they point out sections of the story that the narrator feels are important—the longer the sentence, the more important the part. This sentence, which is made up of twelve lines, indicates the climax of the story.

Lines 49–50 *okfá cobáhcok tallá:katohon, / ohto:cofótlit o:łopótlit* 'and there was a large lake lying there, / and he jumped into the water and forded it'. Water was one of the elements that was considered friendly to people—immersion in water was a way to protect oneself from evil supernaturals. This pattern can also be found in the story, *The Great Lizard*, below.

Lines 54–56 *Má:mo:sin, / athómma:kok ná:son íkbot, / łóykat ółtoho:limpatš* 'Thereupon, / the Indian did not kill any game, / and he returned home, so it is said'. Encounters with evil supernatural forces were thought to affect negatively one's success in hunting. In such a case, one had to return home and be treated by a doctor so that one's good luck in hunting could return.

## THE GREAT LIZARD

narrated by *Sacowáyhki*

This narrative was collected by John R. Swanton (1930) and has never before been edited or published. It tells how hunters accidentally rouse the Great Lizard and how the Indians deal with it. Swanton published a version of this tale as Koasati, with the title "The Monster Lizard" (1929:196). However, it was told by an Alabama speaker, Charlie Thompson, "who thought he knew Koasati" (Swanton, 1912a). Swanton, evidently dissatisfied with the quality of the linguistic material, corrected the texts he had collected with the help of *Sacowáyhki*. However, at present there is no way to tell if any of the tales gathered from Charlie Thompson are authentically Koasati, or are simply versions of Alabama narratives.

The narrative is divided into six scenes. Except for the first scene, which is short and serves as a prologue to the main narrative, the scenes are approximately equal in length. The narrative is divided into halves, each containing three scenes. Unlike other narratives, such as the tale *The Clawed Witches* below, there is no clear arrangement of scenes into pairs.

### Scene 1: A Hunter Finds What He Thinks Is a Bear

A:tik ilanawíhlik á:yatohok,
  ittó:bon híhcok
    ónti:k íhlok ónkak
      "Nitón stąhí:ca:s" káhhan.

A man who was going about hunting,
  catching sight of a hollow tree,
    came returning and said,
      "I have come across a bear."

### Scene 2: The Six Hunters Find the Great Lizard

Má:mo:sin,
  á:ti hanná:lit amá:kat ołáhcin,
    naksó:n nitá ittó:bik stįhaccá:lik.

And then,
  six men went over there
    where the bear's hollow tree stood.

| | |
|---|---|
| Má:mo:sin, | And then, |
| á:ti imaníhtak imonóyyak, | a young man climbed up, |
| ayakhá óhłok, | arrived there nearby, |
| tikbá mastįhókfik ittó:bifa. | and thrust a burning torch into the hollow tree. |
| Má:mo:sin, | And then, |
| ná:sok ittó:bihayó naksą́hkak | something within the hollow tree really made a noise, |
| có:ba ná:ni mánkatoho:limpatš. | it is said that it sounded like a stallion. |
| Má:mo:sin, | And then, |
| á:ti:kok há:lok, | the man, upon hearing it said, |
| "Háw! Niták ǫ́híkko:š!" káhhok, | "Hey! It is not the sound of a bear," |
| óhyak aboyótlit tółkatoho:limpatš. | and they all ran scattering themselves, so they say. |

**Scene 3: The Great Lizard Catches Five of the Hunters**

| | |
|---|---|
| Ma:fó:kon, | After that, |
| hayabincobók ónkatohok imí:safa | the great lizard called out in its nest, |
| i:tachalí:kat pa:haccá:toho:limpatš. | and it came exiting and stood on it [the hollow tree], so it is said. |
| Ma:fó:kap, | Then, |
| á:ti caffá:kan ayakhosín | one man right nearby was standing |
| pa:haccá:litoho:limpatš. | on a branch, as it is said. |
| Ma:fó:kap, | Then, |
| hayabincobák tanátlok, | the great lizard descended, |
| á:ti łóhli:k, | and chased after a man, |
| ihokí:con stí:latoho:limpatš. | and soon brought him back, so it is said. |
| Má:min, | Then, |
| stonóyyat imí:safa ohhókfit, | it climbed up with him, |
| mí:tan łóhlit stí:lat anó:lok. | went and put him into its nest, and finished chasing and bringing back the others. |

**Scene 4: A Hunter Escapes the Lizard**

| | |
|---|---|
| Stacahappá:ka łóhli:fó:kon, | While it was chasing the fifth man, |
| á:ti abá haccá:li:kok tanátlok | the man who had been standing up above |
| walí:katoho:limpatš. | descended and ran, so it is said. |
| Walí:ka:k, | When he ran, |
| hahcifá ó:ła:si:k, | when he really got over to a river, |
| sánkot támmitoho:limpatš. | he could do no more and fell, so it is said. |
| Má:mok, | Then, |
| konótlit okifón ohto:támmok. | he rolled toward the water and went and fell into the water. |

Má:mok,
oktá:yat okí ałí:yafok,
á:tik o:wá:ya:fó:kap,
hayabincobák í:latoho:limpatš.
Má:mok,
okifá o:cofótlit o:łopótlit,
łóykat o:łopótlit wihláhpok
sánkot łóykatoho:limpatš.

Then,
he floated in the water current,
and when the man was going about in the water,
the great lizard arrived, so it is said.
Then,
it jumped into the water and forded it,
it returned fording, just looking for him,
and it could do no more and returned [to its nest], so it is said.

**Scene 5: The Hunter Informs the Old People**

Má:min,
á:ti:kok achalíhkok,
ałí:yak óhłok,
ohta:łí:kat,
athocó:bahak "Tá.
Ohtilhí:calaho:š,"
káhhok,
óhya a:łí:kat anóhlok.
Má:mo:sin,
á:ti imaníhta:kon ónkak,
"Ohkommánkš!" ká:ha:p,
á:ti imaníhtak małátlit małátlitoho:limpatš.
Ma:máhpok,
ałí:yak ółkot łóyhkok
walí:katoho:limpatš.

Then,
the man came out,
went and arrived over there,
went, and told the story,
and the old people said, "Indeed.
We will go and look for it,"
after he had finished telling the whole story.
Thereupon,
they spoke to the young man;
when they said "Go and show it to us!"
the young man was very much afraid.
Nonetheless,
he went not too near and returned,
running, so it is said.

**Scene 6: The Old People Conquer the Great Lizard by Magic and Slay It**

Má:min,
athocó:ba:kok ołáhcok
hayabincobá imí:safon,
má:mok,
tálwat atanáhkatoho:limpatš.

And then,
the old people arrived there to the nest
of the great lizard,
and then,
they circled it singing medicine songs, so it is said.

Onostá:lik fáylok.
Má:mo:sin,
"Tá. Onóhyok tikbá
mastįhókfąh!" káhhan.
A:ti caffá:kat onóyyak mastįhókfin,
naksáhkatoho:limpatš.

They did it four times and stopped.
Thereupon,
"Indeed. Climb up and put a burning
torch in on it!" they said.
One man climbed up and put it in on it,
and it called out, so it is said.

| | |
|---|---|
| Má:mok, | Then, |
| ihokí:con i:tachalí:katoho:limpatš. | soon it came exiting, so it is said. |
| Má:mok, | Then, |
| á:tik notá lokkó:tohon hí:cat, | it saw the people standing below, |
| imóntik cofótlit ittámmin ihá:nifa, | and came jumping at them and came falling to the ground, |
| óhyak swinóhlin, | and they all shook their medicine rattles, |
| ilkoyóhkok, | and it could not move, |
| aballá:katoho:limpatš. | and lay beside them, so it is said. |
| Má:min, | And then, |
| falánkah bànt sánkot, | it tried to get up, but it was unable to do so, |
| aballáhkan, | and as it lay beside them, |
| hakcó stimacóslit | they inserted a weapon into its ear, |
| hóccatoho:limpatš. | and shot it, so it is reported. |
| I:bit apíhlok, | Having killed it and got rid of it, |
| imocóskotohon í:bit apístoho:limpatš. | as for those which were its offspring, they killed and got rid of them, so it is said. |

*Textual emendations*:

The following emendations of the Koasati text as written by Swanton have been made:

| | | |
|---|---|---|
| Line 1 | lanaoihilok | ilanawíhlok |
| Line 13 | toba hayo | ittó:bihayo |
| Line 13 | nakso$^{n}$kak | naksą́hkak |
| Line 18 | toskatoolimpats | tółkatoho:limpatš |
| Line 21 | pahathatcatoolimpa | pa:haccá:toho:limpatš |
| Line 28 | yoketcun | ihokí:con |
| Line 31 | istela kanaholo | stí:lat anóhlok |
| Line 32 | istatcakpaka | stacahappá:ka |
| Line 33 | atlok | tanátlok |
| Line 42 | oyaa fokap | o:wá:ya:fó:kap |
| Line 45 | ołokotlit | o:łopótlit |
| Line 60 | olikatoolimpats | walí:katoho:limpatš |
| Line 62 | połaxtcok | ołáhcok |
| Line 65 | akanaxka toolimpats | atanáhkatoho:limpatš |
| Line 69 | mastehokfakahhan | mastįhókfąh káhhan |
| Line 70 | onuyia | onóyyak |
| Line 73 | okitcun | ihokí:con |
| Line 76 | monte | imóntik |
| Line 76 | eteme | ittámmin |
| Line 76 | ihanik | ihá:nifa |

| | | |
|---|---|---|
| Line 78 | obilakatoolimpats | aballá:katoho:limpatš |
| Line 81 | falankahabant | falánkah bànt |
| Line 86 | motcaskotohon | imocósko:tohon |

*Textual commentary:*

Lines 1–11 These lines give invaluable ethnographic information on how the Koasati hunted bear. Rather than individually hunt free roaming animals, as they did with deer, the Koasati looked for a bear that was denned up and rousted it out, with several hunters at hand to shoot the animal when it emerged. Group hunting seems to have been practiced only when pursuing very large or dangerous animals. Note what happened to the two hunters in *Bear Medicine* (chapter 5), when they wounded a bear in the open.

Line 13 *ná:sok itto:bihayó naksą́hkak* 'something within the hollow tree really made a noise'. In this line, Swanton garbled the Koasati, writing <nasuk toba hayo nakso$^{n}$kak> and glossing it 'something like a horse inside make a neighing noise'. Although the word *hayó* 'inside' can stand alone, most frequently it is fused with the preceding noun as the inessive case suffix. The word written <toba> cannot be *có:ba* 'horse', as the gloss suggests, as *co:bahayó* 'within the horse' is not semantically appropriate. Rather <toba> is a miswriting for *ittó:bi* 'hollow tree'. The writing <nakso$^{n}$kak> is a blend between *na:s-ónka-k* 'making some kind of purposeful noise' and the n-grade of *naksáhka-k* 'making noise of any kind'. Semantically, the n-grade of *naksáhkak* is most appropriate.

Lines 22–24 *Ma:fókap / á:ti caffá:kan ayakhó:sin / pa:haccá:toho:limpatš* 'Then, / one man right nearby / was standing on a branch, as it is said'. Literally, the verb *pa:haccá:lin* means 'to stand on a raised or artificial horizontal surface'. It is frequently used with the understanding that it can also mean 'to stand in a tree'. In this line, the implication is made that the man standing in a tree right nearby was the one who threw the burning torch into the den of the Great Lizard. Quite clearly, when hunters were after a bear, to climb up onto the hollow tree in which a bear was denning would be dangerous in the extreme. Thus, one of the hunters would have to climb a nearby tree to drop the torch in on the animal.

Line 35 *hahcifá ǫ́:ɬa:si:k* 'when he really got over to a river'. The derivational elements consisting of the n-grade and the diminutive/intensive suffix found in *ǫ́:ɬa:si:k* (from *ó:ɬan* 'to be over there') indicate that the action is being performed to the best of the ability of the actor, or is done with the utmost powers of concentration. This concept is not easily translated into English, especially with a verb such as 'to be over there'. In this instance, it indicates that the man got to the river only by exerting himself to his limits.

Lines 40–41 *Má:mok, / oktá:yat okí aɬí:yafok* 'Then, / he floated in the water current'. The verb *oktá:yan* 'to float,' usually refers only to large branches or logs, the verb pair *okpaká:lin* (singular subject)/*okpakáffin* (plural subject) otherwise being used. Its use here may be predicated on the man, being long and cylindrical, being compared to a log, or it may be predicated on the Great Lizard perceiving him as a log, and thus not catching him.

Lines 64–65 *Mamok, / tálwat atanáhkatoho:limpatš* 'And then, / they circled it singing medicine songs, so it is said'. Literally, the line says 'they circled it singing'. However, song in Koasati culture was not secular, but religious. Song accompanied ceremonial dances and was used in curing rituals to aid and give virtue to herbal medicines. Here, the old people are attempting to control the Great Lizard with their mystical powers by means of singing. It is likely that the old people are all *hopá:yi* 'prophets', persons who could foresee the future, find lost persons or objects, and call and control game animals. Since each clan had its own *hopá:yi*, the number of old people who come to handle the Great Lizard implies that all of the clan *hopá:yi* are involved. Throughout this narrative, the gender of the actors is unstated, as gender does not require specific linguistic marking. One can assume, however, from social roles the gender of the actors—the hunters are all male, for example. On the other hand, the *hopá:yi* are probably both male and female, as all ritual roles in Koasati society were open to women as well as men.

Line 66 *Onostá:likfáylok* 'They did it four times and stopped'. Four was the ritual number for the Koasati. All important ritual activities were done four times to ensure their success. A baby had its head shaved when it was four months old, and a widow or widower had to remain unmarried for four years.

Line 77 *óhyak swinóhlin* 'they all shook their medicine rattles'. The verb *swinóhlin* means 'to rattle a rattle'. It is related to the verb *winohlí:cin* 'to rattle something by making small movements of the wrist'. Here, the rattling of the medicine rattles combined with the medicine songs renders the Great Lizard powerless.

Line 82–84 *aballáhkan, / hakcó stimacóslit / hóccatoho:limpatš* 'and as it lay beside them, / they inserted a weapon into its ear, / and shot it, so it is said'. It is of interest to note that, although magic can control the Great Lizard, it cannot kill it, so physical means must be used. Swanton's gloss of *stimacóslit* is 'they had put a gun in', and present-day speakers understand that a gun is meant. However, because the kind of weapon is not mentioned, originally it could well have been a nocked arrow that was put into the Great Lizard's ear.

Line 85–86 *Í:bit apíhlok /. . . í:bit apístoho:limpatš* 'Having killed it and gotten rid of it / . . they killed them and got rid of them, as it is reported'. The verb pair *apí:lin* (singular object)/*apíslin* (plural object) usually means 'to throw something away'. However, it can also be used in the sense of 'to get rid of something unpleasant or unnecessary', as in this case.

## THE GREAT LIZARD

narrated by Martha John

I recorded this narrative on tape in 1992, over sixty years after Swanton recorded the version above. It is an excellent example showing that Koasati narrative is not linguistically fixed, but rather consists of a series of core elements, upon which the narrator elaborates according to her desire. In comparing Miss John's version with that of *Sacowáyhki*, it is possible to determine the necessary plot elements of this narrative. The hunters must be more than two, and the hunter who puts the fire into the hollow tree and rouses the Great Lizard is the one who escapes. That hunter escapes via water, returns to tell the tale, and is compelled by the old people to take them to the Great Lizard's den. Finally, the old people use supernatural power to control the Great Lizard, and the monster is slain using natural means.

This tale seems to have been a favorite of Miss John, who told it without pausing to think about what she was about to say. Linguistically, this resulted in the text consisting of a very few, very long sentences, as the system of anticipatory switch reference keeps the action and the characters clearly in focus. The tale consists of six scenes and an epilogue, and can be divided into two sections. The first section is much longer than the second; this results from Miss John focusing on the escape from the Great Lizard. She seems to have found chase and escape scenes particularly thrilling; in her telling of *The Clawed Witches* below, she elaborates the chase scene in a similar fashion, and even uses the same expressive interjection.

### Scene 1: Four Men Go Hunting

| | |
|---|---|
| Ostá:kat amá:katoho:limpáhcok ilanawíhlá:hik, | Four men went to hunt, so it is said. |
| Ittohayó amá:katohok yomáhli:fó:kap, | They went into the forest, and as they went about, |
| itto:bik haccá:tohon, | there was a hollow tree standing there, |
| hopáhki stalpí:san ilá:ci:fó:kon, | when they had arrived sufficiently far, |
| itto:bik haccá:tohon, | there was a hollow tree standing there, |
| ittimmáhkok, | and they spoke to each other, |
| "Ná:so:kon a:táhco:lima:m," káhhan, | "There must be something living there," they said. |
| Má:mo:sin, | Thereupon, |
| caffá:kat onóyyak mathí:cat, | one man climbed up and looked in, |
| "Káhcot a:táhcon,"káhhan. | "Just like that, there is something living," he said. |

### Scene 2: The Men Rouse the Great Lizard and it Captures Three

| | |
|---|---|
| Mó:lip, | Well, |
| ohtikbahiłi:líhcok, | one went and kindled a fire |
| mastimapíhlik | in order to throw it in, |
| kámmi:fó:kon, | when he did so, |
| "Isná:holaho katík óm," ká:tohok, | "It is the case that you will do it," they said |
| Ná:ho:fó:kap, | When he did it, |
| ohtikbahiłi:líhcok, | when he went and lit the fire, |
| mastapí:li:fó:kap, | and threw it in, |
| achalí:kok, | it [the Great Lizard] came out, |
| mathí:cat ittaí:satohon, | and looked down at those there on the |

łóhlin,
intółkatohon,
óhyak intółkot amá:katohok,
Caffá:kan tábatkak,
ilabaná:lit stíhlok
ittofá ittokohókbi má:lon itpíłkok,

łóykatoho:p mán,
mók mán tabátkak stíhlok,

itpíłkok statoccí:na:fó:kon,
stonostá:kap ałí:ya:fó:kok,
"Hopáhki stalpí:san hináp ó:ło katík óm."

"Ałí:ya:si:má:m,
matáłłalą," á:lok
akkó caffá:kak ittinsá:wafa pa:haccá:lit,
tikbá mastimapí:tohok pa:haccá:tohok,

hiná:p ałí:yat.

ground, and chased them,
and they ran from it,
they all went running from it.
It caught one man,
and brought him back on its shoulder,
and went and put him in the hole of the tree itself,
again when it returned,
once again it caught one man and brought him back,
it went and put in the third man
and when it went for the fourth time,
"It must be the case that it has gone far enough away,
It must be really gone,
I shall go off," he thought,
that one who was standing on the branch,
who, standing on the branch, had put the fire in,
now he went.

### Scene 3: The Fourth Man Tries to Escape and Succeeds

Má:mo:sin,
ittó ittámmit,
ná:hon,
toppón walí:katohon,
hahcík tàmmitohon sobáylisk,
má:fa walí:kat.
Óōōōōōōà!
Hopáhki stalpí:san ó:łat,
o:łá:hi:p íksǫ,
sánko:fó:kap,
sánko:sit anáhkat
konótlit anáhkatoho:limpak.
Má:mo:sin,
"Hiná:p pa:haccá:líhci mó,"á:lot
kostí:nit ilkafíhlíhcotohok,

hahcifók i:to:táhmok,
i:to:táhmok okí ałí:yafok,
o:cokhalí:káhcok
ałí:yatohok.

Thereupon,
he went and threw himself from the tree,
well,
he ran far away,
because he knew there was a river,
he ran over there.
Ooooooooooooh!
He had gone far enough,
but he not yet gotten there,
he wasn't able to do so,
he had become physically incapable,
it is said that he fell rolling.
Thereupon,
"It might be standing there," he thought,
and he came to himself and gathered his strength,
and came and threw himself into the river.
he threw himself into the current,
he entered the water,
and went off.

| | |
|---|---|
| Má:mo:sin, | Thereupon, |
| ná:hok, | well, |
| akkó haybiná:kok óhłok, | that Lizard arrived there, |
| ohhaccáhlok, | it went and stood there, |
| bànnat á:lok, | it wanted him, |
| matwíhlit sánkon, | it searched about, and was unable [to find him], |
| ayóslit sánkon, | it tracked him, and was unable [to find him], |
| łóykat ó:łan, | and it went back, |
| łóykask, | because it went back, |
| łóykháwahá:lok, | since he could hear that it was going back, |
| o:walí:kat hopáhkiná:n, | he went far in the water, |
| ilokmáylitok hahcí:kon. | he swam the river. |

**Scene 4: The Man Returns Home and The Old People Make a Plan**

| | |
|---|---|
| Pa:hókfat ałí:yatohok, | He went to the people he lived with, |
| achalí:kok ałí:yatohok | he went coming out, |
| má ohí:safa óhłok, | he arrived there where they lived, |
| "Akkámmin á:yat hi:calíhcóm acíhban, | "In such a way I, going about, saw something awful, |
| akkámmo:sin á:yalíhc," káhhan. | just like that as I was about," he said. |
| Mó:li:p, | Well, |
| "Ohayyi ittafámmi:fó:kon | "When a year has come and gone, |
| amá:hilkalaho:š. | we shall go. |
| Kǫhiná:tama:mik kosnók ǫhíla:š," | Lead us then, perhaps, and we shall do something," |
| ká:hatoho:limpáhcok á:ti hosíhno:li:s. | it is said that the old people said. |

**Scene 5: The Old People Set Out after the Great Lizard**

| | |
|---|---|
| Á:tok ahissį talibó:tohok, | The people made medicine, |
| talibó:lit anóslitohok, | they made it up completely. |
| himá:yap ohayyí caffá:kan afammíhcon, | Now, one year had come and gone, |
| "Kǫhiná:t!" káhhan, | "Lead us!" they said, |
| małátlhalpí:stik sámmilahókko:s. | and as he was afraid he would not do so. |
| "Matkǫhiná:t!" | "Lead us thither!" |
| Małátlisk, įhiná:tatohok, | And even though he was afraid he led them, |
| ałí:yat ómma:to:k, | after they went, |
| ałí:yatoho:p, | when they went, |
| má ó:łafa ná:hotohon, | there at that place they used it [the medicine] |

| | |
|---|---|
| bókka ná:hotohok | they used the beating of drums, |
| ayókcik onàntohon má ahissón, | they were still making that medicine. |

### Scene 6: The Great Lizard is Drawn Out and Slain

| | |
|---|---|
| "Sáncitohok, | "As you did before, |
| malmámmit pa:haccáhlok! | having stood on the branch, do in the same way! |
| Konná:homá:mik," káhhan, | It will perhaps do something to us," they said. |
| ittó onóyyat, | and he climbed the tree, |
| ittinsá:wafa pa:haccá:lit | and stood on the branch, |
| tto:bifon akkok ohtikbahiłi:lik | and that man into the hollow tree, |
| mastimapíhlin, | having kindled a fire, |
| achalí:ka:fó:k, | put it in, |
| mathi:cat, | and it [the Great Lizard] came out. |
| á:tį hí:catohon, | It looked at the people, |
| "Akkammí:cilitik," á:lot matcofótlik, | "I shall do the same to them," it thought, jumping down, |
| akkón okhayyihmó:cit | but there they had turned it to mud, |
| óhya imilató:batohoyáhlon, | they had really prepared it all, |
| sánkot, | and it was unable to move, |
| haybinco:bá:kok o:pattáhkan, | the Great Lizard lay flat in the mud, |
| sánkon, | and was unable to move, |
| cáklit íhbok, | and they struck it many times with an ax and killed it. |

### Epilogue: War-Medicine is taken from the Great Lizard's Ashes

| | |
|---|---|
| Ná:hon, | Well, |
| ittón óhya ó:tit anóslok, | having completely kindled wood |
| tołkaybí:cit óhyat anóhlok, | having turned it all to coals, |
| ná:ho:p, | when they did it, |
| pa:píłkan ibisnók | they put something on it, |
| ná:hok, | when the Lizard had all turned to coals, |
| haybiná:kok óhya tołkáybit anó:kat | they took something out of the fire |
| ittapíhlit náhho, | to use, |
| ná:hon, | well, |
| ná:sok syomáhtohot | it was something they carried; |
| kammí:cit ŏ:hya stitticaffá:kat anóslok, | they did it, having completely divided up each and every bit of it; |
| ittimáhkáhcotohok, | they told each other about it. |

| | |
|---|---|
| Náksok ittihápli:p, | If some people went to war, |
| akkón sǎ:mmo:sin ilbí ná:hon, | if they used just a little bit of that on their hands, |
| píłka:sin | having fully kept it, |
| o:yó:lifa impa:cikkí:lit, | having put it in and on their fists, |
| sánkot ciłátlit í:bit ostamá:káhco-toho:limpáhcok. | it is said that having habitually carried it they could not fall or be killed. |
| Akkammí:cit ostamá:káhcotoho:limpáhcok athommahak. | Just like that it is said that the Indians used to carry it. |
| Tafhiyám! | Finis! |

*Textual Comments:*

Line 1 *Ostá:kat amá:katoho:limpáhcok* 'Four men went to hunt, so it is said'. Formerly, when the Koasati went hunting, it was customary for two men to hunt together. The fact that four men are hunting suggests that they are going for a very large game animal, such as the bear that is mentioned in *Sacowáyhki*'s version of this tale.

Line 20 *mathí:cat ittaí:satohon* 'and looked down at those there on the ground'. As she uttered these words, Miss John held her head up very straight, opened her eyes widely, and turned her head slowly from side to side, imitating the motions of the Great Lizard.

Line 35 *tikbá mastimapí:tohok pa:haccá:tohok* 'who, standing on the branch, had put the fire in'. Just as in the earlier version of the tale, it is the hunter who dropped the fire into the den of the Great Lizard who is the one to survive.

Line 43 *Óōōōōōōōōà!* 'Ooooooooooooh!'. This expressive interjection is used to heighten the tension of this scene. The listeners do not know if the hunter is still being pursued by the Great Lizard, nor do they know if he will escape.

Line 52 *hahcifók i:to:táhmok* 'and came and threw himself into the river'. In Line 41, the hunter, because he knows where a river lies, runs towards it. Water, especially running water, was considered to be a beneficent element with the power to confuse or thwart evil supernaturals.

Line 74 *Ohayyi ittafámmi:fó:kon amá:hílkalaho:š* 'When a year has come and gone, we shall go'. This line marks a striking difference between Miss John's version of this tale and that of *Sacowáyhki*. In the first version of the tale, the old people go immediately to confront the Great Lizard; in the present version, they will wait for the one year anniversary before going after the monster. There is clearly some magical significance in the anniversary (*ittafámmi*) that will make defeating the Great Lizard possible.

Line 83 *Małátlisk, įhiná:tatohok* 'And even though he was afraid he led them'. Here the two versions closely parallel each other. In both, the surviving hunter is afraid to go back to the den of the Great Lizard, but the old people convince him to lead them there.

Line 87 *bókka ná:hotohok* 'they used the beating of drums'. The two versions here separate again. In *Sacowáyhki*'s version, the old people use medicine rattles against the Great Lizard, and in Miss John's version, they use drums. It would seem that the basic plot of the story only requires that some magical means be used against the Great Lizard; it does not define what kind of means, which are left to the imagination of the storyteller to elaborate.

Line 105 *cáklit íhbok* 'and they struck it many times with an ax and killed it'. Here, too, the variation between the two versions suggests that the plot merely requires the Great Lizard to be slain, and does not define the method of killing it.

Lines 106–23 This epilogue, which is completely absent from the first version, tells how the ashes of the Great Lizard were used as a war medicine. It can be assumed that one of the *hopá:yi* or prophets, who would have been the old people who conquered the Great Lizard, learned of this use for the ashes of the Great Lizard in a dream. In the war stories of Ellisor Battise in Chapter 8, war medicines are frequently used and are necessary for success in war.

## THE CLAWED WITCHES

narrated by Martha John

I recorded this narrative on tape in October, 1990. No Koasati version of this tale had ever been recorded previously, although I later found an English version by *Soyá* (Ellisol Batisse) from 1936 in the papers of Lyda Paz-Taylor (1936). The Koasati text has been slightly emended to remove false starts and slips of the tongue. The word *copoktaykí*, here rendered as 'Clawed Witch', cannot be translated into English. Furthermore, it cannot be interpreted in Koasati, although the element *-tayki* clearly is an old word meaning 'woman'. The interpretation 'Clawed Witch' is based on the physical similarity between the Koasati character and the Clawed Witch of the Tunica (Haas 1950:166–67).

There are twelve scenes in this narrative, a larger number than is common. Note that twelve is a multiple of four, the ritual number. As is typical, the narrative is divided into halves, with six scenes in each half. The scenes are arranged in pairs, with three pairs of scenes in each half. Scenes are paired according to semantic criteria, as opposed to linguistic ones. A linguistic analysis of this story has been published (Kimball 1993:473–88).

### Scene 1: Two Men Set Out to Hunt

| | |
|---|---|
| Copoktaykík ná:hok, copoktaykí: | As for the Clawed Witches, the Clawed Witches: |
| Ilanawíhlit ná:nihak tóklot aswáhcotohok, | There were two men going hunting, and they left their people at their |

halkifá atfáylok,
imí:safa má:lon fáylok,
aɬɬá:citohok.
Hopáhki stalpí:san aɬɬá:ci:fó:kok,
mafíhnat aɬɬá:ci:fó:k,
ilanawíhlik a:yá:citohok.
Ittahó:bat stanóslok,
aɬɬá:citohok,
ilanawíhlit a:yá:citohok í:bitoh.

Ná:hon, fi:tó íhbok,
stilá:ci:fó:kok,
stiláhcin,
stilá:cit a:yá:citoho:limpahcok.

wives' home,
they left them at their own houses,
and the two of them went off.
When the two had gone sufficiently far,
when the two went straight,
the two were going about hunting.
Having finished getting ready,
the two of them went off,
the two went about hunting and killing game
Now, having killed a turkey,
when they brought it,
having brought it,
it is said that the two were going about bringing it.

### Scene 2: They Find Their Wives at Camp

Halkí ná:so:t,
ná:hok, halkík oɬá:citohok,
"Sámmin ohacíntí?" káhhan.
"Inkòh. Komá:tok
poskánkahalpí:sáhcok
ómmin,
olintíhcok óm," ká:hatoho:limpáhcok
tayyí caffák.

And their wives were there,
now, their wives had arrived there,
"Why have you two come?" they said.
"For no reason. It seemed to be the case
that our husbands might be longing
for the taste of meat,
so we have just come," said one of the women, so it is reported.

### Scene 3: The Dogs See Them Eating Raw Meat

Tayyihák imáswan,
"Mó:li:p yón libáthól!" káhhan,
libátt i:tí:sit,
"Poskánka:yóllok halpí:s," ká:hat,
ná:hot, ná:hotik,
ókcan í:pahco:líhcok ómmin,
mán ifák hí:catoh.
Má:mo:sok,
hí:cat ahiccá:citoho:limpáhcok.

The two women stayed with them,
and they said, "Well, cook ye this!"
and they went and took it to cook,
"We are ones who always long for the taste of meat," they said,
now, they did it,
but it was the case that they were
eating it raw, and the dogs saw them.
Thereupon,
it is said that they saw and watched them.

### Scene 4: The Clawed Witches Eat the Meat

Má:mo:sin,
ahiccá:cin,

Thereupon,
they were watching them,

| | |
|---|---|
| "Bołótlįh!" hoká:p, | though the men had said, "Boil it then!" |
| mato:wí:sit í:pat, | they took it out of the water and ate it, |
| kámmin ahiccá:cin. | thus they were watching them. |
| Ná:hok, | Now, |
| "Casámmin," | "I can do it," [one dog said] |
| įfilánkak, | it sneaked off to the side, |
| ifák lómmit immánkatoho:limpak. | a dog hid and told it to them, so it is said. |

**Scene 5: The Dog's First Warning**

| | |
|---|---|
| Akkáhcon, | Thus, |
| "A:tókkok, | "She is not a human being, |
| cihalkókkóhcok, | she is not your wife, |
| á:ti akkáhcok," ká:toho:limpak. | she only looks human," it said, |
| | so it is reported. |
| Má:mo:sok, | Thereupon, |
| "Tánka:si:p, | "When it is fully dusk, |
| okí ittihaplilá:hi:cílkat, | we two will fight over the water, |
| ittalíswat, | and when we spill the water, |
| okí sófhili:fó:kon, | you are to go off to go draw water, |
| ohtokó:cá:hik stałcí:yaha:wan | and we will tell you something," |
| cimmą́hílkalahoh," | |
| ká:hatoho:lit. | it said. |

**Scene 6: The Dogs Act According to Plan**

| | |
|---|---|
| Má:mo:sin, | Thereupon, |
| ná:hon, í:san tánka:fó:kon | now, they were there when it was dusk |
| ná:hot, libátlit, | now, they cooked, |
| ná:hot"Poskánka:yolli móh," | now, "They long for the taste of meat," |
| ká:halpí:sa:mo:liskan, | having said that, |
| ká:hat áswatoho:limpáhcok. | it is said that the two were there saying it. |
| Mók nasókkot libátlit ínkat, | Also, as soon as they had cooked food and given it to them, |
| ifá:kok mán ittiháplit, | the dogs then fought, |
| ná:hon, okí sóffin, | and now, spilling the water, |
| ałí:yatoho:limpáhcok. | one went off, so it is said. |

**Scene 7: The Second Warning of the Dogs.**

| | |
|---|---|
| Má:mo:sok, | Thereupon, |
| immą́hkan, | it just told them, |
| "Akkáhcon ómmi:s. | "Thus it is. |

Naskánkok a:yá:ciscónk.

Hacihalkókkóhcok," káhhok.
Má:mo:sok,
"Isnáp, ittó:bok haccá:lilahǫ,
má:fa isnáp cokhalí:kat cokkó:lįh!"
ká:hatoho:limpáhcok.
Má:mo:sok, má:mok,
"Ittó tóspin ilatóhbok!
Ná:hotískalahok,
tamó:ka isnó:ci:fó:kon,
món isná:holahǫ," ká:hatohon.

It is the case that two evil
supernaturals are going about.
They are not your wives," it said.
Thereupon,
"As for you, where a hollow tree will stand,
over there, enter into it and then stay!"
he said, so it is reported.
Thereupon, then,
"Prepare decayed wood!
You will use it;
tonight, when you are sleeping,
again you will use it," it said.

### Scene 8: The Clawed Witches Slay the Disbeliever

Ná:son caffá:ka immánka:k
á:ton immánka:k,
yínkotoho:limpáhcok óm.

Yínkotohon,
mák í:bitoho:lit

íhbok
í:pat anóstoho:limpáhcok.

Whenever they told things to one of them,
when they told the man,
It is said that it was the case that he did
not believe them.
He did not believe them,
and one can be assured that they
killed him,
and having killed him,
it is said that they ate him up.

### Scene 9: The Other Man Escapes and Flees

Má:mo:sok,
caffá:kap na:sókkot naksáhkat,
ná:hok, í:páhco:lik akkón,
ittotospí,
ilbaksí hobaskíhco:liskat acáslitǫ.

Acáslok sánkon,
ná:hon, ilapíhlok swalí:kan,
tółkat acákkin,
walí:kan á:tok,
tółkat acákkin
wali:káhcotohok.

Oóōōōòò!
hopáhkin ó:ła:fó:kok,
"Yón ǫhílkásk," káhhan,
cokhalí:kat cokkó:lin,

Thereupon,
the one, as soon as they made noise,
then, as they were eating the other,
[he used] the rotten wood,
and because their nails were long,
they tried to impale him.
They tried to impale him, but they failed,
and then, he ran from them,
leading them,
they ran chasing him,
and the man ran,
and they ran chasing him,
and he was running.
Ooooooh!
When he had gone far,
they [the dogs] said "Let us be here!"
And he went in and stayed.

a:tacákki:kak,
akkó obá:li ó:łan,
imittiháplitoho:limpáhcok.

And ones who were following him,
arriving behind that one,
it is said that they [the dogs]
fought with them.

**Scene 10: The Dogs Fight the Clawed Witches and Defeat Them**

Imittihă:plin,
imittihă:plin,
imittihă:plin,
níhtat anó:ka:fó:k
akkók nakáłtoho:limpak,
naskánkok.
Má:mo:sin,
á:ton,
akkáp i:tį̨hóccá:hį̨
ná:sok íksotoho:limpáhcok;

híssi má:łok
cikkí:katoho:limpáhcok.

They really fought,
and they really fought,
and they really fought,
and when it was fully day,
those ones disappeared,
the evil supernatural beings.
Thereupon,
he was there,
that one came to shoot at them,
but it is said that there was nothing
there;
it is said that only
their hair lay in a heap.

**Scene 11: The Survivor Returns Home**

Má:mo:sin,
łóykatohon imistilká,
imalí:tafa ó:ła:fó:kap,
halkík áswatohon,
immánkatoho:limpak.

Thereupon,
he returned to their dwellings,
when he arrived at his house,
their two wives were there,
and he told them the tale.

**Scene 12: The Dogs' Last Request is Honored**

Mó:tohon,
ifák ónkak,
"O:łci:p, kosnók alíswan,
kónkat í:pą̨h!" ká:haton.
Mók áswan,
ínkat í:patohon,
balláskat hápkatoho:limpáhcok óm.

Má:mik,
á:ti má:łik iminnihtáhcotohǫ.

Tafhiyám!

Then,
the dogs had spoken.
"If you return, and we two are there,
feed us then!" they said.
Also the two of them were there,
and he fed them,
and it is the case that the two of them
laid down and died, so it is said.
Thus,
the man alone was saved.

Finis!

*Textual Commentary*:

Line 1 The *copoktaykí*, or Clawed Witch, is a being hitherto unknown in Koasati mythology and, in fact, cannot be found in any of the Southeastern Indian tales gathered and published by Swanton. However, a similar character does appear in Tunica mythology, the Clawed Witch, *tíniko*. The description of the Tunica character is as follows:

> *Hinyátihč, tíhčĭn, ʔóninahpókatɛ́nì. Hinyátihč, lɔ́tawanyátĭhč, tihkʔúčŭhč, ʔamáyisáhkŭn, sáhikatɛ́nì, téhpʔiraháyihtàn. Tíhkentírwašwulɛ́nì. Kánahkutápitĭhč, ʔuhkúnapálahkʔatánì.*
>
> She looks just like a person. When she stands to run, she throws her breasts to either side over her shoulders. Her claws are sharp. When she catches hold of something, she snares it by hooking it (in her claws). [Haas 1950:81]

The following is the Koasati description:

> *Copoktaykík ná:hot, ilbaksík hobaskíhco:limpáhcok. Á:ti yámmitik hísso:tok hobáskit ná:hot. Káhco mók ómmíhcotoho:limpak.*
>
> As for the Clawed Witch, it is said that her nails were long. She was like a human being, but she had long hair. Such indeed is it said that she was.

Other features about the Clawed Witch that can be ascertained from this narrative are that she can assume the appearance of any human woman she wishes, she eats raw meat, she can be thwarted by decayed wood, dogs are her chief enemy, and sunlight at dawn causes her to dissolve, leaving only her hair behind. Additional information about the *copoktaykí* given by Mrs. Iwana Bernard, Miss John's half-sister and foster child, links it to the Tunica *tíniko*. She informed me that the *copoktaykí* had long breasts that she threw over her shoulders as she ran. While she was running her breasts made the sound *ɬa ɬa ɬa ɬa* as they bounced up and down.

Lines 2 and passim This text is notable for the frequent appearance of dual verb forms. This is due to the fact that the narrative contains four pairs of characters: two hunters, two wives, two Clawed Witches, and two dogs (see also Kimball 1993b). Again, one can note the fact that the Koasati ritual number four appears in the structure of this tale.

Lines 3–4 *halkifá atfáylok, / imí:safa má:lon fáylok* 'and they left their people at their wives' home, / they left them at their own houses'. Here, part of the drama is set up by the explicit mention that the hunters left their wives at home. On short hunting trips, it used to be the custom that men traveled without their wives; on longer trips, women would accompany them.

Lines 16–20 The hunters are surprised to find their wives at camp when they return from a day's hunt, but are reassured by their explanations. However, the women are not even human, but rather Clawed Witches who have taken the form of the men's wives. This deception plays to the insecurity that Indians felt in the forest at night, where things are not as they seem and danger can appear when one feels himself to be the most secure. Although it is not explicitly stated, it is understood that the sun is low in the sky and its power is weak enough for the Clawed Witches to materialize.

Line 26 *ókcan i:páhco:líhcok ómmin* 'but it was the case that they were eating it raw'. The fact that the Clawed Witches are unable to restrain themselves from eating raw meat reveals them to be evil supernaturals. The eating of cooked meat is considered a uniquely human characteristic, while monsters of all kinds prefer to eat raw (especially human) flesh.

Lines 27–29 *mán ifák hí:catoh. / Má:mo:sok, / hí:cat ahiccá:citoho:limpáhcok* 'and the dogs saw them. / Thereupon, / it is said that they saw and watched them'. The hunters' dogs now appear as characters in the narrative; they are to try to save their owners from the Clawed Witches. The speaking dog that aids a human is a character found widely in the traditional literatures of the Southeast, among the Creek (Swanton 1929:23–26), Hitchiti (Swanton 1929:92–94), and Natchez (Swanton 1929:243–45). The dog was a very important part of the traditional economy. Dogs helped a hunter track game animals, watched and protected home sites, and disposed of garbage. Dogs were also believed to have power against evil supernaturals, as indicated in this tale and that of Eater-of-the-Living, above. They were given names and were generally well-treated, even to the present day, when Koasati dogs are often former pets abandoned in the woods by non-Indians.

Line 69 *Ittó tóspin ilatóhbok!* 'Prepare decayed wood!' Decayed wood was considered proof against evil magic of all sorts. Swanton (1928:635) records its use in curing a witch. The belief that decayed wood had such power may have arisen from the fact that, since it was used to kindle a new fire, it was a source of fresh light, which is inimical to evil supernaturals.

Lines 73–79 In the preceding lines, the dogs have acted as supernatural helpers; the old Indians felt that one ignored such helpers at one's peril. Here, one of the hunters does not believe the dogs and, in consequence, is slain and devoured by the Clawed Witches.

Lines 80–85 The other hunter uses the decayed wood and escapes the claws of the witches. It is not explicitly stated what he did with it, but it is likely that he threw it upon them, as its touch would have the effect of nullifying their powers.

Line 91 *Oóōōōòò!* 'Ooooooh!' This expressive interjection occurs when the tension in the narrative is at its height: the hunter is fleeing for his life from the Clawed Witches and it is not clear to the listener whether or not he will survive. The interjection therefore increases tension in the listener, so that the relief at his escape, when it comes, is all the greater.

Lines 92–94 *hopáhkin ó:ła:fó:kok, / "Yón o̧hílkásk," káhhan, / cokhalí:kat cokkó:lin* 'When he had gone far, / they [the dogs] said, "Let us be here!" / And he went in and stayed'. The dogs, which have not been mentioned recently, seem to have been running along with the hunter, or to have run ahead to the hollow tree to guide him to it safely.

Lines 98–107 The dogs hold the Clawed Witches at bay until the sun rises and the new light destroys the witches. A parallel occurs in the tale *Peregrine Falcon and Great Horned Owl*, and has been analyzed in a Jungian manner (Kimball 1989:45–74). A Jungian interpretation also seems appropriate here. The Clawed Witches can be interpreted as manifestations of the Shadow, the repressed evil and anarchic characteristics of one's personality. It is of importance that a person's Shadow is of the same sex as he or she is. Since the Clawed Witches are manifestations of a female Shadow, it is not a coincidence that this tale was so well remembered and told by a woman. The psychological power of the Shadow, which grows as it is ignored or avoided, can be broken if the Shadow is brought into consciousness. In this tale, as in *Peregrine Falcon*, daybreak destroys the power of the Shadow manifestations—the light of the sun can be interpreted as the light of consciousness. Thus, this tale could serve as a guide for a woman to acknowledge her own capacity for evil and gain power over it.

Lines 108–12 The surviving hunter returns home to find that his wife and the wife of his partner had never left.

Lines 113–21 The dogs, having made the request to be fed, are given food, after which they die. In the other Southeastern Indian literatures, dogs that have taken on the power of speech to help humans often request a last feeding and then die. This could be the result of the removal of the supernatural helper from the body of the animal it had taken over. It is only here, with the use of the dual verbs *áswan* 'dwell (dual)' and *balláskan* 'lie down (dual)', that it is made explicit that the dogs were two in number.

# 4

# Animal Stories

This category of Koasati narrative is a catch-all for stories that do not fit into the other categories of narrative. However, they are united by the fact that the principal characters are anthropomorphized animals, that is, animals with the power of speech and with human attitudes and emotions. Sometimes, as in Rabbit Stories, these animal-humans inhabit a mythological time before humans, as in *Wolf and Box Turtle Run a Race, Barred Owl and Mouse*, and *The Race of Hummingbird and Great Blue Heron*. In several of these stories, there is the explanation of a natural feature that is typical of origin tales, although such explanations in these tales always seem to be rather after-the-fact and not essential to the narrative. In other tales, these animal-humans coexist peacefully (or not) with true human beings.

In many of these stories, as in Rabbit stories, there is a focus on the overweening pride of a character and its punishment, whether it be the feigned fearlessness of Bear that is belied by Jay's trickery and shaming of him, or whether it be Barred Owl's egotism that is punished by a self-willed death. In other stories, such as *The Traveling Orphan* and *The Orphan and the Bear*, the lesson is that to trust in the advice of the supernatural animals is to receive a reward in the future. Finally, there are tales such as *The Contest of the Elf, Human, Panther, and Wildcat*, the sole purpose of which is to elicit laughter.

### A MAN SWITCHES LIVES WITH VULTURE
narrated by *Sacowáyhki*

This narrative was recorded in Koasati by John R. Swanton in 1930. It has never been published. In traditional narratives, Vulture is a being toward which there are greatly ambivalent feelings. In some narratives, Vulture is the doctor of the animal-humans, but, at other times, he is a false doctor, using his profession to prey on others. The association of vultures with death is a long-standing one in the Southeast and was even more enhanced in the late Mississippian period, when ossuary burials were common. As late as early contact times, the Vulture Men of the Choctaw and the *ʔo·š hecmank* 'taboo vultures' of the Chitimacha had the duty of stripping the flesh off the bones of the dead. Thus, this story—to a non-Indian strange, but innocuous—is to the Indian listener creepy and foreboding, so that the denouement, though shocking, is not unexpected. It is not at all clear to the modern reader why the man, if he merely wants to fly like a bird, should approach such a creature; it may well be that Vulture was considered to have magical powers that could make such an exchange possible.

A somewhat similar tale was recorded among the Cherokee (Mooney 1900:294). However, in the Cherokee narrative, the man profits by the switch in forms by finding more game to hunt, and the wife does not die after associating with the Vulture in human form.

### Scene 1: The Man Convinces Vulture to Switch Lives

Saykí á:ton ittina:łí:kak,
 á:tik ónkak,
"Abák alí:yak stankáhnomá:š,"
 ká:toho:limpatš.
Má:mok,
 á:tik ónkak,
"Komalí:ya ittimo:tamátlit,
 a:yá:cit ilhi:cáskš!" káhhan.
Saykík ónkak,
"Ehé!" káhhan,
 "Nihtá ontoccí:nan," ká:toho:limpatš.

Vulture and a man spoke together,
 and the man spoke.
"The way of life above might be better
 for me," he said, so it is reported.
Then,
 the man spoke.
"Let us try trading our ways of life and
 go about!" he said.
Vulture spoke,
 "Yes!" he said,
 "For eight days," he said, so it is reported.

### Scene 2: The Man Deceives His Wife

Má:min,
 á:ti halkík inna:hóhcon.
Máhmin,
 á:tik immánkak halkí,
"Hiná:p ilanawíhlit ałłalą́,"
 ká:hatoho:limpatš.
"Nihtá ostá:kan áklo:p,
 nihtá ontoccí:nan i:lalahǫ," ká:hat
  ałíytoho:limpatš.

Then,
 the man had a wife.
Right then,
 the man told his wife,
"Now I intend to go hunting," he said,
 so it is reported.
 "If I do not come back in four days,
  I will return in eight days," he said,
   and went off, so it is said.

### Scene 3: The Man Trades Lives with Vulture

Má:min,
 saykí afánkat.
Má:mo:sin,
 á:tik abá áłłan,
  saykík á:ti ná:ni halkifá ółtoho: limpatš.

Then,
 he met Vulture.
Thereupon,
 the man went up,
  and Vulture returned, it is said, to the
  man's wife's house.

### Scene 4: The Vulture-Man Slays His Wife

Má:miyon,
tayyihák sobáykotoho:limpatš,
saykók ómmin.
Mántik,
tayyík ónkak,
“Naksámmin óʔmí saykí:kok
cibosóhka:š?” ká:toho:limpatš.
Má:min,
ná:nik ónkak,
“Ná:sok sánko:š,” ká:toho:limpatš.
Má:min,
inná:nik ɬóykat í:latik nihtá tóklo:sin,
halkík íllitoho:limpatš.
Saykí á:tik apoɬó:kan ommitoho:limpatš,
íllik.

But then,
the woman did not know it, so they say,
that he was Vulture.
But,
the woman spoke.
“Why is it that you stink like a vulture?”
she said, so it is reported.
Then,
the man spoke.
“It’s nothing,” he said, so they say.
Then,
even though her husband returned after only two days,
it is said his wife had died.
It is said that since the Vulture-Man had sexual intercourse with her, she died.

*Textual commentary*:

Lines 6–7 *“Komalí:ya ittimo:tamátlit, / a:yá:cit ilhi:cáskš!” káhhan* ‘“Let us try trading our ways of life and go about!” he said.’ The Koasati concept of *alí:ya* ‘one’s basic thoughts, feelings, and nature’, is here brought into play. The *alí:ya* is that part of a person’s personality that is basically unknowable to others. When a Koasati person is asked what part of the personality is knowable, he or she answers the *alí:ta*, or a person’s observable words and actions. Here, the man thinks that he can change basic natures with Vulture. As is shown by the end of the tale, however, each maintains in his new form the essence of his original form.

Lines 11–18 The man, after making a primary error in wanting to change his being, makes another error in not being truthful to his wife, who probably would have been horrified by her husband’s decision. In not telling her, he makes it possible for her to be doomed by carnal association with the transformed Vulture.

Lines 23–35 The man apparently had no idea that the Vulture would return to the man’s home and pretend to be him. His wife must suspect something, since she asks her apparent husband why he smells like a vulture, but the disguised Vulture reassures her, and within two days he has caused her to die by having sexual intercourse with her. If, as is likely, the Koasati anciently practiced ossuary burial with the preliminary defleshing of the corpse, they also must have had Vulture Men and Women, like the Choctaw and Chitimacha. Since even now association with death is considered defiling (note the disease *onalfapó* ‘suffering from the contagion of death’ incurred by digging in a cemetery), in aboriginal times it must have been the same, and there were probably taboos on marital and sexual relationships between Vulture Men and other persons. The violation of the taboo, as suggested by this narrative, would have been death by contagion for the other party. Even recently, the dead were not to be handled by close family members; Bel Abbey made specific provision before his death that his coffin was to be carried by non-Indian friends, to prevent unwitting violation of this taboo by his younger relatives.

## THE ORPHAN AND THE BEAR
narrated by *Sacowáyhki*

This narrative was recorded by John R. Swanton in 1910 and given the number five in his manuscript "Koasati Texts, Second Series." He published a translation based on the interlinear glosses in Swanton (1929:191–92).

The Orphan is a stock character in Koasati oral literature. Almost universally male, he is unrestricted by kinship ties and is therfore envied for the ability to do what he wants. At the same time, he is also pitied, since he lacks the security of clan and family ties that other people take for granted. The Orphan as a woman occurs only once in Koasati oral literature, as a secondary character in *The Traveling Orphan* (see below).

### Scene 1: The Orphan Is Taken Hunting

| | |
|---|---|
| Athómmak ilanawihlíhcok | It is said that some Indians were going |
| amá:katoho:limpatš hahcí cobá tałón. | hunting on the other side of a great river. |
| Máhmin, | Then, |
| á:ti loká:casik a:tá:sat | an orphan joined with the people |
| á:yatoho:limpatš. | and went about, so it is said. |
| Stibákłoscok, | He was extremely poor, |
| tikboltá ahhí:cok, | and he watched the campfire, |
| mó:tohon, ołá:cok, | and then, on their arrival there, |
| tikboltí ayókcok, | they built a campfire, and they went |
| ohtí:sato:š. | and dwelt there. |
| Tamóhkan, | Night fell, |
| mó:tohok, | and then later, |
| innihtá niłá:li matí:bik amá:kato:š. | in the morning of the next day, they went off to hunt. |
| Ittįfilkóhkat, | They separated from each other, |
| máhmin, | and then, |
| loká:casik á:tato:s má:lon. | the orphan remained alone. |
| Mó:tohon, | Then later, |
| caffá:kat icǫ ilabaná:lit | one of them brought a deer, carrying it |
| stí:latoho:limpatš. | on his shoulder, so it is said. |

Má:mok,
sóplit anó:lok, nipǫ́ tóslit imi:sáhcok,
loká:casikok abóslá:hin tóhnok,
mán ɬóykato:s matí:bá:hik.

Then,
he finished skinning it,
and having cut up the meat for them,
he had the orphan roast it, and again
returned to the hunt.

Máhmin,
loká:casik nipǫ́ abóslik
stittaá:tatoho:limpatš.
Mó:tohon,
pontokkó:lin,
óhyak athómmak ilá:cit anóhkok,
má:mo:sin,
nipók libátkatohon,
i:tohómpat fayáhlok,
máhmin,
mán ɬoyóhkato:š atwíhlik.

Then,
the orphan remained around the fire
roasting the meat.
Then later,
when it was noon,
all the Indians having come,
and then,
the meat was cooked,
they came and finished dining,
then,
again the hunters returned
to the hunt.

## Scene 2: The Orphan Goes on His Own

Má:fó:kon
loká:casik anɬiyá bànnat
bánnatoho:limpatš.
Mántik,
bihí acǫ́:bon ohínkatohon,
stá:yatoho:limpatš.
Mó:tohok,
óhyak wasátka:fó:kon,
bihí acó:ba:kon matíhsok,
ilabanáhlok,
aɬí:yatoho:limpatš.
Mó:tohok,
haso:tammí pilahón aɬí:yato:š.

Afterwards,
the orphan really wanted to go,
it is said.
Therefore,
they gave him an extremely old gun,
and it is said that he took it with him.
Then later,
when they all had gone off,
picking up that old gun,
and carrying it on his shoulder,
he went off, so it is said.
Then,
he went towards the west.

## Scene 3: The Orphan Encounters the Bear

Mó:tohon,
á:yatohon,
niták lónkon cokko:tohon,
mayó:ban hí:catoho:limpatš.
Máhmok,
bihí tafilámmik,
hóccá:hik sbiɬí:toho:limpatš.

Then afterwards,
he went about,
and it is said that he saw by good fortune
a bear that was sitting in hiding.
Then,
he took the gun off his shoulder,
and aimed it at him to shoot him,
it is said.

| | |
|---|---|
| Má:miyon, | But contrary to expectation, |
| niták ónkak, | the bear spoke. |
| “Mánko:š! Cahociccá:š!” | “No! Do not shoot me!” |
| ká:toho:limpatš. | he said, so they say. |
| Káhhok, | Having said that, |
| loká:casi:kon impáhkato:š. | he called to the orphan. |
| “Ontok cokkó:š!” ká:to:š. | “Come and sit!” he said. |
| Máhmin, | Then, |
| ohtcokkó:to:š. | he went and sat. |
| Máhmin, | Then, |
| inna:ɬí:katoho:limpatš. | the bear spoke to him, it is said. |
| Máhmok, | Then, |
| í:sito:š. | the bear took him with him. |
| Máhmin, | Then, |
| cikkį́:kato:š. | the two kept on dwelling together. |

## Scene 4: The Orphan Accompanies the Bear

| | |
|---|---|
| Ma:fó:kap, | Then at that time, |
| athómma:kok loká:casi howíhto:š. | the Indians were looking for the orphan. |
| Nakáɬɬak íklon, | He had disappeared and did not return, |
| howíhlit ohikhí:coto:š. | they looked for him and did not find him. |
| Mó:tohon, | Then, |
| cikkį́:kan ihóhcato:š. | the two kept on dwelling together for a long time. |
| Mó:tohon, | Then, |
| niták ilasá:cit stá:yatoho:limpatš. | the bear went about with him, leading him along, so it is said. |
| Máhmik, | Then, |
| niták ónkak, | the bear spoke. |
| “Cimaka:nóˀsí?” ká:toho:limpatš. | “Are you hungry?” he said, so they say. |
| Máhmin, | Then, |
| loká:casik ónkak, | the orphan spoke. |
| “Amaká:no:š,” ká:toho:limpatš. | “I am hungry,” he said, so they say. |
| Máhmin, | Then, |
| niták nokbaɬkafá matwíhlik, | the bear searched in his armpit, |
| biɬkón matpíhlit ínkan | took out persimmons, and gave him them, |
| í:patoho:limpatš. | and he ate them, so it is said. |
| “Biɬkó libátka alí:laso:š.” | “The persimmons are ripe and good.” |
| Akkámmin, a:yá:cito:š. | In this way the two of them went about. |

### Scene 5: The Orphan and Bear Fight Together

Mó:tohon,
nithák ónkak,
"A:ti ná:ni ammaya:cíhcok akofánka:š
hina:p," káhhok.
"Coyyí impisí ká:nosci ísi:š!"
ká:toho:limpatš.
Máhmin,
loká:casi:kok coyyí impisí ká:noscon
í:sin,
a:yá:citoho:limpatš.
Mó:tohon,
á:ti:kap óntit á:yatoho:limpats afánkat.

Máhmin,
niták ónkak,
"Tá! Hiná:p! A:ti:kok óntit á:yš.
Hiná:p scabakóhlin,
batápli:š!" ká:toho:limpatš.
"Mantik,
himáɬɬifíhnat batapcínna:š!
'Mó:š,' ká:li:p, fáyli:š!"
ká:toho:limpatš.
Mó:tohon,
afánkak,
pa:cofótto:š.
Máhmin,
sta:yá:co:sin,
nitá:kok támmitoho:limpatš.
Má:mo:sin,
loká:casi:kok ittó:kon í:sit maswalí:kak
sbakkí yá:lon bóklitoho:limpatš.
Máhmin,
ma:kok kostínkok,
mattámmin,
atóklon batáplá:hiyon,

nitá:kok ónkak,
"Bókcifíhna:š!" káhhan,
fáytoho:limpatš.

Then afterwards,
the bear spoke.
"A male human stronger than me is
meeting us," he said.
"Take then a good pine knot!"
he said, so they say.
Then,
the orphan having taken a good
pine knot,
the two went about, it is said.
Then afterwards,
that human was coming, moving
toward them.
At that,
the bear spoke,
"Well! Lo! That human is coming.
Now, when he throws me down,
hit him then!" he said, so they say.
"But,
do not then strike him too hard!
When I say 'Enough!' quit then!"
he said, so it is reported.
Then afterwards,
he met them,
and he attacked him from ambush.
Then,
they struggled for a long time,
and the bear fell, it is said.
Thereupon,
the orphan took the wood and ran with it
and struck him on the head, it is said.
Then,
that one was insensible,
and fell down,
and he was about to strike him a
second time,
and the bear spoke,
"Do not beat him too much!" he said,
and he quit, so they say.

### Scene 6: The Bear Fortells His End and the Orphan's Good Fortune

| | |
|---|---|
| Má:mo:sin, | Thereupon, |
| aɬɬá:citoho:limpatš. | the two went off, it is said. |
| Aɬɬá:ci:k, | The two went off, |
| ɬoyóhkat | and they returned |
| incokkó:kafa oɬá:citoho:limpatš. | and arrived at his dwelling place. |
| Máhmok, | Then, |
| niták immánkak á:ti loká:casi, | the bear told things to the orphan. |
| "Hiná:p cifáylilá:š. | "I will leave you now. |
| Naswíhlok hocahí:cá:š. | Hunters will find me. |
| Hiná:p hoca:bá:š. | They will kill me now. |
| Hina:p," ká:hato:s niták. | Lo!" said the bear. |
| Máhmok, | Then, |
| á:ti loká:casi:kon inna:ɬí:kak, | he spoke to the orphan. |
| "Hocá:bi:k, hoci:sá:š. | "When they kill me, they will take you. |
| Mántik aca:nipǫ ispánna:š!" ká:hato:š. | But do not then eat my flesh!" he said. |
| A:tihak ónkak, | "The people will speak, |
| 'Ipš' hoká:tik, caispánna:š! | 'Eat it!' they will say, but do not eat of me! |
| Máhmok, | Then, |
| hocá:bi:k, | when they kill me, |
| ampátka ittohíssi hocáktohok, | my slaughtering bed of fresh leaves, |
| ohampátkok hofayáhlin, | having made it for me, they will leave it, |
| máhmok, | then, |
| ohamá:ka:fó:kon, | when they have gone, |
| ɬóykat íslok, | you are to come back, |
| ittohíssi:kon ittanáhlit cikkí:cok, | you are to carefully gather the leaves together, |
| onóhtok, | set them on fire, |
| ɬóyka:š!" ká:hato:š. | and return later!" he said. |
| "Mó:tohok, | "Then afterwards, |
| nihtá stonostá:ka:fó:kon, | on the fourth day, |
| ithíca:š! | come and look! |
| Máhmin, | Then, |
| kosibá olfáhcok walǫhloscok haccá:lin | when you see a tender pokeweed sprout standing there, |
| ishí:ca:k, | you are to cut it, |
| koyófcok, ittapaɬátlit híca:š! | and splitting it in two, look then! |
| Máhmin, | Then, |
| hayó ná:sok áɬkalaho:š. | there will be something inside. |
| Máhmin, | Then, |
| píhcilaho:š. | you are to take it. |

| | |
|---|---|
| Máhmin,<br>ná:son ascí:lok ísbilaho:š. | Then,<br>whatever you desire you will kill in hunting. |
| Caisbín á:lo:š!" ká:toho:limpatš. | But think not to kill [one like] me!"<br>he said, so it is reported. |
| Mántik,<br>loká:casik imacį́hbatoho:limpatš. | However,<br>the orphan was very sad, so they say. |

*Textual emendations*:

The following emendations of the Koasati text as written by Swanton have been made:

| | | |
|---|---|---|
| Line 19 | abosla´ ha´$^{n}$ tō´hạnok | abóslá:hin tohnok |
| Line 37 | hoạsa´ tgafō̃´gon | wasátka:fó:kon |
| Line 39 | ī´lạbanahạlo | ilabanáhlok |
| Line 45 | nita´$^{3}$ | niták |
| Line 50 | ma´ mī´yạ | má:miyon |
| Line 55 | o´ntotcok´ōskat´s | óntok cokkó:š, ká:to:š |
| Line 64 | af´ōgạp | ma:fó:kap |
| Line 67 | howē̃´mit | howíhlit |
| Line 90 | inipi´ si$^{3}$ | impisí |
| Line 114 | bạtạple´yun | batáplá:hiyon |
| Line 122 | ła´ djitohōlimpats | ołá:citoho:limpatš |
| Line 143 | ona´xtok | onóhtok |

*Textual commentary*:

Lines 1–29 The first scene introduces the orphan as a person who just joined up with the hunters of the tale. He would very much like to be a hunter like the other men, but he lacks the economic capacity, being an orphan, to obtain a gun or ammunition. The other hunters test him by having him take care of the camp and the cooking while they are out hunting, and because of his care, in the next scene they give him a gun and agree to let him try to hunt.

Line 34 *bihí acǫ́:bon ohínkatohon* 'they gave him an extremely old gun'. Unlike the hunters in *Bear Medicine* (chapter 5), these hunters use guns, not bows and arrows. By this, the listener can understand that the actions of this narrative took place within the last couple of centuries and not in the time before European contact.

Line 46 *mayó:ban hí:catoho:limpatš* 'he saw [it] by good fortune'. The meaning covered by *mayó:ban* 'to have good fortune; to occur by good fortune', is a difficult concept to define precisely. It is a more general concept than *na:silbá* 'good luck in hunting' and indicates that the one who receives the good fortune did nothing that would result in the luck. Koasati speakers relate *mayó:ban* to the verb *mámmin* 'to happen by chance', in which the happening is not necessarily good or bad.

Lines 50–61 By speaking, the bear has revealed itself as a supernatural helper. The orphan, by listening to it now and obeying it in the future, will ensure that something good will happen to him.

Lines 64–67 Contrary to the notion that the Orphan is unimportant to others, articulated clearly by the Orphan in the first version of *The First Meeting of the Indians and the Europeans* (see chapter 7), the hunters with whom he had been staying look for him after he has disappeared. The same concern for the Orphan as a human being is expressed by the leader of the Indians in the same version of *The First Meeting of the Indians and the Europeans*.

Lines 85–117 Here the Orphan follows the instructions and commands of the bear to the letter, and thus he shows that he is worthy of receiving a supernatural gift.

Lines 118–61 In this, the final scene, the bear foretells his death and tells the Orphan how to obtain a charm to give himself good luck in hunting after the bear is gone. Since the Orphan has obeyed the bear exactly in the past, there is no likelihood that he will disobey the various taboos the bear lays on him to obtain the good-luck charm.

Line 154 *hayó ná:sok áɬkalaho:š* 'there will be something inside'. What exactly the charm that the Orphan is to find inside the pokeweed shoot is left to the imagination. Swanton (1929:148) mentions the Alabama *sapiya* as being a magic stone found inside a magic plant, and that is likely what this is. A version of *Peregrine Falcon and Great Horned Owl* that I recorded in 1992 and included in this chapter also contains a section telling about the origin of a hunting charm.

Line 161 *loká:casik imacį́hbatoho:limpatš* 'the orphan was very sad, so they say'. This final action of the Orphan, pity for the supernatural bear, clearly states to the listener that the Orphan will receive the hunting charm. In Koasati oral literature, and probably in their aboriginal culture, pity for supernatural beings made those beings willing to give their pitiers special gifts. This contrasts with the adjoining Algonquian cultures to the north, in which the pity of supernaturals for humans was solicited, rather than the other way around.

## THE BEAR-KIDNAPPED CHILD
narrated by Martha John

This narrative, recorded on tape in 1992, has not previously been recorded among the Koasati. The only mythological tradition that shows any similarity to it is found among the Cherokee (Mooney 1900:327–29). Bears, being the largest and most ferocious game animals that the Koasati hunted, were thought to have greater than normal powers, and their behavior towards their cubs and their ability to walk on their hind legs made them appear to be almost human.

This is the only tale so far recorded among the Koasati in which the bear is not the hero. This is certainly very different from the character in *The Orphan and the Bear*, or the more naturalistic *Bear Medicine*. In this tale the bear is not evil, per se, it just wants a human child to raise. This is another example of the dangers that the old Indians felt existed in the world—not only were there monsters that desired to eat human flesh, but there were also beings who wanted to take people out of human society and change them into themselves.

### Scene 1: The Parents Decide to Go Visiting

| | |
|---|---|
| Ná:hok, | Well, |
| tayyihók ná:nok stóklok áswatohok, | There were a woman and a man living together, |
| ocó:sik caffá:kan á:sat píłkáhcotohok. | and they took care of an infant child. |
| Ná:ho, | Well, |
| imbiní:la:hik tałabankak o:łopóhlit | they intended to go visit someone, crossing over the water; |
| tałabankáhco:liskan | they used to cross over. |
| má:fa ittó apatahá, | There by a [standing] tree, |
| ittó tałabankacík ná:ho:fó:kon, | there was a tree to cross over; |
| ittó haccá:tohon, | a tree stood there; |
| má:fa łopóhlíhcotohok, | there they used to cross; |
| o:łopóhlit ittałabanápkok, | they forded, and having crossed, |
| haccá:lin. | one stood there. |

### Scene 2: The Child is Kidnapped

| | |
|---|---|
| "Á:to:si matínkalíhcómm ," á:lok, | "I ought to give the child to someone," one thought, |
| matínkat ómmá:tok, | and after the one gave it to someone, |
| nitón matínkáhcómmitohon, | It was a bear to whom one had given it; |
| niták á:to:si íhsok, | the bear, having taken the child, |
| snakáłłan á:sat, | went off with it in its arms, |
| stóntit stá:yáhcómm. | took it and carried it, so it seems. |
| Mó:tohon | Then, |
| ołá:cito, | they arrived there; |
| ołá:citikap, | when they arrived there, |
| á:tosik íkson. | the child was not there; |
| ittá:sak ółáhcok, | having arrived together, |
| "Naksámmin óʔmí á:to:sik komíksok," | "Why do we not have the child?" |
| á:lot ómmá:ton, | they thought, and afterwards, |
| "Niták stinnakáłłáhcotohon." | "A bear disappeared with it." |

### Scene 3: The Child is Sought After

| | |
|---|---|
| Ná:h, | Well, |
| ifá hokáhno wihlí:cit, | they looked for it with two of the best dogs; |
| akkámmit amá:kat, | so they went; |
| stamá:kat sobayá:lt . | they took them so they might know. |
| Ittó:bifon píłkat, | It [the Bear] had put it into a hollow tree; |
| á:to:sik có:bat anó:kat, | the child was growing larger; |
| ná:hok, | well, |
| á:to:sik łimihkóhcotoho:liyok, | the child had been smooth-skinned, |
| óhyak wohóksit anó:kat | but contrary to expectation it was all furry; |
| nashollo:si yámmit wohóksit anó:kat, | like a dangerous wild animal it was all furry; |
| na:łihilkó:ton sobáykot, | it did not know how to speak, |
| kámmin píłkan. | and so it [the Bear] kept it. |
| Niták ínkat í:pak | The bear fed it |
| lókba caffá:kóhya yámmifa | for a whole year in such a place; |
| ná:so:t matwíhlit | it [the bear] went and looked for things, |
| biłkó:t | such as persimmons, |
| ná:son bànnak onàm | whatever it still wanted, |
| ŏ:hyat, | each and every thing. |
| Ná:ho, | Well, |
| lókbat caffá:kóhya wíhlit | for one whole year, it looked for things; |
| ínkat í:pat | fed it [the child], |
| píłkáhcotohon. | and used to keep it. |

### Scene 4: The Bear is Killed, but the Child is Changed

| | |
|---|---|
| Má:fa ołáhcok, | There they all arrived, |
| nitá:kok ómmi:k, | and as for the bear, |
| ifák hí:cat stimbayátlibá:no | the dogs saw it after having gone in a straight line for it, |
| wíhlib ::notohok. | after really looking for it; |
| Ittó:bi co:báhcok haccá:tohon, | a large hollow tree stood there; |
| món ó:łaston, | also just arriving there, |
| ifák hí:can, | the dogs saw it, |
| á:to:si mók cokkó:litik, | and the child also sat there, |
| niták ittiháplik, | but the bear fought; |
| imittiháplik, | it fought with them; |
| ifá imí:bit kántikap, | it killed their dogs, |

| | |
|---|---|
| nitá mók ohí:bok, | however, they also killed the bear, |
| a:to:si mók ohístik, | and as for the child, they took it, but |
| małatlíīīīīīīį̀! | it was wiiiiiild! |
| Kámmik wohóksit, | In such a way it was furry, |
| nitá wohóksi yámmit | it had become as furry as a bear, |
| anáhkáhcotoho:limpáhcok. | so it is said. |

**Epilogue:**

| | |
|---|---|
| Món mán, | Also, |
| akkó yámmi, | like that, |
| nitáp a:tinkoybóhlimpáhcok atlawísta, | bears used to steal children, so it is said, |
| hokáhco:lik. | so they used to say. |
| | |
| Tafhiyám! | Finis! |

*Textual Comments:*

Line 3 *á:sat piłkáhcok* 'they took care of an infant child'. The verb *á:san* literally means 'to carry in the arms' and here indicates that the child is an infant who cannot yet walk or talk.

Lines 5–13 One is to understand that the parents are going to visit someone across a river or creek; *ittó talabanka:cí* is another way of saying *fílbacá* or 'log bridge,' that is a tree laid across a stream from bank to bank.

Line 14 *"Á:to:si matínkalíhcómm," á:lok* '"I ought to give the child to someone," one thought'. It is tacitly understood that there are a group of people standing by the log bridge. The parent gives the child to someone to hold while she/he crosses over, as she/he might lose her/his balance trying to cross with the child.

Line 16 *nitón matínkáhcómmitohon* 'it was a bear to whom one had given it'. The bear is understood as having transformed itself into human form and is standing with the other people by the log bridge. The parent gives the child to the bear-as-human, and only after the parent has crossed and gone does the bear revert to its true form and run off with the child.

Line 26 This line is spoken by someone who saw the bear take the child when the parents return.

Line 28 *ifá hokáhno wihlí:cit* 'they looked for it with two of the best dogs'. The prefix *ho-* when used with active verbs usually indicates a distributive or plural third person subject. However, with stative verbs, such as adjectival verbs, *ho-* frequently indicates a dual subject.

Lines 34–35 Because the bear is taking care of the child and feeding it bear food, the child becomes furry like a bear. This is the same thing that happens to the hunters in the Cherokee story.

Line 40 *lókba caffá:kóhya* 'for a whole year'. The word *lókba*, literally 'the warm time' is a old-fashioned way of saying *ohayyí* 'summer.' Like *ohayyí*, *lókba* can also mean 'year', and it is fairly certain that the bear keeps the child for a year.

Line 42 *biɬkó:t* 'such as persimmons'. It is interesting that persimmons are mentioned as a typical bear food, as the orphan in the tale *The Orphan and the Bear* (in this chapter) is given persimmons to eat by that bear.

Line 59 *ifá imí:bit* 'it killed their dogs'. One might expect *imifá í:bit*, but in Koasati the focus is not on the possession but the possessor. Thus the dative prefix *im-* is attached to the verb, and the possessive prefix is dropped. This then could be translated literally as 'it killed the dogs on them' with the dative prefix expressing a malefactive.

Line 62 *maɬatlíīīīīīį̄̀!* 'but it was wiiiiiiild!'. This is a rare example of rhetorical lengthening applied to the aorist form of a verb. Its use suggests that the child never afterwards ceased to be wild.

## THE TRAVELING ORPHAN

narrated by Selin Williams

This narrative was recorded by John R. Swanton in 1910 from Selin Williams, and given the number twenty-one in his manuscript "Koasati Texts, Second Series." He published a translation of this narrative based on the interlinear glosses in Swanton (1929:175–77), in which he titled it *The Story of an Orphan*.

There is an unusual secondary character in this narrative, a female orphan. The reason that the character of Orphan is not often a woman is that a woman, by being able to bear children, can create the web of family and clan from out of herself, which a man cannot. In this narrative, the female orphan had begun to create family ties, but was frustrated by her disastrous choice of a marriage partner.

Much of this narrative in structure and content bears a very strong resemblance to the thunder myth of the Tunica (Haas 1950:24–59), which in turn is greatly similar to the Biloxi story of Ṭuhe, the Thunder Being (Dorsey and Swanton 1912:85–106). However, the underlying premise has been completely reshaped to fit Koasati cultural ideas. It is no longer an origin myth for Thunder, one of the principal Tunica deities (an evil supernatural to the Koasati), but a story illustrating how to get supernatural aid, and exploring the nature of a person in society. The intimate contact between Koasati and Tunica traditional narrative is reflected by shared characters, such as Iron Woman (*oconá tayyí*), who is like the Stone Witch (*tíšlina*) of the Tunica, and the Clawed Witches (Koasati *copoktaykí*, Tunica *tínikówi*). The Koasati recall visits by the Tunica to their village in the first half of the twentieth century, and there seems to have been a great deal of contact earlier. The Biloxi were also known to the Koasati, and intimate contact is suggested by the presence of Biloxi loanwords in Koasati, so it is possible that this story was adapted directly from the Biloxi original.

### Scene 1: The Orphan Is Abandoned Overseas

Á:ti loká:casok á:yatohon,
á:tik mí:tok ónkak,
"Okicobá tałón amá:hílkáskš!"
káhhok,
loká:casi:kon ilasá:cik,
stamá:kato:š.
Stamá:ka:k,
tałón stołáhcok,
ohfáyhlok,
yomáhlit ittimmánkatohok,
fáylit piłán ohtáłkok,
sto:wamá:kato:š fáylit.
Má:min,
loká:casi:kok ónkak,
"Himá:ko:š! Cį́!
hacihókfalin," ká:ha:sin,
fáylit sto:wamá:katoho:limpatš.

There was an orphaned man going about,
and other people spoke:
"Let us go to the other side of the ocean!"
they said,
and they took the orphan along,
and they went.
When they went,
when they arrived to the other side,
they went and left him;
they went about speaking to each other,
and they left him, got into a boat,
and sailed off and left him.
Then,
the orphan spoke;
"Wait a minute! This way!
I am to go with you," he merely said,
but they left him and sailed away,
so it is said.

### Scene 2: The Orphan Is Counseled by Red-Bellied Woodpecker

Máhmin,
loká:casi:kok sammá:hik sobáykot,
hahcín apotó:kat á:yatoho:limpatš.

Then,
the orphan did not know what to do,
and it is said that he went about along a river.

Á:yan,
á:yan,
mó:tohon,
tososohkasók ó:lat slappáhlin,

He went along,
and he went along,
and then,
a red-bellied woodpecker, calling,
landed on his chest.

"Hí:yì! Isná:łš!
Í:bit acipí:lillahó:š," káhhan.
"Manko:š!
Ná:son cimmánkallahok ónkali:š,"
káhhan.
"Mó:li:p, ammánkš!" káhhan,
tososohkasí:kok okłihómmon
isbakhamóhtoho:limpatš.

"Hey! You!
I will kill you and dispose of you," he said.
"By no means!
I mean to tell you something,"
it said.
"Well, tell me!" he said,
and the red-bellied woodpecker
rubbed red clay on his head.

| | |
|---|---|
| Máhmok, | Then, |
| ónkak, | he spoke: |
| "Ná:si cobáhcok ciłohlá:š," | "Something large will pursue you," |
| ká:toho:limpatš. | it said, so they say. |
| Káhhok, | Having said that, |
| "Máhmin, | "Then, |
| łakón hasáykan ná:ho:š," ká:to:š. | make then many arrows," it said. |
| Má:mok, | Then, |
| "Á:yatohon, | "It goes about, |
| hasapolóhkon ostá:kan náhhok, | and it has four chunkey stones; |
| ací:yatohok, | when you are about, |
| ittó conokbí ospa:cokkó:citohon, | you are to have gone and sat in a bent tree, |
| ná:si cobák, a:ti:pacobá:kok, ifá hocobáhcon ilapíhli:š." | for the great one, Great-One-Who-Eats-Human-Beings, leads large dogs. |

**Scene 3: The Orphan Encounters Great-One-Who-Eats-Human-Beings**

| | |
|---|---|
| Stółtoho:limpatš. | It is said he arrived there with them. |
| Má:min, | Then, |
| á:ti:kok abá pa:cokkó:to:š. | the man sat in a branch above. |
| Má:min, | Then, |
| hasapolóhki matimo:wapí:lik, | he hurled the chunkey stones in the water after him, |
| kammí:ci:k, | and when he did so, |
| stonostá:ka:fó:k, | when it was the fourth time, |
| ifák amá:híkkot, | the dogs did not move, |
| má:lon o:lokkó:lin, | they just stood in the water, |
| a:ti:pacobá:kok noksíhpok, | and Great-One-Who-Eats-Human-Beings grew angry, |
| ifá hocobá ostá:katohon, | and the four large dogs there, |
| óhya íhbok, | he killed them all, |
| má:mi:k, | and then, |
| aykacosí iskónnascon ilihókfot | he carried a narrow crock on himself, |
| stá:yatohon, | and he took it out, |
| matíhsok, | and he really tapped on it with his knuckles, |
| kǫ́fkan, | and it became quite large, |
| có:bat cobáhcok anáhkan, | and he only lit a fire there |
| má:lon okí apatahá ó:tit náhhok, | by the water, |
| okį́ stittapíłkok, | and he put water on the fire, |

má:mo:sin,
ifahá:kon o:wáłłit hó:łit libátlok,
i:pat óhyan anóhlok,
cofkoní óhyan okifá mato:cikkíhlin,
acán ohhaccáhlok,
ifán hocí:fot impáhkan,
mí:tok ilitáhlit achalí:kat,
kámmik,
óhyak ostá:kak stanóhkan,
impáhkok,
stáłłat nakáłtoho:limpatš.

thereupon,
he put the dogs in the water and boiled
them and having cooked them,
and having eaten and finished them,
he put all the bones out in the water,
and he went and stood out of it,
and naming the dogs, he called them,
and another, shaking itself,
came out,
and so,
having finished with all four,
he called them
and taking them, disappeared,
so it is said.

**Scene 4: The Orphan Rides the Sea Monster back over the Ocean**

Má:min,
á:tik loká:casi:kok tanátlok,
łakí fíhnon ná:hot hasáyhkan,
anóhlok áytoho:limpatš.
Á:yat fó:si hóccat í:bit,
hasaykáhcon íhbok,
abóslit anóhlok,
stałí:yak hahcifá,
pá:nan oshaccáhlok,
"Amawó!" ká:ha:fó:kon,
sattó:t,
albató:t,
sattacó:bo:t,
i:tokpaká:lin,
"Isnókko:š," káhhan,
óhyak stanó:ka:fó:kon,
cintosakcók
i:tokpaká:toho:limpatš.
Máhmin,
"Isnó:š," káhhan,
má:mo:sin,
oktacosóhkat o:ballá:kan,
lapík okcakkóhcon,
intałá hommáhcon,
hoká:not hoka:nóhcon.

Then,
the orphan descended,
and having made many true arrows,
he went about using them, it is said.
He went about, and shot and killed birds,
having killed many,
he completely roasted them,
and took them to the river,
and went and stood on the bank,
and when he said, "O my
grandfather!"
turtles,
and alligators,
and snapping turtles, and
suchlike, came and floated,
and he said, "It is not you,"
and when they were all finished,
the sea monster came
and floated, so it is said.
And then,
"It is you," he said.
Thereupon,
he lay in the water of the river mouth,
and [one side of his] horn was blue,
on the other side, it was red,
and it was very good-looking.

| | |
|---|---|
| Má:min, | Then, |
| pa:cokkó:toho:limpatš. | he sat on his back, so it is said. |
| Má:min, | Then, |
| fó:si:kon matimo:wapíhlin, | he threw a bird in the water for him, |
| sto:walí:kak ohtí:sit, | and he ran in the water and went and took it, |
| í:pat anó:li:k, | and when he ate it up, |
| mí:ton mato:wapí:lit. | he threw another in the water for him. |
| Kámmi:fó:kon, | When he did so, |
| ibisnók baksá hiná:ban stá:yatohok, | he himself carried a strong rope, |
| lapín stinsahlí:cito:š. | and he sawed at his horn with it. |
| Ma:fó:kon, | Meanwhile, |
| mí:ton matimo:wapí:lin, | he threw another for him, |
| stałi:yato:š. | and it was taking him. |
| Ma:fó:kon, | Meanwhile, |
| lapį sahlí:cito:š. | he was sawing the horn. |
| Má:min, | Then, |
| cintosakcók ónkak, | the sea monster spoke, |
| "Calapí, naksancí:cin óʔmí? | "What is it that you are doing to my horn? |
| Wasíhlit wasíhlš," ká:ha:fó:kon, | It really itches," he said. |
| "Mánko:š. | "Nothing. |
| Amalóstik hamohlilíhcon ó:š," | Since I like it, I am rubbing it," |
| ká:toho:limpatš. | he said, so they say. |
| Kámmin, | In this way, |
| ałí:yak, | he went, |
| fó:sik stimanóhkan, | and when the birds were finished up, |
| łakí mashóccan, | he shot off an arrow, |
| swalí:kak, | and he skimmed along with him, |
| coswą́ imí:sit limítkak, | on reaching the arrow, he took it out of the water, |
| sto:nakałat ałí:ya:fó:k, | took off the spinal ligaments and swallowed them, |
| mí:ton kammí:cik, | and when he began to sink into the water, |
| stóhya:fó:k, | he did so with another one, |
| o:patahasį́ łakík | and when he used the last one, |
| ohto:haccáhlin, | the arrow went in near the shore, |
| má:min, | and then, |
| lapín koyoffą́:hostohok, | he had almost cut off the horn, |
| halátkat scofótlik, | and he pulled it and jumped with it, |
| lapį kawáłłit | and he snapped the horn |
| acón stámmito:š. | and fell out of the water with it. |

| | |
|---|---|
| Mántik,<br>stakolká:cin,<br>tałí:yat achalí:kato:š. | But,<br>the bank collapsed with him on it,<br>but he went with the horn and got out. |

**Scene 5: The Orphan Finds His Sister**

| | |
|---|---|
| Mó:tohok,<br>ałí::yak,<br>ifonó:si cokkó:lifon ó:łą́:ho:si:k,<br>okolcá hinifá łakį́ ithaca:lí:cito:š. | Then afterwards,<br>he really traveled,<br>and when he was about to arrive<br>to where his sister dwelt,<br>he went and stood an arrow in the well-path. |
| Má:min,<br>ifonó:si:kok okó:cik íhlok,<br>łakį́ híhcok,<br>"Yóllok ąłakfó:si inłakí fíhna:sǫ,"<br>káhhan. | Then,<br>his sister on arriving to draw water,<br>caught sight of the arrow.<br>"This very thing is truly one of my brother's arrows," she said. |
| "Á:yalahókkon,<br>illitohóhcok ómmo:š, á:loli:p," ká:tohok, | "But he will not be going about,<br>he seems to be long dead, I think,"<br>she said. |
| Ma:fó:kap,<br>įłakfó:si:kap illónkok haccá:tohok,<br>"Hé:! Cakíllot ommáttok í:la:š,"<br>káhhan,<br>inna:łí:kato:š. | At that moment,<br>her brother stood up from in hiding.<br>"Hey! I have come, not yet having died,"<br>he said,<br>and he spoke to her. |
| Máhmin,<br>á:yatohon ohimmánkak,<br>"Opón cifonó:sik íhsok cokkó:lo:š,"<br>hoká:tohon. | Then,<br>people had told him as he went about,<br>"Your sister lives, having married a sorcerer [lit. 'barred owl']," they said. |
| "Á:to:si món opasók ómmo:š,"<br>hoká:tohon. | "The child also seems to be a little sorcerer," they said. |
| Ifonó:si imasilhá:ci:k,<br>"Opón íscin ohónkan," káhhan. | He asked his sister,<br>"They say that you have married a sorcerer," he said. |
| "Í:siliyok, stambakłi:cíhcó:š," káhhan. | "Contrary to expectation, I married him,<br>and it is the case that he mistreats me,"<br>she said. |
| Įłakfó:si:kok noksí:pat<br>noksí:patoho:limpatš. | And her brother was extremely angry,<br>it is said. |

### Scene 6: The Orphan Rescues His Sister

| | |
|---|---|
| Má:mok, | Then, |
| ónkak, | he spoke, |
| "Ó:łalin, | "As I arrive there, |
| okón lahpá:cit stittahaca:cí:citohok, | you will have stood water to heat on the fire, |
| 'Opá!' iská:n, | and you are to say 'Sorcerer!' |
| mathí:ca:fó:kon, | and when he looks, |
| opasí:kon okí láhpafa mato:wapíhlok, | having thrown the little sorcerer into the hot water, |
| matiwwalí:ka:š!" ka:hatoho:limpatš. | run then from him!" he said. |
| Mó:tohon, | Then afterwards, |
| ó:łatohon, | as he arrived, |
| opá:kok cafí apihcí tałkáhcok | the sorcerer was sitting whittling an |
| cokkó:tohon, | ax handle, |
| tayyí:kok ónkak, | and the woman spoke, |
| "Opán!" ká:toho:limpatš. | "Sorcerer!" she said, so they say. |
| Káhhan, | On saying it, |
| mathí:ca:fó:kon, | when he looked up, |
| opasí:kon mato:wapíhlok, | she threw the little sorcerer into the water, |
| matiwwalíhkan, | and ran away from him, |
| opá:kok cafí apihcí má:lon í:sit | and the sorcerer, taking up just |
| masłóhlin, | the ax handle, pursued her with it, |
| stontí:ci:fó:kap, | and when the two came, |
| į̇łakfó:sik lónkat haccá:tohon, | her brother stood in hiding, |
| ifonó:sik i:tatanátkat haccáhlin, | and his sister came around him and stood there, |
| opá:kok stí:latok | and the sorcerer arrived with it |
| batáplá:hik, | in order to strike her, |
| ithíhcok ónkak, | and coming and catching sight of him spoke, |
| "Ó:!" káhhok, | "Oh," he said, |
| "Pí:la mammí:cilíhcok | "It is the case I was merely pretending," |
| ómmi:š," ká:ha:sin, | he said, |
| łá:hit stittacoko:lí:cit | but it is said the other shot him through |
| í:bitoho:limpatš. | the middle and killed him. |

*Textual emendations*:

| | | |
|---|---|---|
| Line 3 | ama´hilka´s | amá:hilkáskš |
| Line 9 | oktą´łkōk | ohtáłkok |
| Line 13 | imalkostcē+ | himá:ko:š. cį́. |
| Line 23 | isna´hełŝ | isná:łš |

| | | |
|---|---|---|
| Line 40 | itạtcinō´kobi | itto conokbí |
| Line 51 | naksi´pō | noksíhpok |
| Line 103 | hina´ wan | hiná:ban |
| Line 130 | kawa´ sit | kawáɬɬit |
| Line 146 | tc´ạkil´ ōmatok | cakíllot ómmáttok |
| Line 172 | mowapi´hi´la | mato:wapíhlok |
| Line 173 | matowalē´hgạ | matiwwalí:kan |
| Line 185 | istitatcukole´ djitohōlimpats | stittacoko:lí:cit í:bitoho:limpatš |

*Textual commentary*:

Lines 1–15 The fact that the travelers are going to the other side of an ocean and do not end up in the land of the Europeans indicates that the location of this narrative is not on the present earth.

Lines 23–24 *"Hí:y'i! Isná:ɬš! / Í:bit acipí:lillahó:š," káhhan* '"Hey! You! / I will kill you and dispose of you," he said.' Despite the Orphan's initial hostility to Red-Bellied Woodpecker, this does not upset the supernatural being, who merely tells the Orphan not to do so. Note that in *The Orphan and the Bear*, the Orphan was on the point of shooting and killing the bear when it spoke to him. Here, Red-Bellied Woodpecker goes on to warn the Orphan directly about Great-One-Who-Eats-Human-Beings, and indirectly prepares him for his return journey overseas by having him make many arrows.

Line 38 *hasapolóhkon ostá:kan ná:hok* 'and it has four chunkey stones'. These chunkey stones, as mentioned in *The Obstacle Flight* (see chapter 3), are used by Great-One-Who-Eats-Human-Beings to track his prey. Although it is not made explicit in the narrative, the Orphan is understood to be sitting in a bent tree over a body of water where his reflection is visible. The chunkey stones are attracted to his image, as are the dogs of Great-One-Who-Eats-Human-Beings. Once all four chunkey stones have failed to catch him, the Orphan eventually is able to escape.

Lines 42–70 In this narrative, Great-One-Who-Eats-Human-Beings is very much still the cannibal monster of *The Obstacle Flight*. But here, because the Orphan has followed Red-Bellied Woodpecker's instructions exactly, Great-One-Who-Eats-Human-Beings is not a threat, but a figure of interest because of his weird and dreamlike behavior.

Lines 71–134 The plot element of the orphan riding the sea monster over the ocean occurs in other Southeastern traditional literatures, including the Alabama (Swanton 1929:126–28) and Natchez (Swanton 1929:234–39). Here, the sea monster is a horned snake, with a single horn that is blue on one side and red on another. Blue and red are ancient ritual colors among the Koasati, associated with the cardinal directions south and west, while white and yellow are associated with the north and the east.

Line 87 *cintosakcók i:tokpaká:toho:limpatš* 'the sea monster came and floated, so it is said'. The Koasati word for sea monster, *cintosakcó*, means literally 'snake-crawfish'. Modern-day literal-minded Koasati speakers have transferred this word to apply to another monster of the ocean, the octopus.

Line 112 *Calapí, naksancí:cin óʔmí?* 'What is it that you are doing to my horn?' As a general rule, the word *lapí* 'horn' is considered alienable in regard to possession, so the usual way of saying 'my horn' is *allapí* 'the horn that I have'. However, linguistic marking of inalienable possession is permitted to those beings for whom horns are a usual part of their anatomy. Such beings do not usually speak. However, the sea monster not only has a horn, but it can also speak, thus it uses the form *calapí*, 'my horn', that is, 'the horn that is part of me'. There may well be some irony intended here, for not long after this statement the sea monster loses its horn to the Orphan.

Line 121 *coswą́ imí:sit limítkak* '[he] took off the spinal ligaments and swallowed them'. Spinal ligaments were aboriginally used to tie arrow points to arrow shafts, as well as to fletch arrows. Here, the sea monster eats the edible portion of the arrow, carrying the Orphan on his back as he goes along after each arrow.

Lines 135–43 The rare female Orphan is introduced here; she is the sister of the male Orphan. It is clear that she had attempted to recreate her family and clan ties by marrying and having children, but she made the unfortunate mistake of marrying a sorcerer, here called *opá* 'barred owl'. As the wife of such a being, she was excluded from the society of normal people. The people of long ago greatly feared sorcerers, who were believed to have the ability to change their shape (*stilahobá:cin*) from a human being into that of a barred owl.

Line 151 *"Á:to:si món opasók ómmo:š," hoká:tohon* '"The child also seems to be a little sorcerer," they said.' The Koasati considered witchcraft to be an hereditary illness, with the ability to work evil magic being passed down from parent to child. In real life, there were ceremonies that could be performed to purge a sorcerer of his evil powers and restore him to the society of human beings. In this tale, however, the punishment for being a sorcerer is death.

## PEREGRINE FALCON AND GREAT HORNED OWL
narrated by Martha John

I recorded this tale on tape in September 1992. John R. Swanton recorded a version of this narrative in 1910 from *Sacowáyhki*; he published a translation based on his interlinear glosses in 1929 as "The Pigeon Hawk's Gift." In 1989, I edited, retranslated, and published the Koasati text that Swanton had collected. Miss John's version of the narrative is interesting as much for its differences as for its similarities. While the two versions are very similar, Miss John elaborates on how the Orphan receives good luck in hunting. In *Sacowáyhki*'s telling, this is not made explicit; however, in Miss John's telling, how the Orphan is to find the charm is made clear. This can be compared to Miss John's telling of *The Great Lizard*, in which the way that the ashes of the Great Lizard can be used as a war talisman is openly described. The reason for Miss John's openness as opposed to *Sacowáyhki*'s reticence is not at all clear. It may be that *Sacowáyhki*, having been born and raised in pre-Christian Koasati society, really believed in the efficacy of these charms and did not wish to impart such information to outsiders. Miss John, on the other hand, was born when half the Indians were already Christian, and the rest converted to Christianity in her girlhood. For her, the charms are just another element of fantastic stories, and including them just adds that much more interest. She was a very practical and down-to-earth woman who did not believe in the truthfulness of *cokfa:łihilká* (Rabbit Stories), but nonetheless enjoyed listening to them and telling them very much.

### Prologue

| | |
|---|---|
| Ałaná:sá:yok kitiní stóklot áswatohok, | There once were the Peregrine Falcon and the Great Horned Owl, |
| áswatohok mók mán. | Again, the two of them existed. |

### Scene 1: The Orphan Goes Hunting

| | |
|---|---|
| Mó:tohon, | Then, |
| á:tok atloká:co:sok cokkó:tohok, | there was a man, an Orphan dwelling there, |
| ałí:yatohok, | and he went off; |
| ilanawíhlik á:yatohok. | he went about hunting. |
| Ná:hok, | Well, |
| ilho:síhcot ómmit. | it was the case he got lost in the woods. |
| Ittohayó có:bapalámmmotohok. | The forest was reeeeally large. |
| Íhlok, | Having gotten somewhere, |
| cokkó:tohok, | he stayed, |
| ittó oltá óhya ó:tit anóhlok, | having completely kindled a campfire, |
| óhcokko:tohon. | he went and sat down. |

### Scene 2: The Peregrine Falcon and Great Horned Owl Arrive and Beg Help from the Orphan

| | |
|---|---|
| Ná:hon, | Well, |
| akkón ałaná:sáyon kitiník í:bá:hik łóhlok, | that Peregrine Falcon, that the Great Horned Owl was chasing to kill, |
| stóntik, | he came with him, |
| stí:la:fo:kap, | and when he arrived with him, |
| ohtittacokko:tohon, | he [Peregrine Falcon] went and sat on the ground, |
| ó:bo:t ná:ho:t, | at his thighs, |
| ittab'ittaltaltá:la itcokkóhlok, | between his legs he came and sat, |
| cokkó:lin, | and stayed there. |

| | |
|---|---|
| Kitiníp itpa:cokkóhlok, | Great Horned Owl came and perched on a branch, |
| "Akká:li matamapí:cįh! | "Throw him then to me there! |
| Ná:hollá; | I shall do it, |
| í:billá," ka:ha:p, | I shall slay him," he said, |
| matimapį́:kot, | but he continued not to throw him [Peregrine Falcon] to him. |
| "Ínko má! | "By no means! |
| Matacapi:cínnąh! | Do not throw me to him! |
| Anók ná:son cimmánkallahok," ká:t ałanák | I have something to tell you," said Peregrine Falcon. |
| "Anók cimmánkallaho:š. | "I am the one who has something to tell you. |
| Matamapí:c!" ká:hat kitiník acokkó:lin, | Throw him to me!" said Great Horned Owl sitting there, |
| cokkó:lin, | and he [Peregrine Falcon] sat there, |
| ahiccá:cit cokkó:lin. | and he [Great Horned Owl] sat watching him. |

## Scene 3: Peregrine Falcon Kills Great Horned Owl

| | |
|---|---|
| Níhtat anó:ka:fó:kon, | When it had become day, |
| kitiník ohįfáylit wáykask, | Great Horned Owl left off [asking him] and flew, |
| ałanák wáykok atakká:kat, | and Peregrine Falcon flew and hovered, |
| tabátkok wáykak, | and caught him flying, |
| abá ó:ła:fó:kap, | when he had gotten up above, |
| iciksá intipáslit, | and he snapped his neck, |
| bakkí má:łin í:sit, | he took only the head, |
| matapí:toho:limpáhcok. | and threw it away, so it is said. |

## Scene 4: The Orphan Receives His Reward

| | |
|---|---|
| Kámmisk íhlok, | Just like that he arrived back. |
| "Yámmilán ónkali:s, | "It is the case that I can do so, |
| amawí:cískatohok," káhhok. | since you helped me," he said. |
| "Cimmánkal hiná:p akkón má:fa, | "Now I tell you that over there, |
| apakón ónka máhcok, | it is somewhat like a passion flower; |
| má:fa ółci:k, | you go there, |
| apakók haccá:lifa ółci:k | where the passion flower stands, you go. |
| má nó:ta ittó má:łok | Under the tree itself, |
| hocíhca:k | you dig, |
| hayó íhsok | and having taken what is inside, |
| ilihocíkfok stá:yąh! | go about, then, wearing it on yourself! |

Ná:hǫ,
ná:si ísbilaho katík óm,
ná:sok cimmakítto:s,
ná:son ísbin,
óhyak cimó:łǫ.
ná:son asíht ałcí:yak," káhhok.
Ínhkan,
ałí:yáhcotohok,
ná:si, ná:si ŏoooohya,
ná:son immakíttok
ná:si í:bipalámmok haccá:líhcotohon.

Well,
it is the case that you will have good luck in hunting,
you will miss nothing,
you will kill things,
all will come to you,
you will go tying things up," he said.
Having given it to him,
he [the Orphan] went off,
and as for simply everything,
he missed nothing,
he really kept on killing things.

**Epilogue**

Má:mok,
kitiní, kitiní iyyíhmok,
kitiní pí:lan imawi:citoho:p
hollóhcok haccá:lihalpí:sayok,
ka:nóhcon ałí:yáhco:toho:limpáhcok.

Then,
had he believed Great Horned Owl,
if he had only helped Great Horned Owl,
he would have been in a state of evil sorcery,
but on the contrary, he did well, [by not doing so] so it is said.

Tafhiyám!

Finis!

*Textual Comments:*

Line 4 *atloká:co:sok cokkó:tohok* 'an Orphan dwelling there'. Here, as in many other tales, the Orphan is the hero of the story. Whenever an Orphan appears as a protagonist in a Koasati narrative, one can be certain that he will succeed.

Line 15 Here the basic premise of the narrative is set up. The Peregrine Falcon, whose power disappears at night, begs for help from the Orphan so that Great Horned Owl, whose power is greatest at night, will not kill him. Why the peregrine falcon was chosen out of all the raptors was not clear to me in 1989 when I published my translation of *Sacowáyhki*'s version of this tale. Only afterwards did I learn that human sorcerers, whose avatars are the owls, tried to capture and sacrifice peregrine falcons for use in their evil magic.

Line 36 *ałnák wáykok atakká:kat* 'and Peregrine Falcon flew and hovered'. This description is based on direct observation of the flight of peregrine falcons while they are hunting.

Lines 39–40 *iciksá intipáslit, / bakkí má:łin í:sit* 'and he snapped his neck, / he took only the head'. This description is also based on direct observation, for when a peregrine falcon catches a bird on the fly, it uses its powerful beak to decapitate its prey.

Line 45 Miss John paused a long time before saying the plant name *apakó*, 'passionflower'. The context suggests rather that the name should be that of a tree, rather than a vine. It seems that Miss John could simply not remember the correct name, so she made a quick creative adaptation to handle the problem.

## WOLF AND BOX TURTLE RUN A RACE
narrated by Sam Thompson

I recorded this narrative on tape in May, 1992. It belongs to the conservative tradition, in which the character Wolf is the one to race against Box Turtle. The innovative tradition, as exemplified by Martin Abbey's *Rabbit and Box Turtle Run a Race* (chapter 1), replaces Wolf, who occurs in no other Koasati traditional narrative, with the culture hero Rabbit.

There are six scenes in this narrative. The first three lead up to the climax of the narrative, in which Box Turtle successfully carries out the strategm he planned in order to win the race.

In traditional narrative, because of the fluid nature of the genre and the high degree of creativity required of the narrator, it is difficult to determine those elements that are required. In the sixth scene of Thompson's first version of this narrative, he neglected to mention that the ants ate all of Box Turtle's fat in repairing him. Other speakers pointed out this lack, and Thompson felt obliged to retell the narrative in order to include this element. Thus, the origin myth features–why the box turtle has a patterned shell and why it has no fat–are considered to be important in this story.

Sam Thompson (1927–1998) was married to one of Bel Abbey's sisters. He was the only child of a single mother and was raised by her and his grandfather, *Simholáhki*, one of the last of the traditional doctors. Thompson learned a great deal about traditional practices from his grandfather, but *Simholáhki* refused to teach him the medicines, songs, and rituals because he felt that they were morally ambiguous and too easily bent to evil.

### Prologue

| | |
|---|---|
| Yók ómmi:k, | As for this, |
| cokfa:łihilkón immánkallahon ónkal. | I mean to tell him a traditional narrative. |
| Ihó:ca há:lolíhcotohok. | I used to hear it long ago. |

### Scene 1: Wolf and Box Turtle Decide to Race

| | |
|---|---|
| Himó:łan, | First of all, |
| sattapolǫ́ wasó ittimilakasá:mo-toho:limpáhcok, | it is said that Box Turtle and Wolf felt hubris in regard to each other, |
| ittimmá:yalahok. | in racing with each other. |
| Má:min, | Then, |
| sattapolók ónkak, | Box Turtle spoke, |
| "Ǒ:! Cimmá:yali:š," ká:hatoho:limpak. | "Oh! I can defeat you," he said, so it is reported. |

| | |
|---|---|
| Wasók ónkak, | Wolf spoke, |
| "Ammáycíkkóhc naksofó:kon," | "At no time can you defeat me," |
| ká:hatoho:limpak. | he said, so it is reported. |
| Má:mo:sin, | Thereupon, |
| ká:hat ittincilítkáhpin, | they spoke, and they just begged each other [to race]. |
| "Mó:li:p, nihtá ma:fó:kon, | "Well, tomorrow then, |
| ittafą́hhílkalaho:š," ká:hatǫ. | after our having met each other," Wolf said. |
| "Mó:lilo:š!" ká:hatǫ sattapolók. | "All right!" said Box Turtle. |

**Scene 2: Box Turtle Prepares to Trick Wolf**

| | |
|---|---|
| Má:mo:sok, | Thereupon, |
| sattapolók imakostinní:cónkatǫ. | it is the case that Box Turtle was canny. |
| Naksó:n isá:cinánnatǫ, | He seated them [other turtles] everywhere, |
| copoksí í:sa yók himá:yatik sobáylisk, | because knowing now where the mountains |
| immá:yalahok bànnáhco:liskan. | were, and because he wanted to win. |
| Má:min, | Then, |
| wasó:kok akkámmin akostinní:cíkkotǫ; | Wolf did not know how it was; |
| ibisná:łóhcit ittimá:ya má:łok sobáytǫ. | he thought that they alone would race. |

**Scene 3: Wolf and Box Turtle Start to Race**

| | |
|---|---|
| Mó:tohon, | And then, |
| nihtá ma:fó:kon ittafą́hkan, | when it was the next day and they had met. |
| "Hiná:p mó:li:p!" ká:n, | "Now, then!" the one said, and |
| "Mó:š!" ká:haton, | "Enough!" said the other, |
| mántik sattapolók imakostinní:cok óm. | but it is the case that Box Turtle was canny. |

**Scene 4: Wolf Is Taken In by Box Turtle**

| | |
|---|---|
| Má:mo:sin, | Thereupon, |
| tółkatǫ. | they ran. |
| Tółkak ómmi:k, | As for when they ran, |
| wasó:kok ataká:katǫ walí:kak, | Wolf hung back in running, |
| mó:tohok, obá:li mathí:ca:p, | and then, when he looked behind, |
| sattapolók | Box Turtle was really sitting there, |
| matpa:cokkǫ́:toho:limpáhcok | so it is said, |
| copoksí pá:na obá:li pǐllllllllahón. | on top of the mountain waaaay behind. |
| Mó:tohok, | And then, |
| ałí:ya:fó:kon, | when he went, |
| anámpok mathí:ca:p íksotǫ. | when he looked back again he was gone. |

| | |
|---|---|
| Mó:tohop, | And then, |
| bikkó mathí:ca:fó:k, | when he looked up ahead, |
| sattapolók bikkó pĭllllllllahón matlapá:tǫ. | Box Turtle was hanging on there waaaaaaaay ahead. |
| Ma:fó:kon, | Thus, |
| obá:lon ataká:katǫ wasók. | Wolf was left behind. |
| Mó:tohok, | And then, |
| ałá:ci:p, | as the two of them went, |
| anámpok ohhí:ca:p, | again Wolf went and looked, |
| mí:tok mán bikko pĭllllllllahón matlapá:tǫ. | and another again was hanging on there waaaaaaaay ahead. |
| Wasó:kok ohtałabanápka:k, | When Wolf went and passed over it, |
| caffá:kat lónkatǫ. | the one hid. |
| Má:min, | Then, |
| wasók ibisná:ło:sit stataká:katǫ. | Wolf, completely by himself, was left behind. |
| Illókbat, | He was tired, |
| na:sókkot stitto:hofáhnat. | he hardly was conscious, and the sweat flowed off him. |

**Scene 5: Box Turtle Defeats Wolf and Goads Him**

| | |
|---|---|
| Mó:tohok, | And then, |
| kammáhpin, | it was merely thus, |
| yá ostanó:kafa ołá:ci:fó:kon, | when the two of them reached the end. |
| hiná:p sattapolók ónkak, | now Box Turtle spoke, |
| wasó immánkak, | he told Wolf, |
| "Hiná:p, sobáycikko:p mó, | "Now, if indeed you do not know, |
| cimmá:yalǫ!" | I indeed have defeated you!" |
| ká:hatoho:limpáhcok. | he said, so it is reported. |
| Wasók illokbáhco:lisk, | Wolf, because he was tired, |
| ná:son íkkotok noksí:patǫ. | did not say anything and became angry. |
| Kántik, | But this being so, |
| ná:son íkkotok, | he did not say anything, |
| kántik, | and this being so, |
| sattapolók fáykóhcok, | Box Turtle did not quit, |
| "Cimmá:yalǫ!" ká:hatǫ. | "I have DEFEATED you!" he said. |
| Ná:son íkkotǫ wasók. | Wolf did not say anything. |
| Mó:tohok, | And then, |
| stóhya:fó:kon, | when for the last time he said, |
| "Cimmá:yalǫ!" | "I HAVE DEFEATED you!" |
| wasók haytanátkak, | Wolf turned, |
| "Êè:! Isnó:li:š má:min!" káhhok, | "Yeaah! It is you then!" he said, |

| | |
|---|---|
| óhyap kacá:lit, | and bit him all up, |
| óhya alwáhtǫ. | and broke him all up. |
| Óhya bosotlíhcok, | Having shattered him all up, |
| wasók matałí:yat nakáłtǫ. | Wolf went off and disappeared. |

**Scene 6: The Ants Repair Box Turtle**

| | |
|---|---|
| Má:mo:sin, | Thereupon, |
| cokbaník ohiláhcok, | some ants arrived, |
| imawí:cito katíkap, | they helped him, but, |
| "Nihasí máłtik, | "Be it a little of your fat, |
| cimílpatíkap, | please let us eat it, |
| óhya cittilapaffí:cílkalahǫ," | and we will put you all back together |
| ká:hatǫ. | again," they said. |
| Kámmiskan, | Just like that, |
| cokbaní iláhcok, | the ants arrived, |
| ittilapaffíhcok, | and having put him together, |
| kámmit polóhkit | it is said that they put him together |
| lapaffí:cómmimpáhcok | in round sections, |
| katikap, | but, |
| nihasíp, | as for his fat, |
| sattapolók naksó:p, | anywhere on a box turtle, |
| nihá cikhí:co:š. | you do not see fat. |
| Nihasík imiksóhcok ómmimpáhcok, | It is said that he does not have even a little fat, |
| cokbaník imanóstǫ. | the ants finished it all up on him. |
| | |
| Tafhiyám! | Finis! |

*Textual commentary:*

Line 5 *sattapolǫ wasó ittimilakasá:motoho:limpáhcok* 'it is said that Box Turtle and Wolf felt hubris in regard to each other'. As in many Koasati narratives recorded in the last half of the twentieth century, the focus in this narrative is on *ilakasamotilká* or hubris. In this narrative, both characters are considered to feel hubris and, in fact, both characters suffer one kind of comeuppance or another on account of it. The overwhelming concern with hubris in modern Koasati oral literature seems to be the result of pervasive economic changes that have made it possible for a few Koasati to be far better off than others and to occasionally look down on their fellow men because of their own success. The prevalence of these hubris stories seems to be a warning to these persons and an encouragement to others: "just you wait, hubris always is punished."

Line 9 *Cimmá:yali:š* 'I can defeat you'. This is an elite speech form, used in this narrative as in others to give an old-fashioned feel to the story, since elite speech was used exclusively by a handful of elderly men and women storytellers (among them the Mr. Thompson's grandfather) up until the 1940s, when the last of them died.

Lines 17–24 In this, the traditional form of the narrative, Box Turtle wins by trickery by getting other box turtles to appear at the various mountains to trick Wolf into thinking that somehow Box Turtle is faster. Note that in Martin Abbey's *Rabbit and Box Turtle Run a Race* (chapter 2), Wolf is replaced by Rabbit and the way that Box Turtle wins is of no importance to the narrative.

Line 42 *satapolók bikkó pílllllllahón matlapá:tǫ* 'Box Turtle was hanging on there waaaaaay ahead'. For expressiveness, Koasati usually uses rhetorical lengthening of a long vowel. Here, however, the word *pilahá* 'towards, away' has no long vowel, and rather than lengthening a short vowel, the phonologically most prominent consonant, the *l*, is the segment that is rhetorically lengthened.

Lines 55–78 Here, Wolf has received his comeuppance for his hubris—he has lost the race to Box Turtle. Now it is Box Turtle's turn to suffer. By not leaving Wolf alone, by goading him into admitting that Box Turtle is the winner, Box Turtle aggravates Wolf to the point that he shatters his shell.

Line 61 *cimmá:yalǫ* 'I indeed have defeated you!'
Line 68 *cimmá:yalǫ* 'I have DEFEATED you!'
Line 72 *cimmá:yalǫ* 'I HAVE DEFEATED YOU!'
The first time this word is used, in line 61, the intonation used is the normal one. The second time the word is used, the accented syllable *-má:-* is spoken with greater loudness. Finally, in line 72, the entire word is almost shouted. This intonation pattern is used to suggest to the listener how obnoxious Box Turtle is being and helps one to understand why Wolf reacts so violently.

Lines 85–94 These lines contain the origin tale elements of this narrative—i.e., how the box turtle got his patterned shell and why the box turtle has almost no fat.

## GREAT BLUE HERON AND HUMMINGBIRD RACE

narrated by Martin Abbey

I recorded this narrative on tape in November, 1981. It is one of several stories of races between animals, the most popular being the two variants *Wolf and Box Turtle Run a Race* (above) and *Rabbit and Box Turtle Run a Race* (chapter 1). A similar tale was recorded among the Cherokee (Mooney 1900:290–91) about the race between Hummingbird and Crane for a wife. The difference between this narrative and the former ones is that this tale is basically didactic and moral in nature, illustrating the idea that overweening pride leads to a downfall. In the former tales, the race is not won or lost on moral grounds, but by simple trickery, and it has as one of its main components the origin myth of how Box Turtle got a patterned shell. Here, the pleasure is found in the assertion of a moral foundation to the universe.

### Prologue

| | |
|---|---|
| Himá:ya mán, | Now again, |
| ná:hok, | well, |
| ittimmá:yatoh wahkacayhák, | Great Blue Heron ran a race; |
| ittimmá:yaton copokłinitkón. | he ran a race with Hummingbird. |
| Copokłinitkák yammit, | Because Hummingbird like so, |
| "búmmm!" ałi:yáhco:liskan, | "boom!" goes, |
| wahkacayhák pí:la yámmo:sin, | but Great Blue Heron just like so; |
| yámmo:sin mán ałí:yat | he goes also like so; |
| yammí:cit ałi:yáhcotohon. | he does so when going. |

### Scene 1: The Race Is Set

| | |
|---|---|
| Má:mo:sin, | Thereupon, |
| "Nihtá ostá:kan ittimmáyhílásk!" | "Let us race for four days!" |
| ká:toho:limpak. | he said, so they say. |
| Má:mo:sin, | Thereupon, |
| copokłinitkák iliyyimmíhco:liskan, | Hummingbird, because he was overconfident, |
| "Mó:tik," ká:hatoh. | "Okay," he said. |
| "Mó:tik," ká:n, | "Okay," the other said, |
| má:mo:sin, | thereupon, |
| imá:tan. | he stayed with him. |

### Scene 2: The Race Begins

| | |
|---|---|
| Má:mo:sin, | Thereupon, |
| áswat ittimmá:yá:hi:p, | the two were there about to race; |
| ohpa:lokkó:lok, | they went and stood on a branch, |
| wahkacayhák cofótlit, | and Great Blue Heron took off, |
| copokłinitkák mán cofótlit, | and Hummingbird also took off; |
| copokłinitkák "tímmm" áłłat nakałłáhcot, | Hummingbird "zoom!" went off and disappeared, |
| wahkacayhák yámmo:sok | and Great Blue Heron in such a way |
| á:ytoho:limpáhcoh. | went about, it is said. |

### Scene 3: The Racers Compared

| | |
|---|---|
| Á:yan, | The one went on, |
| á:yan, | and the other went on, |
| tamó:ka:fó:kap, | and when it was night, |
| tamó:ka:fó:kap copokłinitkák nó:cit | when it was night Hummingbird slept |
| pa:cokkó:toho:limpáhcoh. | sitting on a branch, it is said. |
| Ittó abá pacokkó:lin hí:cat łopótlok | High up in a tree sitting on a branch the other |
| ałí:yatoho:limpáhcoh. | the other saw him as he went passing, |
| | so it is said. |
| Yámmo:sin tamó:ka wahkacayhák | In just this way at night Great Blue Heron |
| ałį́:yak, | kept on going, |
| ałį́:yak, | and kept on going, |
| ałį́:yak, | and kept on going, |
| naksó:n ontamó:ka:p, | and whenever it grew dark on them, |
| copokłinitká:kok ohtí:pat | Hummingbird went and ate and sat |
| pa:cokkó:lik nó:ci:fó:kon, | on a branch, |
| wahkacayhák hí:cat łopótlit | and Great Blue Heron saw him |
| ałí:yatoho:limpáhcoh. | as he went passing, so it is said. |

### Scene 4: The Winner

| | |
|---|---|
| Má:mo:sok, | Thereupon, |
| kámmin tamó:ka ostá:ka áłłat, | so for four nights he went, |
| tamó:ka ostá:ka łopótli:p, | and when he passed him for four nights, |
| wahkacayhák bikkón | Great Blue Heron got there first, |
| ó:łatoho:limpáhcoh. | so it is said. |
| Copokłinitkák obaltámmitoh, | Hummingbird was late |
| nó:cifíhnaskat, | because he slept too much, |
| tamó:kayon nó:ciskat, | because at night he slept, |
| wahkacayhák iknó:cotohok ałí:yak, | and Great Blue Heron did not sleep, |
| fáykotohot, | he did not quit going, |
| tamó:katik, | even though it be night, |
| pálhíkkotik. | even though he be slow. |
| Himá:yap, akkámmo:sin stanó:k. | Now that is the end. |

*Textual commentary*:

Lines 7–8 *wahkacayhák pí:la yámmo:sin / yámmo:sin mán ałí:yat* 'but Great Blue Heron just like so, / he goes also like so'. These words were accompanied by arm and hand gestures imitating the slow graceful sweep of the wings of the Great Blue Heron.

Line 13 *copokłinitkák iliyyimmíhco:liskan* 'Hummingbird, because he was overconfident'. The verb *iliyyímmin* 'to be overconfident', is considered by speakers to be very close in meaning to *ilakasá:mon* 'to suffer from hubris'. Right here, the listener is given notice that one of the participants suffers from overweening pride, and in all Koasati stories, such pride leads to a comeuppance.

Line 23 *copokɬinitkák "tímmm" áɬɬat nakaɬɬáhcot* 'Hummingbird "zoom!" went off and disappeared'. The interjection *tímmm* was accompanied by a gesture consisting of the flat of the hand being struck against the thigh down and off again, to indicate the speed of Hummingbird.

Lines 24–25 *wahkacayhák yámmo:sok / áytoho:limpáhcoh* 'and Great Blue Heron in such a way / went about, it is said'. This line was again accompanied by gestures illustrating the slow flight of the Great Blue Heron.

Lines 28–31 Here Hummingbird shows his personal flaw—by being overconfident in his speed, he feels that he can spend the night sleeping, not realizing that Great Blue Heron, by continuing on sleeplessly, will gain an unbeatable advantage.

Lines 43–49 These lines give the moral of the story, which is very similar to that of the Aesop's fable *The Tortoise and the Hare*: "Slow and steady wins the race."

## BARRED OWL AND MOUSE
narrated by Bel Abbey

I recorded this narrative on tape in February, 1982. I had previously recorded the tale in November, 1981, but a flaw in the recording left the end of the tale indecipherable, so Abbey agreed to a retelling. It is interesting that once Abbey had recorded a traditional narrative, he did not want to rerecord it. Such was not true of his cousin, Martha John, who felt no compunction about rerecording if properly asked. A version of this tale was recorded by John R. Swanton from Selin Williams in 1910. A translation based on his interlinear glosses was published under the title of *The Story of Owl and Little Yellow Mouse* (Swanton 1929:198). This is another hubris narrative—Owl's self-esteem not only leads to losing his mouse dinner, but also his pride and his life.

### Scene 1: Barred Owl Catches Mouse

| | |
|---|---|
| Opák cissí stóklot a:yá:citohon | I am ready to tell you about how Barred Owl |
| cimmánkalá:hi:má:m. | and Mouse went about together. |
| Opák cissí stóklon. | Once there was Barred Owl and Mouse. |
| Má:miyon, | But anyway, |
| opák á:yatohok, | Barred Owl was going about, |
| opák imakáhnok, | and Barred Owl was hungry, |

| | |
|---|---|
| "Ná:so:t í:billahok í:pali:p," á:lok, | "I shall kill and eat something,"<br>he thought, |
| á:yatoho:limpáhcok. | as he went about, it is said. |
| Mó:tohok, | Then afterwards, |
| ittohayó ałí:yatohok, | he went into the forest, |
| cissók á:yan híhcok, | and caught sight of Mouse going about, |
| cissók á:yan híhcok tabátkat, | he caught sight of Mouse going about<br>and caught him, |
| tabátkatoho:limpáhcok opák. | it is said that Barred Owl caught him. |

## Scene 2: Barred Owl Questions Mouse

| | |
|---|---|
| Má:mi:yok, | But contrary to expectation, |
| polá:ki íkbot, | he did not kill him quickly, |
| tabátkok í:sit | he caught him and took him, |
| ittó:bi ayakhá ohcokkó:lok, | and he went and sat near a hollow tree, |
| inna:łí:katoho:limpáhcok | and spoke to him since he caught him, |
| tabátkaskan. | so it is said, |
| Má:mo:sok, | Thereupon, |
| ónkak, | he spoke, |
| opák ónkak imasilhá:citoho:limpáhcok. | Barred Owl spoke and asked him<br>questions. |
| Cissí ná:si ŏ:hya imasilhá:cit, | He asked Mouse simply everything, |
| immánkat anó:li:k, | he told him all kinds [of questions], |
| sobáylá:hi bànnak, | he wanted to know things, |
| sámmit í:sak, | how they lived, |
| sámmit yomahlíhco:lik. | how they went about. |
| Má:mo:sok, | Therefore, |
| imasilhá:citoho:limpáhcok. | it is said that he asked him questions. |

## Scene 3: Mouse Flatters Barred Owl

| | |
|---|---|
| Má:mo:sok, | Thereupon, |
| opák ónkak, | Barred Owl spoke, |
| "Nashocamánkáʔsá?" káhhan. | "By what name do they call me?" he said. |
| Cissík immałátlihónka:sik, | Mouse was excessively frightened of him, |
| naská:hik sobáykok, | and did not know what to say, |
| ká:no:sin immánkatoho:limpáhcok, | but it is said that he spoke to him<br>really well; |
| ayóhbo:sit. | he took very great care. |
| Má:mo:sok, | Thereupon, |
| "Támka Stimmikkó hocimankáhcokš,"<br>káhhan. | "They call you King of Darkness,"<br>he said. |

Opák ónkak,
ayokpá:hostoho:limpáhcok,
"Á! Acayókpat stalpí:s.
Mafíhna:son ónk," ká:toho:limpáhcok opák.

Barred Owl spoke,
it is said he was really happy,
"Ah! I am most pleased.
It is the very truth," Barred Owl said,
so it is reported.

Má:mo:sin,
himá:ya mán łóylit
imasilhá:citoho:limpáhcok,
himá:ya mán immánká:hį bànnak.
Himá:ya mán "Nashocamankahcóˀtó?"
káhhan.
Má:mo:sin,
cissík himá:ya immánkak,
"Támka Stimmikkók óm.
Támka Stimmikko:líhcok.
Támka Stimmikkó hocimankáhcok,"
káhhan.
"M̀hḿ! Acayókpat stalpí:s.
Anók mafíhna:sot Támka Stimmikkó mǫ́.
Anók stimmikkó mǫ́,"
ká:toho:limpáhcok opák.
Stayókpat,
nokcóbkot ká:ha:fó:kon.
Ká:hat imasilhá:cik fáykon.
Ká:hat,
naská:t imasilhá:cá:hik
sobáykotoho:limpáhcok.
Naská:t imasilhá:cá:hik sobáykok,
"Himá:ya mán, nashokáhcóˀtó?"
"Himá:ya mán, nashokáhcóˀtó?"
ká:toho:limpak.

Thereupon,
once again it is said
he asked him again,
once again he wanted him to tell him it.
Once again, "What is it that they call me?"
he said.
Thereupon,
Mouse again told him,
"He is the King of Darkness.
One can deduce that he is King of Darkness.
They call you King of Darkness,"
he said.
"Mhm! I am well pleased.
I in very truth am indeed the King of Darkness.
I am indeed its king,"
Barred Owl said, so it is reported.
He loved it,
and did not stop saying it.
He said it and did not quit asking him.
He said it,
and he did not know what else
to ask him, so it is said.
He did not know what else to ask him,
"Once again, what do they say?"
"Once again, what do they say?"
he said, so they say.

## Scene 4: Mouse Escapes

Cissí imasilhá:ci:k,
mán cissík ká:t immánkáhpok,
mántik cissí mók na:łí:ká:łok,
akostinní:citoho:limpáhcok.
Naksó:n sámmihalpí:sok,
ná:so:t óhya hí:cat imakostinní:cit,
imakostinní:cit anóhlok,
ittó:bik łobáfkatohon híhcok,

When he asked Mouse,
Mouse also just told him the same,
but as Mouse was telling him it again,
he was thinking, so it is said.
About where he could do something,
he thought about all he saw,
and having thought it out,
he saw a pierced hollow tree,

| | |
|---|---|
| cissík mán walí:kat | that Mouse again might run |
| cokhalí:kalaho:lik | and enter into, |
| hí:cat anóhlok, | and having looked it over, |
| sobáylok, | he knew what to do, |
| "Nashocamánkahcóˀtó? | "What is it that they call me?" |
| Himá:ya mán!" káhhan. | "Once again!" he said. |
| "Opá ittiɬhocobák hocimankáhcok," | "You are called Owl-Big-Eyes!" |
| káhhan, | he said. |
| "Opá ittiɬhocobák hocimankáhcok," | "You are called Owl-Big-Eyes!" |
| káhhan, | he said, |
| opák noksíhpok, | and Barred Owl grew angry, |
| má:mik, | then, |
| "Hocimankáhcok," káhhok, | "They call you that," he said, |
| tabátká:hi:fó:kap, | and when he was about to catch him, |
| cissík ká:t immánkat | Mouse said it [again] to him, jumped away |
| incofótlik ittó:bi cokhalíhkan. | from him, and entered into the hollow tree. |
| Má:mo:sin, | Thereupon, |
| "Cifáytákkóhc!" | "I will not leave you alone!" |
| Má:mik, | Then, |
| "Cifáytákkóhc! | "I will not leave you alone! |
| Ittó cokhalí:híska:kon cí:bilik | I will kill and eat you who have gone |
| í:pallahok,"káhhok. | into the tree," he said. |
| Ittofá cokhalí:kan wá:cok | And he sat at the tree waiting for the other to come out, |
| cokkǫ́:toho:limpáhcok. | it is said that he really sat there. |
| Wá:cok cokkǫ́:lin, | He really sat and waited, |
| cissík cokhalí:kat | and Mouse had entered into the hollow tree |
| nakáɬtoho:limpáhcok ittó:bihayo. | and disappeared, so it is said. |
| Mó:tohok, | Then afterwards, |
| mí:ta ɬobafkáhcok ohtachalí:katohon | he saw that there was another hole |
| hí:catoho:limpáhcok. | that he could go and get out of. |
| Wá:cok ohtachalíhkok, | He waited and got out; |
| lónkat innakáɬɬok, | he hid and disappeared from him, |
| achalí:kok innakáɬɬan, | he got out and disappeared from him, |
| opák sobáykot pa:cokkǫ́:lit, | and Barred Owl really sat not knowing it. |
| wą́:cit, | He really waited, |
| wą́:cit, | and he really waited, |
| wą́:cit sánkotoho:limpáhcok. | and he really waited until he could do no more, it is said. |
| Wá:cáhpok sánkon, | He just waited, and could do no more. |
| "Cí:bilik í:pallaho kátik óm," á:lok, | "But it is the case that I will kill and eat you," he thought, |
| pa:cokkǫ̌::lit, | and he really, really sat, |

| | |
|---|---|
| imaká:not, | and he got hungry, |
| ná:so:t íkpot pa:cokkó:lit, | he sat there and did not eat anything; |
| wá:cáhpok sánkon. | he just sat there and could do no more. |
| Imaká:nok, | He got hungry, |
| opák onaíllitoho:limpáhcok, | and it is said that Barred Owl died on the tree, |
| wá:cihónka:sik. | he had waited so hard. |
| Cissí:kok itłopótlok nakáłłan, | Mouse had passed through and hid; |
| íkbot. | he had not killed him. |
| Má:min, | Then, |
| cissí í:bit í:pá:hik sánkot, | he was unable to kill and eat Mouse; |
| imaká:nok, | he got hungry, |
| opák íllitoho:limpáhcok, | and it is said Barred Owl died, |
| món wá:cit pa:cokkǫ́:lit. | again from sitting and waiting. |
| Akkámmo:sin sobáylil. | Just so much is what I know. |
| Tafhiyám! | Finis! |

*Textual commentary:*

Line 1 *Opák cissí stóklot a:yá:citohon cimmánkalá:hi:má:m* 'I am ready to tell you about how Barred Owl and Mouse went about together.' This is the closest that a narrator comes to giving a title to a traditional narrative. A narrative is generally referred to by the names of the two principal characters, joined by the word *stóklon*. Thus, when one asks for the tale *Cokfík nitá stóklon* 'Rabbit and Bear together', *The Bungling Host* (chapter 1) is understood.

Lines 21–27 This elaboration on what Barred Owl was asking Mouse does not occur at all in Abbey's earlier version, nor in Williams's version recorded by Swanton in 1910. Mr. Abbey here seems to be grinding an axe in regard to nosy anthropologists, several of whom he had had to deal with not long before he recorded this narrative. Being well brought up, he did not feel that he could tell them how much they had offended him, so he took this opportunity to obtain literary revenge against them by assimilating their behavior to that of Barred Owl, who comes to a bad end in this narrative.

Lines 31–34 This elaboration on the nature of Mouse's response also does not occur in earlier versions. Here, it seems that Mr. Abbey is identifying himself with Mouse and reflecting with quiet pride on how he had answered the anthropologists well and carefully and did not give anything away.

Line 36 *"Támka Stimmikkó hocimankáhcokš"* '"They call you King of Darkness"'. Here, Mouse is not only buttering up Barred Owl by giving him the sonorous title 'King of Darkness', but he addresses him with elite speech in order to further inflate Barred Owl's opinion of himself.

Lines 39–40 This, Barred Owl's reaction to Mouse's flattery, is very well conceived and rendered; it sounds very much like the reaction to flattery of a person who has an overly high opinion of himself.

Lines 63–73 Mouse does not allow himself to fall into self-absorption as does Barred Owl, but continues to think of ways to escape. Here, once he has figured out how to do so, he prepares a nasty insult to deflate Barred Owl.

Line 76 *"Opá ittiłhocobák hocimankáhcok" káhhan* '"You are called Owl-Big-Eyes!" he said'. Mouse's sudden insult, coming in contrast to his previous flattery, makes listeners laugh. Note here the rare use of the passive (the nominative case suffix *-k* and the verbal prefix *ho-*). The use of the passive here implies that there is no one who does not call Barred Owl by that insulting title.

Lines 84–117 These lines show that Barred Owl has learned nothing from his experience. Instead of being chastened by Mouse's trick, he still thinks so highly of himself that he thinks that he can wait until mouse comes out again from the hollow tree and kill him. He never imagines that there might be another way out, and he sits there so stubbornly that he allows himself to die. Once again, hubris is punished in the end.

## THE CONTEST OF HEAT AND COLD
narrated by Martha John

I tape recorded this tale in 1990. It is a version of the well-known fable of Phaedrus, *The Contest of the North Wind and the Sun*. How the Koasati acquired this tale is unknown. A French version occurs in the fables of La Fontaine. Many Koasati people (including Miss John's stepbrother/cousin Ed John) were fluent in the local dialect of French, so it is quite possible that he, or another French-speaking Koasati person, heard the fable read in French and liked it so much that he or she translated it. In structure and sentiment, it is entirely native. It is interesting to observe the changes that have taken place between the Greek original and the Koasati tale. In the Greek version, the contest between the North Wind and the Sun is simply a given; in the Koasati version, the reason for the contest is explicated—the hubris that the two beings felt toward one another. It is interesting that hubris (Koasati *ilakasamolilká*) is as strong a component in Koasati narrative as it is in ancient Greek literature. The Greek version of the fable is cast in iambic trimeter, a poetic form, rather than in prose. The Koasati version is also in a verse format typical of traditional narrative. While the European version is entirely descriptive, the Koasati version invents quoted speech, since the use of quoted speech in traditional narrative is an indication of good style.

### Scene 1: Heat and Cold Dwell Together

Lókbon Kasátkak stóklot aswáhcotohok,
ittimilakasá:motoho:limpáhcok.

Mó:tohon,
á:ti tóklot áswatohok,
aɬɬá:citohok,
caffá:kat kapó:ta ittalbitlí:cit óhya
anóhlok aɬí:yan.

Heat and Cold were dwelling together,
and it is said that they felt hubris in regard
to one another.
Then,
the two beings dwelt together,
and the two of them went off,
and there was one person going along
all layered up in a coat.

### Scene 2: Cold Tries to Strip a Traveler of His Clothing

Kasátkak nasókkon aɬí:ya:fó:k,
óhya ittalbítlit ómmok aɬí:ya:fó:kon,
Kasátkak ónkak,
"Anók ómmi:p įsíhlilíhc akkó aɬí:ya,"
ká:hatoho:limpáhcok.
"Á:ti caffá:kan,
óhya ittalbitlí:cok aɬí:ya:fó:kon,
įsíhlilíhc," ká:ha:p.
Má:mok,
ompófkak,
pófkak,
ná:hok,
pófka:p,
óhya matilaponáylit,
óhya immá:yan matilaponáylit
aɬí:yak,
hopáhki stóhɬan,
amáhkan,
staɬí:yáhpok sankí:cot,
staɬí:yat fáykon,
immá:yan mastilaponní:cit
staɬí:yan,
fáykotoho:limpáhcok akkó á:tik.

Cold, as soon as the other was going along,
when the one who seemed to be all layered
up was going along,
Cold spoke.
"I am the one who can take the clothes off
of that traveler,"
he said, so it is reported.
"That one person,
when he goes along all layered up,
I can take his clothes from him," he said.
Then,
he blew on him,
and he blew;
he did it,
when he blew,
the other wrapped himself all up,
he continued to wrap himself up
all the more;
he went far with him;
they all went,
and merely going with him,
he was unable to do it;
he went with him and did
not quit,
and he wrapped himself
all up all the more,
he went with him,
and that man did not cease
[wrapping himself up],
so it is said.

### Scene 3: Cold Fails and Heat Decides to Try

| | |
|---|---|
| Síhkot immá:yan, | He did not take any more clothes from him, |
| ná:hot stałí:yat fáyko:fó:kon, | when he did it, went with him and did not quit; |
| stałí:yak | he went with him, |
| hopáhki stalpí:san stó:ła:fó:kok, | when they had gone sufficiently far with him, |
| ohhaytanátkak íhlok, | he went and turned around and having come back, |
| Lokbá ittimmą́hkok, | he spoke to Heat. |
| "Santaká:cǫ anáp," káhhan. | "I am unable to do it," he said. |
| Má:mo:sin, | Thereupon, |
| "Isná:hi:lok cincayínkǫ," káhhan, | "I don't believe it of someone like you," he said. |
| "Anáp įsíhlilíhc akkáp. | "As for me, I can take the clothes off of that one. |
| Holikfá óhya įsíhlilǫ!" káhhok, | I indeed can take off all of his clothes!" he said, |
| ałí:yan, | and he went off, |
| pahlí:citoho:limpáhcok Kasátkak. | and it is said that Cold whistled. |

### Scene 4: Heat Tries and Succeeds

| | |
|---|---|
| Má:mo:sin, | Thereupon, |
| ałí:yatoho:limpáhcok. | it is said that he went along. |
| Ałį́:yak, | He really went along; |
| ałį́:yak, | and he really went along; |
| hopa:kíhcotoho:lik | one can guess that it was far, |
| á:tok pálhíkkot ałí:yáhcotohok. | and there was the man going slowly along. |
| Ałłáhcotohok, | He was going along, |
| páhkan, | and he called out, |
| ółkohá:lon, | and before he arrived there, |
| ohcákkitoho:limpáhcok Lokbák. | Heat went and caught up with him, so it is said. |
| Ałí:yak, | He went along, |
| ikbá:cit stałí:yan, | and began to heat him, |
| síplit, | and the other took off a piece of clothing, |
| holikfá hókfatohok síplit matapí:lin, | he took off a piece of clothing that he was wearing and cast it aside, |
| ikbá:ci:fó:kon, | and when he was heating him, |
| síplit matapí:lik, | he took off a piece of clothing and cast it aside; |
| matapí:lik óhya | he threw it all aside, |

| | |
|---|---|
| óhyan įsíht anóhlin, | and he finished stripping all his clothes from him, |
| įsíht anóhlok, | and having stripped the clothes from him, |
| ɬóykatoho:limpáhcok. | it is said that he returned. |

**Epilogue**

| | |
|---|---|
| Kámmisk,<br>Lokbák holikfá a:tįsíhlitoho:limpáhcok. | Just like that,<br>it is said that Heat stripped all the clothing clothing from someone. |
| Má:min,<br>Kasátkak óhya holikfá ittalbitlí:citoho:yáhlok. | Then,<br>it is said to be the case that Cold really made him layer himself up in clothing. |
| Kámmisk,<br>Lokbák immayá:citoho:limpáhcok Kasátka. | Just like that,<br>it is said that Heat won against Cold. |

*Textual commentary*:

Line 2 *ittimilakasá:motoho:limpáhcok* 'and it is said that they felt hubris in regard to one another'. Once again, hubris is given as the motivation for the behavior of beings in a traditional narrative. Note, however, that even though both characters feel hubris, only one, Cold, suffers on account of it.

Line 22 *amáhkan* 'they all went'. One is to imagine Heat following along quietly as Cold tries to strip clothing from the traveler.

Line 35 *"Isná:hi:lok cincayínkǫ"* '"I don't believe it of someone like you"'. Heat's words here are a subtle dig at Cold's inability to do that which he had bragged about doing.

## THE CONTEST OF THE ELF, HUMAN, PANTHER, AND WILDCAT
narrated by *Sacowáyhki*

This narrative was recorded by John R. Swanton in 1910 and given the number nine in his manuscript "Koasati Texts, Second Series." He published a translation of this narrative based on the interlinear glosses titled *The Giant Elk* (Swanton 1929:185–86). The style of this narrative makes a sudden shift from serious to humorous at the end of the third scene. The very suddenness and unexpectedness of this shift amplifies the humor for the Koasati audience.

### Scene 1: The Quest to Kill the Elk

| | |
|---|---|
| A:tilhicíksok á:yan, | There was an Elf going about, |
| mán yá:li á:ti fíhnok á:yatohon, | also a real human from here was going about, |
| á:ti hocó:bak ónkak, | and the old people spoke: |
| "Icopáyhka có:bok kánkot | "There is a large bad elk around, |
| kankóhcok á:tan, | and people have chased it |
| á:to:t łóhlit í:bih bànnatik | and tried to kill it, |
| sánko:š," káhhan. | but were unable," they said. |
| Máhmin, | Then, |
| hocó:bahak ónkak, | the old people spoke: |
| "Tá. Yón himá:yan, | "Well. This way now, |
| naksók máhmi:k, | when it happens that whosoever, |
| icopáyhka í:bi:k, | kills the elk, |
| ná:si i:bíhco:lilahoš," káhhan. | he will have good hunting," they said. |
| A:tilhicíkson, | And an Elf, |
| á:ti fíhna, | a true person, |
| kowicobón, | a large Panther, |
| kowaknasón, | and a Bobcat, |
| stostá:kan cikkí:katoho:limpats. | the four of them dwelt there. |

### Scene 2: The Hunters Await the Elk

| | |
|---|---|
| Mó:tohon, | Then, |
| nihtá stonostá:ka:kok, | after four days, |
| stonostá:ka:fok, | on the fourth, |
| má:kok óhyat hinhí:cat | those ones were keeping on |
| í:satoho:limpatš. | expecting it. |
| Mó:tohon, | Then, |
| icopáyhka:kok ónkatoho:š. | the elk belled. |
| Ná:si cǫ́:bat cǫ́:bat co:báhcok óntik | Something really big, big, big was coming, |
| mattakí:citoho:limpatš. | and they could hear it from afar, it is said. |
| Má:mo:sin, | Thereupon, |
| má:kok óhya lokkó:toho:limpatš | those ones all stood up to shoot at it, |
| hoccá:hik. | they say. |
| Má:min, | Then, |
| á:ti fíhnok bikkón shaccá:toho:limpatš. | the true human stood up first, they say. |
| Máhmin, | Then, |
| anámpok atilhicíksok, | next the Elf, |
| statoccí:na kowicobák cokkó:lin, | third, the Panther sat there, |
| stonostá:ka kowacosí:kok | and fourth, the Bobcat sat there, |
| cokkó:toho:limpatš. | they say. |

### Scene 3: The Bobcat Is Frightened

Mó:tohon,
ná:si cobáhcok óntitoho:limpatš.
Wononhká:cit,
ma:fó:kon,
hinhí:cak slokkó:lin,
kowacosí:kok małátlihalpí:sat
cokkó:toho:limpatš.
Mó:tohok,
ná:si cobá:kok í:lafíhna:fó:kon,
kowacosík małátlik,
kowacosí:kok, "Tá! Hoppó:lat í:lalok,"
káhhok,
walí:katoho:limpatš.
Małátlik ónkatoho:š.

Then afterwards,
something big was coming, they say.
It was roaring,
whereupon,
they stood up expecting it,
and the Bobcat sat being very afraid,
it is said.
Then,
when the big thing was truly coming,
the Bobcat was very afraid,
the Bobcat, "Well, I am going to shit,"
he said,
and he ran off, so it is reported.
It is the case that he was afraid.

### Scene 4: The Slaying of the Elk and the Return of the Bobcat

Máhmin,
á:ti:kok bikkón shaccá:toho:s sbiłí:lit.
Statóklon a:tilhicíksok shaccá:toho:š.
Mó:tohon,
ná:si:kok matachalí:katoho:limpatš.
Ontik í:la:fó:kon,
á:tik hóccah bànnat
sánkotoho:limpatš.
Máhmin,
obá:li shaccá:tohok ássok
tokóhkatoho:limpatš.
Má:min,
icopáyhka:kok támmit ałí:ya:fó:kon,
kowicobák obá:li cofótlik,
í:sit stittatámmitoho:limpatš.
Ma:fó:kon,
kowacosí:kok walí:kat íhlok,
ohí:bi:fó:kon,
itpa:cofótlok no:yáskatoho:limpatš.

Then,
the human stood up first and aimed at it.
Second, the Elf stood.
Then afterwards,
the thing came out into the open, it is said.
When it came arriving,
the human tried to shoot it,
but was unable.
Then,
the one standing behind [Elf] shot first,
it is said.
Then,
as the elk began to fall,
the big Panther jumped from behind, took it
and threw it to the ground, they say.
Right then,
the Bobcat came running,
as they were killing it,
came and jumped on its back and chewed
on its throat, it is said.

Má:mo:sin,
kowacosí:kok ónkak,
"Hoppó:lat fáytákkoyok,
onakoyóffit matwalí:ka:š,"
ká:toho:limpatš.
Má:mo:sin,
a:tilhicíksok ná:si ílban
stí:sitoho:limpatš.
Mamisk,
ǫ́:hyan immayá:citoho:limpatš.

Thereupon,
the Bobcat spoke,
"I had not yet finished shitting,
but, contrary to expectation, I cut it off and came running,"
he said, so they say.
Thereupon,
the Elf received good hunting,
it is said.
Because of this,
he defeated each and every one of them, so they say.

*Textual emendations*:

| | | |
|---|---|---|
| Line 10 | na´hạnēk | máhmi:k |
| Line 19 | susta´gafō´k | stonostá:ka:fó:k |
| Line 25 | mạt'ē´gē´djitoholimpats | mattakí:citoho:limpatš |

*Textual commentary*:

Line 1 *a:tihicíkso* 'elf'. This is the English term that the Koasati prefer to use to translate their term, which means 'invisible person'. The *a:tilhicíkso* were small supernatural beings believed to dwell in trees distinguished by smooth strips of bark, or in which mistletoe, called *a:tilhicíkso imittó* 'elf's tree', grew. On the whole, they were considered harmless to man, although some people believed that the sight of one presaged the death of someone in one's family.

Line 4 *icopáyhka* 'elk'. This word is an old borrowing from Creek into Koasati to describe an animal that does not exist in Louisiana. The Koasati equivalent would be *icó páhka* 'bellowing deer', but the actual term used at present is *icó lapí pathá* 'wide-horned deer'. The narrator seemed not to have had a good grasp on the term, since he forgot it occasionally and replaced it with *ná:si cobá* 'a big thing'.

Lines 11–12 *"icopáyhka í:bi:k, / ná:si i:bíhco:lilahoš," káhhan* '"when one kills the elk, / he will have good hunting," they said'. What is meant by these lines is that the one who kills the elk will receive good luck in hunting and always be able to find game whenever he hunts. The old people here are not just elderly humans, but beings with supernatural powers of some kind.

Lines 14–32 So far, the narrative has been played as a serious tale. Here, at the mid-point, there is a sudden shift in tone and the tale is played for comedy.

Line 43 *kowacosí:kok "Tá! Hoppó:lat í:lalok" káhhok* 'the Bobcat, "Well, I am going to shit," he said'. At this point of high tension in the narrative, Bobcat not only has to defecate, but uses the Koasati equivalent of a four-letter word to tell the others, which causes listeners to dissolve in laughter. As mentioned elsewhere, the sudden interpolation of a taboo topic, such as sex, death, or excretion into an otherwise serious-appearing narrative causes a great deal of laughter among listeners. If this were a normal conversational situation, a person who had to defecate would actually say *ohłóykalą́* 'I have to go to the bathroom', literally, 'I shall go and return'. Blunt speech such as this is just not used in polite conversation.

Lines 65–66 *"Hoppó:lat fáytákkoyok, / onakoyóffit matwalí:ka:š," ká:toho:limpatš* '"I had not yet finished shitting, / but, contrary to expectation, I cut it off and came running," he said, so they say.' If the previously discussed line causes listeners to laugh, this line puts them in stitches because of its blunt vocabulary and vivid imagery. This statement is so far beyond the pale of politeness that the only possible response to it is laughter.

## BEAR IS TRICKED BY JAY

narrated by Myrna Wilson

I recorded this narrative on tape in November, 1981. Myrna Wilson is the eldest daughter of Bel Abbey, and it was he who taught her the following narrative and encouraged her to have it recorded, with the intention that this would help to fix it in her memory.

This particular narrative was not recorded by Swanton among the Koasati, nor is a similar tale to be found among those recorded for other Southeastern groups. Nonetheless, it is completely within native tradition, both in style and content. This is another tale in which a character expresses overweening pride and because of it receives his comeuppance—in this case, in the relatively mild form of being shamed.

### Scene 1: Bear Boasts Unwisely

Ná:hon,
tiskilón nitón ittá:sat áswatohon.
Má:mo:sin,
niták ómmi:k,
"Na:son incamałatkóhcok anap.
Na:son incamałátko:líhcok," ká:hat,
"Camałatkí:coscok," káhhan.

Well,
Jay and Bear were there together.
Thereupon,
as for Bear,
"As for me, I am not afraid of anything.
I am not afraid of anything." he said,
"Nothing frightens me." he said.

### Scene 2: Jay Decides to Trick Bear

Má:mo:sin,
á:tatohon.
Má:min,
ná:hok ómmi:k,
tiskilák ómmi:k á:tatohok.

Thereupon,
he dwelt there.
Then,
as for that one there,
as for Jay, he was there.

| | |
|---|---|
| Mó:tohok, | Then afterwards, |
| ilanawihkó:łan sobáytohok, | he knew that hunting season was arriving; |
| ilanawihkó:ła:fó:kon sobáytohok. | he knew when hunting season arrived. |
| Má:mo:sok, | Thereupon, |
| ná:hon, | well, |
| nitá:kon małatlí:cih bànnak á:lotoho:limpáhcok. | it is said that he thought that he might frighten Bear. |

**Scene 3: Jay Tricks Bear**

| | |
|---|---|
| Mó:tohon, | Then afterwards, |
| ná:hok, | well, |
| niták ikhí:con, | Bear did not see him, |
| áłłat nakáłtohok, | and he went and disappeared; |
| itpa:cokkó:lok, | he went and sat on a branch; |
| ittó abá itpa:cokkó:lok. | high up in a tree he went and sat on a branch. |
| Má:mo:sok, | Thereupon, |
| ilanawihkó:łaskan, | because hunting season had arrived, |
| má:mo:sin, | thereupon, |
| "Hwíiìw!" ká:toho:limpak á:ti fotfó:ka yámmit. | "Hwíiìw!" he said, like a whistling human, so they say. |
| Á:ti fotfó:ka yámmit káhhan, | Having said something like a whistling human, |
| nitá:kok haytanahká:cit wíhtoho:limpak. | Bear whirled around and looked, they say. |
| Haytanahká:cit wíhláhpin, | He whirled around and just looked. |
| má:mo:sin, | Thereupon, |
| ná:hok, | well, |
| himá:ya mán tiskilák matpa:cokkó:lok, | once again Jay sat afar on a tree branch |
| "Hwíiìw!" káhhan. | "Hwíiìw!" he said. |
| Má:mo:sin, | Thereupon, |
| nitá:kok małátlok má:łok walí:katoho:limpak. | Bear was simply frightened and ran, so they say. |
| Walí:katohon, | He ran, |
| himá:ya mán a:táhpok, | and once again he just stayed there, |
| himá:ya mán nitá ó:łafa, | and once again Jay was at the place he arrived; |
| himá:ya mán ittó pá:na wáykat ohpacokkó:lok, | once again he flew up on a tree and was sitting on a branch; |
| niták ikhí:con ónkan, | it was the case Bear did not see him, |
| pa:cokkó:lok ómmok, | he was sitting on a branch, |

himá:ya mán á:ti yámmit,
"Hwíiìw!"ká:hat sánkon.
Himá:ya mán, "Hwíiìw!"káhhan,
niták walí:kalahotok,
walí:ka:hoscok,
walí:kat ałí:yak fáykot,
naksó:n ohhaccá:lit mathí:cat,

ohhaccá:t mathí:cat
naksó:n lónká:hik á:yat
sámmoscok atlónkat á:yáhpok.

and once again like a human,
"Hwíiìw!" he said and quit.
Once again, "Hwíiìw!" he said,
and Bear would have run,
he really ran,
he continued running and did not quit;
he went and stood somewhere
and looked about;
he went and stood and looked about,
if someone were about in hiding
if in some way a hidden person was about.

**Scene 4: Bear Is Shamed By Jay**

Má:mo:sin,
ná:hok,
himá:ya mán tiskilá:kok wáykat pá:na
pa:cokkó:lok,
wáykatohok pa:cokkó:lok,
himá:ya mán, "Hwíiìw!" káhhan.
Má:mo:sin,
nitá:kok iwwíhláhpok,
hí:catohok,
tiskilák pa:cokkó:t ónkatohon.
Híhcok,
"Isnók oncíˀsá?" káhhan.
Má:min,
"È:," káhhan.
"'Aná:hilok ná:son incamałatkóhci,' iská:son,

hiná:p atcimałátlok,
walí:híska:má:m," ká:toho:limpak.

Tafhiyám!

Túf!

Thereupon,
well,
once again Jay flew up on top
and sat on a branch;
he flew and sat on a branch,
and once again, "Hwíiìw!" he said.
Thereupon,
Bear just looked around for him,
and saw him;
Jay was sitting on a branch making noise.
Having seen him,
"Was it you?" he said.
Then,
"Yes," he said.
"You just said, 'In my case I am not afraid of anything.'
Now, you are afraid of people,
you seem to have run," he said, so they say.

Finis!

Ptooey!

*Textual commentary*:

Lines 1–7 This scene sets the tone for the narrative. Bear boasts about his fearlessness, the kind of boast that it is impossible to believe. Undermining Bear's boast is the task Jay sets for himself as the narrative progresses.

Line 14 *ilanawihkó:łan sobáytohok* 'he knew that hunting season was arriving.' This statement suggests that the narrative was developed fairly recently, since hunting seasons were introduced in Louisiana only in the twentieth century. If this is, in fact, a new story, it would explain why it was not collected by Swanton when he did his fieldwork in 1910.

Line 29 *"Hwíìw!" ká:toho:limpak á:ti fotfó:ka yámmit* '"Hwíìw!" he said, like a whistling human, so they say.' The word that is conventionally transcribed *hwíìw* was actually uttered by the narrator as a loud, piercing whistle.

Lines 31–56 These lines well describe Bear's flight from the whistler and Jay casually following along and tormenting him.

Line 68 *"Isnók oncíˀsá?" káhhan* '"Was it you?" he said.' The pitch on the accented vowels of *oncíˀsá* is at least a third higher than the normal interrogative pitch; this was attributed by listeners to the fact that Bear was ashamed while he spoke.

Line 76 *Túf* 'Ptooey!' It was a traditional custom when anyone told a traditional narrative that he or she had to utter the apotropaic interjection *tafhiyám* and spit once. Very old speakers had a tendency not to bother with either the interjection or the spitting, since the punishment for violation, a hump on one's back, seemed hardly a thing to worry about in advanced age. Younger speakers almost always used the interjection, but since they did not like to spit on their clean floors, they would either ignore the custom or utter a spitting interjection, such as *túf* or *cúh*, both of which can be rendered in English as 'ptooey!'

# 5

# Medicine Origin Tales

From a genre that must have once had many tales, only one has been preserved intact to the present. The purpose of these tales was to illuminate the origin of the various medicinal herbs and plants and to explain how human beings came to use them. These tales seem not to have been preserved partly because native herbal medicine has become a thing of the past, and the lore that accompanied learning how to use the medicines has been lost. Another factor may have been the fact that, since knowledge of useful medicines was often considered private property, such a tale could only be passed on if it were purchased from the owner. With the decline in traditional medicine, such tales may have been lost for lack of an interested buyer. Furthermore, many of these tales seem to have contained elements of the supernatural, and owners of these tales might not have wanted them known to people who would not understand this and be sympathetic to it. Certain doctors also had ethical concerns about their medicines. Sam Thompson's grandfather *Simholáhki*, who was a skilled *alikcí* 'traditional doctor', felt that certain of his medicines, such as bear-strength medicine and wolf-speed medicine, had the potential for abuse in the hands of an unscrupulous person. For this reason, he was unwilling to pass the knowledge of them along to anyone.

Fragments of two other medicine origin tales were recorded by Paz-Taylor (1937:20). Though these are in English, they are worth quoting in full. The words are exactly as Paz-Taylor wrote them, but the arrangement here is as if they had been spoken in Koasati, and the two Koasati words quoted are correctly spelled:

TALE 1

One tree (*łobonó* 'black gum') said,
"I am a great help to women,
whenever she gets sick,
I will help her."
Now they use the bark
whenever they need medicine for a woman.

TALE 2

Another tree (*silhobá* ‘black elm’ [*sic* for ‘cork-winged elm’]) said,
“I will help you
when you help sick people.”

In both of these fragments, the trees themselves speak to people and reveal the medicines that they contain. Note that in the two versions of *The Origin of Deciduous Trees* in chapter 2, the trees were considered to be beings who could speak.

## BEAR MEDICINE

narrated by Bel Abbey

This narrative was recorded on tape in 1977 by Barbara Edmonson and Susan Knowles as part of a class in linguistic field methods at Tulane University; I made the translation directly from that tape. The only fully preserved medicine origin tale, it details the way that the Indians discovered how to use pine resin to staunch cuts and wounds. The reason for the preservation of this particular tale is its very literalness. Because the narrative is cast in such a way that it could actually have happened and contains no supernatural elements, Bel Abbey felt that it was a “true tale” and not one that offended his high standards of authenticity. Furthermore, this medicine was not one that required magical songs or the breath of a doctor to be effective, and in telling the tale, there were no secrets or information deemed pertaining solely to the Koasati that were revealed.

### Scene 1: The Hunters Find a Bear

| | |
|---|---|
| Má:miyok, | Now then, |
| ilanawíhli:fó:kok, | when one hunted, |
| ilanawíhcok haccá:lá:hi:fó:k, | when one was in the state of being about to hunt |
| áswa:fó:k aɬɬá:citǫ. | when there were two people, two went off. |
| Ittobihį́ ittobihí inɬakį́ píhlok, | Having picked up bows and arrows, |
| aɬɬá:ci:fó:k, | when the two went off, |
| ilanawíhlit ittohayó. | they hunted in the forest. |
| Mó:tohok, | Then afterwards, |
| niták á:tatohon híhcok, | having caught sight of a bear being there, |
| “Máp ilbásk!" káhhan, | “Let us kill that one!” they said, |
| í:bá:hik stáswa:fó:kap | and as the two were about to kill it, |
| ná:hotoho:limpáhcok. | it is said that it was there. |
| Hóccatohok, | They shot at it, |
| hóccat ɬáhhin, | and having shot at it and hit it, |
| má:mo:sin, | then, |
| nitá:kok ikíllotohok, | the bear did not die, |
| má tóklot hóccayok itɬáhhin. | even though they had shot and hit it. |

### Scene 2: The Bear Struggles with the Hunters

| | |
|---|---|
| Má:mo:sin, | Thereupon, |
| nitá:kok noksí:patohoma:łok, | the bear was completely angry, |
| ikíllotohok. | and it did not die. |
| A:ti łóhlin, | It chased after a man, |
| á:tik iwwalí:kat iwwalí:kat, | and the man ran and ran from it, |
| náhhon, | well, |
| niták łóhli:fó:kon, | when the bear chased him, |
| iwwalí:kat, | he ran from it; |
| ittó statanahká:cit | he went around and around trees |
| iwwalí:ka:fó:kon, | running from it, |
| caffák illónkat | and the one stood hiding from it, |
| haccá:toho:limpáhcok, | it is said; |
| ittó apatahá illónkan. | he was hiding from it behind a tree. |
| Má:mo:sin, | Thereupon, |
| niták łóhlit łóhlit | the bear chased the one; |
| tabátkah bànnak sankí:con, | he chased him and tried to catch him and could not, |
| á:tik lóhkat anó:ka:fó:kon, | when the man was tired out, |
| istinłopótli:fó:kon, | when he came passing by with it [the bear], |
| caffák illónkat haccáhcok, | the one was standing in hiding, |
| himá:ya mán hócca:fó:kon, | and once again when he shot at it, |
| hóccat łá:hi:fó:kon, | when he shot and hit it, |
| niták máp łóhli:fó:kon, | as the bear was chasing that one, |
| akkó illónkatohok haccá:li:p, | [past] where the hidden one was standing, |
| himá:ya mán lóhkatohok | now again he [the man] was tired, |
| į́fáyt anó:ka:fó:kon, | and when he was about to give up |
| himá:ya lóhkat anó:kak | now that one was completely tired, |
| istinłopótlin, | and came passing by with it [the bear], |
| himá:ya hócca:fó:kon, | now when the other shot at it, |
| máp í:lan, | that one arrived, |
| lóhlit | and the two |
| stáswatoho:limpáhcok. | chased it, it is said. |

**Scene 3: The Bear Doctors Itself**

Mó:tohon,
łakohyá:cit,
koyabí:cit anóslin,
niták ná:hotoho:limpáhcok.
Łakhaninánnat,
sánkot anóhkok,
koyá:bik ómmitǫ.
Má:mo:sok,
nokcóhbok,
ittahóhcat,
ihá:nifa ittahóhcat,
ittasikcí má:mi wíhlit,
pahí asikcí má:mi wíhlit,
í:pat,
kámmit á:tan.
"Ná:son sammíhcok óˀmí?" káhhan.
Má:mo:sin,
"Hociccánnąh!
Ná:son sammihcóˀmí?
Ilhi:cásk máp!" káhhan.
Má:mo:sin,
ałłá:cit,
ayakháhcok,
ohhí:ca:fó:kap,
á:tatohok,
ittahóhcat,
pahí asikcí má:mi í:pat
ilimalikcíhcok a:táhcómmitǫ
sobáyhlok.
Coyyífon óhłok,
niták coyyí afakcó kaláslit,
kacáłłit haccá:lit,
socáffit anóhlok,
coyyí nihá píhlok,
stilihamohlíhcotoho:limpáhcok.

Then afterwards,
they used all their arrows on it,
and had completely wounded it;
it is said the bear was there.
It was covered with blood,
and completely unable to do anything,
it was the case that it was wounded.
Thereupon,
it stopped,
and it dug the ground;
it dug in the ground,
and it looked for things like tree roots,
it looked for things like grass roots,
and it ate them,
and so it kept on.
"What is it that it is doing?" one said.
Thereupon,
"Do not then shoot it!
What is it doing?
Let us watch that!" he said.
Thereupon,
the two went,
and approaching it,
when they went and watched it,
it kept on;
it dug the ground,
and it ate things like grass roots,
and it was the case that they knew
it was doctoring itself.
Having gone over to a pine tree,
the bear scratched the pine bark,
he stood there biting it,
and having debarked it,
and taking the pine resin,
it is said that he was rubbing it
on himself.

### Scene 4: The Indians Learn the Medicine

| | |
|---|---|
| Má:mo:sin, | Thereupon, |
| athómmak, "Coyyí nihá | the Indians [said], "It is the case that |
| stilihamohlíhcok óm. | it is rubbing itself with pine resin. |
| Kosnók akkąhilí:cihalpísco:lǫ. | We too might indeed be able to do the same. |
| Ná:sok kǫho:pá:ci:p, | If something should injure us, |
| kosnók coyyí nihá | we too could rub ourselves with |
| stilihamóhhílihalpíscok," káhhan. | pine resin," they said. |
| Má:mo:sin, | Thereupon, |
| íkbot fayáhlok, | they did not kill it and left it alone, |
| pí:la įsobayáhlok, | they just learned from it, |
| łoyóhkatoho:limpáhcok. | and returned home, so it is said. |
| Coyyí nihá stilihamóhlit, | It rubbed itself with pine resin, |
| łakhaní:citohofa stilihamóhtohon | they saw it having rubbed itself where |
| híhcok. | it was bleeding. |
| Kámmo:sin sobáylil. | Just so much is what I know. |
| Tafhiyám! | Finis! |

*Textual commentary:*

Line 1 *má:miyok*. This conjunction, here translated as 'now then', usually means 'but anyway'. It is used here at the beginning of the narrative because it followed one of Abbey's typical introductory prologues, which is not translated as part of the narrative since it is not germane. However, it is given and translated here:

| | |
|---|---|
| Mó:li:p, immánkalayon, | Well, I will tell them, |
| thátka tayyík sobáyka bànnampan, | the white women say they want to know it, |
| anók, acathómmo:liskan, | I, since I am an Indian; |
| ilanawihlíhcotohok, | they used to hunt; |
| sámmit ilanawíhlitoho:limpáhcok | how it is said that they used to hunt, |
| ohimmánkallahok iscokkó:lin. | I shall tell them as they came and sat here. |

Apparently, Edmonson and Knowles had asked Abbey to tape a simple ethnographic description of traditional hunting; however, Abbey felt that the situation required a more formal tale, so he chose a narrative from his repertoire that included hunting as a component.

Line 5 *Ittobihį, ittobihí inłakį píhlok* 'Having picked up bows and arrows'. The mention of bows, *ittobihí*, literally 'wooden guns', and arrows, *ittobihí inłakí*, literally 'bullets of the wooden gun', places this narrative deep in the past. The Koasati received firearms almost three hundred years ago, and many traditional narratives view hunters as having guns and bullets.

Lines 18–46 This scene describes very nicely what might happen if hunters were only to wound a dangerous animal, such as a bear, rather than kill it outright. In this particular narrative, of course, it is necessary that the bear not die in order for the medicine to be discovered; nonetheless, the concept of one hunter being chased by the bear while the other is hiding behind a tree is a vivid and well-thought-out composition within the narrative. An interesting linguistic note: in Koasati, a person hides 'alongside' (*apatahá*) a tree and not 'behind' (*obá:li*) it. This is because trees are not considered to have front or back sides, so the word *obá:li* is inappropriate.

Lines 58–60 *ittasikcí má:mi wíhlit, / pahí asikcí má:mi wíhlit ,/ í:pat* 'it looked for things like tree roots, / it looked for things like grass roots, / and it ate them'. Note that before the bear uses the pine resin to staunch his wounds, he eats particular herbal medicines that are not elaborated here. Lyda Averill Paz-Taylor learned about a number of herbal remedies from Jefferson Abbey, Bel Abbey's grandfather, and she gives the combination of medicines used to treat gunshot or arrow wounds: "A decoction made by boiling together the barks of *Nyssa sylvatica* [black gum, *łobonó*], *Ulmus americana* [elm, *baksá*] and *Acer rubrum* var. *Drummondii* [red maple, *ipłimithatká*], is drunk and is also applied to the wound" (Paz-Taylor 1940:47).

Lines 62–66 Unlike non-Indian hunters, the Koasati were likely to let a game animal live if it exhibited behavior out of the ordinary—as in this fictional case, or in a case reported by Bel Abbey, in which he allowed a rabbit to live, after it tricked his dogs into thinking it was a stone.

Lines 82–91 Here the hunters learn about the healing properties of pine resin and adopt them for their own use. Notice also that the bear that showed them the medicine is permitted to live because of the value of what it taught them.

# 6

# Christian Tales

Despite extended contact between Europeans and Americans from the sixteenth century onwards, Christianity was not introduced to the Koasati until the 1890s. At that time, they were visited by a peripatetic and charismatic Congregational preacher named Paul Leeds, who converted a number of people. For approximately thirty years, the community was divided into two groups—those who followed the traditional religion (which was strongly linked to traditional medicine), and the Congregational community, whose members nevertheless maintained some degree of practice and belief in their former religion. Finally, however, the inability of traditional medicoreligious practices to stem the 1918–19 influenza epidemic that decimated the population led to widespread disillusionment and the virtual abandonment of traditional religion by the beginning of the 1920s—by which time, the entire community had become Congregational Christians. Nonetheless, certain traditional rites were practiced as late as the 1940s by elders brought up in the traditional religion. But, since their children and grandchildren were raised as Christians, these rites fell into disuse as the elders died.

During the period of evangelization, the vast majority of the people were monolingual in Koasati and almost completely illiterate. Thus, Paul Leeds catechized the Koasati by means of interpreters, who cast Biblical narratives into traditional Koasati forms. Stylistically, then, Christian tales are identical to other Koasati narratives; it is only in their content that they stand out. One significant linguistic feature of Christian tales is the presence of more English loanwords than are actually necessary. This seems to have arisen from the fact that English—more specifically, the English of the King James Version of the Bible—was used as a liturgical language, so, to the Koasati ear, its use in these religious tales provides an aura of sanctity.

## ADAM AND EVE
narrated by Ruth Poncho

I recorded this narrative on tape in November, 1990. Ruth Poncho, who was an excellent speaker of colloquial Koasati, preferred not to relate traditional narratives because she felt that she did not have the talent. However, having been a church-going woman all her life, she felt confident enough to relate the following narrative, which in style, if not content, is traditional in form. She belonged to a family that remained deeply traditional despite their Christian faith. Her father was one of the last persons to use elite speech regularly, and both her parents used their Indian names exclusively. Ruth Poncho herself had an Indian name, *Aktó*, almost alone among her generation.

The Christianization of the Koasati naturally led to familiarity with the contents of the Bible. Bible stories were paraphrased from the King James Version during church services by the Indian interpreters and lay ministers, using traditional Koasati literary forms. The following narrative is one of these paraphrases, covering Genesis 2–3. An unusual feature of this narrative is that it is, in essence, a single sentence, joined together by the various switch-reference markers. Sentence boundaries have been inserted at scene breaks to aid comprehension and for reasons of layout and structure.

### Scene 1: The Creation Of Adam and Eve

| | |
|---|---|
| Ná:hok, | Well, |
| abacokkó:lik ihá:ni talibó:lit, | God made the earth; |
| himá:ka stałí:yak ihá:ni talibóhlok, | in the beginning, having made the earth, |
| abá talibó:litohok, | he made the heavens, |
| ná:hon, | and, well, |
| nasmałahli máhco:t isá:cit, | he caused the wild animals and suchlike to live, |
| na:ho:fó:kok | when he had done that, |
| mán á:ton talibó:litohok, | he also made a human being; |
| á:ti inná:hon, | he made a human being of it; |
| okłí mók na:hot, | he also used clay; |
| okłí hómma má:min ná:hot á:ti stalibóhlok, | he used reddish clay to make the human being, |
| ná:hon, | and, well, |
| talibó:lit ballá:li:fo:kok, | when he made him and laid him out, |
| ico:pófkan, | he blew into his mouth, |
| hifóskat hifóskok náhhon, | and he made that he breathed and breathed, |
| ná:hǫ holcifó inká, | and he gave him a name, |
| ǽdamko:to katík, | it was Adam, |
| atámko athómma į̨holcifó katík, | but the Indians' name for him is *Atámko*; |
| mók ałí:yak ałí:yok á:tayok, | also he went along living, |
| bisná:łik stinkánkon, | but contrary to expectation, he did not like being by himself, |
| "Stinkánkǫ; | "He does not like it, |
| tayyihón mán intalibó:lilą́," káhhok, | I shall also make a woman for him," he said, |
| mók atámko:kon nocí:cit balláhlok, | and he put *Atámko* to sleep and laid him out, |
| nakcí incaffá:kan imíhsok, | and taking one of his ribs from him, |
| tayyihá intalibó:lit anóhlok, | and having finished making a woman of it, |

mók ico:hifóskan,
falkóhkok áswan,
áswan.

he also breathed into her mouth,
and the two awakened and dwelt,
the two dwelt there.

### Scene 2: The Temptation in the Garden

Má:mo:sin,
nashókti má:mi stallá:litohon,
"Hokkí:ta:si haccá:li:p haspánnąh!
Haspáhcok ómmit ná:holahǫ;
haciíllilahok," káhhok
immánkatoho:liyon,
ná:hok,
cintó mók haccá:lit a:yáhcotohot ómmǫ.
Má:mo:sok,
tayyihá inna:łí:kak,
"'Akkáp haspánnąh' ká:hask,"
káhhan,
ná:hot,
"Ó:, háspatík ná:son haciíkillóhc katík
óm.
Pí:la įhaspá:hį bánkok ómmok,"
káhhan,
káhhok,
immánkan,
má:mo:sin,
tayyihá:kok caffák tipáslit íhpok,
atámkok ómmok,
"'Caffá:kat háspatík sankóhc,' ká:ha:s,"
káhhok,
"Í:pahak íllitoho:liyon," ká:hayon,
akkántik,
tipáslit matį́hkan,
íhpok,
holikfíkson aswáhcotohok,
ilisobayáhlok,
bihicobá atónkat áswakap.

Thereupon,
he had laid out a garden,
"Do not then eat what stands in the middle!
If it happens that you eat it,
you will die," he said,
he told them,
well,
the Serpent seemed to go about walking.
Thereupon,
he spoke to the woman,
"Just because he said, 'Do not eat that,'"
he said,
well,
"Oh, please eat it; you cannot die for
any reason.
It seems he just doesn't want you to eat it
from him," he said,
and having said it,
he told it to her,
and then,
the woman picked one and having eaten it,
as for *Atámko*,
"'Even though you eat but one,' he said,"
he said,
"The eaters will die," he said,
but this being so,
she picked one and having given it to him,
and he having eaten it,
that the two were naked,
they realized it,
and they hid their genitals
behind the fig.

### Scene 3: The Discovery of the Fall

Ná:ho mók
Cisáskok ómmok,
ohłok impáhka:p,

Well also,
as for Jesus, when he arrived there
and called them,

impáhkat á:ya:p,
bihicobá tałá á:tok atónkat lokkó:lin,

lokkó:lin híhcok,
"Hacimmánkali:sáyon
ná:hotáskok ómmik," káhhan.
ná:hok,
"Naksók káhhan háspá?" káhhan.
"Cintok ónkask,
ká:hat kómmánkat,
'ka:nóhco:liyon ónk,' káhhan,
ílhpok óm," káhhan.

when he went around calling them,
on the other side of the fig, the human
beings were standing hiding their genitals,
and seeing them standing there,
"It is the case that you have done
what I told you about," he said.
well,
"Who told you to eat?" he said.
"Because the Serpent said it,
he told us saying it,
'But it is good,' he [Serpent] said,
we have eaten it," he [Adam] said.

**Scene 4: The Curse on the Serpent, Adam, and Eve**

Má:mo:sin,
cintó:kon,
"Isnók ittasalátlit,
sancó íspamá:łok ałcí:yalahǫ
himá:yap," káhhok,
ittíɬɬit apíhlok,

atámko:kon ónkak,
"Isnók iltocíhnot,
hiná:bat stalpí:san iltocíhnot,
scillókbat,
stibi:hofáhnabáhnok,

cįfámli ínkat í:pat stałcí:yalahǫ,"
káhhok,
ná:ho mók,
í:fa:kok ná:hon,
"Holpá có:ban íscibáhnok,
atlawísta isá:cit stałcí:yalahǫ isnók.
Akkąhací:citoho:liskan," káhhok,

askáhká:hik bánko:fó:kon,
bihicobá híssi má:lon
óhyat ittacó:t anóhlok,
holikfán talibó:lin,
hókfok askáhkatǫ.

Kámmo:simá:m sobáylil.

Thereupon,
to the Serpent,
"As for you, you shall crawl on the ground,
and now [you] shall go about eating
sand," he said,
and coming and pushing him,
threw him away,
and to *Atámko* he spoke,
"As for you, you shall work,
you shall work quite hard,
you will be hot,
sweat shall regularly flow down
your face,
and you will begin to feed your family,"
he said,
well, also,
to *Í:fa* [Eve] who was there,
"As for you, a great illness will take you
regularly, when you cause children to live.
It is because of what you two have
done," he said,
and when they did not want to leave,
they sewed together fig leaves,
and made clothing,
and having put them on,
they left.

Just so much, perhaps, is what I know.

*Textual commentary*:

Line 2 *abacokkó:li* This is a common term for 'God' and is now understood to mean 'dweller in heaven'. Nonetheless, the term seems to have been an old epithet of the sun, meaning 'she who sits in the sky'.

Line 11 The idea that Adam was created of red clay goes back to an old interpretation of the name that connected it to the Hebrew word for 'red'. Nonetheless, there is a striking parallel between this passage and a similar paraphrase written in Naragansett by Roger Williams (1643:125):

| | |
|---|---|
| Wuttàke wuchè wuckeesittin pausuck Enìn, | Last of all he made one Man |
| Wuche mishquòck, | Of red Earth, |
| Ka wesuonckgonnakaûnes Adam, | And call'd him Adam, |
| túppautea mishquòck | or red Earth |

Line 22 *tayyihón mán intalibó:lilą́* 'I shall also make a woman for him'. Here is another example of plural for singular, such as is found in "The Creation of Crow" and "The Two Winds" (Chapter 2).

Lines 30–57 Note that the thing that is eaten by Adam and Eve is never mentioned by name, except that it is some kind of plant. The Koasati seem to have avoided absorbing the non-Biblical popular tradition that the forbidden fruit was an apple.

Line 57 The verb *atónkan*, the intransitive of *atómmin* 'to protect', has the specific meaning of 'to protect or hide one's genitals from view'.

Lines 57–62 Note that Adam and Eve are seen as hiding behind the fig tree and only later creating clothing out of fig leaves.

Line 74 *sancó íspamá:łok ałcí:yalahǫ himá:yap*. 'and now [you] shall go about eating sand'. This is a misunderstanding of the verse "dust shall thou eat all the days of thy life."

Line 81 *cįfámli* 'your family'. This word, although borrowed from English, is not in this narrative because of the religious connotations of English. Rather, the Koasati aboriginally did not have a concept of the bilateral family, focusing rather on the matrilineal clan, the *ayiksá*, which excludes the paternal side of the family, or on the extended family, *ittolihyá*, which could include nonrelatives. Thus, the English word covering the nontraditional concept has been borrowed into Koasati.

# THE ORIGIN OF THE RACES

narrated by Solomon Battise

I recorded this text on tape in November, 1992. Solomon Battise was a lay minister of St. Peter's Congregational Church for many years, where he served as an interpreter for non-Indian ministers and as minister before his non-Indian son-in-law was chosen as minister in 1992. He was the son of *Soyá* (Ellisol Battise), who was an excellent teller of traditional narratives and who served as a consultant for Lyda Paz-Taylor in the 1930s (see Chapter 8). Solomon Battise had long been suspicious of any non-Indian trying to learn Koasati, and this was the first time that any text of his had been recorded with his full permission and cooperation.

A notable feature of Solomon Batisse's narrative is the liturgical use of English. The English word 'God' is borrowed as *Gádka*; one of the several Koasati equivalents is not used. In addition, in line 78, God speaks English in a Koasati context, and the English phrase is translated in the following lines. This is parallel to the way the Bible used to be read in church services: first the passage was read in English and then it was translated and commented upon in Koasati.

## Prologue

| | |
|---|---|
| Má:mik, | Well then, |
| hacimmánkatáks! | let me tell you something! |
| Pí:la a:łihilká cimmá:mo:scon | It is just a little story that I heard; |
| há:lolitohoskak, | |
| dákta ráysik kómmánkahco:lik | Doctor Rising told it to us when he |
| ciká:kofon | came from Chicago. |
| óntok ómmoh. | |

## Scene 1: God Tries to Make Human Beings

| | |
|---|---|
| Gádkak ónka:k, | God spoke, |
| "Á:ton talibó:hilask!" ká:haton. | "Let us make a human being!" he said. |
| Má:mo:sok, | Thereupon, |
| á:ti ómmi:k talibó:li:k | as for when he made the human being, |
| (sámmit tálwat casobáykotikap), | (I do not know how he sang) |
| oktawóhkat anóhlok, | when he had mixed it up, |
| oconafá ohtittaklískatoh. | he put it into the oven. |
| Matacapíłkatohok, | He had taken it out, |
| ikbá:ci:k, | when he was warming it, |
| stittaí:sit ómmok ikbáhcok, | it seems he took it out of the oven when it was warm, |
| mastittaí:sit ómmáttok, | and after taking it out of the oven, |
| ihokí:cofíhn stittaí:sitoh. | he had taken it out of the oven too soon. |

Má:mo:sin,
á:to:kok ómmi:k alpískok onàmmit,
yabóhlimá:mit,
hátkamá:mik onàmmiton.
"Ḿmm̀!" Gádkak ká:hatoh.
"Alpískotohoh," ká:hatoh.

Thereupon,
as for the human being, it was still underdone,
it was somewhat soft,
and it was still somewhat white.
"Mmm!" God said.
"It is underdone," he said.

### Scene 2: God Tries a Second Time

Má:mo:sin,
"Himá:ya mán talibó:lilik," ká:hatoh.
Má:mo:sok,
talibó:li:k,
malmammí:cit talibóhlok,
oconafá mastittapíłkatoh.
Á:táhpok,
ilhó:sitoh.
Ilhóhsok á:tatohok,
"Ǒ:, calhóstoh!" káhhok,
walí:kok ałí:yatohok,
ostimitto:tamá:tlin,
iskocinánnatoh oconafá.
Á:ti:kok himá:ya talibó:lin ihó:cafíhnan,
ittapíłkatohon,
atiní:kat,
locamá:mit,
ná:hon,
matacapíłkatoho:limpáhcok.

Thereupon,
"Once again I will make one," he said.
Thereupon,
when he made it,
he made it in the exact same way,
and put it into the oven.
He just stayed there,
and he forgot it.
Having forgotten it, he stayed there.
"Oh! I've forgotten it!" he said,
and he went running,
he went to exchange it,
and there was nothing but smoke in the oven.
Now the human being had been made too long
before he took it out of the fire,
it was burned;
it was somewhat black,
well,
he took it out, so it is said.

### Scene 3: God Tries a Third Time

Má:mo:sin,
mastalláhlok,
híhcok,
haccá:láhpok,
sámmik sobáykotikap,
"Ḿm̀! Himá:ya,
kántik caffá:kak ómmi:k alpískon

Thereupon,
he laid it down,
and looked at it,
and just kept on standing,
but he did not know how to do it,
"Mm! Now,
but as for the one, I made it underdone,

| | |
|---|---|
| talibó:lilik, | again, |
| mán caffák stimayóffiton, | the other is overdone, |
| caffá:kat kommámmi mók talibó:lilik mán." | one also like us I will again make." |
| "Himá:ya mán, mí:tan talibó:t ilhí:cą̨h!" | "Now again, let us try to make another!" |
| káhhok, | he said, |
| mán á:ti:kon talibó:toh. | and again he made a human being. |
| Atoccí:na talibo:lí. | For the third time he was making one. |
| Má:mo:sok, | Thereupon, |
| mastittapíłkatoh mán. | he put it into the oven again. |
| Talibó:k anóslok, | When they had finished, |
| mastittapíłkok á:táhpok, | when he had just kept it in the fire enough, |
| himá:yap mastittaíhsok, | now having taken it out of the fire, |
| hí:cat ómmátton, | after looking at it, |
| "Ḿm̀!" Kanomá:min hí:catoh. | "Mm!" he found it beautiful. |
| Má:mo:si:kok ómmi:k, | And then it was the case, |
| maspíłkatohok, | he laid them down, |
| alpískomá:mik hátkamá:min, | the one that was somewhat underdone and white, |
| alpísat immá:yak ómmi:k, | and the one that was overdone, |
| ló:cat ittakló:camá:min, | that was black and somewhat blackened on the outside, |
| cattá:lak ómmi:k hommáhcok, | and as for the last, it was red, |
| athómmo:tohok ómmi mók. | it was also the Indian. |
| Kosnón kontalibó:lit ómmitohok Gádkak. | It was the case that God made us. |

**Scene 4: God Keeps All the Human Beings He Created**

| | |
|---|---|
| Kámmit ilhicá kanomá:min, | Thus, as for the beautiful looking one, |
| mascikí:lok, | he took it up, |
| hí:cat lokkó:lon, | and he stood looking at them [the others]. |
| "Sammí:cká:himáhcok? | "Why must it be this way? |
| Intalibó:ci:sak tóklok alpískon, | Of the ones that you made, two were wrongly done: |
| caffák imma:yáhco:lik, | the one was too much, |
| incaffák alpiskóhco:lin, | and another was underdone, |
| incaffák káhno:mo:liskan. | and the other was best. |
| "Sámmickáʔhí?" | "Why must it be so?" |
| ká:toho:limpáhcok. | he said, so it is reported. |
| "Óǒ, áy lúvəm á:l!" ká:hatoho:limpáhcok Gádkak. | "Oh, *I love them all*!" *God* said, so it is reported. |
| "Óhya stimacayokpáhcok, | "I love them all, |
| óhya cikí:liláh," | and I intend to keep them all," |
| ká:hatok ómmin. | is what he said. |

Himá:yan á:ti ilhicá hátkamámmi,

locá,
hommá,
naksók ittimmałá:híkkon
istilkáhcóm
Gádka stimalyokpá.
Kámmisk,
Gádkak skomayókpatohon,
himá:yap kosná:lok
skomayókpatoho:liskan,
kosáhcoto mók,
kohalpískohcoto mók.
Kántik,
mattafílkok stimayókpa:p,
skomayókpatoho:liskan,
ínko mók, immá:yafįton.
Akkó a:pihcí ló:cato mók,
kántik mók a:pihcí locá stimayókpat,
ibisnók skomayókpatoho:liskan,
kopíhlilahok ónkok,
kopíhlok kocikí:lok.
Akkámmik,
kosnók kokáhnotoho:mo:liskat mók,
malmámmo:sin stimayókpa-
toho:liskan,
matapílkok,
stimayokpáhcok ómmi:p,
malmámmo:sin kopíhlin,

imístílkalahon.
Kámmin,
imatlawístak ístílkalahon,
kotalibó:tohok ómmok.

Now, the appearance of human beings
is whitish,
is black,
is red,
we are living in *God*'s love,
not as ones different
from each other.
Just like that,
*God* loves us,
Now, he loves ourselves alone,
because he has loved us,
also as we are,
even though we are unworthy.
But this being so,
he does not turn away if he loves someone,
because he has loved us,
if not so, it has been too much more.
Those ones whose bodies are black,
but he also loves the black bodied ones,
and because he himself has loved us,
it is the case that he gathers us,
he gathers us, and he keeps us.
Thus,
because we also are become much better,
because he loves them in just the
very same way,
he does not discard them,
if it is the case that he loves them,
in the very same way that he
gathers us,
and we will live with him.
Thus,
we will live as his children,
of the one who made us.

**Epilogue**

Himá:yap, akkámmit ilkón
kommánkaton
imalóstitohoskayok,
ima:łí:kalíhcok yá na:łihilká.

Now, because contrary to expectation,
he is interested in how He told us the Word,
I have told the story to him
in these words.

Móh!

Enough!

*Textual commentary*:

Lines 1–2 *Má:mik, / hacimmánkatáks!* 'Well then, / let me tell you something!' Note the use of elite speech here at the beginning of this narrative. In addition, the narrator uses the second person plural indirect object marker *haci-* instead of the second person singular, even though he was dictating the narrative to one person alone. This may be due to the phrase being a stereotypical introduction to a sermon, or it may simply be due to the fact that Mr. Battiste's wife was in the room while the recording was being made.

Lines 2–4 Mr. Battise here disclaims it being an original Koasati narrative by attributing it to a member of the Moody Bible Institute, whose members have made regular missionary visits to the Koasati for years. Nonetheless, the tale is curiously similar to one told by a Seminole Chief to the Governor of Florida in the nineteenth century (Swanton 1929:75):

> The Master of Life said,
> "We will make man."
> Man was made;
> but when he stood up before his Maker he was *white*!
> The Great Spirit was sorry;
> he saw that the being he had made was pale and weak,
> he took pity on him,
> and therefore did not unmake him,
> but let him live.
> He tried again,
> for he was determined to make a perfect man;
> but in his endeavor to avoid making another white man,
> he went into the opposite extreme,
> and when the second being rose up, and stood before him, he was *black*!
> The Great Spirit liked the black man less than the white,
> and he shoved him aside to make room for another trial.
> Then it was that he made the *red man*;
> and the red man pleased him.

There is a striking structural parallel between these two tales, so there may well be aboriginal ideas incorporated into Mr. Battise's narrative, whatever the source. See also Dundes (1962) and Sturtevant (1963) for discussion of the Seminole narratives.

Line 6 *"Á:ton talibó:hílásk!" ká:haton* '"Let us make a human being!" he said'. Throughout this narrative, God varies between using the singular or the plural for himself. Here, it seems the theological concept of God as a triune being, separate but commingled, creates semantic problems with the highly number-sensitive Koasati verbal system.

Line 9 *sámmit tálwat casobáykotikap* 'I do not know how he sang'. This is a clear aboriginal intrusion. God, in his creation, is compared to a traditional doctor who created medicines out of disparate items, joining them together with magic songs.

Lines 17–22 God here is given the tone of a housewife whose meal has come out wrong. The audience finds the gentle humor in this most appealing.

Line 35 *iskocinánnatoh oconafá̆* 'and there was nothing but smoke in the oven'. This descriptive and droll line continues the housewife imagery.

Line 60 *"Ḿm̀!" Kanomá:min hí:catoh* '"Mm!" he found it beautiful'. The Koasati use the term *kanomá:min* 'to be beautiful', much more frequently than the parallel term is used in English. Anything from the natural world, when it is properly shaped, healthy, good sounding, or good smelling, is termed 'beautiful'. An entirely different word, *stipí:lan*, is used for human beauty, which refers to attractiveness as well as physical beauty.

Lines 78–80 The use of an English phrase in a Koasati context, followed by a translation of that phrase, is taken from the traditional Indian Congregational Church service, in which a Biblical text was read in English and then translated and commented upon in Koasati.

Lines 85–110 The remainder of the narrative is a sermon on God's love and on how all human beings who were created are intended to be God's children.

## HOW FAR IS IT TO HELL?
narrated by Asa Poncho

In addition to biblical or semibiblical narratives, the Koasati developed nonbiblical narratives with a Christian content. The following story, *How Far Is It to Hell?*, is a good example. I recorded it in March, 1982, from Asa Poncho (1900–1984), father-in-law of Ruth Poncho. Asa Poncho was considered to be eccentric by the other Indians, with the reputation of being both untalkative and without anything to say. To me, however, he was both helpful and informative, having a strong memory of people and happenings of long ago and a wide vocabulary of obsolete words. However, the other Indians were correct, insofar as his storytelling abilities were concerned. He could tell only two stories—how his leg was ruined in an accident in the 1920s, and this one. Nonetheless, short as it is, it still fulfills what is necessary for a well-formed Koasati narrative. Note here again the use of English loanwords in a religious context.

### Scene 1: The Encounter

Ná:hok,
a:timanihtok á:yatohok,
mo:tosíkilka pa:cokkó:líhcok a:yatoho:k,
prí:ca:kok hínifa á:tatohon,
nokcóhbok,
imasilháhciha.

Well,
there was a young man going about,
he was going about riding on a motorcycle,
and there was a preacher by the roadside,
and having stopped,
one could hear him [the motorcyclist]
asking him things.

Prí:cak,"Naksó:n ałcíˀyá?" káhhan.
"Hélkafon ałí:yal," káhhan.
"Hopáhkit naksammo:scóˀlí?" káhhan.
Prí:cak ónkak,
"Ǒ:, hélkap yá:lon na:hóhcok óm.
Ihokí:co:sin ałcí:yalaho katík óm,"
káhhan.

The preacher said, "Where are you going?"
"I am going to Hell," he said.
"How far is it?" he said.
The preacher spoke.
"Oh, it is the case that Hell is right here."
"But it is the case that you shall soon
go there," he said.

### Scene 2: The Denoument

Mo:tosíkilka pa:cokkóhlok,
stałí:ya:k,
haywéykafa ó:ła:fó:kap,
trúkka cobók íhlok,
batáplit,
stafíllit,
í:bit.
Prí:ca:kok hí:cak haccá:láhpok,
"Hélkafap imapí:ci mók,"
ká:toho:limpah.

Having gotten on the motorcycle,
he drove off,
and when he got to the highway,
a large truck having arrived,
it struck him,
overturned him,
and killed him.
The preacher seeing it, just stood there;
"You threw him to him in Hell,"
he said, so they say.

Móh, ká:mo:s.

Enough. Done.

*Textual commentary*:

Lines 3–4 *mo:toskílka pa:cokko:líhcok á:yatoho:k / prí:ca:kok hínifa á:tatohon* 'he was going about riding on a motorcycle / and there was a preacher by the roadside.' The very twentieth-century setting of this narrative is enhanced by the use of English words for 'motorcycle' and 'preacher'. Although no one knows for sure, it seems likely that the narrator created this tale himself.

Lines 7–8 *Prí:cak "Naksó:n ałcíˀyá?" káhhan. / "Hélkafon ałí:yal," káhhan* 'The preacher said, "Where are you going?" / "I am going to Hell," he said.' The shocking and ill-mannered reply of the young man to the preacher, who would be distinctively dressed and identifiable as such, gives another strong feeling of the modernity of this tale. Note also that the first syllable of *hélkafon* was spoken much more loudly than normal, to emphasize the insulting nature of the reply.

Line 21 *"Hélkafap imapí:ci mók," ká:toho:limpah* '"You threw him to him in Hell," he said, so they say.' It is unclear to whom the preacher is speaking. It is possible that he is speaking to the truck driver, who just ran over the motorcyclist, or he could be speaking to God. The one to whom the motorcyclist has been thrown in Hell is, of course, the Devil. Even though this is the most modern in content of any traditional narrative, it still illustrates a basic theme of Koasati traditional literature: hubris will be punished.

# Part Two

# Semihistorical Narratives

# 7

# Encounter Stories

For the members of an American Indian group, their first encounter with Europeans was of earth-shaking importance, since their history and way of life would have been utterly changed, and their relations with the Europeans would have had an impact on their eventual survival or destruction. This is true of the Koasati, who were encountered by the Spanish in the sixteenth century, and who, by the time they had moved within the orbit of the French in the eighteenth century, had lost about 90 percent of their precontact population. Because of the continuing importance of the encounter, it is not surprising that such stories are well known.

There are two encounter traditions among the Koasati. The first, illustrated by the two versions of *The First Meeting of the Indians and the Europeans,* sees the Europeans through Indian eyes as they first arrived off the coast by boat. This tradition must have been borrowed from another Indian group, since the Koasati at no time in their history have ever lived near the coast and, indeed, at the time of contact lived in the upper Tennessee River valley, west of the Appalachian Mountains. The other tradition, illustrated by *The Origin of the Name "Koasati"*, has the Indians happening upon a European settlement during the Koasati's years of wandering. In terms of historical fact, this narrative is closer to reality, since after the Koasati were forced out of their traditional homeland during the little-known Beaver Wars of the 1690s, they ended their first migration by settling near the French outpost of Fort Toulouse in Alabama.

An interesting feature of both these traditions is that there is never any elaboration on the hostilities between the Indians and the Europeans. The Koasati seem to have managed, through political astuteness and flexibility, to avoid armed conflict with Europeans throughout their history—with the exception of a breakaway band in nineteenth-century Texas that took up hostilities against the Texans and was all but exterminated. In fact, avoidance of conflict has been the hallmark of the Koasati's policy with regard to the Europeans, and it has allowed the survival of a people that have never numbered more than a thousand since the seventeenth century.

In addition to the all-important European encounter, there is another encounter of much less direct importance, but of no less interest to the Indians—that with Africans. This is dealt with in the narrative *The Origin of Black People*, which deals primarily with the life of African slaves that the Indians seem to have viewed with horrified fascination. During part of their history the Koasati were incorporated into the Creek Confederacy, many of the towns of which had African slaves. However, the members of the Koasati town in the 1832 census are recorded as never having any slaves. Still, the encounter with Africans is of importance to the Koasati, as the descendants of Africans form a large minority of the population of the area in which the Koasati now live.

## THE FIRST MEETING OF THE INDIANS AND THE EUROPEANS (First Version)
narrated by Bel Abbey

I recorded this narrative on tape in February, 1982. Bel Abbey was somewhat nervous in the presence of the tape recorder and made several slips of the tongue. At his request, these have been edited out of the following text.

As in other traditional narratives, this narrative contains certain core occurrences or scenes that cannot be eliminated and that are expected to occur in a fixed sequence. However, the degree of elaboration given to the scenes varies according to the speaker's interest and to the conditions under which the narrative is told.

The required elements are the following: (1) The life of the Indians before the coming of the Europeans; (2) the flight of the Indians at the sight of the Europeans; (3) the Europeans devise a plan for speaking to the Indians; (4) the Europeans leave a barrel of whiskey and retire to a hidden location; (5), the Indians return and debate with each other whether or not the whiskey might be good to drink or poisonous; (6) a man (sometimes, as here, an orphan) insists on being the one to drink the whiskey; (7) the Indians observe the effects of alcohol on the man; (8) all of the Indians drink themselves into a stupor; and (9) the Europeans capture two drunken Indians, take them to their ship, and sail out onto the ocean where, on their recovery, the Europeans convince them of their good intentions. These elements can be combined into scenes according to the desire and interest of the narrator.

A Cherokee tale similar to this one was mentioned by Mooney (1900:350), but was not fully elaborated. It is very likely that this narrative passed to the Koasati from the Cherokee in the sixteenth century when they were still neighbors in the upper Tennessee River Valley.

### Prologue

| | |
|---|---|
| Athómmak i:sáhcotohon, | The Indians once were dwelling; |
| yá:li ihá:nifa i:sáhcotohon. | here in this land they dwelt. |
| Thátkak ilá:ci:fó:kok, | When the white people arrived, |
| thátkak ilá:ci:fó:k, | after the white people came, |
| ná:hotoho:limpáhcok, | they existed, so it is said, |
| athómmak illónkat | and they knew that the Indians |
| intółkamá:min sobayáhlok. | might run and hide from them. |
| Mántik, | But, to change the subject for a moment, |
| athómmak i:sáhcotohon, | the Indians were dwelling; |
| athómmak yá:li í:sat ilanawíhlit | the Indians dwelt here, and they hunted for game, |
| ná:so:t í:bit í:pat i:sáhcotohon. | and lived by killing and eating various sorts of things. |

### Scene 1: The Meeting and Flight

| | |
|---|---|
| Thátkak kotałá naksofón | Wherever the white people were going |
| yomáhlihcómmitǫ ilá:ci:fó:k, | about on our side of the ocean when they arrived, |
| himá:k afánka mán ómmot ómmitǫ. | it seems to also have been the first meeting. |
| Himá:k ilá:cin, | On first arriving, |
| món itto:tamátlitǫ iláhcok. | they also came to trade with them. |
| Thátkak ilá:ci:fó:k, | When the white people arrived, |
| piłón áłkat sto:wilá:ci:fó:kon, | when within a boat they arrived over the water, |
| athómmak í:satohok, | the Indians dwelling there, |
| híhcok | on seeing them, |
| intółkatoho:limpáhcok. | ran from them, so it is said. |
| Intółka:fó:kon, | When they ran from them, |
| intółka:fó:k, | after they ran from them, |
| afą́híkkon. | they did not meet them. |
| "Ná:sommo:líˀsá? | "Whatever could it be? |
| Sámmin intółkó?" | Why must they run off?" |
| ká:hatoho:limpáhcok thátkak. | the white people said, so it is reported. |
| Má:min, | And then, |
| intółkat akkánt í:san, | they kept on fleeing from them so; |
| naksámmi:p intółkana:nan, | sometimes they all ran from them, |
| illónkana:nan. | at other times they all hid from them. |
| Athómmak immałáhlik ómmitohok, | The Indians were afraid of them, |
| akkó á:tik ná:si akkámmin | because they had never seen such |
| ikhí:comáhco:lisk. | people as those. |
| Immałáhlik ómmitoho:limpáhcok. | It is said that they were afraid of them. |
| Intółkat í:san. | They kept on fleeing from them. |

### Scene 2: The Dilemma of the Europeans

| | |
|---|---|
| Mó:tohon, | Then, |
| thátkak ónkak, | the white people said, |
| "Sámmíhcok afánkok | "How can we get to know them before |
| inna:łí:kílkohá:lok?" hoká:ha:p, | we speak to them?" |
| intółkah illónkanánnan. | as they all ran hiding from them. |
| Imistilkafá hí:ca:p, | If they looked into their dwellings, |
| iha:nó:bi máhcotohok inná:hon, | (those they had were somewhat sunken in the earth), |
| imí:sintíwwo:tok, | they who were the openers of their houses, |
| ná:hon, | well, |
| i:sáhcotohon, | that those others dwelt in, |
| thátkak hí:ca:p | if the white people looked into |
| athómma imistilkafón má:lok, | the Indian's own dwellings; |

| | |
|---|---|
| á:ti imistilkafa má:lok | people's own dwellings were looked |
| hohí:cayon, | into, but contrary to expectation, |
| athómma ná:sok íksot, | there were no Indians of any kind, |
| imaskáhkat tółkat illónkat | they had gone out and run and |
| wasátkatohon. | hid from them and disappeared. |
| Má:mo:sin, | And then, |
| "Sammǐ::cíhcok afą̂hkok | "How ever would it be possible for us |
| inna:łí:hílká:mo:líhc," á:lot í:satohon. | to meet and speak with them?" they kept on thinking. |
| Sánkon, | It was impossible; |
| sammí:cá:hik sobáykot thátkak. | the white people did not know how they might do it. |

**Scene 3: The Leaving of the Whiskey**

| | |
|---|---|
| Ishilkák syomáhlitohok, | They [the white people] went around with liquor; |
| okohomí syomáhtohok. | they carried whiskey with them. |
| Tokofkasí caffá:kan stołá:cok | They brought over one keg, and went and |
| ostintallá:toho:limpáhcok. | laid it down for them, so it is said. |
| Ostintallá:li:fó:kok, | When they laid it down for them, |
| koplót ómmi:k, | as for the drinking glass, |
| ínko:p, | if it were not such, |
| kafí stishilká máhcot ommitǫ | it was more or less like a coffee cup, |
| casobáykotik, | but I do not know; |
| námpon intállitǫ casobáykotik, | how many they laid down for them, |
| intáhlok | I do not know, |
| łoyóhkatoho:limpáhcok. | but having laid them down for them, they returned [to their ship], so it is said. |

**Scene 4: The Return and Debate of the Indians**

| | |
|---|---|
| Má:min, | And then, |
| athómmak wasátkan, | the Indians who had gone off, |
| athómma:sáyok łoyóhkat ilá:cok hí:ca:p, | these Indians returned and came arriving, and when they saw it, |
| athómmak łoyóhkat ístohǫ. | the Indians kept on returning. |
| Athómmak hasaykáhcok í:satohok. | There were many Indians there. |
| Łoyóhkat iláhcok, | Having returned and arrived back, |
| hí:ca:kap stallá:katohon, | they who saw it [the keg] lying with it [the liquor], |
| tokoyofkasí caffá:kat tallá:kan híhcok, | upon seeing the one keg lying there, |
| hohí:ca:p, | when they saw it, they said, |

"Ná:sok óˀmí?" ká:ha:k.
"Ínkǫ! Ayakha:caskán!"
"Ná:sot ómmitohok cįho:pá:cilahǫ!"
"Ná:sot ómmitohok hacií:bilahǫ!"
ká:hat imaybá:citoho:limpáhcok
alahká.
Má:miyon,
atanáhkat hí:cat í:sat,
atanáhkat hí:cat í:sat,
kánt í:sahpin,
ná:hotoho:limpah,
akkánt í:sáhpin;
má:mo:sin,
"Na:sóˀlí?"
"Casobáykotik yáhcok
stalla:káhcok ónk,"
káhhan.
Má:mo:sin,
caffák ónkak,
"Ískot híhcaták," ká:ha:p,
"Ínkǫ! Ishiskán! Kankóhcot ómmin.
Naskánkot ómmin,
ishhískok ciíllilahǫ," káhhan.

"What is it?"
"No! Do ye not approach it!"
"Whatever it is will hurt you!"
"Whatever it is will kill ye!"
they said, forbidding the rest,
so it is reported.
But then, contrary to expectation,
they kept on turning and looking at it,
turning and looking at it,
and they kept on so,
er, so it is said,
they kept on so;
thereupon [one said],
"What is it?"
"I do not know, but it is lying there
with it [the liquor] just like that,"
said another.
Thereupon,
when one person said,
"Let me test it by drinking!"
"No! Do not drink it! It is bad by nature!"
"As it is a bad thing, upon your drinking
it, you will die," the other said.

### Scene 5: The Intervention of the Orphan

Má:mo:sin,
"Anók ómmilą́!
Anók ómmilą́!" ká:hatoho:limpáhcok
á:ti loká:casok á:yatohok.
Imaláhka íksot,
ibisnă::loscok,
atpa:hókfat a:táhcotohok,
imaláhkak íksot,
loká:casok ómmók á:tatohok.
"Anók ómmilą́, mó:li:p.
Anók ískolá:hinò," ká:ha:p,
"Ínko:š" ká:hat, "Ishiskán!
Ná:sik kankóhcot ómmitohok,
ciíllilahok," káhhan.
Ká:ha:p,
á:ti loká:casik cilítkat
fáykotoho:limpáhcok
ískoh bànnak.

Thereupon,
"I shall be the one! I shall be the one!"
said an orphaned man who was passing by,
so it is reported.
Being without living relatives,
he was completely and utterly alone;
he used to live by joining up with people;
his relatives were no more;
it was as an orphan that he lived.
"Well, I will be the one!"
When he said, "I might just drink it,"
"Nay!" said another. "Do not drink it!
As it is something bad by nature,
you will die!"
When he said this,
the orphan man would not quit begging
to try drinking it,
so it is said.

| | |
|---|---|
| “Kántik, | “But all the same, |
| ískotik, | if it be drunk, |
| amaláhkak íksoskan, | because my relatives no longer exist, |
| á:ti ná:sok ná:son imacikíhbo:s. | no one at all can feel sorry about anything. |
| Ná:sok stimacíhbalahókko:s. | Nothing will sadden anyone. |
| Ana:łóhco:liskat, | Because I have been habitually alone, |
| á:ti ná:sok amacikíhbǫ. | no one sorrows for me. |
| Ískot ammáttat | It will be a good thing if I err |
| ka:nóhco:lilahǫ. | in drinking it. |
| Sántohon hacimmánkalá:s. | I want to tell you how it is. |
| Sobáylilik,” káhhan. | I will know,” he said. |
| Stilapíhlik, “Ínko:š! | The leader said, “Nay! |
| Ná:sosco íscíkkotík. | Please do not drink even a little bit. |
| Isnómma á:tok ací:tahalpí:sǫ,” ká:hok, | You as well deserve to live,” |
| imaybá:ci:p, | and when he forbade him, |
| ikhá:lok, | the other did not listen, |
| cilítkat fáykáhpin, | and just did not quit pleading. |
| “É:, ísk má:mik,” ká:hok, | “All right, drink it then,” he said, |
| ohįfáylin. | and the other left off [begging]. |
| “Ískot híhc sámmitohon kommánka:k,” káhhan. | “Take a drink of it that you might tell us how it is,” he said. |

**Scene 6: The Results of Drinking**

| | |
|---|---|
| Má:mo:sin, | Thereupon, |
| įfáyhlin, | having left off with him, |
| á:ti loká:casikok áłłok | the orphan man filled up a container |
| ískotoho:limpáhcok. | and drank, so it is said. |
| Ískok, | He drank, |
| ískot ałí:yak, | and continued to drink, |
| incokfolóhlit stanó:ka:fó:kap, | and now, when he was completely dizzy, |
| na:sókkotoho:limpáhcok. | it is said that he was insensible. |
| Na:sókkot á:tatoho:limpáhcok. | He was in a state of insensibility, as it is reported. |
| Má:mo:sok, | Thereupon, |
| incokfolóhlit anó:ka:fó:kap, | when he was completely dizzy, |
| himá:ya mán naksáhkat, | now also, he made noise, |
| naská:hak sobáyhíkkotik, | and what he said was unintelligible, |
| ałí:yatoho:limpak. | but he went on, so it is said. |
| Himá:ya mán, “Ískok kokámmin.” | Now also they said, “Drinking does so to us!” |
| “Máh! Hacikámmilahohónka:sin.” | “Listen! That is completely and utterly what will happen to ye!” |
| “Hiná:p hashicá.” káhhan. | “Now you see it,” they said. |

Na:sókkot á:tatoho:limpáhcok.

Iskó,
ałí:yat ískot háktok,
ískon háktot ómmitohok.
Má:mo:sok,
ískot háktik táhmok,
ittaballá:kok nóhcin hí:cok,

ĭ::satoho:limpáhcok óhyak.

"Íllá:p;
íllilahok,
komíllin,
íllilahok káhcok óm," ká:hok,
wá:cok ístoho:limpáhcok híhcok.

Má:mo:sin,
káhcok hí:cok í:san,
ittatàmmitoho:limpáhcok.
Tă:mmin,
ihó:ca sámmin tàmmit kostí:nitohon
casobáykotik,
tàmmáhpok,
falą́hkok,
tàmmáhpok
ilihá:lok ilkoyóhlin.
"Máh! Hiná:p! Falánká:himá:m!"
Ilihamóhlit ómmitohon falą́hkok.

Má:mo:sin,
falánká:hin,
imasilhá:citoho:limpáhcok,
"Sáʔmí? "
"Ná:sok sáʔmí?"
"Cisammíʔcí?"
"Sámmin onciʔsáʔ?" káhhan.
Má:mók,
yaʔá:sáyày,
"Ka:ná:hostohon stinnocók.
Stinnocók ká:nopalámmotohon,
kámmisk ishók!
Íshílko:li:p,
stinnocók ká:nopalámmotohon.

It is said that he was in a state of insensibility.
He drank,
went on drinking and became drunk;
he drank and was drunk.
Thereupon,
they watched him as he drank and got drunk,
fell down, and lay down on the ground
and fell asleep;
they all were really keeping on watching him.
"He is almost dead.
He will die,
he is dying on us; such is the case,
he is going to die," they said,
and watching him, they kept on waiting for it, so it is said.
Thereupon,
they kept on watching him in the same way;
he was lying on the ground, so it is said.
He really lay there;
I do not know how long he lay there
before he regained consciousness,
but he just lay there,
and he awoke;
he just lay there,
woke up, and moved.
"Look! Lo! He is about to awaken!"
He was continuing to rub himself as he was awakening.
Thereupon,
as he was awakening,
it is said that they asked him,
"How is it?"
"What is it like?"
"How was it for you?"
"How are you?" they said.
Then,
this one here, contrary to expectation, said,
"It was a very good soporific.
It was an extremely good soporific,
and this being so, drink ye it!
If we were to drink it,
it would be a very good soporific.

| | |
|---|---|
| Stanka:nă::ho:sin, | I liked it very, very much; |
| nó:co:tok ká:nopalámmotohok," | it was an extremely good sleep," |
| káhhan. | he said. |

**Scene 8: The Return of the Europeans and the Capture of the Indians**

| | |
|---|---|
| Thátka:sáyok iláhcok, | The aforementioned white people,<br>upon arriving |
| ittabá:katoho:limpáhcok, | came and caught some of them, |
| toklóhcot ómmǫ. | about two in number. |
| Tabá:kok słoyóhkok | They caught them, returned with them, |
| piłáfá stołá:cok áłłitohok. | and, getting over there to the boat, put<br>them into it. |
| Kostí:nit anó:ka:p, | After they regained consciousness, |
| inna:łí:ka:fó:k, | when the others spoke to them, |
| intółkah bànnatik, | they tried to run away, |
| okó:liskan sánkon. | but because they could tell that they were<br>on the water, they were unable to do so. |
| Fayáhláhpok, | Their having given up [trying to escape], |
| hiná:yap ponná:cit inna:łí:kat | now they spoke to them and taught them; |
| inna:łí:kat holikfó:t hokfí:cit, | they spoke to them and dressed them in<br>them in things such as clothing; |
| hokfí:cit anóstohomá:łok. | they would have dressed them completely. |
| Ná:son aláhka mók immą̀híkká:hin, | The rest also would tell them nothing<br>more than, |
| "Ilacití:k holikfó:t cínkat na:hotilká," | "Belt on the clothing and so forth that we<br>made and gave you." |
| káhhan. | |
| Ittimmą̀hkan, | Having spoken to each other, |
| óhya thátkak athómma ostacákkin, | all the white people went along<br>accompanying the Indians, |
| holikfó:t hokfí:cit stimóklat, | they gave them things such as clothing |
| ishilkók á:sat stafą̀hkan, | and made friends with them by means of<br>it [clothing], |
| iskóhcot ómmin. | as liquor was with them, and having<br>met them with it, they [the Indians] were<br>now habitual drinkers. |

*Textual commentary*:

Lines 7–10 Mr. Abbey, possibly because of nervousness, launched straight into scene 1 after only two introductory verses. After a few moments, he clearly felt that the introduction was insufficient, so he stopped and inserted these verses introduced by the conjunction *mántik*, which indicates a change in the subject being discussed.

Lines 24–25 *“Ná:sommo:lí?sá? / Sámmin intółkó?” ká:hatoho:limpáhcok thátkak* ‘“What-ever could it be? / Why must they run off?” the white people said, so it is reported.’ It is a stylistic fiction in the genre of *cokfa:łihilká* that non-Indians speak Koasati. In other kinds of narratives, when a non-Indian speaks Koasati, an explicit statement is usually made as to whether or not the non-Indian really spoke the language.

Lines 40–41 *Imistilkafá hí:ca:p, / iha:nó:bi máhcotohok inná:hon* ‘If they looked into their dwellings, / (those they had were somewhat sunken in the earth)’. It is unclear what the narrator means exactly by *iha:nó:bi máhcotohok*. The word *iha:nó:bi* usually means ‘hole in the ground, such as is made by digging’. At times, it is used also to mean ‘cave’. If ‘cave’ were meant, however, one would not expect the modifier *máhco* ‘sort of’. What is more likely is that here is a remembrance of semisubterranean dwellings, such as are found in archaeological contexts in former Koasati territory in Tennessee (Bauxar 1957:414).

Lines 50–52 *Má:mo:sin, / “Sámmĭ::cíhcok afą́hkok / inna:łí:hílká:mo:líhc,” á:lot í:satohon* ‘And then, “How ever would it be possible for us to meet and speak with them?” they kept on thinking.’ The Koasati verb *á:lon* ‘to think’ requires that the thought be expressed as a quotation, rather than as a subordinate clause as in English.

Line 93–95 The figure of the Orphan is a stock character in Koasati narrative. Kimball (1989:49–50) discusses the sources of this fascination with the Orphan. By being free of kinship ties, an orphan is free to do things that such ties restrain others from, such as helping Corn Woman or, as in this narrative, drinking an unknown substance.

Lines 108–17 This monologue by the orphan helps to explain why he feels free to do what others dare not to; it also indicates the isolation of a kinless individual in a kinship-based society.

Line 118 *stilapíhlik* ‘the leader’. In Koasati narrative, the word *stilapíhli* ‘leader’ is preferentially used over *mikkó* ‘chief’. Although the evidence is not clear, it seems likely that *stilapíhli* is a separate role from *mikkó*. Certainly in the 1820s and 1830s in Alabama, the leader of the Koasati, *Ka·cca Ha·co*, was not the chief, who was named *Mikko Hatka*. It also seems likely that the *stilapíhli* was also known as *inkapitaní*, a borrowing from the Spanish word *capitán*.

Lines 150–52 Here, the differing syntax of Koasati and English leads to a fusion of lines in the English translation. The final word of line 151 is a verb upon which the previous part of the line and the previous line depend. In English, however, a dependent clause must follow such a verb. Thus, the verb *hí:cok*, the last word in line 151, must be translated at the beginning of line 149. For this reason, lines 149–52 are fused in the English translation.

Lines 178–84 The unexpected response of the Orphan to the questions of the other Indians, that the whiskey “was a very good soporific,” is extremely amusing to listeners of this narrative, who laugh after each of these lines.

Line 196 *inna:ɬi:kat holikfó:t hokfí:cit* 'they spoke to them and dressed them in things such as clothing'. This seems to be another very archaic feature of this narrative. When the Spanish first contacted the Indians of the Southeast, clothing was among the first things that they gave them. This is reflected in a letter written in 1688 to the King of Spain by the Apalachee Indians of Florida:

| | |
|---|---|
| yak gobernadori | This governor |
| don diego quiroga ka nakayo | Don Diego Quiroga by name |
| lat ibitacoko tafon | arrived at the town of Ibitacoko |
| man ihtipicat | again they saw each other |
| yalilka fihla imakat | and he gave them good speech |
| nakahlos min imakat. . . | and also he gave them bolts of cloth. . . |
| | |
| yap piholoci ihkana pihka | As we are being loved by this one |
| pinbalayɬli | he has dressed us, |
| naka yakomin pinbalayɬit | he has dressed us in things of cloth, |
| alinci ancina amali min apinciɬlit | he has also given us to wear clothing |
| pikomahlihka. | and wearing apparel of all kinds, |
| | and thus we are. [Kimball 1987a,166–67] |

THE FIRST MEETING OF THE INDIANS AND THE EUROPEANS (Second Version)
narrated by Martha John

I recorded this narrative on tape in March, 1989. It comes from the same tradition as that of Bel Abbey; however, the focus is completely different. The eight scenes of Abbey's version are here reduced to six, followed by two epilogues—the first of which continues, in an abbreviated fashion, the history of the Indians and the Europeans to the present, while the second presents a sketch of the prophecies in which the old Indians told about the coming of the Europeans and the marvels of modern technology.

**Scene 1: How the Indians Used to Live**

| | |
|---|---|
| Athómmak yá:li i:sáhcotohok. | The Indians used to live here. |
| Yá:li í:sak ómmi:k, | As for the people who lived here, |
| ilanawíhlit, | they hunted game, |
| na:sacíhlit, | and they planted crops; |
| ná:so:t ilanawíhlik | whatever they hunted, |
| má:ɬik ohómpat. | that is only what they ate. |
| Nayincá:kap sobáykotik, | Although they were ignorant of writing, |
| ná:hǫ, | well, |
| niɬahasó:t hí:ca:p, | when they watched the moon, |

| | |
|---|---|
| hociłó:t hí:ca:p, | and when they watched the stars, |
| na:sacíhlit amá:ka mók, | they also knew exactly how and when to begin planting; |
| ná:sok sámmihalpí:sa, | they used to continue to find out everything. |
| óhya sobayá:lit | |
| ama:káhcotohok. | |
| Hopáhki ná:sok sámmihalpí:sa | How things were at a distance, |
| mastakostinní:cik amá:kat, | they kept on finding out from afar; |
| ittinkáhcotohok, | they used to give things to each other, |
| ittimalíkcit, | and they doctored each other, |
| kámmit ama:káhcotohon. | and so they used to continue. |
| Í:sak ómmi:k, | As for those who lived [here], |
| łałó:t í:bit, | they killed fish and suchlike, |
| ná:so:t í:bit, | they killed various things, |
| icó:t í:bit, | they killed deer and suchlike, |
| nitó:t í:bit, | they killed bear and suchlike, |
| ná:so:t í:bit í:pat, | whatsoever they killed they ate, |
| ná:so:t intállit i:sáhcotohoh athómmahak. | the Indians used to keep on trapping things. |

### Scene 2: The Meeting and Flight

| | |
|---|---|
| Kántoho:liyon, | This is the way things used to be; however, |
| thátkak ilmá:katohok, | the white people came; |
| ittałá i:sáhcotohok ilmá:kak, | those who used to live on the other side came; |
| ilmáhkok, | and having come, |
| ilá:cik ómmi:k i:tí:san, | those who arrived came and dwelt, |
| iláhcok i:tí:satohok. | having arrived they used to come and dwell. |
| Mó:tohok, | And then, |
| piłák ómmi:k stilma:káhcok, | they were coming by boat, |
| stilmá:katohok, | and they came; |
| piłá námpot ilmá:katohon mók | I do not know how many boats came, |
| casobáykotik, | but when they came, |
| ilmá:kak ilá:ci:k, | when they arrived, |
| iláhcok i:tí:san, | having arrived they came and dwelt, |
| intółkok, | and the Indians fled from them, |
| illónkatohok, | and hid from them, |
| ikhí:cotohok. | and did not look at them. |

### Scene 3: The Dilemma of the Europeans

| | |
|---|---|
| Himá:ka ikhí:cotohok, | Now since they did not see them, |
| íkkotohok, | and did not speak, |
| pí:la í:sat. | they merely dwelt. |
| Má:miyon, | But, |
| illónkaskan, | because the Indians hid from them, |
| ikhí:cotohok, | and the Whites did not see them, |
| íkkotohok, | nor speak, |
| anámpon iláhcok. | they came again [to try]. |

### Scene 4: The Leaving of Liquor and the Debate of the Indians

| | |
|---|---|
| Ishilkó:t ómmitohot istintállok, | It was some kind of liquor that the Whites came and laid down for them, |
| łoyóhkat, | and they went back, |
| ahiccá:cit i:sáhcotoh. | and they watched the Indians. |
| Mó:tohok, | Then, |
| ishilká istintállin | they had come and laid down the liquor for them, |
| caffá:kat ómmi:k, | and as for one Indian person, he said, |
| "Íská:hik," ká:p, | "One might drink it." |
| "Imíská:hik," ká:p, | "One might drink of it," he said. |
| "Ínkon!" | "No!" |
| "Ná:so:t ómmitik, | "Whatever it may be, |
| ishaskánnąh!" | do ye not then drink it!" |
| Má:mit, | Then, |
| stilapíhlik ká:hat, | the leader spoke; |
| immikkók káhhan, | their chief spoke, |
| immikkók, "Ná:son," ká:hak, | "Nothing," the chief said, |
| "Ná:son mankí:cóhcotoh." | "Nothing is to be done by chance." |
| Kámmiskan, | Just like that, |
| hawá:lo:sin hí:cáhcotohok. | they were looking at it intently. |

### Scene 5: The Drinking of the Liquor

| | |
|---|---|
| Má:mo:sin, | Thereupon, |
| caffá:kat ómmi:k, | as for one person, |
| "Ískot híhcalá:hin, | "I intend to taste it by drinking, |
| sámmi mók sámmilaho:s," káhhok, | how it is and also how it will be," he said, |
| ískotoho:limpáhcok ishilká. | and it is said that he drank the liquor. |
| Má:mo:sok, | Thereupon, he drank, |
| ískon, | and after he drank, |
| ískot ómmá:tok nó:citoho:limpak. | it is said that he fell asleep. |

| | |
|---|---|
| Má:mo:sin, | Thereupon, |
| nó:cit ómmá:ton, | after he slept, |
| "Ka:nă::ho:stohon, | "It was really good! |
| stinnocák ka:nă::ho:stoho:li:s!" | One can deduce that it is a really |
| káhhok. | good soporific!" he said. |
| Mí:tok ískot amá:katoho:limpáhcok. | And it is said that the others began to drink. |

### Scene 6: The Return of the Europeans and the Capture of the Indians

| | |
|---|---|
| Mó:tohon, | Later on, |
| kánt amáhkan, | it having happened to them in the same way, |
| tabá:katoho:limpak. | it is said that the white people caught some of them. |
| Athómmak tóklon tabáhkok, | They caught two Indians, |
| honó:cin tabáhkok, | they caught them after they had fallen asleep, |
| stamá:kat, | and they took them off; |
| illónkatohok tabáhkok, | they had hidden from them, caught them, |
| stamá:kan, | and taken them, |
| piłá matáłłok, | and they put them into the ship |
| stama:káhcotohok. | and went off with them. |
| Stamá:kak, | They took them, |
| ná:hoh, | and well, |
| okí o:hokki:tá:ci:fó:kon, | when they were in the midst of the sea [they awakened]; |
| okhołkók sámmá:hik sobayá:kot | and they were ignorant of what the waves were like, |
| ohacikkí:katik, | and they sat there on the water. |
| "Sámmilahókko:š," ká:t acikkí:kak, | "It is not such a thing one has experienced," they said, as they went sitting on the ship, |
| tałá amá:katoh. | and they went on to the other side. |
| Okí tałá má:lon stamá:katok, | The white people verily took them to the other side of the ocean, |
| stiláhcok, | they arrived with them there. |
| cikkí:lit paka:má:cit stanóslok, | The white people kept them, and having completely civilized them, |
| stí:sáhpok, | they just lived with them; |
| pakamá:cit anósli:fó:kok, | when they had completely civilized them, |
| masłoyóhkat stilmá:katoh yá:li. | they returned with them from afar, they brought them here. |
| Stilmá:katohok, | They had brought them, |
| stiláhcin, | and arrived with them, |
| i:sáhcotohon. | and the white people dwelt here. |

### First Epilogue: What Happened After

| | |
|---|---|
| Ittóhyak í:satik, | Although they all dwelt together, |
| ittiháplit, | they went to war; |
| athómmak ittiháplin, | the Indians went to war, |
| thátka mók ittiháplin, | and the white people also went to war; |
| athómmak ittiháplin, | the Indians went to war, |
| thátkak ittiháplin, | and the white people went to war, |
| kánt amá:kan. | and so they continued. |
| Má:fó:ka mók, | Also then, |
| ihó:ca mók, | also long ago, |
| thátkak athómma tayyí í:siscotohok, | a white person married an Indian woman, |
| athómma tayyí í:siscotoho:yá:lon, | and after he married an Indian woman, |
| "Ałí:yap akkámmilahot ómmoh," | "In the future such will be the case, it seems," |
| hokáhco:lik. | they used to say. |
| Mó:tohoskap, | Then because of this, |
| himá:yámmi mók thátka tayyi, | also nowadays white women, |
| athómmahak thátka tayyí í:sin, | Indians marry white women, |
| thátka tayyihá mók immałáhliha í:sin. | and White women also marry the Uncivilized People. |
| Kánt ama:káhcommíhcok. | And so it goes on. |

### Second Epilogue: The Prophecies

| | |
|---|---|
| Kámmisk, | Just like that, |
| "Akkámmilahok, | "It will be so, |
| oho:łá:cot, | they all will arrive there, |
| oho:łá:cot ómmoh," hohá:lot | it seems they all will be there," |
| hona:łi:káhcok himá:yámmip. | people heard them say at that time. |
| Kámmisk, | Just like that, |
| "Ínkolahoh," hoká:tik, | "It will not be," some said, |
| "Akkámmilahoh," hokáhco:lik. | but, "It will be so," others used to say. |
| "Himá:kon himó:ła:sin akkántoho:liskan, | "Because first once it happened, |
| akkámit ałį́:yah. | it indeed continues in the same way. |
| Ostanó:kalahot ómmin ómmoh," | It seems that it [the Indian way of life] |
| hokáhcok mí:tak. | will be coming to an end," some said. |
| Mí:tak hobánkotikap, | Others, they did not like it, |
| "Kámmiyáhlilaho:limá:š" hokáhcok, | "One can deduce that it must perhaps be so then," they said, |
| hohá:lot hona:łi:káhco:líhcok. | people used to hear them telling it. |
| Kámmisk, | Just like that, |
| sámmo:sin immakittóhco:líhcok, | at times they used not to err, |
| athómma mók kán sobayá:lit | because the Indians also continued |
| ama:káhcotoho:liskan, | to know how it is, |
| hokáhcok yá himá:ya yámmip. | they spoke of these modern times. |

| | |
|---|---|
| Kámmisk, | Just like that, |
| himá:yá:hi:lok ná:sok wayóhkat yomáhlit, | in the case of these modern days, things go about flying, |
| ná:ho:t, | such as, well, |
| piłá wáyko:t wayóhkan, | such as flying canoes [airplanes], |
| piłó:t amá:kan, | and things such as boats go crossing the ocean, |
| o:łopótlit ittótik amá:kat. | even though they be of wood, they go. |
| Kámmisk, | Just like that, |
| himá:ya yámmip, | nowadays, |
| ná:sok ómmi:p sha:láhkan, | as for objects, they move them, |
| apokí:to:sin ama:káhco:lik. | they used to go moving them with difficulty. |
| Kámmik ama:káhco:lik. | So they used to go. |
| Himá:yap acikí:bo:sin, | Now it is easy, |
| ahó:ban ama:káhcok. | they go likewise. |
| Kámmisk, | Just like that, |
| ihó:cap, | long ago, |
| má:łin ihó:ca | only long ago, |
| o:łopohlíhcoto katik, | the white people used to cross the ocean, |
| athómmak sobayá:kot | but the Indians did not know how. |
| Kámmo:sin sobáylilimá:m. | It is just so much that I know. |

*Textual commentary*:

Lines 7–13 In John's narrative, what is covered by a short prologue in Abbey's version is given full treatment as a scene. Here, John focuses on the natural knowledge of the Indians—namely, their celestial observations—and associates it with their knowledge of planting. It is of interest that when Abbey speaks of the way of life of the precontact Indians, he focuses entirely on hunting, while John gives equal weight to agriculture. This may well be due to the fact that in traditional Koasati society agriculture was carried on by women.

Lines 14–17 Here, in oblique fashion, John refers to the ritual specialists known as *hopá:yi*—in English, 'prophets'. These ritual specialists were able to see the future, find lost objects or persons, call game animals or people telepathically, and see things at a distance. Here, also, she obliquely refers to the traditional religion, which was tied to traditional medical practices.

Line 61–62 *stilapíhlik ká:hat, / immikkók káhhan* 'their leader spoke; their chief spoke'. Unlike Abbey, who does not mention a chief at all in his narrative, John here equates the leader and the chief. In her view, both roles could be carried out by the same person.

Lines 67–71 Unlike Abbey, John does not focus on the kind of person who wants to taste the liquor or his motivations. When asked, she did say that the person was an orphan, but for her the character apparently did not have the psychological resonance that it did for Abbey.

Line 83 *Athómmak tóklon tabáhkok* 'they caught two Indians'. It is interesting that the number of Indians captured remains the same in both versions of the narrative, especially in light of the fact that Sir Walter Raleigh's first expedition to Virginia in 1584 brought two Indians back to England.

Line 98 *cikkí:lit pakamá:cit stanóslok* 'they [the white people] kept them, and having completely civilized them'. Note the metaphor for 'to civilize', *paka:má:cin* 'to tame'. The metaphor is continued in the expression 'to be uncivilized', which is *małáhlin* 'to be wild', as in line 120, where the Indians are termed *immałáhliha* 'the Uncivilized People'.

Lines 105–16 This epilogue, in summary fashion, describes the conflict between the Indians and the Europeans after their first peaceful contacts, and suggests that intermarriage was the reason for terminating hostilities. We should note that John was a strong supporter of intermarriage, since her own desired marriage had been thwarted by traditional clan exogamy, and she had observed over the years the physical problems (primarily, repeated miscarriage) arising from marriages among the Indians, all of whom are related to each other to one degree or another due to the small size of their population.

Lines 122–59 The second epilogue is a highly oblique account of the prophecies of the ancient Indians about the coming of the Europeans and the wonders of Western technology, including a debate between those people who believed that these things were to occur and those who did not, followed by a description of some of the things that have since come to pass. Some versions of the prophecies focus on the destructive potential of technology, while others simply emphasize the verity of the prophecies. The following is a short example of the last, recorded by the author in 1988 from Tom John, a first cousin once removed of Martha John:

| | |
|---|---|
| Ná:hǫ, | Well, |
| cacokí:bo:si:fó:kap, | when I was young, |
| ampicík ammankáhco:lik. | my mother used to tell me things. |
| "Nihtá caffá:káhcon, | "One day, |
| á:tiha tóklot ilkafíhlihónka:sik | there will be two excessively powerful people, |
| ittimilakasá:mok, | they will feel hubris in regard to each other, |
| niłahasí hóccalahǫ," ka:háhco:lik. | and they will shoot the moon," she used to say. |
| Mó:tohon, | Then, |
| cacokí:boskat | because I was young, |
| incayímmá:hik casankóhco:lik. | I used to be unable to believe her. |

| “Yók bihí | “This gun, |
|---|---|
| bihosí hí:cali:p, | this pistol that I see; |
| niłahasí łá:hilahókkomá:m,” | it cannot in any way shoot the moon,” |
| á:lolíhco:lik. | I used to think. |
| Mó:tohon, | Then, |
| amokcaliyyák stanó:híkkok onàmmin, | my life has not yet come to an end, |
| Amérika Rúša ittá:sak | and America and Russia both, |
| niłahasí onahóccan hí:calik, | I saw them send rockets to the moon, |
| Amérika a:ti:bí:nok | and America, alone of all people, |
| ohpa:haca:lí:cik | went and stood someone |
| niłahasifá. | on the moon. |
| Akkámmiskan | Just like that, |
| akostinní:cili:p | I understand |
| athómmahak hokostíhnitohok ommíhcok. | how very wise the Indians were. |
| | |
| Ká:mo:s. | The end. |

## THE ORIGIN OF THE NAME “KOASATI”

narrated by Bel Abbey

I recorded this narrative on tape in March, 1989. The previous two narratives form one tradition of the first meeting of the Indians and the Europeans; this illustrates the second tradition. While the previous narratives are apparently Cherokee in origin, a tale similar to the second tradition is found among the Caddo (see the textual commentary for lines 209–53) as the origin for the name Koasati. As for the historical content of this narrative, it is much closer to the Koasati's actual experience, since from 1690 to 1886 they regularly chose (or were forced) to move from their homes. And the sudden encounter with a European settlement is quite plausible, since settlement was well advanced when the Koasati began their migrations.

### Prologue Part 1: The Word “Koasati”

| Mó:lip, mó:li:p, anók cimmánkalǫ. | Well, well, I will tell you. |
|---|---|
| Naksó:n mafíhnokkóhcotohomo:lik sobáylilik cimmánkalǫ. | Somewhere, it can be deduced that it is not true, but I will tell you what I know. |
| Anok caKowassá:tǫ anáp. | As for me, *I* am a Koasati. |
| Kámmiskan, | Just like that, |
| anók sámmit caKowassá:titoho:bí:nok | how I am merely a Koasati, |
| casobáykotik, | I do not know, |
| “caKowassá:ton,” hoká:tohon, | but people say, “I am a Koasati.” |
| “Kowassá:ti,” ká:t a:talíhcok. | I continue to say “Koasati.” |
| Má:mo:sok, | Thereupon, |
| “Kowassá:ti” ká:halíhcok anáp, | as for me, I say “Koasati,” |
| mamí:yon mí:tok ónkak, | but, on the contrary, others say, |

mí:tok ónkak má:lon,
hona:łí:kan mó:tohon,
"Košá:ta" ka:háhcok.
Kámmiskan,
anáp "Kowassá:ti" ká:halíhcok.
Kámmiskan,
naksofák má:lo:li casobáykotik,
"caKowassá:tǫ," ká:halíhcok.

others say differently,
they speak then,
they say "Coushatta."
Just like that,
as for me, I say "Koasati."
Just like that,
I do not know which is correct,
but I say, "I am a Koasati."

### Prologue Part 2: The Origin of the Tale

Má:mo:sok,
má:łon ammánkak,
ná:hon, amawocó:bo:tok,
amawó:tot ómmo:liskan,
ná:ho ónkan,
"Jéfka," hokáhcon,
"Jefæ̃bi," hokáhcon.
A:táhcok,
acó:bok a:táhcotohoskap.
caffá:kan ambiní:lik,
má:mo:sok,
kommánkak,
iswaylí cokkó:t ammánka:fó:k
imasilháhcilin,
ammánkak:

Thereupon,
only he told me,
well, my late great grandfather,
actually my late grandfather,
well, they said
"Jeff[erson]," they called him,
"Jeff Abbey," they called him.
He was dwelling,
for he had become an old man.
Once he visited me;
thereupon,
he told it to us,
when he was sitting on the porch, he told me,
I having asked him,
and he told me:

### Scene 1: Where the Indians Dwelt

Má:mo:sok,
athómmap i:sáhcotohok
naksó:n hopá:kifon.
Ó:lap holcifó hocíftákkok,
casobáykok.
Ó:lafak komi:sáhcotohok,
hahcí apatahó:t i:sáhcot ómmǫ,
o:lafokkóhcot mafíhnak.
Hahcí, okfamá:mifo:t,
hahcí apatahó:t,
naksó:n i:sáhcotohok ómmǫ.
Má:miyok,
i:sáhcot ónkamáhcok.

Thereupon,
the Indians used to dwell
somewhere far away.
I do not name the town;
I do not know it.
It was in the town that they dwelt with us,
they seem to have dwelt by a river,
perhaps not in a real town.
On a river, or on some kind of lake,
by some kind of river,
it seems that they dwelt somewhere.
But this being so,
it was the case that they were dwelling.

### Scene 2: How the Indians Lived

| | |
|---|---|
| Má:mo:sok, | Thereupon, |
| í:sat ilanawíhlit, | they dwelt, and they hunted, |
| ná:si í:bit í:pak i:sáhcotohon. | and they continued to kill and eat things. |
| Okík ná:hoskan, | Because there was water, |
| okí apatahá | by a river, |
| okí má:lon matískot, | they went and drank just water; |
| hopó:nit, | they cooked with it, |
| o:hápkat i:sáhcotohok, | and they continued to swim in it, |
| naksó:n hahcí apatahá. | somewhere by a river. |
| Má:mi:p, | When it was thus, |
| ná:homáhcot, | well, |
| icó:t í:bit, | they killed deer and suchlike, |
| fi:tót í:bit, | they killed turkey and suchlike, |
| ná:so:t "ilpá" ilká í:bit í:pat | and things that are called "edible" they killed and ate |
| í:sahcómmíhcotohok. | and were continuing so to live. |
| Kámmisk, | Just like that, |
| nipó ittaklaná:cit solóhlit, | they smoked and dried meat; |
| hasaykáhcot í:bit ittaklá:nat solóhlit. | having killed many [animals], |
| | they smoked and dried them. |
| Akkammí:citohok, | They did it so, |
| hocikkí:t í:pá:hik ómmitǫ. | perhaps they kept some that they might eat them. |
| Mó:tohok, | Then, |
| kánt i:sáhcotoho:liyon, | thus they used to live, |
| ná:si í:sa małáhlihak í:bit anoslíhcot ómmitik, | but even though it was the case that these uncivilized people finished killing anything living, |
| ittaksolohkáhcon ómmitǫ; | it was the case that they smoked it [all], |
| sámmin ómmito casobáykotikap. | but I don't know how it was. |

### Scene 3: The Chief Proposes a Move

| | |
|---|---|
| Ná:hǫ, | Well, |
| immikkók ónkak. | their chief spoke. |
| "Ha:láhhílkalahǫ nihtá niłá:lik," | "We shall move away tomorrow morning," |
| ká:hat immánkatǫ á:ti í:sa. | he said, telling the people that dwelt there. |
| Má:miyon, | But then, |
| á:ti óhya immánkan, | he told everyone, |
| óhyak ha:láhká:hik, | all who were about to move, |
| "Stilatóbtáskatohon, | "You all having gotten ready, |
| nihtá niłá:lik amá:hílkalahǫ olíhyak," | tomorrow morning, we all will go," |
| káhcon. | he said. |

### Scene 4: A Few Are Unwilling to Go

| | |
|---|---|
| A:timmánkak á:ya:fó:kap, | Now, when he went around telling people, |
| scaffá:kat, ná:hǫ, | there were a few, well, |
| scaffá:kat á:ti imistilká | a few of the people dwelling there |
| | with him, |
| scaffá:kat ónkak, | a few spoke. |
| "Kosnók ama:hilká kosánkǫ." | "As for us, we are unable to go." |
| Mí:ta má:lik, | Others, in the same way, told him, |
| "Amá:hílkahalpískǫ," ká:hat immánkatǫ. | "We cannot go." |
| Má:miyon, | But then, |
| "Amá:hilkalahon cabànna:š," káhhok | "I intend that we go," he said, |
| immánka:p, | and when he told them so, |
| "Kosankǫ kosnáp amá:kak nihtá má:łip. | "As for us, we can not go just tomorrow. |
| Sámmin ihóhcat stokomą̀híkkok ómmik, | Howsoever long it was, we weren't told, |
| mák ihó:cat immáhíkkok ómmik," | that is how long it wasn't told," |
| ká:hak. | they said. |
| Immą̀hilkáhcon, | He had told them, |
| "Nihtá mán, | "Now, tomorrow, |
| nihtá mán amá:hílká:hik cabànna:š," | now, tomorrow I intend for us to go," |
| ká:hatǫ. | he said. |
| "Ó:la toppón ha:láhhílkalahǫ." | "We will move to a foreign land." |
| Imponha:lohíkko:p, | If they did not listen, he said, |
| "Amá:hílkalahon cabànna:š," káhhan. | "I intend that we will go." |
| Má:mo:sin, | And then, |
| caffák ónkak, | one said, |
| "Nihtá má:lik amá:hílkahalpískǫ kosnáp." | "We cannot go just tomorrow." |
| Á:ti ná:sok sámmit ónkatot casobáykǫ; | I do not know what kind of persons they were, |
| ínko:p, | or if it were |
| halkó:t, | their wives or suchlike, |
| ínko:p, | or if it were |
| imá:toso:t ho:páhcot | their children or such were sick, |
| ínkoto:p, | however, |
| sámmin mók ómmitǫ | it was that they |
| ha:láhka bánkotoho: | did not want to move, |
| limpáhcok. | so they say. |
| Inko:p, | Or if not, |
| ná:sok ittahóbkoscot ómmǫ, | perhaps they did not have things ready; |
| ínko:lá:pi, | or whatever, |
| ha:láhka bánkotoho:limpáhcok. | they did not want to move, so they say. |

### Scene 5: The Unwilling Are Given an Alternative, and the Majority Go

| | |
|---|---|
| Má:mo:sin, | And then, |
| “Mó:li:p, cimittahó:bat anó:ka:k, | “Well, when you are all ready, |
| haciká:not anó:ka:p, | when you are all well, |
| amá:hiíkatohotik, | even though we have gone, |
| obá:lit akocakhók!” | follow ye us behind!” |
| a:timmánkatoho:limpáhcok mikkók. | it is said that the chief told the people. |
| Má:mo:sin, | And then, |
| “Intallá mó:li:p sámmin sobáyka | “On the other hand, well, how are we |
| ama:hilká naksón ómmik | to know where you have gone?” |
| ama:haská?tó?” káhhan. | they said. |
| “Ná:holit ɬóykallaho katík óm, | “It is the case that I will go back and do something, |
| cimmą́hilkálahǫ amá:hílkatohofap.” | we will tell you where we went.” |
| “Ná:hǫ, cimincáhhíllahǫ, | “Well, we will make marks for you on various things, |
| ná:so:t, | like on trees, |
| ittofó:t | we will do things, |
| ná:so:t akkammí:cit | you will see things on trees |
| ittofón hashí:cak amá:háskat” káhhok, | as you go,” he said, |
| immą́hkat amá:katoho:limpak. | and having told them so, he went off. |
| Má:min, | Then, |
| “Món hashí:cak obá:li ashací:lo món, | “You looking and expecting things behind also, |
| acakháska:k óɬhacilahǫ obá:li,” káhhan. | following, you will arrive behind,” he said. |
| “Mó:li:p, ónɬalaho katík óm. | “Well, we are going there, |
| Kámmit stamá:háskatohok, | in such a way when you have come along, |
| obá:li á:talahok kosnók.” káhhan. | I will remain behind us,” he said. |
| Inníhta:p, | On the next day, |
| nihtá niɬá:lon, | on the next morning, |
| niɬá:lo:son, | early in the morning, |
| óhyak wasátkatoho:limpáhcok. | they all went off, so it is said. |
| Óhyak amą́hkan, | All having gone, |
| akkáhcok í:satǫ. | the others dwelt on. |
| Akkámmik, | Having done this, |
| sámmo:sin ihó:cat í:saton casobáykotik, | I do not know how long they dwelt there, |
| í:satǫ. | but they dwelt there. |
| Mó:tohok, | Then afterwards, |
| amá:katǫ obá:lį. | they went off behind. |

### Scene 6: The Afterfollowers Get Lost

| | |
|---|---|
| Má:miyon, | But then, |
| ittó:t imincá:litohofa hí:ca:k, | when they saw where they had marked trees for them, |
| accákkit amá:katǫ. | they went following. |
| Mó:tohok, | Then, |
| ká:non amá:katoho:liyok, | even though they were going well, |
| akkó imincá:t amá:katoho:liyon, | even though the others went making the marks, |
| iminca:lí:cíkkot amá:katok amá:katon, | suddenly, they went without marking where they went. |
| naksofón amá:ka:k. | where they went. |
| Yomáhtoho:liyok, | The others went about, |
| kánt ama:káhcotohon, | but so they went, |
| nasyomáhlit, | they went about, |
| ná:son ilatóbkon, | and nothing was prepared; |
| nasyomáhlit | they went about; |
| ǫ́:hya syomahlíhcotohon, | they all were wandering about; |
| sha:láhkat syomáhlitoho:liyok. | they went about moving. |
| Má:mo:sok, | And then, |
| incá:lit obá:li amá:kayok, | even though they followed the marks that they had made them for them, |
| intalibó:lit ihiní:cit, | they had made paths, |
| hínosi intalibó:lit amá:katǫ. | they had gone making paths. |
| Mó:tohon, | Then, |
| ká:not amá:kan | they had gone well, |
| obá:li hí:cat amá:kat, | they went looking behind, |
| amá:kak yomáhli:fó:kap, | when they went wandering, |
| ká:noh hí:cat stamă::kat, | they really went around looking carefully; |
| acákkit amá:kat amá:kat, | they went on and on following them, |
| hopáhkin ha:láhkat ómmit ómmǫ, | they seemed to have moved far, |
| hopáhkipalá:mmǫ. | it was excessively far. |
| Mó:toho:liyok, | But then, |
| naksofón amá:kak sobáyko-toho:limpáhcok, | it is said that they did not know where the others had gone; |
| innakaɬɬá. | they had disappeared. |
| Incá:litohok, | The others had made marks, |
| incá:híkkon wíhlit, | but they looked and they had not made marks, |
| naksó:n amá:kato sobáykot | they did not know where they had gone; |
| mǫ́ wáylo:sin wíhlit, | they kept on looking just so far, |
| wíhlit sánkon, | they kept on looking, |
| ikhí:cotoho:limpáhcok wíhli:k. | but were unable to find them, they say. |

| | |
|---|---|
| Má:mo:sok, | And then, |
| sámmoson sobayá:kon, | they all did not know how it was, |
| ínkok, | or if not, |
| ibisnók bikkó yomáhli mók, | as for those who had gone ahead, |
| ínko:p, | it may have been, |
| ná:so:t immałáhlok lónkat | something perhaps frightened |
| tółkatot ómmǫ, | them, and they ran and hid, |
| ínko:p, | or if not, |
| imí:safo:t wasátkatǫ, | they died in their dwellings, |
| sobayá:kotoho:limpáhcok má | and the others did not know |
| wáylo:sin. | any more than that. |

### Scene 7: The Afterfollowers Find a White Settlement

| | |
|---|---|
| Máhmin, | At that, |
| akkók má wáylo:sin onnokcóhbok, | those people stopped only as far as there, |
| naksó:n imaláhką sobáylá:hik, | when they went about, they tried to find |
| wíhlih bànnak yomáhli:fó:kap, | their relatives that they knew somewhere, |
| á:tok ittinna:łí:kahá:watoho:limpáhcok. | it is said that they heard people speaking together. |
| Hahcí apatahá naksáhkat í:sahawan há:lok, | By a river, they heard the sounds of people dwelling, |
| "Máh! Yá:fon sáhcok í:saha," káhhok, | "Listen! There, one can hear people living so!" they said, |
| amá:kat o:łá:cit ómmá:ton, | and after they went arriving there, |
| amá:kat o:łá:cit ómmá:ton, | and after they went arriving there, |
| á:ti mí:tak i:sáhcotohon | it was the case that other people |
| ómmitoho:limpak. | were dwelling there, so they say. |
| Á:ti hatkáhcok, | They were people who were white; |
| á:ti hohatkáhcok í:satot ómmitohon | it was the case that they were all white, |
| ohłá:citǫ. | and they arrived there. |
| Akkántik á:ti mí:to:li sobáyliyok | But this being so, even though they knew that they were different people, |
| ohtayakhá:cit, | they went and approached them, |
| óhyak amá:katikap | even though they all went, |
| immałáhlitoho:limpáhcok á:ti hátkak, | the people who were white were afraid of them, so they say. |
| immałáhliyok kántik ohtimo:łá:ciyok | Even though they were afraid, but still the same they went over to them; |
| o:łá:cit ayakhá:citoho:limpáhcok. | they arrived there and approached them, so they say. |

### Scene 8: The Afterfollowers Receive the Name "Koasati"

| | |
|---|---|
| Amá:katok wasáthkok, | They went having been lost, |
| o:łá:cok, | they arrived there, |
| holokkó:lin, | and they stood there, |
| thátkak híhcok, | and the white people seeing them, |
| thátkak ónkak, | the white people spoke, |
| "Ná:son hacibànnok | "What is it that you are going |
| yomaháʔcí?" | about wanting?" |
| káhhan. | they said. |
| Athómmak ónkak, | The Indians spoke, |
| athómma:sáyok ónkak, | these Indians spoke, |
| "Kowasátkok yomáhhílk" | "*Kowashatkok yomahilk* [We are going |
| ká:toho:limpak. | about lost]" they said. |
| "Kowasátk," ká:toho:limpak. | "*Kowashatk* [We are lost]," they said. |
| "Kowasátk," káhhan. | "*Kowashatk* [We are lost]," they said. |
| Má:mo:sin, | And then, |
| thátkak ónkak, | the white people spoke, |
| "Náʔsí?" ká:toho:limpak. | "What?" they said. |
| "Nasháskat ǫháská?" káhhan. | "What is it that you are saying?" |
| | they said. |
| Má:mi:yon, | But then, |
| athómmak inna:łí:kamá:lon ónkak, | the Indians only spoke to them saying, |
| "Kowasátk," ká:toho:limpáhcok. | "*Kowashatk* [We are lost]" they said. |
| Má:mo:sin, | And then, |
| thátkak ónka:k, | the white people spoke, |
| "Ná:son ónká?" sobáyktoho:limpak. | "What does it mean?" They did not |
| | know the language, it is said. |
| "Kowasátk," káhhan. | "*Kowashatk* [We are lost]" they said. |
| Má:mo:sok, | And then, |
| ká:ha:p, | when they said it, |
| athómmak fáykotoho:limpáhcok. | the Indians did not quit, so it is said. |
| "Kowasátk," ká:hak, | "*Kowashatk* [We are lost]" they said. |
| "Ná:son, ná:son hacibànnak ǫháská?" | "What, what is it what you want?" |
| ká:ha:p, | they said, |
| athómmak, "Kowasátk," ká:hak | and the Indians did not quit saying |
| fáykotoho:limpak. | "*Kowashatk* [We are lost]." |
| Má:mo:sin, | And then, |
| thátkak ónka:k, | the white people said, |
| "Ǒ! Kowas . . . Kowaš á:ti athómmok | "Oh! Kowas . . . Kowash people are |
| yomahlíhcok óm. | the Indians going about, |
| Athómmak Kowaš á:tok yomahlíhcok óm," | The Indians going about are Kowash people," |
| káhhok. | people," they said. |

"Kowašá:ton," káhhok,
incá:tohok ómmin,
"Kowassá:ton" koho:cí:fotohok ómmin,
yomáhhilíhcotoho:limpáhcok.
Kántik,
"Kowasátk," ká:ha:p, "kolhó:s."

"Kowasátk,
naksó:n amá:hílkak sobáykílkot
yomahhilíhcóm," ilkáhcok immanká.
Ka:háhcok immankáhco:liyon,
thátkak, "Kowassá:ti athómmak
yomahlíhcok óm," ká:hok incá:tohon,

Kowassá:ton
syomahilíhcómmimpáhcok.

"Kowashaton" they said,
and they were writing it down.
"Koasati" is what they named us,
while we were wandering, so it is said.
But this being so,
when they said "*Kowashatk* [We are lost],"
[it meant] "We are lost in the woods."
"*Kowashatk* [We are lost],"[it meant]
"we are wandering not knowing where we
are going," they said, telling them.
Saying, so they told them,
but the white people, "Koasati are the
Indians going about," they said
and wrote it down,
and as Koasati we are going about,
so it is said.

## Epilogue

Hokáhcotik,
mafĩ:hnasokkóhcot ómmǫ,
má:lon ammánkak,
amawocó:botok "Jéfka" hoká:k,
"Jefǽ bi" hoká:k ammánkak.

Má:mo:sin,
ká:t a:łi:kalit a:łi:kalit,
fáykat stamahó:bat
ká:t a:łí:kalibá:no:líhcotohok.
Thátkak há:lo:fó:k,
amasihá:citohok,
immánkalitikap,
ma:lókkoscot ómmǫ,
ínko:p,
mafíhnascot óm,
ínko:p,
pí:la fáyhílkot ammánkatot ómmǫ.
Akkáhcon ammánkáhcon.
Thátkak imalóstit amasilháhcin,
immánkalíhcómmi yín.

They said it so,
but perhaps it is not the whole truth;
he just told me,
my old grandfather, Jeff, they called him,
Jeff Abbey, they called him;
he told me so.
And then,
telling the story again, I say it,
and I leave off, and I say it,
telling the story repeatedly.
When white people hear about it,
they ask me,
and I tell it to them,
but perhaps it is not correct,
or if not,
it is the whole truth,
or if not,
they just told me it in jest.
So they told me,
and white people are interested
and having asked me, I tell them this.

| | |
|---|---|
| Má:misk, | Because then, |
| stammáttato mók, | I may have erred in some way; |
| anók sobáylilá:hik cabànnak, | I, too, want to know it; |
| pí:la fáyhílkot ónkalik ómmók, | I may be telling it in jest, |
| ná:sok katíkap. | what has been said. |
| Thátkak ná:son sámmí:cit cikkí:lit, | White people keep things how they were, |
| ná:si a:łí:kalahok ómmi casobáykotik, | I do not know how the story will be told, |
| imalóstik amasilháhcin, | but as they are interested and having |
| immánkalíhcok mǫ. | asked me, I tell them enough. |
| Mó:li:p, | Well, |
| akkámmo:sin immánkalá:himá:m; | this is just so much that I am prepared to tell; |
| kámmo:sin sobáylil. | just so much is what I know. |

*Textual commentary*:

Lines 20–26 It is extremely unusual for a traditional narrative to be ascribed to a particular person for, as a rule, no such background is given. In this case, since Abbey seems to have had more confidence in the veracity of his version of *The First Meeting of the Indians and the Europeans*, by ascribing this narrative to his grandfather, he was removing the onus of proof from himself. Although specifying the origin of a tale is not done by narrators of the elder generation, younger ones, such as Bertney Langley (*How Bat Received His Wings*, chapter 2) always ascribe their tales to older relatives. In doing so, they imply that a member of the older generation would have told it better.

There is a nice descriptive passage in the prologue that describes Abbey's grandfather sitting on the porch and Abbey listening to him. Thus, the listener is taken back in time to be an audience to an older telling of the tale.

Line 43 *hahcí, okfamá:mifo:t* 'on a river, or on some kind of lake'. It is interesting that a lake is mentioned here, since there was a Koasati village established on the shore of Lake Bisteneau in northwestern Louisiana around 1800, near a Caddo village.

Lines 48–70 This scene describes the way of life of the Indians before contact. Abbey describes only hunting activities, as he did in his version of *The First Meeting of the Indians and the Europeans*. This contrasts with John's telling of the same narrative, in which she included agricultural activities. Abbey's focus on hunting may well reflect the fact that hunting was primarily a man's job, whereas agriculture was performed by women.

Line 66 *hocikkí:t í:pá:hik ómmitǫ* 'perhaps they kept some that they might eat them'. This line refers to animal husbandry. By the second decade of the nineteenth century, the Koasati kept herds of cattle, horses, and hogs, and a family's wealth, even well into the twentieth century, was measured by the size of its herds. Nonetheless, because animal husbandry was not considered typical of the 'Indian of long-ago' (*athómma ihó:ca*), Abbey downplays it here.

Line 69 *maɬáhɬihak* 'these uncivilized people'. This metaphor, literally 'the wild people', is used by the Indians to describe themselves. It is not necessarily pejorative.

Lines 72–79 The chief's decision to have the Indians move is given as a fait accompli. Some older people say that a vision of the future seen by a *hopá:yi* 'prophet' would be the underlying reason for making such a move.

Lines 80–145 These two scenes portray a very interesting situation, in which the authority and wishes of the chief conflict with the desires of a minority. Rather than forcing them to do his will, at first he tries to persuade them to do as he says. But when they remain adamant in their opposition, he works out a compromise with them so that they can have their way and yet still follow his command.

Lines 90–91 *"Sámmin ihóhcat stokomąhíkkok ómmik / mák ihó:cat immąhíkkok ómmik" ká:hak.* '"Howsoever long it was, we weren't told, / that is how long it wasn't told," they said.' The exact interpretation of these lines is not clear. The general sense is that the people wanted to have the time to think the move over and to prepare for it.

Lines 181–89 These lines contain speculations about the fate of the people who had gone on ahead with the chief and why they had stopped marking the trail for the others. Neither speculation is pleasant, one being that they had been frightened by something and scattered, and the other being that they had somehow died. By the time the Koasati came into intensive contact with Europeans, they were indeed only a remnant of a much larger body, and this narrative contains their understanding of how this situation came to be.

Lines 195–208 Here the Indians encounter white people for the first time. Note that the phrase *á:ti hátka* 'person who is white' is used here instead of the usual apocopated form *thátka* 'white person'. Although there is tension in this scene between the two parties, the tension dissolves in the following scene.

Lines 209–53 This entire scene is almost a farce, with the Indians and white people doing an Abbot and Costello "Who's on first"-type repartee. The Indians speak to the white people as if they understood, and the white people speak back to them in their own language, as if the Indians were to understand. (The white people's language is here translated into Koasati, according to the stylistic criteria that all characters are speaking Koasati even when they are not.) The Indians are trying to tell the white people that they are lost, and the white people want to know what the Indians are saying, but neither gets their message across. The upshot is that the white people think that the Indians are trying to tell them their tribal name, and they concoct it out of the Koasati word *kowasátk* 'we are lost'.

Here is where the Caddo version of the narrative presents an interesting parallel. In that narrative, a group of Caddo have gotten lost and, encountering Europeans, say the Caddo word *kuyašadah* (<*ku-* 'first person singular subject' + *-yašad-* 'be lost' + *-ah* 'temporal suffix') 'I am lost.' Thus, the Caddo call the Koasati *kuyašadah* (Wallace Chafe, p.c.1990). The Caddo narrative was recorded in English in the mid-1970s by Claude Medford from Sadie Bedoka Weller, and it is worth quoting in full (my transcription from the tape):

Years back,
when old man *Támnat* was living,
probably about 1932 or '33,
well, we were talking about the Alabama-Coushatta Indians,
and at that time,
he stated,
why, there was a small band
that strayed away from the main band
of the people of the Caddo tribe,
and they went to look for sinew.
So these people were taken by some stray people of the Spanish,
and there were some French there.
So they kept asking them,
"Who are you?" and "Where are you from?"
and they kept saying "*kuyašadah*."
So the word *kuyašadah* means "I'm lost,"
and so up to that time;
why, then, when they finally located somewhere,
they were noted as the Alabama-Coushattas,
who are really a part of the band of the Caddos.
And they were supposed to have gone to hunt,
and they were lost,
and that's where that. . .
and the Caddos call the Alabama-Coushattas
*ˀa:ba:mah kuyašadah.*
So that's where the root,
the word came from.
It means "I'm lost."
That's all.

Lines 239–44 Abbey here intentionally mispronounces the tribal name to show how the white people derived "Koasati" from *kowasátk.*

Lines 246–49 These lines illustrate the ability of Koasati speakers to develop the concept of definition. First, *kowásatk* is glossed with a verb of similar meaning, *kolhó:s* 'we are lost in the woods'. Then, it is glossed with the phrase *naksó:n amáhhílkak sobáykilkot yomáhhílihcom* 'we are wandering not knowing where we are going'. The Koasati language has rich resources for doing definitions, and it seems likely that the science of definition was developed aboriginally, and not due to European contact.

Line 280 *ná:si a:ɬí:kalahok ómmi casobáykotik* ‘I do not know how the story will be told’. Here, Abbey states that he does not know what the true story might be, but he suspects that the white people will ferret it out. The latest suggestion (see Kimball 1994b) is that the name comes from that of the precontact chiefdom to which the Koasati belonged in the sixteenth century, known in the literature as “Coosa” or, in Koasati, as *Kowassá*. Thus, *Koasati* is *Kowassá* ‘Coosa’ + *á:ti* ‘people’.

## THE ORIGIN OF BLACK PEOPLE
narrated by Martha John and Ed John

This narrative, which I recorded in October, 1982, is unusual in both content and origin. It gives the Koasati view of black people and of their relationship with white people—a view that is surprisingly sympathetic to black people, considering the almost complete lack of all but the most casual social relations between the black community and the Koasati. This narrative does not really focus on the origin of black people, but primarily on what black people had to endure during the time of slavery. There is little chance that the content of this narrative was influenced by the media. Neither narrator was well educated; both were able to read English only poorly. Moreover, as both were poor and lived far from any movie theaters, is it unlikely that films could have been the origin for any of the content. On the whole, the narrative seems to preserve actual Koasati tradition about how black life appeared to them during the period of slavery. Certainly, the supernatural explanation for the achievement of freedom by black people is aboriginal in origin—the Koasati maintain no traditions concerning the Civil War, which was fought entirely away from the lands they occupied during that period.

The origin of this narrative is unusual in that it was a joint effort of Martha John and her older cousin and brother Ed John (the Johns were brought together as brother and sister by the levirate marriage of their parents). Martha John dictated the narrative, but only after discussing many points with her brother, and after they had come to a consensus on what should be said.

### Scene 1: The Origin of Black People and How They Were Sold

| | |
|---|---|
| Ihó:ca atlocák iksóhcotohok yá:li ihá:nifa. | Long ago, black people used not to exist here in this land. |
| Mó:tohon, | Then, |
| thátkak có:pat, | white people bought them, |
| stilá:cit, | came with them, |
| onapahlíhcotǫ yá:li. | and enslaved them here. |
| Caffá:kak tokná:wan námpo | What the price was for one, |
| casobáykotik, | I do not know, |
| tokná:wa cóhban sco:páhcotohon. | but they were sold for a great deal of money. |
| | |
| Có:bo:t, | When one kept things such as horses, |
| wá:ko:t cikkí:li:p, | and such as cows; |
| incá:lit cikkí:liton, | one kept them and branded them, |

akkó yámmi,
atlocá mók incá:lit cikki:líhcotohon,
intohnó:ci:k.

and it was like that:
they kept and branded black people also,
and forced them to work.

Má:mik,
mí:tok mán stilá:cit isco:pat yá:li,
piɬá áɬɬit stilá:cíhcotǫ yá:li.

Then,
others came with more and came and sold them here,
they put them in a boat and brought them here.

Stilá:ci:fó:kok,
stinco:patǫ yá:li í:san.

When they brought them,
they sold them to the people living here.

**Scene 2: How the Black People Were Forced to Work**

Ma:fó:kon,
intohnó:ci:k,
có:ba cikkí:li yámmit
ɬómmit cikkí:lik
intohnó:cit,
caffá apáslit,
holihtá:cit,
wilaplí:cit,
acíhlit paykahatká atlocá:sáyok.

Then from that,
when they were made to work,
they were like kept horses;
they kept them and beat them
and made them work;
they cleared fields,
they made fences,
they plowed,
and they planted cotton, the black people.

Mók ómmitǫ:
acíhlin oná:po:li:s.

Thus it was:
one can deduce that they were slaves for planting.

Ifi:hilkák iksóhcotohon,
įfi:hilkák íkson,
intohnóhcotohon,
pí:la ohompá:cit,
koyófkat cassí tabáhka caffá:ka:sin,
í:pak lokkó:tǫ,
co:ba intohnó:ci yámmi:s.

Their pay used not to exist;
they were not paid;
they used to work,
and they just fed them;
having cut just one piece of corn bread,
they ate it standing,
just like a work horse.

**Scene 3: How They Were Treated**

Holikfá inká,
hokfá:cit ama:káhcotǫ.
Atlocá:sáyok hó:pa:p,
imí:sasi má:lon ballá:kan,
imalíkcitik,
lókbatik,
kasátkatik,
kántik imí:sasifa.

They gave them clothing,
and they made them put in on.
If a black person fell ill,
he lay merely in his little house,
even when they doctored him,
and even though the weather were warm,
even though it were cold,
all the same in his little house.

| | |
|---|---|
| Kántik, | This being so, |
| mí:tak íllin, | some died, |
| mí:tak falánkan, | others recovered, |
| aláhkak intóhnoscotohon. | and, having recovered, they used to work. |
| Paykahatkák hókti:fó:kon, | When the cotton was ripe, |
| í:mo:k, | when they gathered it, |
| paykahatkán í:mo:fó:kon, | when they gathered the cotton, |
| mók baybá baybá:ci:fó:k, | also when they weighed out the weight, |
| námpon stóɬko:fó:kon, | if it did not arrive to just so much, |
| imá:ti:sáyok ɬommíhcotohon | the black people were beaten |
| atlocá. | by their masters. |
| Kámmisk, | Just like that, |
| acíhban i:sáhcotǫ atlocák. | the black people lived in misery. |

### Scene 4: How God Helped Them Escape and How They Live Now

| | |
|---|---|
| Mó:tohon, | Then, |
| atlocá:sáyok tamó:ka í:sa:k, | as the black people were in the night, |
| Imililliksók matinna:ɬi:káhcotohon, | the Deathless One kept on speaking to them from afar, |
| sánt í:sat stibákɬik. | how they lived in poverty. |
| Mó:tohok, | Then, |
| ohtaskáhkatǫ. | they got out [of slavery]. |
| Imililliksók awí:ciskan, | Because the Deathless One helped them, |
| ohtaskahkáhcotohon. | they went and got out of slavery. |
| Mó:tohon, | Then, |
| imaskáhkatohok | having gotten out of slavery, |
| himá:ya í:sak atlocahák. | the black people now are dwelling. |
| Himá:ya í:sak ohtaskáhkan, | Now they live, having gone and gotten out of slavery, |
| himá:ya thátka immayá:cit ama:káhcok óm. | and now they are in the process of winning against the white people. |
| Atlocahák na:sinca:kitsobáykafa pa:náɬkat ama:káhcok óm. | Black people are in the process of joining in at school. |
| Má:mók, | Then, |
| oholimpá scó:pafo:t cokkáhkatohómpat, | they enter places such as restaurants and dine, |
| kafó:t onaískot, | they drink coffee and suchlike from the counter, |
| bítlifo:t oɬá:cit pa:náɬkat | they go over to dance halls and join in, |
| thátka tayyí sbítlit, | and dance with white women, |
| himá:yap i:sáhcok óm. | and now they are so living. |

Thátkak ómmi:p,
ilimmayá:cok i:sáhcok himá:yap.

As for white people,
they are now in the process of defeating themselves.

*Textual commentary:*

Lines 6–7 *Caffá:kak tokná:wan námpo casobáykotik, / tokná:wa cóhban sco:páhcotohon* 'What the price was for one, I do not know / but they were sold for a great deal of money'. This statement points to this description of slavery coming from traditional observation, since slaves used to be sold for a thousand dollars or more, an incredible price for anything by Indian standards.

Line 12 *atlocá mók incá:lit cikki:líhcotohon* 'they kept and branded black people also'. Branding of slaves is another feature of slavery that is not usually mentioneed in the modern media descriptions of slavery.

Lines 23–27 Here, the narrator points out that slaves were used for all kinds of agricultural labor, not just for the planting of cotton.

Lines 30–33 Because the idea of forced slavery is so foreign to the Koasati hearer, the idea that the black slaves might have been paid is brought to the fore to be dismissed; their only pay, as far as the Indians could determine, was what they were fed.

Line 54 *imá:ti:sáyok łommíhcotohon atlocá* 'the black people were beaten by their masters'. The Koasati verb here is an active verb, not passive, since a passive with an agent is not possible in Koasati. Rather, the passive here is used to translate the unusual subject-verb-object construction, which is used to bring extra attention to the verb in the sentence. Here, it focuses attention on the fact that the masters of the black people beat them when they did not pick enough cotton; the purpose is to arouse surprise in the listener.

Lines 55–56 *Kámmisk, / acíhban i:sáhcotcǫ atlocák* 'Just like that, the black people lived in misery'. As far as the Indians could perceive, there was no redeeming feature about life as a slave.

Line 59 *Imililliksók matinna:łi:kácotohon* 'the Deathless One kept on speaking to them from afar'. The Deathless One, *Imililliksó*, is one of the Koasati names for God. The Koasati believe that *Imililliksó* gives power to people through dreams; this line implies that this is what God did for the black people.

It is interesting that the narrators ascribe the eventual freedom of black people to divine intervention, implying that slavery was against the will of God. Note that there is no mention of Lincoln, or the Civil War, or any of the other happenings that a non-Indian historian would focus on.

Line 69 *himá:ya thátka immayá:cit ama:káhcok óm* 'and now they are in the process of winning against the white people'. The narrator also includes all the years after the Civil War through the period of the Civil Rights legislation as part of the period of slavery, which is actually close to the de facto situation even if the de jure situation was much different. The narrator sees the advances made by black people in the area of civil rights and integration as a contest between them and the white people—one which the black people are winning.

Line 75 *thátka tayyí sbítlit* 'and dance with white women'. Given that within the memory of the narrators a black man could be murdered for speaking the wrong way to a white woman, the fact that a black man can now dance with a white woman freely is a sign of how far the black people have advanced.

Lines 77–78 *Thátkak ómmi:p / ilimmayá:cok i:sáhcok himá:yap* 'As for white people, / they are now in the process of defeating themselves.' The narrator does not see the advances of black people as only due to their struggles, but also as the result of white people breaking their united front against black people. With a large proportion of white people no longer opposing black people, the latter are more able to advance in society.

# 8

# War Stories

War stories form a subcategory of semihistorical narratives. The Koasati have not been seriously involved in armed conflict as a people since the 1830s. Although war stories were passed on from generation to generation, as time passed, these stories became less and less relevant to a people who had given up armed conflict. Thus, they were almost forgotten.

War stories were still being told to some degree earlier in the twentieth century. These war stories focused mostly on the Comanche. According to Paz-Taylor (1937:16), "That they ever met the Comanche seems doubtful, but in most of their stories, the Comanche are always the traditional enemy." Taylor was unaware of the fact that the Koasati and Comanche did actually make raids on one another in the 1830s; however, she preserved in her manuscripts several of these stories, albeit only in English. Taylor records that the Koasati had conflicts with a number of tribes other than the Comanche. It is of interest that the Tonkawa are not mentioned by her, yet one of the two preserved stories about war concerns the Tonkawa.

At the present time, it is difficult to discern the causes of conflict, although the evidence points toward a defensive reaction to attacks from outside. The Koasati must once have participated in the warrior culture that spread across the Southeast with the Southern Cult; however, by the end of the eighteenth century, all of the ranks and paraphernalia of warriors had been abandoned; all that is left at present is the obsolete word *kaskí* 'warrior' and the plant name *kaskimilpá* 'yaupon', which literally means 'warrior's food', reflecting the former ritual use by warriors of the 'black drink' made of yaupon (see Hudson 1979 for more details).

An interesting feature of the first two narratives included here is that both were told by women. One might expect that men would be more interested in war and violence than women, but I have heard far more stories of murder, rape, and suicide from female narrators than from male ones. It is hard to understand this feature of Koasati culture—it seems hardly likely that the matrilineal organization and the relatively higher status of women in Koasati culture has anything to do with it. It may well that be since war and violence are things that upset a well-ordered social life—something with which women are greatly concerned—they show an interest in it. By understanding violence and discussing it with others, women may then be able to work toward preventing its occurrence. Certainly, it can be noted that in all Koasati narratives in which violence is practiced upon one human being by another, that violence is neither justified nor idealized; it occurs, it is unpleasant, and if it presents a serious threat to the social fabric, it must be dealt with. The use of violence in response to violence is presented only as a last resort.

A final note of interest is that these first two narratives tell only of the beginnings of the conflicts with the Tonkawa and Comanche—the ends of the conflicts are not discussed. The basic structure seems to consist of an introduction, which sets the stage, and then the initiation of hostilities by the other group. One would expect, if the narratives were fully preserved, that the Koasati reaction would be included, terminating with a Koasati victory over the enemy. Although it is unfortunate that so little of this genre has been preserved, what is presented here is of both historical and cultural interest.

## THE ATTACK OF THE TONKAWA CANNIBALS

narrated by Azilie Langley

This narrative was recorded on tape by the late James M. Crawford in 1970, during his investigation of the Mobilian Trade Language. A copy of this tape was given to Claude Medford, Jr., Langley's grandson-in-law, who in turn gave a copy to Eugene Burnham of the Summer Institute of Linguistics, who then gave me a copy. This is a rather difficult text, due in part to the condition of the recording and in part to the way the narrator spoke. In addition, Langley was having her granddaughter attempt to interpret for her, even though she was perfectly able to speak English. The interruptions and asides made by her granddaughter have been edited out of this text.

Azilie Langley, whose name was an anglicization of her Indian name *a:silí*, was a Choctaw born in 1883 among a band of that people who lived between the Calcasieu River and Bayou Nezpique in southwestern Louisiana. Her first husband was said to be a Frenchman, but after his apparent death, she and her young daughter joined the Koasati community, into which they both intermarried. During her years in the community, Langley developed a native fluency in Koasati, although she had traces of a Choctaw accent. Langley was known as a *traiteur* 'curer' among all races of the local people, although the Koasati considered her to be a Choctaw doctor, as opposed to one of their own. Although this narrative and *The Drought* (chapter 9) are her only preserved tales, she apparently had a wide knowledge of Koasati traditional narrative and a distinctive narrative style. This narrative is one of the rare survivals of a tale pertaining to the wars in which the Koasati participated during the first third of the nineteenth century. While no direct evidence survives of hostilities between the Tonkawa and the Koasati, a letter of Stephen Austin written in 1823 (Barker 1924:735–36) speaks of the possibility of persuading the Koasati to exterminate the Tonkawa. Thus, the approximate date of the incident related in this narrative is 1820.

This short story has a relatively simple organization. It consists of only two scenes, with a prologue and epilogue. It can be divided into two sections, with the prologue and scene 1 forming the first section, which set the stage for the climax and aftermath in scene 2 and the epilogue, which forms the second section. Nonetheless, for all its organizational simplicity, the narrative is not especially clear. The attack of the cannibals is indicated by the reaction of the old woman seeing one of her relatives die, rather than by a description of the action. The number of actors is also unclear. Scene 1 indicates that there are six Koasati protagonists, and scene 2 indicates that all but one are killed or captured. However, lines 27–28 imply that there is a group of other Koasati at a distance, watching the attack take place. The number of cannibals is not made clear, although the use of plural verbs implies that there were more than one.

**Prologue**

| | |
|---|---|
| Má:mok, | Then, |
| á:tik ittiháplik í:sa:fó:kon, | when people continued to make war, |
| athómmak ittihaplíhcotoho:limpáhcok. | it is said that the Indians used to habitually make war. |
| Mó:tohon, | Then, |
| Tankawí, Tankawí hokáhcon a:tí:pa. | Tonkawa, Tonkawa is what they called the cannibals. |

**Scene 1: A Koasati Family Is Wandering About**

| | |
|---|---|
| Á:tip í:satohon. | There were people dwelling. |
| Hopá:yik atná:son sobáykan onkahcí. | A prophet is someone who knows things. |
| Akkó hopá:yik, hopá:yik á:tatohon, | That prophet, the prophet was dwelling, |
| hopá:yik á:yatohon, | and the prophet was going about, |
| halkík á:yan, | his wife was going about, |
| ocó:sik á:ya:fó:kap | his son was going about, |
| mán ima:pók á:ya:fó:kap, | also his grandmother was going about, |
| mán ippokó:sik tóklon imaníhtaha. | also his two young granddaughters. |

**Scene 2: The Tonkawa Attack**

| | |
|---|---|
| Kámmi:fó:kok, | This being so, |
| a:tí:pak tółkatohon | the cannibals began to run after them, |
| ałí:yatoho:limpáhcok. | so it is said. |
| Kámmi:fó:kon, | This being so, |
| coyyí ahóccafa yámmo:sit haccá:lin, | shooting from behind a pine tree one stood thus, |
| a:tacó:bak ónkak, | and the old woman spoke: |
| "Ŏ::! Á:ti ná:nip illikí!" ká:h. | "Oh! The man is dead," she said. |
| Akkók ónkak, | That one [the old woman] spoke, |
| "Mathóccąh!" ká:hak, | "Shoot them then!" she said, |
| "Mathóccąh!" káhhan, | "Shoot them then!" she said, |
| mathócca:fó:kon, | and after they shot at them, |
| a:tí:pak sán í:bit anó:lá:hostoho:limpak | it is said that the cannibals so killed |
| akkó á:tih, | almost all of those people, |
| a:timaníhtak á:tatohok. | the young people that were there. |
| Mó:tohok, | Then, |
| akkó pittiya:thaccá:li óhyak | those all standing at a distance, |
| akanáhkatoho:limpak. | it is said that they watched, |

Mó:lin,
sakbá yámmin inɬá:hi:p,
sakbá inɬá:hi:fó:kok,
sakbá yámmin tóɬkat iláhcok.

It was that way,
if someone was shot in the arm,
when someone was shot in the arm,
with their arms in such a way they came running back.

Á:ti sámmik a:timaníhta í:bit anó:lin,

The people like that killed all the young people,

ima:pocó:bak á:tatoho mán,
íhbok.

their great grandmother still lived,
after they had been killed.

## Epilogue

Táyyi imaníhta tóklot áswatohon,
mastóɬkatoho:limpak,
staɬí:yak ohtí:pá:hih.

The two young women that were there,
it is said that they ran off with them,
they each took one so that they might eat them.

*Textual commentary*:

Line 5 *Tankawí, Tankawí hokáhcon a:tí:pa* 'Tonkawa, Tonkawa is what they called the cannibals'. Cannibal characters occur in other oral literatures of the Southeast, such as that of the Natchez (Swanton 1929:218–21). Here, the cannibals are real people and not mythical characters. There is no evidence, in fact, that the Tonkawa ever were cannibals. When the relatively advanced Muskogean-speaking peoples moved into southwest Louisiana and eastern Texas, they looked upon the primitive hunter-gatherers native to the region with disdain; "cannibal" was apparently an ethnic slur. The Choctaw named the natives of the southwest Louisiana prairies and marshes *hattak apa* 'cannibals'—this is the origin of the English tribal name Atakapa. In this story, the slur is no longer understood as an insult, but rather as truly descriptive of the Tonkawa.

Line 7 *hopá:yi* 'a prophet'. As mentioned elsewhere, the *hopá:yi* was a ritual specialist who led traditional ceremonies. He or she was considered to have the ability to see the future, to call game animals, and to find lost people or objects. Each clan had its own *hopá:yi* and some had more supernatural power than others.

Line 17 *coyyí ahóccafa yámmo:sit haccá:lin* 'shooting from behind a pine tree one stood thus'. This literally means 'where they shot by a pine tree'. This is not a standard Koasati expression and may show Choctaw influence. Although the locative prefix *a-* occurs with the same meaning in Choctaw and Koasati, its use is greatly restricted in Koasati by comparison to Choctaw and suggests Choctaw interference in Langley's Koasati. The gloss 'behind' has to be supplied because in Koasati a tree does not have a front or back, being round, so a person stands 'at' or 'beside' a tree.

Lines 20–25 Here a complex sequence of events is taking place, with only switch-reference markers tracking which subject is doing which action. The old woman tells her companions to shoot the cannibals, her companions shoot at them, and then the cannibals kill all the young people. Thus, the Koasati fought back, though in vain.

Line 27 *akkó pittiyathaccá:li óhyak* 'those all standing at a distance'. The word *pittiyathaccá:li* seems to be a hybrid Choctaw-Koasati form. The element *pittiy-* looks to be composed of *pit-*, the Choctaw equivalent of *mat-* 'afar', and *itti-* 'reciprocal' with the Choctaw glide *-y-* used between a prefix that ends in a vowel and a word that begins with a vowel. It is here translated as if it were *matathaccá:li.* A rendering that would capture the foreign feel of this phrase might be 'those all standing *von weiter*', translating the Choctaw element with German, since German is related to English in approximately the same way that Choctaw is related to Koasati.

Line 38 *stałí:yak ohtí:pá:hih* 'they each took one so that they might eat them'. Here, in the epilogue, the cannibals kidnap the two young women. Langley assumes that their purpose was to eat them. However, if this story is based on an actual event, it is more likely that they were kidnapped to serve as wives to their captors, just as with the Koasati girl who was kidnapped by the Comanche in Ellisol Batisse's *Rescuing the Kidnapped Girl*, below.

## COMANCHE HORSE-STEALING RAIDS

narrated by Martha John

I recorded this narrative on tape in October, 1988. Miss John felt a little uncertain about her command of this narrative; clearly, it is only part of a longer tale that related the wars of the Koasati and Comanche. Similarly, there were tales about the wars of the Koasati and Tonkawa; only part of one is preserved. These wars took place in the days of the grandparents and great-grandparents of the oldest generation now living. Other speakers recall having heard tales about these wars, but they were not interested enough to have bothered to learn them.

This is one of the few semihistorical narratives that can be fixed securely in time. In his *Journey to Mexico during the Years 1826 to 1834,* Jean Louis Berlandier (1980:561) notes that the Koasati raided the Comanche in 1832 and 1833. Thus, this narrative relates events that took place in the early 1830s and seems to focus on the beginning of the conflict between the Koasati and the Comanche, started by Comanche raids on Koasati horses.

**Prologue**

| | |
|---|---|
| Ná:hok, | Well, |
| mafíhnok óhyan, | all that is true |
| sobáytákkóhcot ómmo katík | I perhaps do not know, but it is the case, |
| sombáylilo:simá:łi:p | that merely all that I remember, |
| cimmankalíhcot ómmoh. | I am perhaps telling you. |

### Scene 1: The Koasati and Comanche Are at War

| | |
|---|---|
| Má:misk mók, | Also just like this, |
| Kowassá:tik Komancí stóklok í:satohok, | the Koasati and Comanche dwelt together, |
| ittapa:cóffit. | and they made raids on each other. |
| Ittapa:cóffá:hi:fó:kok, | When they were about to make raids on each other, |
| ná:sok ómmi:k, | as for things, |
| ŏ:hyak ittahobá:cit, | all prepared them, |
| imahissí óhya. | all the medicines. |
| Óhyan stittaho:bá:cit anóst ná:hotohon. | Having finished preparing them all,<br>they used them. |
| Ná:hok ómmi:k, | As for using them, |
| Komancík ómmi:k, | as for the Comanche, |
| ilmá:kak ilá:ci:p, | when they came arriving, |
| ilmá:katikap, | even though they came, |
| naksó:n ilá:cin | the Koasati also used to know |
| sobaya:líhcotohok Kowassá:tiha mók. | where they came [by means of medicines]. |
| Kámmisk, | Just like that, |
| sobayá:lit ná:ho:fó:kok mók, | they also knew it when they used them, |
| imakostí:nik malmámmit í:san. | they continued being aware of them<br>in the same way. |

### Scene 2: How the Comanche Raid

| | |
|---|---|
| Komancí mók malmámmit í:sat | The Comanche dwelt also in the same way, |
| ilmá:katohok | and they came; |
| tamo:káhcotohon ilmá:kak ilá:cit, | at night they came arriving, |
| níhta:p ilmá:híkkotoh. | if it were day, they did not come. |
| Tamó:ka:sin, | Just after dark, |
| ilmá:ka:sin, | they really came on, |
| ilá:citoho:p, | when they arrived, |
| ittahobá:cit anóstoh. | they had completely prepared. |
| Tamó:ka:k, | When it was night, |
| pa:cóffitikap, | they made raids, |
| Kowassá:ti mók malmámmit í:satohok, | but the Koasati also dwelt in the same way, |
| món malmámmit imahissík, | again their medicine was just the same, |
| malmámmit íst stohyá:łok. | in the same way they took them [all]. |

### Scene 3: The First Comanche Raid

| | |
|---|---|
| Ná:hok, | Well, |
| ittapa:cóffin, | they made a raid; |
| có:bak pa:í:sat ittapa:cóffiskan, | they made a raid because there were horses there, |
| có:bak ómmi:k, | as for the horses; |
| óhya stamałáhkok słoyóhkatohok Kowassá:tiha. | they looted them all from the Koasati and returned with them. |
| Słoyóhka:k imó:lafa, | When they returned with them to their town, |
| sto:łáhcok, | having arrived there with them, |
| óhya ohtonokbáhlok í:satohon. | they kept them all corralled up. |

### Scene 4: The Second Comanche Raid and Its Aftermath

| | |
|---|---|
| Ná:hok óm, | Well, they did it, |
| Komancí:kok łoyóhkatohok. | the Comanche returned. |
| Mán ilmá:kak, | Again, they came, |
| nihtá mán ilmá:katohok. | the next day, they came again. |
| Tamó:ka:sin, | It was just night, |
| ittahó:bá:hit anóstohok, | they had just finished preparing; |
| tamó:kak pa:cóffit, | they made a raid at night, |
| ná:hok, | well, |
| óhya málman có:ba i:timpíhlok, | in the same way, they [the Comanche] came and took all the horses, |
| słoyóhkat stołá:citik. | they returned with them and arrived there with them. |
| Akkánt ittapa:cóffit amá:katohok ałí:yan, | But, thus, they began to go making raids on each other, |
| ná:hok, | well, |
| Kowassá:tik immayá:ciscotoho:limpáhcok. | it is said that the Koasati defeated them. |

*Textual commentary*:

Lines 11–12 *ŏ:hyak ittahobá:cit, / imahissí óhya* 'all prepared them, / all the medicines'. These medicines were preparations with supernatural virtues, prepared by doctors and prophets to help secure victory in battle.

Lines 17–18 *naksó:n ilá:cin / sobaya:líhcotohok Kowassá:tiha mók* 'even though they came, / the Koasati also used to know where they came'. This is an oblique reference to the powers of the *hopá:yi*, who was believed to be able to follow events from afar by telepathic means.

Lines 23–24 *tamo:káhcotohon ilmá:kkak ilá:cit, / níhta:p ilmá:híkkotoh* 'at night they came arriving, / if it were day, they did not come'. Comanche raiders were more interested in horses than in Koasati captives, probably because horses were economically more valuable and more easily transported back to the Comanche home territory.

Line 36 *có:bak pa:í:sat ittapa:cóffiskan* 'they made a raid because there were horses there'. The Comanche raided the Koasati because they possessed horses. In their years of contact with Europeans, the Koasati had adopted stock-raising, primarily of cattle, hogs, and horses. Stock possession was an indication of wealth, but animals were allowed to range freely, possession being indicated by ear notches. When the Koasati moved into Texas, their casual stock-management practices must have made them a tempting target for the Comanche.

Line 38 *óhya stamałáhkok słoyóhkatohok Kowassá:tiha* 'they looted them all from the Koasati and returned with them'. The verb *stamałáhkan* in the meaning of 'to loot something from someone' is now unusual. The generally understood meaning at present is 'to get something from someone by guile or by inspiring pity'.

Line 54 *Kowassá:tik immayá:ciscotoho:limpáhcok* 'it is said that the Koasati defeated them'. The narrator did not remember all that she had heard of this narrative. Quite clearly, the narrator could not end the narrative with the Koasati losing to the Comanche, especially since she knew that the Koasati won in the end, so rather than continue awkwardly, she ended the narrative with this line, which summarizes the rest of the tale.

## OUTWITTING THE COMANCHE
narrated by *Soyá*

In the summer of 1936 Lyda Paz-Taylor did fieldwork among the Koasati in preparation for writing her master's thesis at Yale University, "A Comparative Study of Southeastern Cultures" (1937). The thesis does not give her consultants' names; however, in 1993 I discovered her manuscripts in the National Anthropological Archives of the Smithsonian Institution (MS 4658), where they had been deposited by her husband after her death. Among these papers are a series of typescript pages, dated July 31 through August 4, headed at the beginning "Alison Baptise," then simply "Ellison." These contain English versions of a number of Koasati traditional narratives including *The Great Lizard* and *The Clawed Witches*, as well as the war stories transcribed below.

Ellisor Battise, known to the people who remember him by his Indian name, *Soyá*, was born in 1881 in the old Koasati village near Shepherd, Texas and died in 1943; he was 52 years old when Paz-Taylor worked with him. Little that is remarkable is said about him, except that he was old-fashioned in speech (for example, using the term *akakanahhilká* 'looking glass' for *stililhicá* 'mirror'), and worked, as many of his contemporaries did, for the sawmill owner R.E. Powell (*Pawilkacó:ba*). The fact that he was an excellent storyteller was remembered by his son, Solomon Battise, who recalled as a child how his father would hold him while he entertained those around him with story after story, until he fell asleep in his father's arms. It is likely that *Soyá* taught his literary techniques to his son, who was for many years the lay minister at St. Peter's Congregational Church and the narrator of the tale *The Origin of the Races* (chapter 6).

This narrative was the first one recorded by Paz-Taylor on August 4, 1936. In common with all *Soyá*'s war stories, this one has a strong magical and fantastic element. The reticence that Martha John felt in explaining the effect of the medicines the warriors used to have is not shared by *Soyá,* for possession of strong magic power is the key to victory in all of his tales.

Originally, Paz-Taylor wrote these tales as straight prose. However, like the Koasati-language tales, they can be divided into scenes and verses. In this and the following transcriptions, the wording and punctuation of the original manuscript have been maintained, only the text has been rearranged in Koasati verse form very much as the original must have been. The only changes are the silent correction of typographical errors and the italicization and proper spelling of Koasati words.

### Scene 1: A Man Kills a Comanche Woman

A group of men were going out into the woods to hunt
and the *inkapitaní* was leading them.
They had gone very far
and so made a camp.
The *inkapitaní* told them
that they had to behave,
not to kill anyone
because they were hunting near the Comanche.
There was one man
who would never mind the *inkapitaní*,
so he went out to thc woods
and saw a Comanche woman.
He killed her
and took off her scalp
and brought the scalp back to camp.
The *inkapitaní* said,
"I told you to behave
and not do that."

### Scene 2: The Long Walk

The next morning
the *inkapitaní* told them
he was going to do something
to make up for this
so he said,
"Next morning,
I am going to make you take a long walk."

Early the next morning
  he called them to start before the sun rose.
They were to walk all day
  and not eat anything.
About noon,
  they were very hungry,
    but he wouldn't give them anything
      and made them keep on walking.

### Scene 3: One Looks and Sees the Comanches

The *inkapitaní* told them
not to look back while on this trip.
In the afternoon,
  about four,
    the same man who had killed the woman
      was very tired and hungry
        and he looked back.
When he did this,
  he saw that the Comanches were coming after them.
He got scared
  and couldn't move,
    so the *inkapitaní* whipped him
      until he got up and started again.
This happened a second time
  and the *inkapitaní* whipped him again.

### Scene 4: They Find a Hiding Place

About sunset,
  they were going under two trees.
They stopped there
  and the *inkapitaní* told them,
    "This is the place where
      our bones will stay and get rotten."
There was a cave here
  and a gully,
    so they stepped in there
      and sat down.
While they were sitting there,
  the Comanches came up
    and circled around them.
The people found a big rock in the cave
  and hid under it.

The Comanche tried to kill them,
but couldn't do [and]
went off to wait until after supper.

**Scene 5: The Magic Duel**

After supper,
the *inkapitaní* came out of the cave,
got some kind of dry mud,
and spat on it to make it soft,
then rubbed it all over his face.
Then he took a buffalo tail
and facing north,
waved it in the air.
The Comanche had an *inkapitaní*
who sat there watching the other *inkapitaní.*
As soon as he had finished,
the Comanche *inkapitaní* said,
"*Tá.*" (Thank you)
He was thinking about the kind of punishment
he was going to give.
Soon as the *inkapitaní* had finished waving the buffalo tail
they saw a little cloud coming.
When it came where the people were,
it started to rain.
It put out the Comanches's fire.
Their *inkapitaní* was mad,
so he pawed the ground
and rolled over the ground
like a bull
and immediately the rain stopped.
The other Indians didn't have enough rain,
or enough water in the cave,
so their *inkapitaní* came out of the cave,
rolled on the ground
and waved the buffalo tail
and it began to rain again,
then it began to hail.
But the Comanche had no clothes or cover.

### Scene 6: The Escape

By then,
the cave was full of water
and was running out down the gully.
The people in the cave turned into leaves [through the magic of the *inkapitaní*],
their *inkapitaní* leading them.
The Comanche were standing by the gully
getting ready to shoot,
they didn't know the leaves were the people,
so they passed on safely.
They floated several miles down the river,
but had to come out of the water
before they got too far from camp.
When they were getting out of the water,
they heard the Comanche shooting in the cave.
Then they went back to their own camp.
The Comanche stayed around the cave
all night long without sleep watching.
Then they tried to move the stone,
but they found that the people were not there.
The other people had already gone home.

That is all.

*Textual commentary*:

Line 2 The person titled *inkapitaní* has a major role in Battise's stories. This title comes from the Creek language, and ultimately from the Spanish word *capitán* 'captain'. The word *inkapitaní,* as well as the role itself, is now obsolete in Koasati language and culture; very old people glossed the word with *mikkó imawí:ci* 'helper of the chief'. In traditional society, the *inkapitaní* seems to have been a subchief, with powers and responsibilities bestowed on him by both the chief and the society.

Lines 13–14 *He killed her / and took off her scalp*. Scalping (*isbakkí įsoffí:cin*, among other expressions) seems to have been a historic-period adaptation of the Mississippian custom of trophy head taking.

Lines 16–18 *The* inkapitaní *said, / "I told you to behave / and not do that*." Commission of warlike acts seems to have been considered incompatible with good hunting. Thus, the *inkapitaní* has to devise a way to overcome the negative supernatural forces aroused by this incident.

Lines 67–98 These lines contain the most explicit description of "weatherworking" (*oybacilká*) that has survived. Martha John's grandfather was the last acknowledged weatherworker (*oybá:ci*); few contemporary Koasati know of the practice, and fewer still have been willing to discuss it with outsiders.

Here begins the duel between the Koasati leader and his Comanche counterpart, with the one with the greatest supernatural power being the victor.

Lines 103–4 *The people in the cave turned into leaves, / their* inkapitaní *leading them.* The Koasati leader shows his consummate magical prowess by changing himself and his followers into leaves, which escape the notice of the surrounding Comanche. Thus, the Koasati leader is victorious.

## THE GRANDFATHERS' REVENGE

narrated by *Soyá*

This is the second war story narrated by *Soyá* on August 4, 1936. The first scene, in which a Comanche raid on a Koasati camp leads to the murder of the Koasati children, bears a marked resemblance to *The Attack of the Tonkawa Cannibals* above, especially in lines 1–7. Just as certain common themes can be found in Koasati Rabbit stories, there may well have been such themes in war stories.

### Scene 1: The Murder of the Children

There was a man,
his wife,
their children,
and his parents.
The grandparents wanted to go hunting
so asked the son and grandchildren
to go along.
They got several miles from home
and made a camp in the woods.
The grandparents said,
"We are too far away,
we had better go back next morning."
Before going back,
there was a young man who had a dream.
He told the old men
that he had had a bad dream.
While he was telling about it,
one of the grandfathers said,
"We better go hunting a little bit more
before we go home."

The rest of the people went hunting,
but the young man wouldn't go with them,
he took his gun and walked a little ways.
While they were all out hunting,
the young man heard somebody
shooting a gun and hollering.
Soon he saw some men passing
with their guns.
When he came back to the camp,
he saw that the camp fire was still burning,
but the women had all scattered into the woods,
the babies were dead
and were placed in sticks over the fire
the same way as they placed meat to roast it.

### Scene 2: The Grandfathers Vow Revenge

Soon the other men returned
and saw the same thing.
The grandfathers got mad.
They told everyone else to go home
and said,
"We are going to find out
who did this to our grandchildren,
but you all go home."
The rest went home.
The grandfathers walked out into the prairie,
one of them took his gun
and shot twice
to find out where the Comanches were.
It was sunset,
then the old men went to sleep.

### Scene 3: The Grandfathers Take Revenge

Just before daybreak,
they shot the gun twice again.
They sat down to eat.
Soon they saw the Comanches coming.
There were so many of them
you couldn't tell how many.
They gathered around.
The grandfathers finished eating
and started mending their moccasins.

The Comanches all came to them
and told them to hurry up
and get up
so they could have some fun.
When the old men finished mending the moccasins,
their guns weren't ready to use,
so they had to work on them.
The Comanches all had bundles
and all put them on the ground
before the two men.
The Comanches knew
that they could kill those two men easily.
The old men had some kind of medicine
so rubbed that on the end of the gun
while fixing it.
They were very slow about fixing the gun,
but soon it was ready to shoot.
He shot it
and the gun made a noise like thunder.
The Comanches were scared
and the whole earth shook
so that they fell down.
The grandfathers then took a hatchet,
as the Comanches tried to get up,
they chopped off their heads with the hatchet.
They killed some of them,
but some got away.
Then the old men opened the bundles
that the Comanches had brought.
They took out the pretty blankets,
but put everything else on a pile
and set fire to it with a piece of fat pine wood.

### Scene 4: The Grandfathers Finish Up

The old men didn't go away right away,
but stayed there another day
and called the cold weather from the north.
Before it got cold,
it rained,
then came the wind and the storm
and everything got icy.
Then it snowed
until it got about four feet deep.

The gun shot had made some of the Comanches faint,
and when they ran away,
they ran in the opposite direction from their camp.
They hadn't stopped
to pick anything up
when they ran.
After the snow,
the grandfathers were sleeping,
then they got up
and said,
"I guess we have to chase the rest of the Comanches."
They could trace them
by their tracks in the snow.
[They] found some of them
leading to a tree
but couldn't see the man
only the tracks.
Then
they went back home to their people.
"It wasn't enough,
but we paid the Comanche
for what they did to our grandchildren."

That is all.

*Textual commentary*:

Lines 15–16 *He told the old men / that he had had a bad dream*. Dreams were very important in traditional Koasati society. Since dreams were considered to be the sendings of supernatural powers, they were ignored at one's peril.

Lines 32–33 *the babies were dead / and were placed in sticks over the fire*. The murder of a child is the most heinous crime a Koasati person can think of. In fact, such a crime has not been committed by a Koasati within living memory. The fact that the Comanche would kill children shows them in this tale to be especially villainous.

Line 38 *They told everyone else to go home*. The reason that the grandfathers are the ones to take responsibility for the revenge is that they were the ones who ignored the young man's dream and therefore are in part responsible for the deaths of their grandchildren.

Lines 59–63 *The Comanches all came to them / and told them to hurry up / and get up / so they could have some fun*. The "fun" the Comanches are talking about is torture. In such a position, where they had a seemingly insurmountable numerical advantage, they would banter with their intended victims. In this case, the Comanche do not realize that the two old man have strong magical powers.

Line 88 *They took out the pretty blankets*. These "pretty blankets" may have been Navajo blankets. During their sojourn in Texas, the Koasati became acquainted with and learned to make Pueblo-style coiled basketry (very different from their aboriginal woven cane), quite possibly as loot from raids on the Comanche.

Line 93 *and called the cold weather from the north*. The grandfathers also are weatherworkers, in addition to their other magical abilities.

## RESCUING THE KIDNAPPED GIRL
narrated by *Soyá*

This is the third and final war narrative told by *Soyá* on August 4, 1936, to Lyda Paz-Taylor. The magical elements are much subdued in this narrative as compared to the other, the only examples involving an invisible Koasati uncle and a Comanche sitting in a tree in the form of a turkey. In this narrative, as in the previous narrative and Langley's *The Attack of the Tonkawa Cannibals*, the uncertainity of life in proximity to enemy peoples is brought out forcefully. A person never knew, each time he or she left the safety of the group, whether or not he or she would return safely or even survive.

### Scene 1: A Girl Is Kidnapped

There was an old Koasati
  who had some girls.
The Comanche stole one of the girls
  while she was away from camp,
    probably getting some water.
The Koasati were looking for her
  around the camp;
    while doing this
      they saw a muddy place
        with a footprint in it.

### Scene 2: She Is Found and Rescued

The *inkapitaní* led them
  to go after her.
When they got there,
  and it had taken them four days
    to find the Comanche camp,
      they hid behind bushes.

They saw the Comanche
  sitting around the fire,
    and saw the girl sitting with them
      making a moss blanket.
The *inkapitaní* asked one man,
  "Go without being scared
    over to the girl;
      nobody will see you."
He went over to her,
  touched her on the back
    and she turned
      and saw it was her uncle.
He didn't speak to her,
  but made signs
    that they were coming for her.
The Comanche didn't see him.

### Scene 3: The Flight from the Comanches

He took the girl to his people,
  they were all on horseback,
    and they took her with them.
This all happened during the afternoon,
  but it turned dark
    before they had gone far.
Just before sunset,
  they made a fire in the woods,
    fixed camp
      and were getting supper.
They heard a turkey
  and one of the men went out to get it.
He didn't return,
  so they sent another man out
    to see what had happened.
The first man who went out
  found a big tree with two branches.
It wasn't a turkey,
  but a Comanche in the shape of a turkey
    sitting in the tree.
The Comanche didn't see the man,
  but the man saw him
    and killed him.

As soon as the Comanche fell off the tree,
 the man ran back to camp
  because the rest of the Comanches were coming up.
The men who had been sent to follow him
 were in the bushes
  and they came up to the Comanches with guns.
The Comanches fled when they saw them.

### Scene 4: The Return

Then
 the man who had killed the turkey
  came back to camp
   and told that he had killed one Comanche
    and all the rest got ready
     to go out with him.
He wanted to take the scalp off
 the Comanche he had killed.
When he got there,
 the scalp was already gone,
  this had been done by the other Comanche
   because they didn't want
    any other people to have their scalps.
The next day,
 they all went home
  and the girl was very happy
   to see her people again.

That is all.

*Textual commentary*:

Lines 9–10 *they saw a muddy place with a footprint in it.* The footprint obviously must have been that of the Comanche warrior who captured the girl.

Lines 17–20 *They saw the Comanche / sitting around the fire, / and saw the girl sitting with them / making a moss blanket.* In contrast to the Tonkawa, who stole girls to eat, the Comanche steal them in order to adopt them into their tribe. The moss blanket used to be woven on a standing frame using the dried strands of Spanish moss. The geographical location of this narrative cannot be far from the forests of east Texas where Spanish moss could be gathered.

Lines 21–28 It is through the magical power of the *inkapitaní* that the girl's uncle is able to approach her in broad daylight and not be seen.

Lines 29–30 *He didn't speak to her, / but made signs.* This may refer to the common sign language of the Plains, which was in use by the Comanche and probably learned by the Koasati during their sojourn in Texas.

Lines 50–51 *It wasn't a turkey, / but a Comanche in the shape of turkey.* This Comanche in the form of a turkey is a scout for the rest of the Comanche searching for the girl and her rescuers. The ability to change one's form into that of a bird or animal was restricted to evil sorcerers (*athollö*).

# 9

# Other Semihistorical Stories

This collection of narratives is of tales that most probably occurred at some time in the past, but whose historical basis is uncertain. They do not fall into any major category. In fact, *The Boy and the Pygmy Rattlesnake* and *How a Man Lost His Breechcloth to a Bull* could be considered as anecdotes rather than as historical narratives. The reason for their inclusion is their innate interest and the stylistic abilities shown in them by their narrators. These final stories bring this collection of Koasati tales to a close, and it is fitting that the last two stories should be anecdotes from Indian life, both of which involve danger and ludicrous incidents, features of life everywhere.

## THE DROUGHT

narrated by Azilie Langley

This narrative was recorded on tape by the late James M. Crawford in 1970, at the same time that he collected the narrative *The Attack of the Tonkawa Cannibals* (chapter 8). The history of this tape is the same as that of the former. As seems to be typical of Langley's narratives, this one is as difficult as it is interesting. For reasons of her own, Mrs. Langley refused to speak English, even though she was familiar with the language. She used her young granddaughter as an interpreter. Langley's granddaughter's interpolations, which do not add clarity or content to the narrative, have been deleted.

It is unclear when this drought took place. Langley places it before her birth in the time of her grandfather. Assuming that he was forty-five years old at her birth, the drought took place some time between 1840 and 1880. An earlier time is suggested, since the only Indians mentioned by name are the Choctaw; however, since the Indians trade for water, the presence of non-Indians in the area is also suggested.

### Scene 1: The Drought Occurs

| | |
|---|---|
| Món ihó:ca hona:łi:káhcotoh, | Again, long ago, they told this: |
| ná:hoh, | well, |
| amawó:tok hí:catoho:limpáhcoh. | it is said that my late grandfather saw it. |
| Ohayyí toccí:nan okíybotoho:limpáhcok. | For three years, it did not rain, it is said. |

| | |
|---|---|
| Ohayyí toccí:nan okíybon, | For three years, it did not rain, |
| Talbó:ni káhcoh, | and thus in the Calcasieu River, |
| okó:t okhaytánatkat, | the water went down, |
| okhayóhkipală::::mon, | the water reeeeeealy went down deep, |
| talla:káhcotohok okíybon. | it [the river] lay like that, and it did not rain. |

**Scene 2: How the Indians Lived**

| | |
|---|---|
| Á:tip, okíybon ohayyí toccí:naskat, | As for people, because it did not rain for three years, |
| ná:si yámmit íksot, | there were no things like this, |
| na:sacíhkak íksot, | there was no harvest, |
| na:sókkop íksot, | there was nothing at all, |
| okíp íksot, | and there was no water, |
| okíp íksot. | there was no water. |
| Ohayyí toccí:nan kolossosín wá:ko:t stałí:yatoho:limpah. | For three years, it is said that they took the chickens and cows. |
| Wá:ka stó:lat stá:yat scó:pamá:mit | They took and brought them and must have sold them, |
| stó:łat scó:pama:mit | they took them and must have sold them, |
| stó:łatohok, | they took them, |
| okí ískok | and drinking water, |
| okí ískok má:lon, | only for drinking water, |
| fó:sosi yă::::nkohc; | there was nooooothing like little birds [left]; |
| stáłtohok óm. | it is the case that they took them [all]. |

**Scene 3: How the Deer Lived**

| | |
|---|---|
| Icó:tok món okí i:tískok imaláhtoha. | Deer at that time came to drink the water that was left to them. |
| Okí i:tískon, | They came to drink water, |
| ná:si pasáhkak kánkomá:mit, | it was an ugly thing and must have been been bad; |
| okí i:tískot, | they came to drink water, |
| mí:tot ǫhíkkot, | and some did not, |
| ohtískot yámmih. | they went thus to drink. |

**Scene 4: How the Choctaw Lived**

| | |
|---|---|
| Cahtahák má:fa í:sak | The Choctaw who were dwelling there, |
| imaka:nóhcok í:saskan, | because they continued to be hungry; |
| icó:t ohilabánnit ilá:ci:fó:kok | things like deer when they brought them back over their shoulders, |

mók í:pak
hopakí:ci:fó:kon o:támmih.

they also ate it,
when they went far away [hunting]
to the west.

Món pa:tabáhko:t,
okí íksoskan,
a:nipó mă::::łon í:sat
okí ískon,
má ískon ohayyí toccí:natohok.
Mó:tohok,
okíyboskan,
ihó:cak "innokšila" mók atná:hot.

Also, things were crusty on top,
because there was no water,
they lived oooonly on meat,
drinking water,
they drank that for the three years.
Then,
because it did not rain,
long ago people also had thirst.

### Scene 5: The Wildfires

Okíybon,
ittó:tok ibisná:lok hiłí:lit,
ittó:tok hiłí:lit,
ittó:tok óhyak hiłí:lit
óhyak kánkomá:mit,
ḿmm̀, kánkostalpístoho:limpáhcok.

It did not rain,
and the trees at that time caught fire of themselves;
the trees at that time caught fire;
all the trees at that time caught fire;
everything must have been bad.
Mmm! It is said that it was sufficiently bad.

### Scene 6: Where the Water Was

Ná:hoh,
kámmi:fó:kon,
okí mă::::łok imí:son yá:fa
ohayyí toccí:natoho:limpáhcoh.
Okí má:łok,
okíp sámmo:sop,
Talbó:nik yáp o:haytanátkak
kofókbik ná:ho:kon
akkáhcotohá.

Well,
this being so,
they lived ooooonly by water there,
for three years, it is said.
Only water,
there was only a little water,
in the Calcasieu here in the meanders;
there was some in pits;
thus it was.

### Scene 7: The State of the People

Ohayyí toccí:nan cahták stibákłitohok,
imaká:not,
imaká:nok,
icó:to:t ilabaná:t ilá:ci:k,
món í:patohoh,
hokáhcotoho:limpáhcok.

For three years, the Choctaw were impoverished,
they were hungry,
they were hungry,
and, when they brought back deer
and suchlike on their shoulders,
they also ate it, so it is reported.

| | |
|---|---|
| Ihá:ni yámmok | The earth was like so, |
| hahcí yámmit, | the rivers were like so, |
| faská:cik ná:hotoho:limpáhcok. | it is said they were flaking off. |
| Okhayóhkik, | In the depths of the water, |
| okík íkso:fó:kap, | when there was no water, |
| wakahkaciscí ihá:nik. | the earth was cracking up. |
| Kámmik, | Thus, |
| hahcí yámmit bálkatoho:limpáhcok | it is said that the rivers lay so, |
| okíybo:fó:kap. | when it did not rain. |
| Ohayyí toccí:na:fó:kon okíyboskat, | Because it did not rain for three years, |
| stibákɬitoho:limpak, | it is said that they were impoverished: |
| imakásnok athómmahak. | the Indians were hungry. |

**Scene 8: The Rains Return**

| | |
|---|---|
| Mó:tohon, | Then, |
| ohayyí toccí:na:fó:kon, | after three years, |
| o:locik sǎ::::mo:sit | soooome clouds |
| í::::lat ónti:fó:kok, | arriiiiived, and when they came, |
| óybaton má:ɬok, | it merely rained, |
| óybat, | and it rained, |
| óybat, | and it rained, |
| óybat, | and it rained, |
| óybat, | and it rained, |
| óybat, | and it rained, |
| óybat, | and it rained, |
| óybat, | and it rained, |
| óybat, | and it rained, |
| óybat. | and it rained, |
| Fápli:fó:kon, | When it stormed, |
| ɬóykat, | it returned; |
| ókik tanátkatoho:limpáhcok. | the water descended, so it is said. |
| Ohayyí toccí:nan amawó:tok | My late grandfather saw it after three |
| hí:catoho:limpáhcok. | years, it is said. |
| Na:sóhyak ká:notoho:limpáhcok. | It is said that everything was good again. |

*Textual commentary*:

Line 6 *Talbó:ni* 'the Calcasieu River'. The use of this toponym gives a definite location where the drought took place. *A:sili*'s ancestors were a wandering band of Choctaw who had entered Louisiana at the end of the eighteenth century. The place name *talbó:ni* is of interest because it is the only Koasati place name that is not a borrowing from another language. The English place name Calcasieu is a borrowing from Atakapa, the native language of the area; the lexeme is *katka siw* 'screaming eagle'. The Koasati term seems to have been applied by them to whatever major river on which they were living; thus the name *talbó:ni* seems to have been applied to the Trinity River in Texas, and it probably was used for the Alabama River in the eighteenth century. It is not unlikely that the original referent for *talbó:ni* was the Tennessee River, on which the Koasati dwelt at the beginning of the historical period.

Line 8 *okhayóhkipalǎ:̄:̄:̄:̀mon* 'the water reeeeeealy went down deep'. The use of the intensive, which involves a vowel being lengthened and marked with a rising-falling pitch contour, was used extensively by Langley. Her rhetorical extension of the intensive, along with her tendency to lower the vowels *a* and *o* and to pronounce *s* in all positions as *š*, makes her speech instantly identifiable to anyone who was familiar with her. Further examples of this rhetorical intensive can be found in lines 23, 38, 52, 79, and 80.

Lines 26–27 *Okí i:tískon, / ná:si pasáhkak kánkomá:mit* 'They came to drink water / it was an ugly thing and must have been bad'. These verses seem to refer to the fact that the waterholes that were left were all trodden and muddy, besides being polluted with dead fish.

Line 31 *Cahtahák má:fa í:sak* 'The Choctaw who were dwelling there'. The Choctaw are the only people mentioned by name in this narrative. That there were other people, presumably non-Indians, is implied by the fact that the Indians sold animals for drinking water. But for the narrator, these people are not important to her, as her ancestors, the Choctaw, are the ones on whom she wishes to focus.

Line 43 *ihó:cak "innokšila" mok atná:hot* 'long ago people also had thirst'. The word *innokšila* is a Choctaw word meaning 'thirst'. The Koasati equivalent of Choctaw *nokšila, noksolothilká* is quite rare, as the use of 'thirst' as an abstract notion is generally subsumed in the term *balissá* 'famine'. This is an interesting example of Azilie's first language interfering with her otherwise impeccable Koasati.

Lines 44–45 *Okíybon, / ittó:tok ibisná:lok hiłí:lit* 'It did not rain, / and the trees at that time caught fire of themselves'. These lines begin the fifth scene, which, by its placement at the beginning of the second half of the narrative, is marked as the climax of the narrative. The fact that lines 44 through 49 form one single phrase, with the lines separated from each other by intonational and morphological clues, also indicates that what is being said is important. Considering the fact that the forest at that time consisted of virgin long-leaf pine, a wildfire in the forest would have been most impressive and terrifying.

Lines 53–57 *okíp sámmo:sop, / Talbó:nik yáp o:haytanáltak / kofókbik ná:ho:kon / akkáhcotohá* 'there was only a little water, / in the Calcasieu here in the meanders, / there was some in pits, / thus it was'. This is a free translation of the Koasati text, which is much more involved. A more literal translation would be, 'Now, there was only just so much water, and the Calcasieu had these meanders, and pits is that which they [the meanders] had, and the other thing [the water] was indeed so [i.e., in the pits]'. Here, the morphological feature of reference indexing keeps the Koasati unambiguous without the continuous repetition of nouns as required by English in the same context.

Lines 80–88 *óybat,* etc. 'it rained', etc. Although repetition of a phrase is typical in Koasati traditional narrative, Langley uses one variety of repetition to an extent that no other speaker uses. The identical repetition of a verb phrase indicates that the action is more intense than normal, very much as in colloquial English *it rained and it rained*. Each repetition indicates the intensity is greater. Thus, Langley, in repeating the phrase eight times (note that eight is twice the ritual number four), verbally indicates that the returning rains were far more intense and prolonged than what would be considered normal. Langley's idiosyncratic use of intensive repetition may be related to her similar use of the extended intensive internal change, as mentioned above.

## THE DROWNED VILLAGE (First Version)

narrated by Martha John

This narrative was recorded by dictation in May 1992. For reasons she did not discuss, she was unwilling for it to be tape recorded. This story is widely known, but not often told to outsiders, as most people accept this to be a true story and do not wish to be criticized about their belief in it. Although the story does contain a supernatural component, the sudden collapse of the ground into a subsurface lake is quite plausible, especially in an area of karst topography (limestone or dolomite that has been eroded by subsurface drainage), such as is found in central Florida or central Texas. The magic lake (*okí holló*) into which the village was submerged is a dangerous place to which evil supernaturals descend from the sky, riding on bright meteors, or fireballs, called *kowí hómma* 'red panthers'. This is the only body of water that the Indians of long ago considered to be dangerous to human beings; all other lakes, streams, and rivers were considered to be helpful to people.

### Scene 1: The Indians Dance and the Land Submerges

| | |
|---|---|
| Athómmak bítlik í:sáhcotohon | The Indians continued to dance; |
| bítlin í:satohon, | they danced and continued on, |
| ihá:nik o:nakáɬɬan | and the land was drowned, |
| okí hollók tallá:katohon, | and the magic lake lay there; |
| okík mataská:káhcok, | the water had burst out, |
| athommák ho:cí:fok, "okí holló" | and the Indians name it, saying: |
| hokáhcon. | "the Magic Lake." |

### Scene 2: The Sounds of Singing and Drumming Can Be Heard to This Day

| | |
|---|---|
| Mó:tohon, | Then, |
| nihtá sáhmi:p, | some days, |
| aykacabonohkák b$^{o}$kkan, | drums are really beaten, |
| á:tik naksą̨hkan, | and people really make noise, |
| tálwat aykacabonóhka stintálwat$^{o}$. | they sing, and they sing to the drums. |

Kámmi:fo:kon,
  ná:ho:t
    kolosó:t ó:lan,
      wá:ko:t páhkan,
        sohkó:t naksąhkan,
          káhco:limpáhcok má:fa.
Anta:tanahkák kommánkáhco:lik
kánto má:fa.

When this is so,
  well,
    chickens and so forth squawk,
      cows and so forth bellow,
        pigs and so forth squeal;
          that is the way it is there, so they say.
My stepfather used to tell us how it was
there.

*Textual Comments:*

Note the following description from Martha John:

Abá ishí:catohon
  sámmin wíhhíli:p,
    skalafkáhci.
Skaláfka:fó:kon,
  nashollók acákkit amá:kan
    (nasholló holcifó kowí hómma).

If you look up,
  sometimes when we look for it,
    there is a meteor trail.
When there is a meteor trail,
  evil supernaturals go following it
    (the evil supernaturals are named Red
    Panthers).

Akkámmi:fó:kon,
  ihá:nifa hahcosík tintí:bit yámmit ałi:yá.
    (mók kowí hómma įhíno:limpáhcok)
O:támmi:p
  má:fa okí hollók tallaká.
Nashollók o:wisá ka:háhco:lik.

This being so,
  on earth a stream goes twisted like so.
    (This is said to be the Red Panther's path.)
When it falls into the water,
  there the magic lake lies.
The evil supernaturals dwell in the water
there, they used to say.

Lines 14–17 The animals are disturbed and make noise when they hear the sounds coming from the drowned village below the surface of the magic lake.

Line 18 *Anta:tanahkák* 'my stepfather'. This was Alfred John (1872-1941), Miss John's paternal uncle (father of her cousin/stepbrother Ed John), who, as a widower, took Miss John's widowed mother in the levirate marriage that was expected in traditional Koasati culture.

## THE DROWNED VILLAGE (Second Version)
narrated by Sam Thompson

This narrative was told to me and recorded on tape by Mr. Thompson in May 1992, in part as an elaboration on the narrative of Miss John, after having heard it read to him. For him, the drowned village was a real place that could be found in Texas. It is interesting that Mr. Thompson thought that the inhabitants of the village might not have been Koasati; the karst areas of Texas, in which a sinkhole could form, are somewhat more to the west of the westernmost Koasati settlements in Texas.

### Prologue: About the Village

| | |
|---|---|
| Ihó:cak ómmi:p, | As for long ago, |
| oha:łí:kan há:loli:p | as I heard them tell the tale, |
| Kowassá:tihot ómmǫ, | they were perhaps Koasati, |
| ínko:p | or if not, |
| athómma ná:sihot imayiksá katíkap | Indians of some other tribe, |
| sto:nakáłtoho:limpáhcok | but is is said that they drowned. |
| Ihá:nik stonàmmit katík | But it was the whole land, |
| masto:nakáłłak ómmi:k, | that disappeared into the water, |
| sto:nakáłłak ómmi:k | that drowned, |
| niłá ostá:kan hobítt athómmak imbítka | after the Indians danced their dance for four nights. |

### Scene 1: The Indians Dance, and the Land Submerges

| | |
|---|---|
| Aláhka má:min, | It seems there were other people, |
| ilmá:káhcotohok imbini:líhcot | and they came to visit them; |
| ilo:tałán athómmak ístǫ, | there were Indians living on this side, |
| Liwistóntiksiffí:non. | around Livingston, Texas. |
| Albá:mok í:san má:fa, | The Alabama live there, |
| imbiní:t ilmá:katohot ómmǫ aláhkap. | and it seems that some of them came to visit. |
| Má:min, | Then, |
| aláhkak ilmá:kat bítlik, | the others came to dance; |
| niłá ostá:kan ístǫ. | they stayed there four nights. |
| Mó:tohok má:łon, | Only then, |
| niłá ostá:ka:fó:kon, | when it was the fourth night, |
| bítka kankóhcot, | the dance was wrong. |
| hotálwak bítlíhcot ómmǫ. | and it seems they sang and danced it. |
| Ŏ:hya:si sto:nakáłtoho:limpáhcok athómmak óhyak. | All the Indians utterly and completely drowned with the land, they say. |

### Scene 2: The Village Still Exists

| | |
|---|---|
| Kámmiskan, | Just like that, |
| akkó athómmak sto:nakáłtohok, | those Indians drowned with the land, |
| tallá:kak onàmmimpáhcok hokáhcok. | but they say, it is said, that it is still there. |
| Gúdrictiksiffí:namá:min, | Around Goodrich, Texas, |
| matịhaso:támmiffí:namáhcok ómmǫ. | it seems to be somewhat towards the west of there. |
| Naksó:n oha:łí:kak onàmmimpáhcok. | Somewhere, they say, they still tell the story. |

| | |
|---|---|
| Thátko:t, | People such as white people, |
| atlocó:t, | people such as black people, |
| akkó yámmik hohá:lo:fó:kok. | people like those have heard it. |
| Kámmisk | Just like that |
| tallá:kak onàmmo katík, | it still exists, |
| á:tok sobayá:kǫ, | but people don't know about it, |
| yá imaníhtaha yámmip katík, | such as these young people, |
| anáp sombáylilik onáhcok. | but as for me, I still remember it. |
| Ohhí:callaho:litik | I had intended to go and see it, |
| ohtakhí:cóhcok món. | but I was unable to find it. |
| | |
| Ká:mo:s. | The end. |

*Textual comments:*

Line 10 Dancing was an integral part of traditional Koasati religion. When asked about what the Indians did before they went to church, Martin Abbey said, "*Pí:la niɬá ostá:kan hobíttow* 'They just danced for four nights'." Note that in Abbey's statement, and in the text of the narrative, the use of the obsolete word *niɬá* 'night' for the modern word *tamó:ka*, which originally meant 'darkness'.

Line 21 *bítka kankóhcot* 'The dance was wrong'. Unlike the great creative freedom that Koasati storytellers have in crafting their tales, words used in ritual speech were highly stereotyped and had to be repeated without error, or the ritual would be in vain. Jameson Poncho (son of Asa Poncho and husband of Ruth Poncho) in his childhood attended a New Field Inauguration Ceremony given by his grandfather, Sacowáykhi, who warned those attending:

> *"Aykacabonohkasí bóklili:p, afa:li:caskánnąh!" ká:hat ocóski immanká. "Kánkopalámmǫ; faplicobó:t í:lalahǫ afa:li:cáska:p," ká:hat. "Ínko mók, ihá:no:t sto:ɬibítlilahǫ," ká:hat.*
>
> "When I beat the small drum, do ye not then laugh!" he said, telling it to his children. "It would be very wicked. A great wind [hurricane] will come if you laugh," he said. "Or if not, the earth will collapse," he said.

The belief expressed in this statement suggests that in the narrative the collapse of the land occurred because the ritual dances were wrongly performed.

Lines 30–32 The fact that white people and black people, as well as Indians, have heard the sounds coming from the drowned village attests to Mr. Thompson that this story is not a mere fable.

# THE BOY AND THE PYGMY RATTLESNAKE

narrated by Bel Abbey

I recorded this narrative on tape in May, 1987. Like the tale *How a Man Lost His Breechcloth to a Bull*, this narrative is more anecdotal than historical. It is set in a timeless past, the anonymity of the human characters indicating that the original incident took place in a time out of memory of the person from whom Abbey got the tale. Similar semihistorical narratives that can be dated indicate that most incidents occurring in the nineteenth century are old enough for their participants to have been forgotten. It is likely that the original incident that provides the content of this narrative is from that period.

Nevertheless, the possibility remains that this narrative is actually autobiographical. The protagonist, a young boy with an intense curiosity about the natural world, bears a striking resemblance to Abbey, a man with an equally intense interest in nature. In addition, the boy lives with his mother and grandmother; after Abbey's father's early death, he and his brother lived with his own mother and grandmother. These features, although suggestive, may merely indicate the reason that Abbey kept this narrative in his repertoire. Because it contains a character and situation with which he could identify strongly, Abbey may have felt attracted to this narrative, and thus interest, rather than personal experience may have been the reason he "took" (the Koasati idiom) this narrative.

## Scene 1: A Boy Wanders About

| | |
|---|---|
| Á:tosi cokí:boscok, | There was a little child, |
| ohayyí námposco:li casobáykotik, | I do not know how old he was, |
| á:tosik cokí:boscok á:tatohok. | but there once was a little child. |
| Á:yatoho:limpáhcok hínosi apatahá. | It is said that he was going about alongside a path. |
| Hínosi apatahá, | Alongside a path, |
| naksó:n imí:sa ayakhá, | somewhere near his house, |
| matáytohok. | he was there wandering. |
| Á:yat naswíhlit nashí:cat, | He went about looking for things, looking at things: |
| ná:son sammíhcommito a:yáhcotohok á:tatohok. | he continued to go about [seeing] how things were. |

## Scene 2: He Finds a Pygmy Rattlesnake

| | |
|---|---|
| Hí:catoho:limpáhcok. | It is said that he found something. |
| Ná:hot cokkó:tohon cintosók. | It was there, sitting, a little snake. |
| Cintosí mók holcifók hacolaycótohon, | Also, the name of the little snake was "pygmy rattlesnake"; |
| hacolaycosík ómmitǫ. | it was a small pygmy rattlesnake. |

| | |
|---|---|
| Mó:tohon, | Then, |
| cokkó:ton híhcok, | on seeing it sitting there, |
| "Amalostă::ho:s!" | "I find it really interesting!" |
| ká:hatoho:limpą́hcok | the boy said, |
| ná:no:sik. | so it is reported. |
| Imaló:stit á:ta:fó:k, | As he kept on being interested in it, |
| hí:catoho:limpak. | it is said that he watched it. |

**Scene 3: The Boy Picks Up the Pygmy Rattlesnake**

| | |
|---|---|
| Má:mo:sok, | Thereupon, |
| "Tabáthkalok słóykalą́," á:lok, | "Having caught it, I shall take it back," he thought, |
| tabátkok słóykah bànnok, | and he tried to catch it and take it back, |
| á:ta:p, | as he stayed there, |
| hí:ca:p, | as he watched it, |
| sánkon, | but he was unable to do it, |
| ná:hotoho:limpak. | it is so said. |
| Ittó afakcó, | It was bark, |
| hałbón, | pine bark; |
| ittó afakcó, | it was the bark |
| hałbík ilkáhcok, | that is called pine bark; |
| ittó afakconánnamá:min, | it seems that there was bark all over; |
| hałbón wíhlit híhcok, | he looked for and found pine bark, |
| ná:hotoho:limpak. | and it is said that he used it. |
| Ayakhá impa:tállok, | Having laid it down for it nearby, |
| ná:hon, | well, |
| hacolaycosík matpa:cokko:líhcok, | the pygmy rattlesnake went over and sat on it, |
| stíhsok, | and he picking it up, |
| stonàmmi salátlin | it having slid completely on, |
| stíhsok, | he picked it up, |
| óntitoho:limpak imí:safa. | and it is said that he came to his house. |

**Scene 4: The Boy Arrives Home with the Pygmy Rattlesnake**

| | |
|---|---|
| Imí:safa stíhlok, | Having brought it to his house, |
| ittimpáhkatoho:limpak. | it is said that he called out to them there. |
| Ima:pót ómmitǫ ittimmánkak, | It was, perhaps, his grandmother he told, |
| ima:pó mǫ, | indeed his grandmother, |
| immá:mo:tot ómmǫ, | or perhaps his mother, |
| naksón casobáykotik, | which one I do not know, |
| stíhlok, | but he brought it. |

| | |
|---|---|
| "Yáhcon, | "It is like so; |
| yáhcok ká:noscon, | like this, it is really good, |
| cintosík ka:nóhcon í:silok stí:lal," | I picked up and brought a real good |
| káhhan. | little snake," he said. |
| "Ǒ:, kankóhc! | "Oh, it is bad! |
| Apí:l! | Get rid of it! |
| Kánkopalámmot aci:yáhcóm! | You are being excessively wicked! |
| Apí:l!" hoká:ha:p, | Get rid of it!" they said; |
| mán, ná:hok, | and again, well, |
| "Cintosík ónkak, | "The little snake spoke to me. |
| 'cího:pá:cákkolahǫ. | 'I will not injure you. |
| cího:pá:cákkolaho katík óm,' | It is the case that I will not |
| káhhok," | injure you,' it said," |
| káhhan. | he said. |
| "Pa:cokkó:lin | "It sat on it [the bark] |
| słóykat stóntit sti:lalíhcok ómmil," | and I have come bringing it back," |
| ká:ha:fó:kap, | he said. |
| "Apí:l! | "Get rid of it! |
| Apí:l!" ká:ha:p, | Get rid of it!" she said; |
| ima:pók ká:ha:p, | his grandmother said it, |
| apí:kotoho:limpáhcok. | and it is said that he did not get rid of it. |
| Ma:fó:kon, | Thereupon, |
| sámmitik sobáyko:fó:k, | as he did not understand how it was, |
| ima:pók ayakhá sbatáplit | his grandmother struck it away from him nearby, |
| stimapí:toho:limpáhcok. | and it is said that she got rid of it on him. |
| Má:mo:sin, | Thus, |
| cintosík hacolaycosótoho:limpáhcok. | it is said that the little snake was a pygmy rattlesnake. |

## Epilogue

| | |
|---|---|
| Má:mo:sin, | Thereupon, |
| sammí:citot | I do not know how it went, |
| casobáykó; í:bitot ómmǫ, | perhaps they killed it, |
| imapí:tot ómmǫ. | perhaps they [just] got rid of it. |
| Sammí:citot ómmo casobáykotik, | I do not know how it perhaps was, |
| á:ti ná:nosok tábatkat stóhłan, | but the boy caught it and brought it there, |
| iyyawópkat ómmitoho:limpáhcok | and it is said that he startled them, |
| immá:mak ima:pók stóklok. | both his mother and his grandmother. |

Kámmo:sin sobáylil hiná:p. — Just so much is what I know now.

*Textual commentary*:

Lines 1–9 These lines give a succinct description of a young boy wandering about, amusing himself on his own. As mentioned in the introduction to this narrative, this character is very similar in personality to Abbey, who made a life-long study of the natural world and was highly educated in traditional knowledge about it. If it is not autobiographical, the scene is an example of keen observation of child behavior.

Line 13 *Cintosí mók holcifók hacolaycótohon, / hacolaycosík ómmitǫ* 'Also, the name of the little snake was "pygmy rattlesnake," / it was a small pygmy rattlesnake.' Venomous snakes are endemic in southwestern Louisiana, including the cottonmouth or water moccasin, the canebrake rattlesnake, and the coral snake. The pygmy rattlesnake is particularly dangerous because it is common, small, and relatively docile. The dangers of the real world could be just as frightening to the Indians as those of the supernatural world.

Lines 19–37 This scene forms the climax of the tale for the narrator. This clearly shows that the indigenous concept of climax differs from the Western notion. For one used to western stylistics, the climax of this narrative occurs when the boy brings the rattlesnake into the house. To a Koasati person, however, the boy wanting to catch the snake and figuring out how to bring it home is what is important. This is marked linguistically by the scene consisting of three long sentences, each containing six or seven lines.

Lines 38–65 This scene contains an extremely well-crafted confrontation between the boy and his grandmother. He is merely interested in showing her the wonderful thing he found; she, who realizes the danger he has placed himself in, reacts in a fashion that would be familiar to a mother or grandmother in any culture. The combination of boyish naiveté and adult horror is considered highly amusing, as are all sudden, sharp contrasts in emotions.

Lines 49ff *Apí:l!* "Get rid of it!" Every time this word is spoken, the pitch is at least a sixth higher than normal, and the *p* is strongly aspirated. These are linguistic markers of excitement and fear.

Lines 54–56 *"Cintosík ónkak* '"The little snake spoke to me"' Here, the boy tries to reassure his grandmother that the snake is all right because it spoke to him, very much in the manner that the animals in Rabbit stories speak to people. This is a deft picture of a young child's psychology, for such a child is not yet able to understand that his mental projections on an outside object come from himself, and not from the object.

Linguistically, the child's phraseology is exactly parallel to that found in Rabbit stories, as in the comparison below:

The Boy and the Pygmy Rattlesnake, line 56:

*"cího:pa:cákkolaho katík óm," káhhok.* "It is the case that I will not injure you," it said.

The Bungling Host, line 70:

*"imalíkcillaho katík óm," káhhan.* "It is the case that I will doctor him," he said

Lines 61–64 Because it finally becomes clear to the grandmother that the boy is unable to understand the danger, she strikes the snake out of his hands and removes the danger from him. It should be noted that the grandmother does this not out of anger, but only as a last resort. The Koasati permit corporal punishment of children, but only in the case of persistent and wilful disobedience and lying. If a child admits to wrongdoing and expresses remorse for his actions, he usually receives a short lecture on proper behavior and then is allowed to go on his way.

## HOW A MAN LOST HIS BREECHCLOTH TO A BULL

narrated by Bel Abbey

I recorded this narrative on tape in May, 1987. It is of stylistic interest because although its form is consistent with traditional narrative, its content is more similar to semihistorical narratives. Since this narrative has no speaking animal characters, and the incident related could well have occurred, it is classified as a semihistorical narrative.

The narrative contains only six scenes, but, as usual, they can be grouped into two sections, with the first half setting the situation for the climax to occur, and the second half containing the climax and denouement. The only stylistic fault in this narrative is the interpolation in the middle of the third scene. The need to explain the way the men were dressed has only been necessary since traditional clothing was given up in the late nineteenth century; originally, this would not have been necessary. Thus, the narrator has to insert it as some point. Here, he chooses the last scene of the first half, since knowing the manner of dressing is vital to understanding the climax in the next scene.

The approximate date of the incident related can only be guessed at. Abbey explained that it happened in one of the prairies to be found formerly in southwest Louisiana. The bent tree is likely to be a blackjack oak, found in the woods and fields at the present. Since the Koasati had returned to Louisiana in large numbers in the 1840s and 1850s; it is probably that this incident happened between 1860 and 1870.

### Scene 1: Two Men Are out in the Woods

| | |
|---|---|
| Á:tik a:yá:citoholimpáhcok. | It is said that two people were going about. |
| Łopohlíhcok, | They were passing through; |
| naksó:n ałła:cíhcommíhcok, | it was the case that the two of them were going somewhere, |
| ínko:p, | or if not, |
| ilanawíhcot ómmitǫ. | they must have been hunting. |
| Ittohayó a:yá:citǫ. | The two of them were going about in the forest. |
| Wá:ka małáhlik í:san, | The wild cattle that were dwelling there; |
| hí:cat łopóhlit a:yá:citǫ. | the two of them saw them as they were passing by. |

### Scene 2: They Come across Wild Cattle

| | |
|---|---|
| Wá:kak małáhlotoho:limpáhcok, | It is said that the cattle were indeed wild, |
| wá:kok małáhlotoho:limpáhcokittohayó isá. | it is said that cattle that were indeed wild were dwelling in the forest. |
| Mó:tohok, | Then, |
| wakná:nik lapó:t hobáskit, | the bulls had long horns; |
| wá:ka lapí hobáskit o:láhcotohok, | the long-horned cattle were lowing, |
| i:sáhcotohok. | as they were standing there. |
| Có:ba małáhli mók malmámmit ístoho:liyon, | Wild horses also lived in just the same way, |
| ittohayó a:yá:cit łopóhli:fó:k, | but as the two of them were passing by in the forest, |
| hínosok ałí:yatohon, | the path went that way; |
| hínosi ałłá:ci:k, | when the two of them were going on the path, |
| a:yá:ci:fó:kap, | when they were going about, |
| wá:kak mathí:catoho:limpáhcok. | it is said that the cattle saw them from afar. |

### Scene 3 Part 1: An Ill-Tempered Bull Chases the Men

| | |
|---|---|
| Mó:tohon, | Then, |
| wakná:nik kánkok á:sat á:tatohok, | an ill-tempered bull that was dwelling with them, |
| hí:catohomá:łok, | after it saw them, |
| ná:hotoho:limpáhcok, | well, it is said, |
| matwalí:katoho:limpáhcok. | it is said that it ran at them from afar. |

| | |
|---|---|
| Má:mo:sin, | Thereupon, |
| óntitohok, | it was coming, |
| óntitohok áttohomá:łok, | after it kept on coming, |
| intółkatoho:limpáhcok. | it is said that they ran from him. |
| Wá:ka ná:ni intółka:fó:kap— | When they ran from the bull— |

### Interpolation: How the Men Were Dressed

| | |
|---|---|
| Ihó:cap, | Now long ago, |
| wiló:tok íksot, | shoes at that time did not exist, |
| stiliyófkak ómmi:k, | and as for trousers, |
| iboksó:sit yomáhcotoho:limpáhcok. | it is said that they went about wearing short breechcloths. |
| Iboksó:sit, | They wore short breechcloths; |
| wiló:tok íksot, | shoes at that time did not exist, |
| ittobihí syomáhlit | they carried bows with them, |
| kámmiscotoho:liyok | and, contrary to what one might think, they were like that, |
| atyomáhtohok. | people went about so. |

### Scene 3, Part 2: The Ill-Tempered Bull Chases the Men

| | |
|---|---|
| Yá tóklot a:yá:citohok, | These two who were going about, |
| a:yá:citohon, | they were going about, |
| wakná:nik híhcok matwalí:kan, | and a bull, catching sight of them came running; |
| hołohlíhcok óm. | it is the case that it was chasing them. |
| Hiná:p hołohlíhcok óm, | Now, it is the case that it is chasing them; |
| "Intółhílkásk!" káhhan. | "Let us run from him!" they said. |

### Scene 4: One Loses His Breechcloth

| | |
|---|---|
| Mó:tohop, | Then, |
| ittók nampotíkkon shi:báhkatohon, | there were a few trees that were standing there, |
| matwalí:ka:fó:kap, | when it was running from afar, |
| caffák walí:kat imonóyyan, | one man ran and climbed up away from it, |
| caffák ilimonoyyá:cit ałí:ya:fó:kap, | when the other was beginning to get himself to climb, |
| wakná:nik cákkostoho:limpáhcok łóhli:k. | it is said that the bull was upon him in chasing him. |
| Wakná:nik cákko:si:fó:kap, | When the bull was almost upon him; |
| immayá:cit walí:kahonká:sit, | he really ran more than it, |
| ittó conokbíhcok haccá:litohon, | and there was a bent tree standing there, |

mafíhna walí:kak,
imó:łok ałí:ya:fó:kok,
wakná:nik cákkoston,
cofótlit ittinsá:wafa
ataká:ka:fó:kap,
cofótlit ataká:ka:fó:k,
ná:nik "Caficípkalahǫ,"
á:lotohok,
ficípkat ómmá:tok,
ittó ittimataká:kan,
iboksí má:łon ficípkat,
imí:sit,
słopótlok,
swalí:kat,
lapí imataká:kat
swalí:kat
snakáłtoholimpak.

and he ran straight there;
when he was just getting there
the bull was almost upon him,
when he jumped and was hanging
from a branch;
when he jumped and was hanging,
"I shall be gored,"
he thought,
and after it gored at him,
as he was hanging from the tree,
it gored only his breechcloth;
it took it from him,
went past with it,
and ran off with it;
it ran with it hanging
from its horn,
and it is said that it
disappeared.

## Scene 5: The Men Return to Camp

Má:mo:sin,
á:ti:kok matcóffitohomá:łok,
cóffit ałła:cíhcok,
łoyohkáhcok intółkatoho:limpáhcok.
Má:mo:sok,
iboksí-íksot caffák łóykat,
łóykatohok hoká:k,
"Ná:sok?"
"Wá:ka ná:ni kánkok á:tatohok,
iboksí ąsíplit," ká:ha:p,

itta:łí:katoho:limpáhcok
tikboltifá.
Ittaí:san,
łóykat í:la:p,
káhcok í:sa:s;
inkostí:nitohą,
immałáhlitoho:limpáhcok má
wakná:ni.

Thereupon,
the men merely jumped down;
the two of them went jumping,
and they went back running, so it is said.
Thereupon,
one came back without his breechcloth,
he came back, and they said,
"What in the world?"
"There was an ill-tempered bull,
and he took my breechcloth off of me,"
he said,
and it is said that they told the story
at the campfire.
They were sitting by the fire,
when he came returning,
and so they stayed;
they were cautious;
it is said that they were afraid of
those bulls.

### Scene 6: Epilogue

| | |
|---|---|
| Kámmisk, | Just like that, |
| ittohayó ihó:cap, | in the forest long ago, |
| acíhbapalammotoho:limpáhcok alí:tak. | it is said that life was excessively difficult. |
| Kámmisk, | Just like that, |
| alí:yo:tok małáhlik í:sa:fó:kon, | they lived uncivilized lives at that time, |
| wakná:nik atłóhliskan, | because bulls chased after people; |
| ná:ni iboksí ísíptoho:limpáhcok yáp. | thus it is said a man had his breechcloth taken off of him. |
| Kámmo:sin hacimmánkalá:himá:m. | Just so much is what I am ready to tell you. |
| Tafhiyám! | Finis! |
| Ká:mo:s. | The end. |

*Textual commentary*:

Lines 1–7 This scene introduces the human actors in this narrative. The use of the dual verbs *a:yá:ci-* 'for two to go about' and *ałłá:ci-* 'for two to go' indicates that they are two in number. It was customary for hunters to travel in pairs, especially when searching for large game animals, since the strength of both might be necessary to carry back a large buck or bear.

Line 10 *wá:kok małáhlotoho:limpáhcok ittohayó isá* 'it is said that cattle that were indeed wild were dwelling in the forest'. It is not known when domestic cattle turned feral in Louisiana. Cattle were almost certainly brought to Louisiana by the Spanish or French. In the seventeenth century, the Spanish had established cattle ranches in Florida and it is not unlikely that the French established stock raising in their territory. By the end of the eighteenth century, the Koasati and other Indians are recorded as raising hogs. By the third decade of the nineteenth century, when they lived in Texas, they are recorded as raising horses and cattle. Thus, the wild cattle of the southwestern Louisiana prairies could have come from either French, Spanish, or Indian herds.

Lines 35–39 *Iboksó:sit, / wiló:tok íksot, / ittobihí syomáhlit / kámmiscotoho:liyok / atyomáhtohok* 'They wore short breechcloths, / shoes at that time did not exist, / they carried bows with them, /and, contrary to what one might think, / they were like that, / people went about so.' The narrator here focuses on the fact that all the protagonists are wearing are breechcloths, a fact that is important later in the narrative. At present, the Koasati dress extremely modestly, especially when outsiders are present. Thus, the habitual near-nudity of their ancestors is remarked on as something that is beyond expectation.

Lines 46–67 This scene forms the climax of the narrative. It is marked as the climax, not only by being the first scene of the second half of the narrative, but by the fact that it consists of only two very long sentences, the second one containing fifteen lines. Because of the use of reference indexing, in which the subject of a following phrase is marked on the preceding phrase as being either the same or different, Koasati narrators are able to accurately track participants without having to come to a full stop or having to repeat an excessive number of nouns. This makes for a difficulty in translating into English because English lacks even the rudiments of such a system and presents difficulties in disambiguating two third-person actors, especially in cases such as here where they are of the same number and gender.

Lines 62–67 *ittó imataká:kan, / iboksí má:łon ficípkat, / imí:sit / słopótlok, / swalí:kat, / lapí imataká:kat swalí:kat snakáłtoholimpak* 'as he was hanging from the tree, / he gored only his breechcloth, / he took it from him, / went past with it, / and ran off with it; / it ran with it hanging from its horn, and it is said that it disappeared'. The breechcloth was a single strip of cloth or deerskin that was passed between the legs and tied with a cord around the waist so that flaps of material fell from the front and behind. The bull's horn caught on the back flap of the man's breechcloth, and pulling on it broke the waist cord, so that the bull carried it off. Present-day listeners find this ludicrous end to a dangerous situation both relieving and amusing.

Line 88 *alí:yo:tok małáhlik í:sa:fó:kon* 'they lived uncivilized lives at that time'. The Koasati term *małáhli*, which usually means 'wild (pl.)' is colloquially used to mean 'uncivilized', in contrast to *paká:ma,* which means 'tame; civilized'. Occasionally, the Koasati will refer to themselves as *immałáhliha* 'the wild people; the uncivilized people'. However, this term is more humorous than self-deprecating, and illustrates the basic difference that they still feel exists between them and Western culture. This is reinforced by the word for 'life' used here, *alí:ya,* which refers to interior life, personality, or mental attitudes, as opposed to *alí:ta,* used two lines above, which refers to external behavior.

Line 92 *Tafhiyám!* 'Finis!' The use of this apotropaic interjection indicates that the speaker considers the preceding tale to be a member of the class of traditional narratives, and thus not necessarily a true tale. The use of this interjection is not limited only to these narratives; at one time Martha John was relating her life as a child, and when she finished this personal narrative, her equally elderly stepbrother/cousin, Ed John, who had heretofore been quietly listening, burst out with "*tafhiyám*!", sending both himself and his stepsister/cousin into gales of laughter.

# Appendices

# References

# Appendix 1

# Linguistically Analyzed Texts

## (for Marianne Mithun)

The following are linguistic analyses of five of the narratives included in this collection: *Corn Woman, The Great Lizard (First Version), Barred Owl and Mouse, The Boy and the Pygmy Rattlesnake*, and *How a Man Lost His Breechcloth to a Bull.* Two other narratives included in this volume have been linguistically analyzed elsewhere: *The First Meeting of the Indians and the Europeans* (Kimball 1991:580–603) and *The Clawed Witches* (Kimball 1993b).

The linguistic terminology used is from Kimball (1991), with the difference that singular verbs are not specially marked, the two subjunctives are not distinguished, and no differentiation is made between the various elements that fall into the adverbial and modal slots.

### CORN WOMAN

| Tayyí | sihnóhcok | á:yatoho:limpatš. |
|---|---|---|
| tayyí | sihno-V́hco-k | á:ya-toho-:li-mpa-t-š |
| woman | old-HABIT-SS | go:about-REALIS-DEDUC-HEARSAY-PAST-PH:TR |

| Ho:tinannáhcok, | pasá:kascok, |
|---|---|
| ho:ti-nanna-V́hco-k | pasá:ka-:si-V́hco-k |
| sores-NOTHING:BUT-HABIT-SS | be:dirty-DIM-HABIT-SS |

| ohimpalátka:sin. | Á:yatohok, |
|---|---|
| oh-im-palátka-:si-n | á:ya-toho-k |
| DISTR-3DAT be:cross-DIM-SW | go:about-REALIS-SS |

| atlawístanannáhcok, | loká:caskok |
|---|---|
| at-lawísta-nanna-V́hco-k | loká:ca-si-k-ok |
| person-small(pl)-NOTHING:BUT-HABIT-SS | orphan-DIM-ART-SS:FOC |

í:satohon. Óhłan, atlawístak
í:sa-toho-n ó,h,ła-n at-lawísta-k
dwell(pl)-REALIS-SW be:there,H:GRADE,-SW person-small(pl)-NOM

ayyihó:cihónkan cokkó:toho:limpatš.
ayyihó:ci-hónka-n cokkó:li-toho:-li-mpa-t-š
have:pity-ADV-SW sit(sg)-REALIS-DEDUC-HEARSAY-PAST-PH:TR

"Koncokkǫ:li:š," káhhan.
kom-cokkó:,N,li-V̨h-š ká,h,ha-n
3DAT-sit(sg),N:GRADE,-DELAY:IMP-PH:TR say,H:GRADE-SW

Má:mo:sin, tayyí síhnok ónkak, "Ná:son
má:mo:si-n tayyí síhno-k ónka-k ná:s-on
be:then-SW woman old-NOM SAY-SS something-ACC:FOC

shopónhácíhcotohok i:talloko:líhcok!"
s-hopón-háci-V́hco-toho-k i:t-am-loko:li,h,c-ok
INSTR-cook-2PL:SUBJ(2AI)-HABIT-REALIS-SS COME:&-1DAT-stand(pl),H:GRADE,-SS:FOC

káhhan. I:tilloko:líhcin. Má:mo:sin,
ká,h,ha-n i:t-im-loko:li,h,ci-n má:mo:si-n
say,H:GRADE,-SW COME:&-3DAT-stand(pl),H:GRADE,-SW be:then-SW

ibisnók cassók a:yáhcok ómmitohok,
ibisnó-k cass-ók á:ya-V́hco-k ómmi-toho-k
3:pronoun-NOM corn-NOM:FOC go:about-HABIT-SS be-REALIS-SS

ilisahlí:cit i intabáhlin í:pat
ili-sahlí:ci-t im-tabáhli-n í:pa-t
3REFLEX-scrape-CONN 3DAT-make:bread-SW eat-CONN

í:satoho:limpatš. Mó:tohon,
í:sa-toho-:li-mpa-t-š mó:toho-n
dwell(pl)-REALIS-DEDUC-HEARSAY-PAST-PH:TR be:then-SW

ónkak, "Cassík hiná:p hiná:bat
ónka-k cassí-k hiná:p hiná:ba-t
quoth-SS corn-NOM now be:hard-CONN

hinábš," káhhan. "Pitáhkok
hiná:ba-DEL-š ká,h,ha-n pitáhk-ok
be:hard-PH:TR-PH:TR say,H:GRADE,-SW storage:house-NOM:FOC

| acó:bok | haccá:tohon, | yón | páslit | anóslok, |
|---|---|---|---|---|
| acó:b-ok | haccá:li-toho-n | yón | pásli-t | anósl-ok |
| old-NOM:FOC | stand(sg)-REALIS-SW | here | clean-CONN | finish(pl)-SS:FOC |

| onokbáhlok | nocitóka:š!" | káhhok. | "Anók |
|---|---|---|---|
| onokbáhl-ok | noci-tóka-V̨h-š | ká,h,h-ok | anó-k |
| close-SS:FOC | sleep(imp)-2PL:IMP-DELAY-PH:TR | say,H:GRADE,-SS:FOC | I-NOM |

| hacimpicí | mó:š, | káhhok, | "Cassí | hátką," |
|---|---|---|---|---|
| hacim-picí | mó-š" | ká,h,h-ok | cassí | hátka |
| 2PL:POSS-mother | indeed-PH:TR | say,H:GRADE,-SS:FOC | corn | white |

| Ónkak, | "Tabáhlit | háspalaho:š," |
|---|---|---|
| ónka-k | tabáhli-t | hás-pa-laho-š |
| quoth-SS | make:bread-CONN | 2PL:SUBJ(1A)-eat-IRREALIS-PH:TR |

| ká:hatohon. | Tamóhkan, | hobálka:p, | pitáhkak |
|---|---|---|---|
| ká:ha-toho-n | tamó,h,ka-n | ho-bálka-:p | pitahká-k |
| say-REALIS-SW | be:night,H:GRADE,-SW | DISTR-lie(pl)-SUBJUNC | storage:house-NOM |

| kobohlí:cit | nakáłtohok. | Níhtan, |
|---|---|---|
| kobohlí:ci-t | nakáłła-toho-k | níhta-n |
| make:noise-CONN | be:lost-REALIS-SS | be:day-SW |

| ohtohintiwáptohon, | cassík | alotó:kat |
|---|---|---|
| oht-oh-im-tiwápli-toho-n | cassí-k | alotó:ka-t |
| GO:&-DISTR-3DAT-open-REALIS-SW | corn-NOM | be:full:up-CONN |

| shaccá:toho:limpatš. |
|---|
| s-haccá:li-toho-:li-mpa-t-š |
| INSTR-stand-REALIS-DEDUC-HEARSAY-PAST-PH:TR |

## THE GREAT LIZARD

| Á:tik | ilanawíhlik | á:yatohok, | ittó:bon |
|---|---|---|---|
| á:ti-k | ilanawíhli-k | á:ya-toho-k | ittó:b-on |
| person-NOM | hunter-NOM | go:about-REALIS-SS | hollow:tree-ACC:FOC |

| híhcok | ónti:k | íhlok | ónkak |
|---|---|---|---|
| hí,h,c-ok | ónti-:k | í,h,l-ok | ónka-k |
| see,H:GRADE,-SS | come-SUBJUNC | arrive,H:GRADE,-SS | quoth-SS |

"Nitón stą́hí:ca:s" káhhan.
nit-ón st-am-hí:ca-:s ká,h,ha-n
bear-ACC:FOC INSTR-1DAT-see-IPAST say,H:GRADE,-SW

Má:mo:sin, á:ti hanná:lit amá:kat
má:mo:si-n á:ti hanná:li-t amá:ka-t
be:then-SW person be:six-CONN go(pl)-CONN

ołáhcin, naksó:n nitá ittó:bik
ołá,h,-ci-n naksofón nitá ∅-ittó:bi-k
be:there,H:GRADE,-PL-SW where bear 3POSS-hollow:tree-NOM

stįhaccá:lik. Má:mo:sin, á:ti imaníhtak
st-in-haccá:li-k má:mo:si-n á:ti imaníhta-k
INSTR-3DAT-stand-SS be:then-SW person young-NOM

imonóyyak, ayakhá óhłok, tikbá
im-onóyya-k ayakhá ó,h,ł-ok tikbá-∅
3DAT-climb-SS near be:there,H:GRADE,-SS:FOC fire-ACC

mastįhókfik ittó:bifa. Má:mo:sin, ná:sok
mast-im-hókfi-k ittó:bi-fa má:mo:si-n ná:s-ok
INSTR-3DAT-put:in-SS hollow:tree-LOC be:then-SW something-NOM:FOC

ittó:bihayo naksą́hkak có:ba ná:ni
ittó:bi-hayo naksá,N,hka-k có:ba ná:ni
hollow:tree-INESS make:noise,N:GRADE,-SS horse male

mánkatoho:limpatš. Má:mo:sin,
mánka-toho-:li-mpa-t-š má:mo:si-n
be:like-REALIS-DEDUC-HEARSAY-PAST-PH:TR be:then-SW

á:ti:kok há:lok, "Háw! Niták ǫ́híkko:š!"
á:ti-k-ok há:lo-k háw nitá-k ón-híkko-:š
person-ART-NOM:FOC hear-SS hey bear-NOM be-3NEG(3A)-PHT:TERM

káhhok, óhyak aboyótlit
ká,h,h-ok óhya-k aboyótli-t
say,H:GRADE,-SS:FOC all-NOM scatter-CONN

tółkatoho:limpatš. Ma:fó:kon,
tółka-toho-:li-mpa-t-š ma:fó:k-on
run(pl)-REALIS-DEDUC-HEARSAY-PAST-PH:TR after:that-SW:FOC

| hayabincobók | ónkatohok | imí:safa | i:tachalí:kat |
|---|---|---|---|
| hayabin-cob-ók | ónka-toho-k | im-í:sa-fa | i:t-achalí:ka-t |
| lizard-big-NOM:FOC | quoth-REALIS-SS | 3POSS-house-LOC | COME:&-exit-CONN |

| pa:haccá:toho:limpatš. | Ma:fó:kap, | á:ti |
|---|---|---|
| pa:-haccá:li-toho-:li-mpa-t-š | ma:fó:ka-p | á:ti |
| LOC-stand-REALIS-DEDUC-HEARSAY-PAST-PH:TR | after:that-NEW:TOP | person |

| caffá:kan | ayakhosín | pa:haccá:litoho:limpatš. |
|---|---|---|
| caffá:ka-n | ayakh-osí-n | pa:-haccá:li-toho-:li-mpa-t-š |
| one-SW | near-DIM-ACC | LOC-stand-REALIS-DEDUC-HEARSAY-PAST-PH:TR |

| Ma:fó:kap, | hayabincobák | tanátlok, | á:ti |
|---|---|---|---|
| ma:fó:ka-p | hayabin-cobá-k | tanátl-ok | á:ti |
| after:that-NEW:TOP | lizard-big-NOM | descent-SS:FOC | person |

| łóhli:k, | ihokí:con | stí:latoho:limpatš. |
|---|---|---|
| łóhli-:k | iho,ki,:c-o-n | st-í:la-toho-:li-mpa-t-š |
| chase-SUBJUNC | be:long,3NEG(2B),-NEG:COMP-SW | INSTR-arrive-REALIS-DEDUC-HEARSAY-PAST-PH:TR |

| Má:min, | stonóyyat | imí:safa | ohhókfit, |
|---|---|---|---|
| má:mi-n | st-onóyya-t | im-í:sa-fa | oh-hókfi-t |
| then-SW | INSTR-climb-CONN | 3POSS-house-LOC | GO:&-put:in-CONN |

| mí:tan | łóhlit | stí:lat | anó:lok. |
|---|---|---|---|
| mí:ta-n | łóhli-t | st-í:la-t | anó:l-ok |
| another-ACC | chase-CONN | INSTR-arrive-CONN | finish-SS:FOC |

| Stacahappá:ka | łóhli:fó:kon, | á:ti | abá | haccá:li:kok |
|---|---|---|---|---|
| stacahappá:ka-∅ | łóhli-:fó:k-on | á:ti | abá | haccá:li-:k-ok |
| fifth-ACC | chase-WHEN-SW:FOC | person | above | stand-ART-NOM:FOC |

| tanátlok | walí:katoho:limpatš. | Walí:ka:k, |
|---|---|---|
| tanátl-ok | walí:ka-toho-:li-mpa-t-š | walí:ka-:k |
| descend-SS:FOC | run(sg)-REALIS-DEDUC-HEARSAY-PAST-PH:TR | run(sg)-SUBJUNC |

| hahcifá | ó:ła:si:k, | sánkot |
|---|---|---|
| hahci-fá | ó:ła-:si-:k | sám-ko-t |
| river-LOC | arrive-SIM-SUBJUNC | be:able-3NEG(2AII)-CONN |

| támmitoho:limpatš. | Má:mok, | konótlit |
|---|---|---|
| támmi-toho-:li-mpa-t-š | má:m-ok | konótli-t |
| fall-REALIS-DEDUC-HEARSAY-PAST-PH:TR | then-SS:FOC | roll-CONN |

| okifón | ohto:támmok. | Má:mok, | oktá:yat |
|---|---|---|---|
| oki-fón | oht-o:-támm-ok | má:m-ok | oktá:ya-t |
| water-ALL | GO:&-LOC-fall-SS:FOC | then-SS:FOC | float-CONN |

| okí | ałí:yafok, | á:tik | o:wá:ya:fó:kap, |
|---|---|---|---|
| okí | ałí:ya-f-o-k | á:ti-k | o:w-a:ya-:fó:ka-p |
| water | current-LOC-BE-SS | person-NOM | LOC-go:about-WHEN-NEW:TOP |

| hayabincobák | í:latoho:limpatš. | Má:mok, |
|---|---|---|
| hayabin-cobá-k | í:la-toho-:li-mpa-t-š | má:m-ok |
| lizard-big-NOM | arrive-REALIS-DEDUC-HEARSAY-PAST-PH:TR | then-SS:FOC |

| okifá | o:cofótlit | o:łopótlit, |
|---|---|---|
| oki-fá | o:-cofótli-t | o:-łopótli-t |
| water-LOC | LOC-jump-conn | LOC-cross-CONN |

| łóykat | o:łopótlit | wihláhpok |
|---|---|---|
| łoyka-t | o:-łopótli-t | wíhl-áhp-ok |
| return-CONN | LOC-cross-CONN | look:for-MODAL-SS:FOC |

| sánkot | łóykatoho:limpatš. | Má:min, |
|---|---|---|
| sám-ko-t | łoyka-toho-:li-mpa-t-š | má:mi-n |
| be:able-3NEG(2AII)-CONN | return-REALIS-DEDUC-HEARSAY-PAST-PH:TR | then-SW |

| á:ti:kok | achalíhkok, | ałí:yak | óhłok, |
|---|---|---|---|
| á:ti-:k-ok | achalí,h,k-ok | ałí:ya-k | ó,h,ł-ok |
| person-ART-NOM:FOC | exit,H:GRADE,-SS:FOC | go-SS | arrive:there,H:GRADE,-SS:FOC |

| ohta:łí:kat, | athocó:bahak | "Tá. | Ohtilhí:calaho:š." |
|---|---|---|---|
| oht-a:łí:ka-t | at-ho-có:ba-ha-k | tá | oht-il-hí:ca-laho-:š |
| GO:&-tell:story-CONN | person-PL-old-PL-NOM | indeed | GO:&-1PL (1A)-see-IRREALIS-PH:TR |

| káhhok, | óhya | a:łí:kat | anóhlok. |
|---|---|---|---|
| ká,h,h-ok | óhya | a:łí:ka-t | anó,h,l-ok |
| say,H:GRADE,-SS:FOC | all | tell:story-CONN | finish,H:GRADE,-SS:FOC |

| Má:mo:sin, | á:ti | imaníhta:kon | ónkak, |
|---|---|---|---|
| má:mo:si-n | á:ti | imaníhta-:k-on | ónka-k |
| be:then-SW | person | young-ART-ACC:FOC | quoth-SS |

| "Ohkommánkš!" | ká:ha:p, | á:ti | imaníhtak |
|---|---|---|---|
| oh-kom-mánk-š | ká:ha-:p | á:ti | imaníhta-k |
| GO:&-1PL:DAT-tell(imp)-PHT:TERM | say-SUBJUNC | person | young-NOM |

| małátlit | małátlitoho:limpatš. |
|---|---|
| małátli-t | małátli-toho-:li-mpa-t-š |
| be:afraid-CONN | be:afraid-REALIS-DEDUC-HEARSAY-PAST-PH:TR |

| Ma:máhpok, | ałí:yak | ółkot | łóyhkok |
|---|---|---|---|
| ma:m-áhp-ok | ałí:ya-k | ół-ko-t | łóy,h,k-ok |
| then-MODAL-SS:FOC | go-SS | arrive:there-3NEG(2AI)-CONN | return,H:GRADE,-SS:FOC |

| walí:katoho:limpatš. | Má:min, |
|---|---|
| walí:ka-toho-:li-mpa-t-š | má:mi-n |
| run(sg)-REALIS-DEDUC-HEARSAY-PAST-PH:TR | then-SW |

| athocó:ba:kok | ołáhcok | hayabincobá |
|---|---|---|
| at-ho-có:ba-:k-ok | ołá,h,-c-ok | hayabin-cobá |
| person-PL-old-ART-NOM:FOC | arrive:there,H:GRADE,-PL-SS:FOC | lizard-big |

| imí:safon, | má:mok, | tálwat | atanáhkatoho:limpatš. |
|---|---|---|---|
| im-í:sa-fon | má:m-ok | tálwa-t | atanáhka-toho-:li-mpa-t-š |
| 3POSS-house-ALL | then-SS:FOC | sing-CONN | circle(pl)-REALIS-DEDUC-HEARSAY-PAST-PH:TR |

| Onostá:lik | fáylok. | Má:mo:sin, | "Tá. |
|---|---|---|---|
| onostá:li-k | fáyl-ok | má:mo:si-n | tá |
| do:four:times-SS | quit-SS:FOC | be:then-SW | indeed |

| Onóhyok | tikbá | mastįhókfįh!" |
|---|---|---|
| onóy,h,y-ok | tikbá-Ø | mast-im-hókfi-V̨h̲ |
| climb,H:GRADE,-SS:FOC | fire-ACC | INSTR-3DAT-put:in-DELAY:IMP |

| káhhan. | Á:ti | caffá:kat | onóyyak | mastįhókfin, |
|---|---|---|---|---|
| ká,h,ha-n | á:ti | caffá:ka-t | onóyya-k | mast-im-hókfi-n |
| say,H:GRADE,-SW | person | one-CONN | climb-SS | INSTR-3DAT-put:in-SW |

| naksáhkatoho:limpatš. | Má:mok, |
|---|---|
| naksáhka-toho-:li-mpa-t-š | má:m-ok |
| make:noise-REALIS-DEDUC-HEARSAY-PAST-PH:TR | then-SS:FOC |

| ihokí:con | i:tachalí:katoho:limpatš. |
|---|---|
| iho,kí,:c-o-n | i:t-achalí:ka-toho-:li-mpa-t-š |
| be:long,3NEG(2B),-NEG:COMP-SW | COME:&-exit-REALIS-DEDUC-HEARSAY-PAST-PH:TR |

| Má:mok, | á:tik | notá | lokkó:tohon | hí:cat, |
|---|---|---|---|---|
| má:m-ok | á:ti-k | notá | lokkó:li-toho-n | hí:ca-t |
| then-SS:FOC | person-NOM | under | stand(pl)-REALIS-SW | see-CONN |

| imóntik | cofótlit | ittámmin | ihá:nifa, |
|---|---|---|---|
| im-ónti-k | cofótli-t | it-támmi-n | ihá:ni-fa |
| 3DAT-come-SS | jump-CONN | COME:&-fall-SW | ground-LOC |

| óhyak | swinóhlin | ilkoyóhkok |
|---|---|---|
| óhya-k | swinóhli-n | ilkoyóh-ko-k |
| all-NOM | shake:medicine:rattle-SW | move-3NEG(2AII)-SS |

| aballá:katoho:limpatš. | Má:min, |
|---|---|
| aballá:ka-toho-:li-mpa-t-š | má:mi-n |
| lie:beside-REALIS-DEDUC-HEARSAY-PAST-PH:TR | then-SW |

| falánkah | bànt | sánkot, | aballáhkan, |
|---|---|---|---|
| falánka-h | bànna-t | sám-ko-t | aballa,h,ka-n |
| get:up-CONN | want-CONN | be:able-3NEG(2AII)-CONN | lie:beside,H:GRADE,-SW |

| hakcó | stimacóslit | hóccatoho:limpatš. |
|---|---|---|
| hakcó-∅ | st-im-acósli-t | hócca-toho-:li-mpa-t-š |
| ear-ACC | INSTR-3DAT-insert-CONN | shoot-REALIS-DEDUC-HEARSAY-PAST-PH:TR |

| Í:bit | apíhlok, | imocóskotohon |
|---|---|---|
| í:bi-t | apí,h,l-ok | im-ocós-k-o-toho-n |
| kill-CONN | throw:away,H:GRADE,-SS:FOC | 3POSS-offspring-PAUC-BE-REALIS-ACC |

| í:bit | apístoho:limpatš. |
|---|---|
| í:bi-t | apísli-toho-:li-mpa-t-š |
| kill-REALIS | throw:away(pl)-REALIS-DEDUC-HEARSAY-PAST-PH:TR |

## BARRED OWL AND MOUSE

| Opák | cissí | stóklot | a:yá:citohon |
|---|---|---|---|
| opa-k | cissí | stóklo-t | á:ya-:ci-toho-n |
| owl-NOM | mouse | together-CONN | go:about-DU-REALIS-SW |

| cimmánkalá:hi:má:m. | Opák | cissí | stóklon. |
|---|---|---|---|
| cim-mánka-l-á:hi-má:m | opá-k | cissí | stóklo-n |
| 2DAT-tell-1SS-INTENT-DUBIT | owl-NOM | mouse | together-SW |

| Má:miyon, | opák | á:yatohok, | opák |
|---|---|---|---|
| má:mi-y-on | opá-k | á:ya-toho-k | opá-k |
| then-BUT-SW | owl-NOM | go:about-REALIS-SS | owl-NOM |

imakáhnok, "Ná:so:t í:billahok
im-aká,h,n-ok ná:s-o:t í:bi-l-laho-k
3DAT-be:hungry,H:GRADE,-SS something-LIST kill-1SS-IRREALIS-SS

í:pali:p" á:lok, á:yatoho:limpáhcok.
í:pa-li-:p á:lo-k á:ya-toho-:li-mpa-V́hco-k
eat-1SS-SUBJUNC think-SS go:about-REALIS-DEDUC-HEARSAY-HABIT-IVPAST

Mó:tohok, ittohayó ałí:yatohok, cissók
mó:toho-k itto-hayó ałí:ya-toho-k ciss-ók
be:then-SW tree-INESS go-REALIS-SS mouse-NOM:FOC

á:yan híhcok, cissók á:yan
á:ya-n hí,h,c-ok ciss-ók á:ya-n
go:about-SW see,H:GRADE,-SS:FOC mouse-NOM:FOC go:about-SW

híhcok tabátkat, tabátkatoho:limpáhcok
hí,h,c-ok tabátka-t tabátka-toho-:li-mpa-V́hco-k
see,H:GRADE,-SS:FOC catch-CONN catch-REALIS-DEDUC-HEARSAY-HABIT-IVPAST

opák. Má:mi:yok, polá:ki íkbot,
opá-k má:mi-y-ok polá:ki ík-b-o-t
owl-NOM then-BUT-SS:FOC quickly 3NEG(1A)-kill-NEG:COMP-CONN

tabátkok í:sit ittó:bi ayakhá ohcokkó:lok,
tabátk-ok í:si-t ittó:bi ayakhá oh-cokkó:l-ok
catch-SS:FOC take-CONN hollow:tree near GO:&-sit-SS:FOC

inna:łí:katoho:limpáhcok tabátkaskan.
in-na:łí:ka-toho-:li-mpa-V́hco-k tabátka-ska-n
3DAT-speak-REALIS-DEDUC-HEARSAY-HABIT-IVPAST catch-BECAUSE-SW

Má:mo:sok, ónkak, opák ónkak
má:mo:s-ok ónka-k ópa-k ónka-k
be:then-SS:FOC quoth-SS owl-NOM quoth-SS

imasilhá:citoho:limpáhcok Cissí ná:si
im-asilhá:ci-toho-:li-mpa-V́hco-k cissí ná:si
3DAT-ask-REALIS-DEDUC-HEARSAY-HABIT-IVPAST mouse something

ŏ:hya imasilhá:cit, immánkat anó:li:k,
o,V̌:,hya-∅ im-asilhá:ci-t im-mánka-t anó:li-:k
all,INTENS,-ACC 3DAT-ask-CONN 3DAT-tell-CONN finish-SUBJUNC

sobáylá:hi bànnak, sámmit í:sak, sámmit
sobáyl-á:hi bànna-k sámmi-t í:sa-k sámmi-t
know-INTENT want-SS be:how-CONN dwell(pl)-SS be:how-CONN

yomahlíhco:lik. Má:mo:sok, imasilhá:citoho:limpáhcok.
yomáhli-V́hco:li-k má:mo:s-ok im-asilhá:ci-toho-:li-mpa-V́hco-k
go:about(pl)-HABIT-IVPAST be:then-SS:FOC 3DAT-ask-REALIS-DEDUC-HEARSAY-HABIT-IVPAST

Má:mo:sok, opák ónkak, "Nashocamánkáˀsá?"
má:mo:s-ok opá-k ónka-k nas-ho-ca-mánka,V́ˀV́,-:sa
be:then-SS:FOC owl-NOM quoth-SS STH-DISTR-1S:ACC-call-Q-IPAST

káhhan. Cissík immałátlihónka:sik, naská:hik
ká,h,ha-n cissí-k im-małátli-hónka-:si-k nas-k-á:hi-k
say,H:GRADE,-SW mouse-NOM 3DAT-fear-ADV-DIM-SS STH-say-INTENT-SS

sobáykok, ká:no:sin immánkatoho:limpáhcok,
sobáy-ko-k ká:no-:si-n im-mánka-toho-:li-mpa-V́hco-k
know-3NEG(2AII) good-DIM-SW 3DAT-tell-REALIS-DEDUC-HEARSAY-HABIT-IVPAST

ayóhbo:sit. Má:mo:sok, "Támka Stimmikkó
ayóhb-o:si-t má:mo:s-ok támka st-im-mikkó
take:care-DIM-CONN be:then-SS:FOC darkness INSTR-3DAT-king

hocimankáhcokš," káhhan. Opák ónkak,
ho-ci-mánka-V́hco-k-š ká,h,han opá-k ónka-k
DISTR-2S:ACC-call-HABIT-SS-PH:TR say,H:GRADE,-SW owl-NOM quoth-SS

ayokpá:hostoho:limpáhcok, "Á! Acayókpat
ayókp-á:ho:si-toho-:li-mpa-V́hco-k á ca-ayókpa-t
be:happy-VERY-REALIS-DEDUC-HEARSAY-HABIT-IVPAST ah 1SSTAT-be:happy-CONN

stalpí:s. Mafíhna:son ónk," ká:toho:limpáhcok
stalpí:s mafíhna:s-on ónk ká:-toho-:li-mpa-V́hco-k
be:enough very:truth-ACC:FOC be say-REALIS-DEDUC-HEARSAY-HABIT-IVPAST

opák. Má:mo:sin, himá:ya mán łóylit
opá-k má:mo:si-n himá:ya mán łóyli-t
owl-NOM be:then-SW now again do:again-CONN

imasilhá:citoho:limpáhcok, himá:ya mán
im-asilhá:ci-toho-:li-mpa-V́hco-k himá:ya mán
3DAT-ask-REALIS-DEDUC-HEARSAY-HABIT-IVPAST now again

immánká:hį bànnak. Himá:ya mán
im-mánk-á:hi-n bànna-k himá:ya mán
3DAT-tell-INTENT-SW want-SS now again

"Nashocamankahcóˀtó?" káhhan. Má:mo:sin,
nas-ho-ca-mánka-V́hco,V́ˀV́,-to ká,h,ha-n má:mo:si-n
STH-DISTR-1S:ACC-call-HABIT,Q,-IIIPAST say,H:GRADE,-SW be:then-SW

cissík himá:ya immánkak, "Támka Stimmikkók
cissí-k himá:ya im-mánka-k támka st-im-mikkó-k
mouse-NOM now 3DAT-tell-SS darkness INSTR-3DAT-king-NOM

óm. Támka Stimmikko:líhcok. Támka
óm támka st-im-mikk-o-:li-V́hco-k támka
be darkness INSTR-3DAT-king-BE-REALIS-HABIT-SS darkness

Stimmikkó hocimankáhcok," káhhan.
st-im-mikkó ho-ci-mánka-V́hco-k ká,h,ha-n
INSTR-3DAT-king DISTR-2S:ACC-call-HABIT-SS say,H:GRADE,-SW

"M̀hḿ! Acayókpat stalpí:s. Anók mafíhna:sot
m̀hḿ ca-ayóka-t stalpí:s anó-k mafíhna:s-o-t
Mhm 1SSTAT-be:happy-CONN be:enough I-NOM very:truth-BE-CONN

Támka Stimmikkó mǫ́. Anók stimmikkó
támka st-im-mikkó mǫ́ anó-k st-im-mikkó
darkness INSTR-3DAT-king indeed I-NOM INSTR-3DAT-king

mǫ́," ká:toho:limpáhcok opák. Stayókpat,
mǫ́ ká:-toho-:li-mpa-V́hco-k st-ayókpa-t
indeed say-REALIS-DEDUC-HEARSAY-HABIT-IVPAST INSTR-be:happy-CONN

nokcóbkot ká:ha:fó:kon. Ká:hat imasilhá:cik
nokcób-ko-t ká:ha-:fó:k-on ká:ha-t im-asilhá:ci-k
stop-3NEG(2AI)-CONN say-WHEN-SW:FOC say-CONN 3DAT-ask-SS

fáykon. Ká:hat, naská:t imasilhá:cá:hik
fáy-ko-n ká:ha-t nas-ká:-t im-asilhá:c-á:hi-k
quit-3NEG(2AII)-SW say-CONN STH-say-CONN 3DAT-ask-INTENT-SS

sobáykotoho:limpáhcok. Naská:t
sobáy-ko-toho-:li-mpa-V́hco-k nas-ká:-t
know-3NEG(2AII)-REALIS-DEDUC-HEARSAY-HABIT-IVPAST STH-say-CONN

imasilhá:cá:hik sobáykok, "Himá:ya mán,
im-asilhá:c-á:hi-k sobáy-ko-k himá:ya mán
3DAT-ask-INTENT-SS know-3NEG(2AII)-SS now again

nashocakáhcóˀtó?" "Himá:ya mán,
nas-ho-ca-ká:-V́hco,V́ˀV́,-to himá:ya mán
STH-DISTR-1S:ACC-say-HABIT,Q,-IIIPAST now again

nashocakáhcóˀtó?" ká:toho:limpak.
nas-ho-ca-ká:-V́hco,V́ˀV́,-to ká:-toho-:li-mpa-k
STH-DISTR-1S:ACC-say-HABIT,Q,-IIIPAST say-REALIS-DEDUC-HEARSAY-IVPAST

Cissí imasilhá:ci:k, mán cissík ká:t
cissí im-asilhá:ci-:k mán cissí-k ká:-t
mouse 3DAT-ask-SUBJUNC again mouse-NOM say-CONN

immánkáhpok, mántik cissí mók na:łí:ká:łok,
im-mánk-áhp-ok mántik cissí mók na:łí:k-á:ło-k
3DAT-tell-MODAL-SS:FOC but mouse again speak-AGAIN-SS

akostinní:citoho:limpáhcok. Naksó:n
akostinní:ci-toho-:li-mpa-V́hco-k naksofón
think-REALIS-DEDUC-HEARSAY-HABIT-IVPAST where

sámmihalpí:sok, ná:so:t óhya hí:cat
sámmi-halpí:s-ok ná:s-o:t óhya-∅ hí:ca-t
be:how-MODAL-SS:FOC something-LIST all-ACC see-CONN

imakostinní:cit, imakostinní:cit anóhlok,
im-akostinní:ci-t im-akostinní:ci-t anó,h,l-ok
3DAT-think-CONN 3DAT-think-CONN finish,H:GRADE,-SS:FOC

ittó:bik łobáfkatohon híhcok, cissík
ittó:bi-k łobáfka-toho-n hí,h,c-ok cissí-k
hollow:tree-NOM be:pierced-REALIS-SW see,H:GRADE,-SS:FOC mouse-NOM

mán walí:kat cokhalí:kalaho:lik hí:cat
mán walí:ka-t cokhalí:ka-laho-:li-k hí:ca-t
also run(sg)-CONN enter-IRREALIS-DEDUC-SS see-CONN

anóhlok, sobáylok, "Nashocamánkahcóˀtó?
anó,h,l-ok sobáyl-ok nas-ho-ca-mánka-V́hco,V́ˀV́,-to
finish,H:GRADE,-SS:FOC know-SS:FOC STH-DISTR-1S:ACC-call-HABIT,Q,-IIIPAST

Himá:ya mán!" káhhan. "Opá ittiɬhocobák
himá:ya mán ká,h,ha-n opá ittiɬ-ho-cobá-k
now again say,H:GRADE,-SW owl eye-DU-big-NOM

hocimankáhcok," káhhan, "Opá ittiɬhocobák
ho-ci-mánka-V́hco-k ká,h,ha-n opá ittiɬ-ho-cobá-k
DISTR-2S:ACC-call-HABIT-SS say,H:GRADE,-SW owl eye-DU-big-NOM

hocimankáhcok," káhhan, opák
ho-ci-mánka-V́hco-k ká,h,ha-n opá-k
DISTR-2S:ACC-call-HABIT-SS say,H:GRADE,-SW owl-NOM

noksíhpok, má:mik, "Hocimankáhcok,"
noksí,h,p-ok má:mi-k ho-ci-mánka-V́hco-k
be:angry,H:GRADE,-SS:FOC then-SS DISTR-2S:ACC-call-HABIT-SS

káhhok, tabátká:hi:fó:kap, cissík ká:t
ká,h,h-ok tabátk-á:hi-:fó:ka-p cissí-k ká:-t
say,H:GRADE,-SS:FOC catch-INTENT-WHEN-NEW:TOP mouse-NOM say-CONN

immánkat incofótlik ittó:bi cokhalíhkan.
im-mánka-t in-cofótli-k ittó:bi cokhalí,h,ka-n
3DAT-tell-CONN 3DAT-jump-SS hollow:tree enter,H:GRADE,-SW

Má:mo:sin, "Cifáytákkóhc!" Má:mik, "Cifáytákkóhc!
má:mo:si-n ci-fáy-tákko-V́hc má:mi-k ci-fáy-tákko-V́hc
be:then-SW 2S:ACC-quit-1NEG(2AII)-CAN then-SS 2S:ACC-quit-1NEG(2AII)-CAN

Ittó cokhalí:híska:kon cí:bilik í:pallahok,"
ittó cokhalí:-hiska-:k-on ci-í:bi-li-k í:pa-l-laho-k
tree enter-2SS(3A)-ART-ACC:FOC 2S:ACC-kill-1SS-SS eat-1S-IRREALIS-SS

káhhok. Ittofá cokhalí:kan wá:cok
ká,h,h-ok itto-fá cokhalí:ka-n wá:c-ok
say,H:GRADE,-SS:FOC tree-LOC enter-SW wait-SS:FOC

cokkǫ:toho:limpáhcok. Wá:cok cokkǫ:lin,
cokko:,N,li-toho-:li-mpa-V́hco-k wá:c-ok cokko:,N,li-n
sit,N:GRADE,-REALIS-DEDUC-HEARSAY-HABIT-IVPAST wait-SS:FOC sit,N:GRADE,-SW

cissík cokhalí:kat nakáɬtoho:limpáhcok
cissí-k cokhalí:ka-t nakáɬɬa-toho-:li-mpa-V́hco-k
mouse-NOM enter-CONN disappear-REALIS-DEDUC-HEARSAY-HABIT-IVPAST

| ittó:bihayo. | Mó:tohok, | mí:ta | łobafkáhcok |
|---|---|---|---|
| ittó:bi-hayo | mó:toho-k | mí:ta | łobáfka-V́hco-k |
| hollow:tree-INESS | then-SS | another | be:pierced-HABIT-SS |

| ohtachalí:katohon | hí:catoho:limpáhcok. |
|---|---|
| oht-achalí:ka-toho-n | hí:ca-toho-:li-mpa-V́hco-k |
| GO:&-exit-REALIS-SW | see-REALIS-DEDUC-HEARSAY-HABIT-IVPAST |

| Wá:cok | ohtachalíhkok, | lónkat | innakáłłok, |
|---|---|---|---|
| wá:c-ok | oht-achalí,h,k-ok | lónka-t | in-nakáłł-ok |
| wais-SS:FOC | GO:&-exit,H:GRADE,-SS:FOC | hide-CONN | 3DAT-disappear-SS:FOC |

| achalí:kok | innakáłłan, | opák | sobáykot |
|---|---|---|---|
| achalí:k-ok | in-nakáłła-n | opá-k | sobáy-ko-t |
| exit-SS:FOC | 3DAT-disappear-SW | owl-NOM | know-3NEG(2AII)-CONN |

| pa:cokkǫ́:lit, | wą́:cit, | wą́:cit, |
|---|---|---|
| pa:-cokkó:,N,li-t | wá:,N,ci-t | wá:,N,ci-t |
| LOC-sit,N:GRADE,-CONN | wait,N:GRADE,-CONN | wait,N:GRADE,-CONN |

| wą́:cit | sánkotoho:limpáhcok. |
|---|---|
| wá:,N,ci-t | sám-ko-toho-:li-mpa-V́hco-k |
| wait,N:GRADE,-CONN | be:able-3NEG(2AII)-REALIS-DEDUC-HABIT-IVPAST |

| Wá:cáhpok | sánkon, | "Cí:bilik |
|---|---|---|
| wá:c-áhp-ok | sám-ko-n | ci-í:bi-li-k |
| wait-MODAL-SS:FOC | be:able-3NEG(2AII)-SW | 2S:ACC-kill-1SS-SS |

| í:pallaho | kátik | óm," | á:lok, | pa:cokkǫ̌:lit, |
|---|---|---|---|---|
| í:pa-l-laho | kátik | óm | á:lo-k | pa:-cokko:,N,,V̌,li-t |
| eat-1SS-IRREALIS | PARTICLE | be | think-SS | LOC-sit,N:INTENS,-CONN |

| imaká:not, | ná:so:t | íkpot |
|---|---|---|
| im-aká:no-t | ná:s-o:t | ík-p-o-t |
| 3DAT-be:hungry-CONN | something-LIST | 3NEG(1A)-eat-NEG:COMP-CONN |

| pacokkó:lit, | wá:cáhpok | sánkon. |
|---|---|---|
| pa:-cokkó:li-t | wá:c-áhp-ok | sám-ko-m |
| LOC-sit-CONN | wait-MODAL-SS:FOC | be:able-3NEG(2AII)-SW |

| Imaká:nok, | opák | onaíllitoho:limpáhcok, |
|---|---|---|
| im-aká:no-k | opá-k | ona-ílli-toho-:li-mpa-V́hco-k |
| 3DAT-be:hungry-SS | owl-NOM | LOC-die-REALIS-DEDUC-HEARSAY-HABIT-IVPAST |

| wá:cihónka:sik. | Cissí:kok | itłopótlok |
|---|---|---|
| wá:ci-hónka-:si-k | cissí-:k-ok | it-łopótl-ok |
| wait-ADV-DIM-IVPAST | mouse-ART-NOM:FOC | COME:&-pass-SS:FOC |

| nakáłłan, | íkbot. | Má:min, | cissí |
|---|---|---|---|
| nakáłła-n | ík-b-o-t | má:mi-n | cissí-∅ |
| disappear-SW | 3NEG(1A)-kill-NEG:COMP-CONN | then-SW | mouse-ACC |

| í:bit | í:pá:hik | sánkot, | imaká:nok, |
|---|---|---|---|
| í:bi-t | í:p-á:hi-k | sám-ko-t | im-aká:no-k |
| kill-CONN | eat-INTENT-SS | be:able-3NEG(2AII)-CONN | 3DAT-be:hungry-SS |

| opák | íllitoho:limpáhcok, | món |
|---|---|---|
| opá-k | ílli-toho-:li-mpa-V́hco-k | món |
| owl-NOM | die-REALIS-DEDUC-HEARSAY-HABIT-IVPAST | again |

| wá:cit | pa:cokkǫ́:lit. | Akkámmo:sin | sobáylil. |
|---|---|---|---|
| wá:ci-t | pa:-cokkó:,N,li-t | akkámmo:si-n | sobáyli-l |
| wait-CONN | LOC-sit,N:GRADE,-CONN | just:so-SW | know-1SS |

## THE BOY AND THE PYGMY RATTLESNAKE

| Á:tosi | cokí:boscok, | ohayyí |
|---|---|---|
| á:t-osi | co,kí,:b-o-:si-V́hco-k | ohayyí |
| person-DIM | big-3NEG(2A)-NEG:COMP-DIM-HABIT-SS | year |

| námposco:li | casobáykotik, | á:tosik |
|---|---|---|
| námpo-:si-V́hco-:li | ca-sobáy-ko-tik | á:t-osi-k |
| be:so:many-DIM-HABIT-DEDUC | 1SS-know-3NEG(2AII)-BUT | person-DIM-NOM |

| cokí:boscok | á:tatohok. |
|---|---|
| co,kí,:b-o-:si-V́hco-k | á:ta-toho-k |
| big-3NEG(2A)-NEG:COMP-DIM-HABIT-SS | dwell-REALIS-IVPAST |

| Á:yatoho:limpáhcok | hínosi | apatahá. |
|---|---|---|
| á:ya-toho-:li-mpa-V́hco-k | hín-osi | apatahá |
| go:about-REALIS-DEDUC-HEARSAY-IVPAST | road-DIM | alongside |

| Hínosi | apatahá, | naksó:n | imí:sa | ayakhá, |
|---|---|---|---|---|
| hín-osi | apatahá | naksofón | im-í:sa | ayakhá |
| road-DIM | alongside | somewhere | 3POSS-house | near |

matáytohok. Á:yat naswíhlit
mat-á:ya-toho-k á:ya-t na:s-wíhli-t
AFAR-go:about-REALIS-IVPAST go:about-CONN STH-look:for-CONN

nashí:cat, ná:son sammíhcómmito
na:s-hí:ca-t ná:s-on sámmi-V́hco-k ómmi-to
STH-see-CONN something-ACC:FOC be:how-HABIT-CONN be-IIIPAST

a:yáhcotohok á:tatohok. Hí:catoho:limpáhcok.
á:ya-V́hco-toho-k á:ta-toho-k hí:ca-toho-:li-mpa-V́hco-k
go:about-REALIS-SS dwell-REALIS-IVPAST see-REALIS-DEDUC-HEARSAY-HABIT-IVPAST

Ná:hot cokkó:tohon cintosók. Cintosí mók
ná:ho-t cokkó:li-toho-n cint-os-ók cint-osí mók
well-CONN sit-REALIS-SW snake-DIM-NOM:FOC snake-DIM also

holcifók hacolaycótohon, hacolaycosík
∅-holcifó-k hacolayc-ó-toho-n hacolayc-osí-k
3POSS-name-NOM pygmy:rattler-BE-REALIS-SW pygmy:rattler-DIM-NOM

ómmitǫ. Mó:tohon, cokkó:tohon híhcok,
ómmi-to-V̨ mó:toho-n cokkó:li-toho-n hí,h,c-ok
be-IIIPAST-PH:TR be:then-SW sit-REALIS-SW see,H:GRADE,SS:FOC

"Amalostă::ho:s!" ká:hatoho:limpáhcok
am-aló:st-a:,V̌:,ho:s ká:ha-toho-:li-mpa-V́hco-k
1SS-be:interested-ADV,INTENS say-REALIS-DEDUC-HEARSAY-HABIT-IVPAST

ná:no:sik. Imaló:stit á:ta:fó:k,
ná:n-o:si-k im-aló:si-t á:ta-fó:k
man-DIM-NOM 3SS-be:interested-CONN dwell-WHEN

hí:catoho:limpak. Má:mo:sok,
hí:ca-toho-:li-mpa-k má:mo:s-ok
see-REALIS-DEDUC-HEARSAY-IVPAST be:then-SS:FOC

"Tabáthkalok słóykalą́," á:lok,
tabát,h,ka-l-ok s-łóyka-l-á-V̨ á:lo-k
catch-,H:GRADE,-1S-SS:FOC INSTR-return-1S-INTENT-PH:TR think-SS:FOC

tabátkok słóykah bànnok, á:ta:p,
tabátk-ok s-łóyka-h bànn-ok á:ta-:p
catch-SS:FOC INSTR-return-CONN want-SS:FOC dwell-SUBJUNC

| hí:ca:p, | sánkon, | ná:hotoho:limpak. |
|---|---|---|
| hí:ca-:p | sám-ko-n | ná:ho-toho-:li-mpa-k |
| see-SUBJUNC | be:able-3NEG(2AII)-SW | do-REALIS-DEDUC-HEARSAY-IVPAST |

| Ittó | afakcó, | hałbón, | ittó | afakcó, | hałbík |
|---|---|---|---|---|---|
| ittó | Ø-afakcó | hałb-ón | ittó | Ø-afakcó | hałbi-k |
| tree | 3POSS-skin | pine:bark-ACC:FOC | tree | 3POSS-skin | pine:bark-NOM |

| ilkáhcok, | ittó | afakconánnamá:min, |
|---|---|---|
| ílka-V́hco-k | ittó | Ø-afakco-nánna-má:mi-n |
| be:called-HABIT-SS | tree | 3POSS-skin-NOTHING:BUT-DUBIT-SW |

| hałbón | wíhlit | híhcok, |
|---|---|---|
| hałb-ón | wíhli-t | hí,h,c-ok |
| pine:bark-ACC:FOC | look:for-CONN | see,H:GRADE,-SS:FOC |

| ná:hotoho:limpak. | Ayakhá | impa:tállok, |
|---|---|---|
| ná:ho-toho-:li-mpa-k | ayakhá | im-pa:-táll-ok |
| use-REALIS-DEDUC-HEARSAY-IVPAST | nearby | 3DAT-LOC-lay-SS:FOC |

| ná:hon, | hacolaycosík | matpa:cokko:líhcok, |
|---|---|---|
| ná:ho-n | hacolayc-osí-k | mat-pa:-cokkó:li-V́hco-k |
| well-SW | pygmy:rattler-DIM-NOM | AFAR-LOC-sit-HABIT-SS |

| stíhsok, | stonàmmi | salátlin | stíhsok, |
|---|---|---|---|
| st-í,h,s-ok | stonàmmi | salátli-n | st-í,h,s-ok |
| INSTR-take,H:GRADE-SS:FOC | entirely | slide-SW | INSTR-take,H:GRADE-SS:FOC |

| óntitoho:limpak | imí:safa. | Imí:safa |
|---|---|---|
| ónti-toho-:li-mpa-k | im-í:sa-fa | im-í:sa-fa |
| come-REALIS-DEDUC-HEARSAY-IVPAST | 3POSS-house-LOC | 3POSS-house-LOC |

| stíhlok, | ittimpáhkatoho:limpak. |
|---|---|
| st-í,h,l-ok | ittim-páhka-toho-:li-mpa-k |
| INSTR-arrive,H:GRADE,-SS:FOC | RECIP:DAT-call-REALIS-DEDUC-HEARSAY-IVPAST |

| Ima:pót | ómmitǫ | ittimmánkak, |
|---|---|---|
| im-a:p-ó-t | ómmi-to-Ṿ | ittim-mánka-k |
| 3POSS-grandmother-BE-CONN | be-IIIPAST-PH:TR | RECIP:DAT-tell-CONN |

| ima:pó | mó, | immá:mo:tot | ómmǫ, |
|---|---|---|---|
| im-a:pó | mó | im-má:m-o:t-o-t | ómm-o-Ṿ |
| 3POSS-grandmother | indeed | 3POSS-mother-ART-BE-CONN | be-BE-PH:TR |

| naksón | casobáykotik, | stíhlok, |
|---|---|---|
| naksó-n | ca-sobáy-ko-tik | st-í,h,l-ok |
| who-ACC | 1SS-know-3NEG(2AII)-BUT | INSTR-arrive,H:GRADE,SS:FOC |

| “Yáhcon, | yáhcok | ká:noscon, |
|---|---|---|
| yámmi-V́hco-n | yámmi-V́hco-k | ká:no-:si-V́hco-n |
| be:thus-HABIT-SW:FOC | be:thus-HABIT-SS:FOC | be:good-DIM-HABIT-SW |

| cintosík | ka:nóhcon | í:silok | stí:lal,” |
|---|---|---|---|
| cinto-sí-k | ká:no-V́hco-n | í:si-l-ok | st-í:la-l |
| snake-DIM-NOM | be:good-HABIT-SW | take-1S-SS:FOC | INSTR-arrive-1S |

| káhhan. | “Ŏ:, | kankóhc! | Apí:l! |
|---|---|---|---|
| ká,h,ha-n | ŏ: | ká:n-ko-V́hc | apí:l |
| say,H:GRADE-SW | oh! | be:good-3NEG(2AI)-CAN | throw:away(IMP) |

| Kánkopalámmot | aci:yáhc | óm! | Apí:l!” |
|---|---|---|---|
| ká:n-ko-palámm-o-t | a,cí,:ya-V́hco-k | óm | apí:l |
| be:good-3NEG(2AI)-ADV-BE-CONN | go:about,2S(2A)-HABIT-SS | be | throw:away(IMP) |

| hoká:ha:p, | mán, | ná:hok, | “Cintosík | ónkak, |
|---|---|---|---|---|
| ho-ká:ha-:p | mán | ná:ho-k | cinto-sí-k | ónka-k |
| DISTR-say-SUBJUNC | again | well-SS | snake-DIM-NOM | quoth-SS |

| cįho:pá:cákkolahǫ. | cįho:pá:cákkolaho katík |
|---|---|
| cim-ho:pá:c-ákko-laho-V̧ | cim-ho:pá:c-ákko-laho=katík |
| 2SDAT-injure-1SNEG(3B)-IRREALIS-PH:TR | 2SDAT-injure-1SNEG(3B)-IRREALIS=ENCL |

| óm,’ | káhhok,” | káhhan. | “Pa:cokkó:lin |
|---|---|---|---|
| óm | ká,h,h-ok | ká,h,ha-n | pa:-cokkó:li-n |
| be | say,H:GRADE,-SS:FOC | say,H:GRADE,-SW | LOC-sit-SW |

| słóykat | stóntit | sti:lalíhcok | ómmil,” |
|---|---|---|---|
| s-łoyka-t | st-ónti-t | st-í:la-li-V́hco-k | ómmi-l |
| INSTR-return-CONN | INSTR-come-CONN | INSTR-arrive-1S-HABIT-SS:FOC | be-1S |

| ká:ha:fó:kap, | “Apí:l! | Apí:l!” | ká:ha:p, |
|---|---|---|---|
| ká:ha-:fó:ka-p | apí:l | apí:l | ká:ha-:p |
| say-WHEN-NEW:TOP | throw:away(IMP) | throw:away(IMP) | say-SUBJUNC |

| ima:pók | ká:ha:p, | apí:kotoho:limpáhcok. |
|---|---|---|
| im-a:pó-k | ká:ha:p | apí:-ko-toho-:li-mpa-V́hco-k |
| 3POSS-grandmother-NOM | say-SUBJUNC | throw:away-3NEG(2AII)-REALIS-DEDUC-HEARSAY-HABIT-IVPAST |

Ma:fó:kon, sámmitik sobáyko:fó:k,
má:fó:k-on sámmi-tik sobáy-ko-:fó:k
then:from:that-SW:FOC be:how-BUT know-3NEG(2AII)-WHEN

ima:pók ayakhá sbatáplit
im-a:pó-k ayakhá s-batápli-t
3POSS-grandmother nearby INSTR-strike-CONN

stimapí:toho:limpáhcok. Má:mo:sin,
st-im-apí:li-toho-:li-mpa-V́hco-k má:mo:si-n
INSTR-3DAT-throw:away-REALIS-DEDUC-HEARSAY-HABIT-IVPAST be:then-sw

cintosík hacolaycosótoho:limpáhcok.
cinto-sí-k hacolayc-os-ó-toho-:li-mpa-V́hco-k
snake-DIM-NOM pygmy:rattler-DIM-BE-REALIS-DEDUC-HEARSAY-HABIT-IVPAST

Má:mo:sin, sammí:citot casobáykǫ;
má:mo:si-n sammí:ci-to-t ca-sobáy-ko-V̨
be:then-SW do:how-IIIPAST-CONN 1SS-know-3NEG(2AII)-PH:TR

í:bitot ómmǫ, imapí:tot ómmǫ.
í:bi-to-t ómm-o-V̨ im-apí:li-to-t ómm-o-V̨
kill-IIIPAST-CONN be-BE-PH:TR 3DAT-throw:away-IIIPAST-CONN be-BE-PH:TR

Sammí:citot ómmo casobáykotik,
sammí:ci-to-t ómm-o ca-sobáy-ko-tik
do:how-IIIPAST-CONN be-BE 1SS-know-3NEG(2AII)-BUT

á:ti ná:nosok tábatkat stóhłan,
á:ti ná:n-os-ok tabátka-t st-ó,h,ła-n
person male-DIM-NOM:FOC catch-CONN INSTR-be:there,H:GRADE-SW

iyyawópkat ómmitoho:limpáhcok
im-yawópka-t ómmi-toho-:li-mpa-V́hco-k
3ss-be:startled-CONN be-REALIS-DEDUC-HEARSAY-HABIT-IVPAST

immá:mak ima:pók stóklok.
im-má:ma-k im-a:pó-k stóklo-k
3POSS-mother-NOM 3POSS-grandmother-NOM together-SS

Kámmo:sin sobáylil hiná:p.
kámmo:si-n sobáyli-l hiná:p
just:so:much-SW know-1S now

## HOW A MAN LOST HIS BREECHCLOTH TO A BULL

| Á:tik | a:yá:citoholimpáhcok. |
|---|---|
| á:ti-k | á:ya-:ci-toho-:li-mpa-V́hco-k |
| person-NOM | go:about-DU-REALIS-DEDUC-HEARSAY-HABIT-IVPAST |

| Łopohlíhcok, | naksó:n | aɬɬa:cíhcommíhcok, |
|---|---|---|
| łopóhli-V́hco-k | naksofón | áɬɬa-:ci-V́hc-ómmi-V́hco-k |
| pass(pl)-HABIT-SS | somewhere | go-DU-HABIT-be-HABIT-SS |

| ínko:p | ilanawíhcot | ómmitǫ. |
|---|---|---|
| ínko:p | ilanawíhli-V́hco-t | ómmi-to-V̨́ |
| or:if:not | hunt-HABIT-CONN | be-IIIPAST-PH:TR |

| Ittohayó | a:yá:citǫ. | Wá:ka | małáhlik | í:san, |
|---|---|---|---|---|
| itto-hayó | á:ya-:ci-to-V̨́ | wá:ka | małáhli-k | í:sa-n |
| tree-INESS | go:about-DU-IIIPAST-PH:TR | cow | wild(pl)-NOM | dwell-SW |

| hí:cat | łopóhlit | a:yá:citǫ. | Wá:kak |
|---|---|---|---|
| hí:ca-t | łopóhli-t | á:ya-:ci-to-V̨́ | wá:ka-k |
| see-CONN | pass(pl)-CONN | go:about-DU-IIIPAST-PH:TR | cow-NOM |

| małáhlotoho:limpáhcok | wá:kok |
|---|---|
| małáhl-o-toho-:li-mpa-V́hco-k | wá:k-ok |
| wild(pl)-BE-REALIS-DEDUC-HEARSAY-HABIT-IVPAST | cow-NOM:FOC |

| małáhlotoho:limpáhcok | ittohayó | isá. |
|---|---|---|
| małáhl-o-toho-:li-mpa-V́hco-k | itto-hayó | isá |
| wild(pl)-BE-REALIS-DEDUC-HEARSAY-HABIT-IVPAST | tree-INESS | dwell(AOR) |

| Mó:tohok, | wakná:nik | lapó:t | hobáskit, | wá:ka |
|---|---|---|---|---|
| mó:toho-k | wak-ná:ni-k | lap-ó:t | ho-báski-t | wá:ka |
| then-SS | cow-male-NOM | horn-LIST | DU-be:long-CONN | cow |

| lapí | hobáskit | o:láhcotohok, | i:sáhcotohok. |
|---|---|---|---|
| lapí | ho-báski-t | ó:la-V́hco-toho-k | í:sa-V́hco-toho-k |
| horn | DU-be:long-CONN | low-HABIT-REALIS-ss | dwell-HABIT-REALIS-SS |

| Có:ba | małáhli | mók | malmámmit | ístoho:liyon, |
|---|---|---|---|---|
| có:ba | małáhli | mók | malmámmi-t | í:sa-toho-:li-y-on |
| horse | wild(pl) | also | same:way-CONN | dwell-REALIS-DEDUC-BUT-SW:FOC |

| ittohayó | a:yá:cit | łopóhli:fó:k, | hínosok |
|---|---|---|---|
| itto-hayó | á:ya-:ci-t | łopóhli-:fó:k | hín-os-ok |
| tree-INESS | go:about-DU-CONN | pass(pl)-WHEN | road-DIM-NOM:FOC |

| ałí:yatohon, | hínosi | ałłá:ci:k, | a:yá:ci:fó:kap, |
|---|---|---|---|
| ałí:ya-toho-n | hín-osi | áłła-:ci-:k | á:ya-:ci-:fó:ka-p |
| go-REALIS-SW | road-DIM | go-DU-SUBJUNC | go:about-DU-WHEN-NEW:TOP |

| wá:kak | mathí:catoho:limpáhcok. | Mó:tohon, |
|---|---|---|
| wá:ka-k | mat-hí:ca-toho-:li-mpa-V́hco-k | mó:toho-n |
| cow-NOM | AFAR-see-REALIS-DEDUC-HEARSAY-HABIT-IVPAST | then-SW |

| wakná:nik | kánkok | á:sat | á:tatohok, |
|---|---|---|---|
| wak-ná:ni-k | kán-ko-k | á:sa-t | á:ta-toho-k |
| cow-male-NOM | be:good-NEG(2AI)-SS | be:with-CONN | dwell-REALIS-CONN |

| hí:catohomá:łok, | ná:hotoho:limpáhcok, |
|---|---|
| hí:ca-toho-má:ł-ok | ná:ho-toho-:li-mpa-V́hco-k |
| see-REALIS-MODAL-SS:FOC | er-REALIS-DEDUC-HEARSAY-HABIT-IVPAST |

| matwalí:katoho:limpáhcok. | Má:mo:sin, |
|---|---|
| mat-walí:ka-toho-:li-mpa-V́hco-k | má:mo:si-n |
| AFAR-run(sg)-REALIS-DEDUC-HEARSAY-HABIT-IVPAST | be:then-SW |

| óntitohok, | óntitohok | áttohomá:łok, |
|---|---|---|
| ónti-toho-k | ónti-toho-k | á:ta-toho-má:ł-ok |
| come(sg)-REALIS-SS | come(sg)-REALIS-SS | dwell-REALIS-MODAL-SS:FOC |

| intółkatoho:limpáhcok. | Wá:ka | ná:ni |
|---|---|---|
| im-tołka-toho-:li-mpa-V́hco-k | wa:ka | ná:ni |
| 3DAT-run(pl)-REALIS-DEDUC-HEARSAY-HABIT-IVPAST | cow | male |

| intółka:fó:kap— | Ihó:cap, | wiló:tok |
|---|---|---|
| im-tółka-:fó:ka-p | ihó:ca-p | wil-ó:to-k |
| 3DAT-run(pl)-WHEN-new:top | long:ago-NEW:TOP | shoe-ART-NOM |

| íksot, | stiliyófkak | ómmi:k, | iboksó:sit |
|---|---|---|---|
| íkso-t | stiliyófka-k | ómmi-:k | iboksó:si-t |
| not:exist | trousers-NOM | be-SUBJUNC | wear:short:breechcloth-CONN |

| yomáhcotoho:limpáhcok. | Iboksó:sit, |
|---|---|
| yomáhli-V́hco-toho-:li-mpa-V́hco-k | iboksó:si-t |
| go:about(pl)-HABIT-REALIS-DEDUC-HEARSAY-HABIT-IVPAST | wear:short:breechcloth-CONN |

wiló:tok íksot, ittobihí syomáhlit
wil-ó:to-k ískso-t itto-bihí s-yomáhli-t
shoe-ART-NOM not:exist-CONN wood-gun INSTR-go:about(pl)-CONN

kámmiscotoho:liyok atyomáhtohok.
kámmi-s-V́hco-toho-:li-y-ok á:ti-yomáhli-toho-k
be:so-DIM-HABIT-REALIS-DEDUC-BUT-SS:FOC person-go:about(pl)-REALIS-NOM

Yá tóklot a:yá:citohok, a:yá:citohon,
yá tóklo-t á:ya-:ci-toho-k á:ya-:ci-toho-n
this two-CONN go:about-DU-REALIS-SS go:about-DU-REALIS-SW

wakná:nik híhcok matwalí:kan, hołohlíhcok mó
wak-ná:ni-k hí,h,c-ok mat-walí:ka-n ho-łóhli-V́hco-k mó
cow-male-NOM see,H:GRADE,-SS:FOC AFAR-run(sg)-SW DU-chase-HABIT-SS indeed

Hiná:p hołohlíhcok óm, "Intółhílkásk!"
hiná:p ho-łóhli-V́hco-k óm im-tół-hílk-ásk
now DU-chase-HABIT-SS be 3DAT-run(pl)-1PLS(3A)-1PL:EXHORT

káhhan. Mó:tohop, ittók nampotíkkon
ká,h,ha-n mó:toho-p ittó-k námpo-tíkko-n
say,H:GRADE,-SW then-NEW:TOP tree-NOM be:many-3NEG(3CI)-SW

shi:báhkatohon, matwalí:ka:fó:kap, caffák
s-hi:báhka-toho-n mat-walí:ka-:fó:ka-p caffá-k
INSTR-stand:erect-REALIS-SW AFAR-run(sg)-WHEN-NEW:TOP one-NOM

walí:kat imonóyyan, caffák ilimonoyyá:cit
walí:ka-t im-onóyya-n caffá-k ilim-onoyyá:ci-t
run-CONN 3DAT-climb-SW one-NOM REFLEX-make:climb-CONN

ałí:ya:fó:kap, wakná:nik cákkostoho:limpáhcok
ałí:ya-:fó:ka-p wak-ná:ni-k cákk-o:si-toho-:li-mpa-V́hco-k
go-WHEN-NEW:TOP cow-male-NOM catch:up-DIM-REALIS-DEDUC-HEARSAY-HABIT-IVPAST

łóhli:k. Wakná:nik cákko:si:fó:kap,
łóhli-:k wak-ná:ni-k cákk-o:si-:fó:ka-p
chase-SUBJUNC cow-male-NOM catch:up-DIM-WHEN-NEW:TOP

immayá:cit walí:kahonká:sit, ittó conokbíhcok
im-mayá:ci-t walí:ka-hónka-:si-t ittó conókbi-V́hco-k
3DAT-be:more-CONN run(sg)-ADV-DIM-CONN tree be:bent-HABIT-NOM

haccá:litohon, mafíhna walí:kak, imó:łok
haccá:li-toho-n mafíhna walí:ka-k im-ó:ł-ok
stand(sg)-REALIS-SW truly run-SS 3DAT-arrive:there-SS:FOC

ałí:ya:fó:kok, wakná:nik cákkoston, cofótlit
ałí:ya-:fó:k-ok wak-ná:ni-k cákk-o:si-to-n cofótli-t
go-WHEN-SS:FOC cow-male-NOM catch:up-DIM-IIIPAST-SW jump-CONN

ittinsá:wafa ataká:ka:fó:kap, cofótlit ataká:ka:fó:k,
ittinsá:wa-fa ataká:ka-:fó:ka-p cofótli-t ataká:ka-:fó:k
branch-LOC hang-WHEN-NEW:TOP jump-CONN hang-WHEN

ná:nik "Caficípkalahǫ," á:lotohok, ficípkat
ná:ni-k ca-ficípka-laho-V̨ á:lo-toho-k ficípka-t
man-NOM 1S:ACC-gore-IRREALIS-PH:TR think-REALIS-SW gore-CONN

ómmá:tok, ittó ittimataká:kan, iboksí má:łon
ómm-á:to-k ittó ittim-ataká:ka-n iboksí má:ło-n
be-AFTER-SS tree RECIP-hang-SW breechcloth only-ACC

ficípkat, imí:sit, słopótlok, swalí:kat, lapí
ficípka-t im-í:si-t s-łopótl-ok s-walí:ka-t lapí
gore-CONN 3DAT-take-CONN INSTR-pass-SS:FOC INSTR-run(sg)-CONN horn

imataká:kat swalí:kat snakáłłtoholimpak.
im-ataká:ka-t s-walí:ka-t s-nakáłła-toho-:li-mpa-k
3DAT-hang-CONN INSTR-run(sg)-CONN INSTR-disappear-REALIS-DEDUC-HEARSAY-IVPAST

Má:mo:sin, á:ti:kok matcóffitohomá:łok,
má:mo:si-n á:ti-:k-ok mat-cóffi-toho-má:ł-ok
be:then-SW person-ART-NOM:FOC AFAR-jump(pl)-REALIS-MODAL-SS:FOC

cóffit ałła:cíhcok, łoyohkáhcok
cóffi-t áłła-:ci-V́hco-k łoyóhka-V́hco-k
jump(pl)-CONN go-DU-HABIT-SS return(pl)-HABIT-SS

intółkatoho:limpáhcok. Má:mo:sok,
im-tółka-toho-:li-mpa-V́hco-k má:mo:s-ok
3DAT-run(pl)-REALIS-DEDUC-HEARSAY-HABIT-IVPAST be:then-SS:FOC

iboksí-íksot caffák łóykat, łóykatohok
iboksí-íkso-t caffá-k łóyka-t łóyka-toho-k
breechcloth-not:exist-CONN one-NOM arrive-CONN arrive-REALIS-SS

| hoká:k, | "Ná:sok?" | "Wá:ka | ná:ni | kánkok |
|---|---|---|---|---|
| ho-ka:-k | ná:s-ok | wá:ka | ná:ni | kán-ko-k |
| DISTR-say-SS | what-SS:FOC | cow | male | good-3NEG(2AI)-NOM |

| á:tatohok, | iboksí | ąsíplit," | ká:ha:p, |
|---|---|---|---|
| á:ta-toho-k | iboksí | am-sipli-t | ká:ha-:p |
| dwell-REALIS-SS | breechcloth | 1S:DAT-take:off-PAST | say-SUBJUNC |

| itta:łí:katoho:limpáhcok | tikboltifá. |
|---|---|
| itt-a:łí:ka-toho-:li-mpa-V́hco-k | tikbolti-fá |
| RECIP-tell:story-REALIS-DEDUC-HEARSAY-HABIT-IVPAST | campfire-LOC |

| Ittaí:san, | łóykat | í:la:p, | káhcok | í:sa:s; |
|---|---|---|---|---|
| itta-í:sa-n | łóyka-t | í:la-:p | kámmi-V́hco-k | í:sa-:s |
| RECIP-dwell-SW | return-CONN | arrive-SUBJUNC | be:so-HABIT-CONN | dwell-IPAST |

| inkostí:nitohą, | immałáhlitoho:limpáhcok |
|---|---|
| im-kostí:ni-toha-V̌ | im-małáhli-toho-:li-mpa-V́hco-k |
| 3DAT-be:careful-REALIS-PH:TR | 3DAT-fear(pl)-REALIS-DEDUC-HEARSAY-HABIT-IVPAST |

| má | wakná:ni. | Kámmisk, | ittohayó | ihó:cap, |
|---|---|---|---|---|
| má | wak-ná:ni | kámmi-sk | itto-hayó | ihó:ca-p |
| that | cow-male | be:so-BECAUSE | tree-INESS | long:ago-NEW:TOP |

| acíhbapalammotoho:limpáhcok | alí:tak. |
|---|---|
| acíhba-palamm-o-toho-:li-mpa-V́hco-k | alí:ta-k |
| be:difficult-ADV-BE-REALIS-DEDUC-HEARSAY-HABIT-IVPAST | life-NOM |

| Kámmisk, | alí:yo:tok | małáhlik | í:sa:fó:kon, |
|---|---|---|---|
| kámmi-sk | alí:y-o:to-k | małáhli-k | í:sa-:fó:k-on |
| be:so-BECAUSE | life-ART-NOM | uncivilized(pl)-NOM | dwell-WHEN-SW:FOC |

| wakná:nik | atłóhliskan, | ná:ni | iboksí |
|---|---|---|---|
| wak-ná:ni-k | at-łóhli-ska-n | ná:ni | ∅-iboksí |
| cow-male-NOM | SOMEONE-chase-BECAUSE-SW | man | 3POSS-breechcloth |

| įsíptoho:limpáhcok | yáp. |
|---|---|
| im-sípli-toho-:li-mpa-V́hco-k | yá-p |
| 3dat-take:off-REALIS-DEDUC-HEARSAY-HABIT-IVPAST | this-NEW:TOP |

| Kámmo:sin | hacimmánkalá:himá:m. | Tafhiyám! |
|---|---|---|
| kámmo:si-n | hacim-mánka-l-á:hi-má:m | tafhiyám |
| just:so-SW | 2PL:DAT-tell-1SS-INTENT-DUBIT | finis |

# Appendix 2

# Transcriptions of Swanton's Texts

The following are examples of two texts transcribed as they are found in the manuscripts and typescripts of John R. Swanton. Both these texts are analyzed linguistically in Appendix 1.

THE GREAT LIZARD

The following is a transcription of the tale *The Great Lizard*, as found in Swanton's (1930) manuscript, showing his Koasati version with English glosses. This was retranscribed into the form found in chapter 4.

[Page 1]

Story of the Haiabintcuba

| Atî′$^{3}$ | lana′oihî′lok | a′iatohok | î′tobûn |
|---|---|---|---|
| man | hunting | was going | ~~tree~~hole |

| hî′xtco o′ntek | îhî′lo | o′nka | | nîtû′n |
|---|---|---|---|---|
| he found | came | came back | he said | bear |

| îstanhe′tcas | ka′ha | ma'mō′sîn | ati′$^{3}$ |
|---|---|---|---|
| I have found | said | & then | person |

| hanā′lî | amā′kak | oła′xtcîn | naksûn |
|---|---|---|---|
| 6 | went | got there | something |

| nî′ta$^{3}$~~sti~~ | îtō′bi | îsti$^{n}$hatcā′lî | ma'mō′sîn |
|---|---|---|---|
| bear | hole | where it is | & then |

| ati′$^{3}$ | manî′xta | îmanō′ya | ayakha′ |
|---|---|---|---|
| man | young | climbing | near |

o´ɬok   tî´kaba   maste$^{n}$ho´kfî   îto´bifa
he got   fire   he put in   in the hole

mā'mo´sîn   nā´sūk   toba   hayo´
& then   something   like a horse   inside

nakso$^{n}$´kak   tcubana´ni   ma´ɛka-
make a neighing noise   male horse   it sounded

toolîmpats   maamo´sîn   ā´tîkok
like   & then   the man

hā´lōk   hao   nîtako$^{n}$hî´kūs   kā´xok
heard   here [*heu*?]   that is not a bear   he said

o´hiyak   abuyu´tlî   toskatoolîmpats
all   scattered   all around running

[page 2]

mafo´gon   hayabîntcubok   o´ɛkatohok
thereupon   the lizard   made a noise

îmī´safa   ītatchale´kat   pahathatcā´-
in his hole   he come out of the hole   & stood up

toolîmpats   $^{m}$afo´gup   atitcafa´kan   ayak-
outside &   then   person one   near

hosi   pahat_tcalîtoolîmpats   mafō´kap
stood up close to the hole   then

ayabî´ntcubak   tana´tlok   atî$^{n}$   ɬoho-
the lizard   got down   person   after

lē´k   yokē´tcûn   îstē´latoholîmpats
ran   a little while   it brought him back

maamîn   îstono´yat   îmi´safa   oho´kfît
& then   he($^{with}$man$_{up}$)climbed   his hole   he put him in

tana´tlît   metan   ɬo´holît îste´la   kana-
came down   another one   ~~af~~ran   after   ~~cameb~~came with was

| holo | îstatca´kpā´ka | ɬo´holefogūn | a´ti$^{3}$ |
|---|---|---|---|
| all done | the 5th one | when he pursued | man |

| a´ba$^{3}$ | atcā´lekūk | atlok | walē´ka- |
|---|---|---|---|
| up | who stood | got down | & ran |

| toolîmpats | wale´kak | ha´xtcîfa | ō´nłasik |
|---|---|---|---|
| | he ran | to a river | got close to |

| ca´ɛkūt | tamîtoolîmpats | maamok | kūno´tlît |
|---|---|---|---|
| he got tired | was falling down | & then | he rolled on |

[page 3]

| o´kîfan | oxtota´mok | mamok | oktā´yat |
|---|---|---|---|
| to water | he went in | then | floated down |

| okî | ałe´yahok | atî | oya´a | fōkap | hayabî- | |
|---|---|---|---|---|---|---|
| water | went on | man | water was bringing | | then | the |

| tcubak | ilatoolîmpats | maamok |
|---|---|---|
| lizard | came | & then |

| o´kifa | otcufû´tlît | ołoko´tlît | ɬoikat |
|---|---|---|---|
| in water | went on in | went across | back |

| ołoko´tlît | we´helapok | ca´ɛkût | ɬoika- |
|---|---|---|---|
| went across | hunted for him | couldn't find him | went |

| toholîmpats | maamîn | a´tîkok | atc- |
|---|---|---|---|
| back | & then | the person | came |

| hale´xko | ałe´ya | o´xłok | oxtāłe´xkat |
|---|---|---|---|
| out of the river | went back | got home | told all people |

| at hotcōbaha | ta$^{3}$a | hoxtîlîtcalahōs |
|---|---|---|
| old people | well | we will go to look |

| ka´xok | o´hia | ałī´kat ano´holo | mamosin |
|---|---|---|---|
| they said | all | he told to come | & then |

| atîmanî´xtakon | oɛka | oxkoma´ɛks | kaha´p |
|---|---|---|---|
| the young ~~people~~ man | they said | go & show us | saying |

| atîmanî´xta | mała´tlît mała´toolîm- |
|---|---|
| young man | was very much afraid |

| pats | mama´xpo | ałē´ya | ołkût | łoi´xko |
|---|---|---|---|---|
| | well | I'll go | didn't go close | went back |

[page 4]

| olī´katoolimpats | maamin | at- |
|---|---|---|
| on the run | & then | the |

| hotcō´bakok | poła´xtcok | ayabî´ntcuba |
|---|---|---|
| old people | got there | the lizard |

| îmī´safan | maamok | ta´lwat |
|---|---|---|
| in his hole | & then | they sang (& made medicine) |

| akana´xka | toolîmpats | ħonostā´lî |
|---|---|---|
| went around in circles | | 4 times |

| fai´ilo | ma'mō´sîn | ta[3] | onohî´yok |
|---|---|---|---|
| it was done | & then | well | one (he) climbed up |

| tî´kaba | masteho´kfakahan | atî |
|---|---|---|
| fire | & put the fire in it | person |

| tcafa´kat | onū´yīa | maste´hō´kfîn |
|---|---|---|
| one | who went up | putting fire in |

| naksakatoolîmpats | ma´amok |
|---|---|
| he shouted | & then |

| okītcûn | intatcalē´katoolimpats | $^{ma}$amo´k |
|---|---|---|
| quickly | it came out | & then |

| atî´k | nûta´ | loko´tohon | hē´tcat |
|---|---|---|---|
| persons | under | standing | looking |

| mo´nte | tcofo´tlît | ete´me | iha´nîk |
|---|---|---|---|
| it came | and jumped | down | the ground |

| o´hia | îswinoholît | înkoyō´xkût obilakatoolimpats |
|---|---|---|
| all | shook | & the thing could not move |

[page 5]

maamîn fala´nkahaba´nt sa´ɛkût
& then he wanted to get up couldn't

abala´xkat ha´ktco îstimatcō´slît
he lay down ear they had put a gun in ~~& shot~~

hotcîtoolîmpats îbîta´pîhe´lo
shot they killed

motcasko´tohon îbîta´pistoolîmpats
the little ones (lizards) they killed also

## CORN WOMAN

The following is a transcription of the tale *Corn Woman*, as found in Swanton (1910).

XLVII

Tai´ye sehe´noxtcok ai´atohō´limpats. Hōtinạ´nạxtcōk
woman old traveled had sores all over

pạsa´gastcok ohimpạla´tgaasin a´yạtohok atlawi´stạ nạ´nạstok
was very dirty they didn't want to see her she traveled little children only

lokatcạ´skok ī´satohon ō´xłan atla´wistạk ayihō´tcihō´ñgạn
orphans stayed she came children she took care of them

tcokō´toholimpats. Kontcokō$^{n}$´lēskạhạn ma´mōsin tai´ye sē´henōk
she sat down you stay with us they said then woman old

ō´ñgak na´sun sō´pon hạ´tcitcōtō´k itạlạgō´litcōk ga´xạn
said something what [x-ed out]have you? you have to cook with come and set it up she said

itillogōlē´'tcin ma´mō´sin ibisnō´k tca´suk a´yatcokō´mitōhok
they set it up then she corn she is (that is what corn is)

īlī´sạhalē´tcit intạba´hạlin ē´pạt īsạtohō´limpats. Mō´tohon
scratched herself (like a roasting-ear) and made bread with it and they stayed and ate. then

| ō´ñgak | tcạsi´k | hina´p | hina´bạthina´bs | ga´xạn | pita´xgok | |
|---|---|---|---|---|---|---|
| said | | corn | now (old) | it is getting hard | said | corncrib |

| ạtcō´buk | hạtca´tohon | yun | pasli´t | ạnōslōk | onokba´hạlōk | nōtci- |
|---|---|---|---|---|---|---|
| old | stood | this | sweep out | finished | shut it up | and go and |

| tokas | ga´xōk | anō´k | hạtcimpi´tcimōs | gaxō´k | tcạsi´[3] | ha´tka$^{n}$ |
|---|---|---|---|---|---|---|
| sleep | said | I | am your mother | she said | corn | white |

| ō´ñgak | tạba´hạlit | hạ´spạlahōs | ka´tohon | tạmōxgạn | hoba´lap |
|---|---|---|---|---|---|
| she said | for bread | you can eat | said | night came | they lay down |

| pita´xgạ | kōbōhilē$^{n}$´djit | xxxnạga´łtohok | ni´xtạn | oxtohi´ntiwạ´p- |
|---|---|---|---|---|
| corncrib | heard something rapping | was gone | next day | they went there |

| tohon | tcas´k | ạlotō´gạt | sạtcatohō´limpats. |
|---|---|---|---|
| and opened door | corn | full | was there |

# References


Barker, Eugene C., ed.

1921 *The Austin Papers.* Part I. Annual Report of the American Historical Association, 1919. Washington.

Bauxar, J. Joseph

1957 Yuchi Ethnoarchaeology. *Ethnohistory* 4:279–301, 369–464.

Berlandier, Jean Louis

1980 *Journey to Mexico during the Years 1826 to 1834.* Austin: Texas State Historical Association and The Center for Studies in Texas History, University of Texas at Austin.

Clifton, James A.

1984 *Star Woman and Other Shawnee Tales.* Lanham, Md.: University Press of America.

Dorsey, James Owen, and John R. Swanton

1912 *A Dictionary of the Biloxi and Ofo Languages, Accompanied with Thirty-One Bioloxi Texts and Numerous Biloxi Phrases.* Bureau of American Ethnology Bulletin 47. Washington.

Dundes, Alan

1962 Washington Irving's Version of the Seminole Origin of the Races. *Ethnohistory* 9:257–64.

Haas, Mary R.

[1939] [Koasati texts.] Mary R. Haas Papers, American Philosophical Society Library, Philadelphia, Penn.

[1940] [Koasati-English vocabulary.] Mary R. Haas Papers, American Philosophical Society Library, Philadelphia, Penn.

1950 Tunica Texts. *University of California Publications in Linguistics* 6:1–174. Berkeley and Los Angeles: University of California Press.

Hudson, Charles M.

1979 *Black Drink: A Native American Tea.* Athens: University of Georgia Press.

Hymes, Dell H.

1981 *"In Vain I Tried to Tell You". Essays in Native American Ethnopoetics.* Studies in Native American Literature: Philadelphia: University of Pennsylvania Press.

Jackson, Jason Baird

2003 *Yuchi Ceremonial Life: Performance, Meaning, and Tradition in a Contemporary American Indian Community.* Lincoln: University of Nebraska Press.

Kimball, Geoffrey D.

1987a A Grammatical Sketch of Apalachee. *International Journal of American Linguistics* 53:136–74.

1987b Men's and Women's Speech in Koasati: A Reappraisal. *International Journal of American Linguistics* 53:30–38.

1989 Peregrine Falcon and Great Horned Owl: Ego and Shadow in a Koasati Tale. *Southwest Journal of Linguistics* 9:45–74.

1990 A Further Note on "Men's" Speech in Koasati. *International Journal of American Linguistics* 55:158–61.

1991 *Koasati Grammar.* Lincoln: University of Nebraska Press.

1993a Koasati Narrator and Narrative. In *New Voices in Native American Literary Criticism*, edited by Arnold Krupat, 3–36. Washington, D.C.: Smithsonian Institution Press.

1993b Two Hunters, Two Wives, Two Dogs, and Two Clawed Witches: The Use of the Dual in a Koasati Narrative. *International Journal of American Linguistics* 59:473–88.

1994a *Koasati Dictionary.* Lincoln: University of Nebraska Press.

1994b Making the Connection: Is It Possible to Link the Koasati to an Archaeological Culture? In *Perspectives on the Southeast: Linguistics, Archaeology, and Ethnohistory*, edited by Patricia B. Kwachka, 71– 79. Athens: University of Georgia Press.

1995 Two Koasati Traditional Narratives. In *Coming to Light*, edited by Brian Swann,704–13. New York: Random House.

1997 Bel Abbey: Koasati Stories: Thątkak ilą:ci:fǫ:kok (The First Meeting of the Indians and the Europeans) and Hacinmąnkalą:himą:m (A Man Loses His Breechcloth to a Bull) in *Swapping Stories: Folktales from Louisiana*, Carl Lindhal, Maida Owens, and C. Renęe Harvison, eds., 92–98, 100–3. Jackson: University Press of Mississippi.

Mooney, James

1900 Myths of the Cherokee. *Nineteenth Annual Report of the Bureau of American Ethnology*. Washington.

Nicklas, Thurston Dale

1974 *The Elements of Choctaw.* Ph.D. diss. University of Michigan.

Paz-Taylor, Lyda Averill

1936 [Ethnographic and ethnobotanical field notes]. MS 4658, National Anthropological Archives, Smithsonian Institution, Washington, D.C.

1937 A Comparative Study of Southeastern Cultures. M.A. thesis, Yale University.

1940 *Plants Used as Curatives by Certain Southeastern Tribes.* Cambridge, Mass.: Botanical Museum of Harvard University.

Speck, Frank G.

1904 *Ethnology of the Yuchi Indians*. Philadelphia, Penn.: University Museum.

Surtevant, William C.

1963 Seminole Myths of the Origin of Races. *Ethnohistory* 10:80–86.

Swadesh, Morris

[1950] Chitimacha-English Dictionary. MS 30(G6.1), Franz Boas Collection, American Philosophical Society Library, Philadelphia, Penn.

Swanton, John R.

1912a Koasati Texts, First Series. MS 4154, National Anthropological Archives, Smithsonian Institution, Washington, D.C.

1912b Koasati Texts, Second Series. MS 1818, National Anthropological Archives, Smithsonian Institution, Washington, D.C.

1924 The Muskhogean Connection of the Natchez Language. *International Journal of American Linguistics* 3:46–75.

1928 Religious Beliefs and Medical Practices of the Creek Indians. In *Forty-Second Annual Report of the Bureau of American Ethnology for 1924–25*, pp. 473–672. Washington.

1929 *Myths and Tales of the Southeastern Indians.* Bureau of American Ethnology Bulletin 88. Washington.

1930 Koasati Linguistic Material from Jackson Langley. MS 4153, National Anthropological Archives, Smithsonian Institution, Washington.

Tedlock, Dennis

1972 *Finding the Center: Narrative Poetry of the Zuñi Indians*. New York: Dial Press.

Williams, Roger

1643 *A Key into the Language of America*. London: Gregory Dexter.

www.ingramcontent.com/pod-product-compliance
Lightning Source LLC
Chambersburg PA
CBHW081131300726
48982CB00005B/929

* 9 7 8 0 8 0 3 2 2 7 2 9 3 *